About the Auth

Dale Dawson is a married man with two children. He is immensely proud of them and is devoted to his sensible, caring wife. He was bought up on the outskirts of Glasgow in a small countryside village setting. Life was tough in his early years like many others bought up with council backgrounds.

Dedication

I wholeheartedly dedicate this book to my beautiful and loving wife, without your support during the dark years, I do not know where I would have been (I need your grace, to remind me to find my own). Your sensible approach to events helped me enormously and I know that it helped the others who were also on this journey with me.

To my beloved R&R, you are my world and always will be – so proud of you both.

To my three brothers, I hope this helps you to understand what life was like for me and my family during what can only be described as "dark times".

Dale Dawson

FINGER OF SUSPICION

AUSTIN MACAULEY PUBLISHERS™

LONDON • CAMBRIDGE • NEW YORK • SHARJAH

A CIP catalogue record for this title is available from the British Library.

ISBN 9781398408555 (Paperback)
ISBN 9781398408562 (Hardback)
ISBN 9781398408579 (ePub e-book)

www.austinmacauley.com

First Published 2022
Austin Macauley Publishers Ltd®
1 Canada Square
Canary Wharf
London
E14 5AA

Table of Contents

"Point a gun at a cop and everyone runs to his side; point a finger at him and no one wants to know."

Factual events of a city detective with one of Scotland's largest police forces.

Chapter 1
Living in a Bubble

It appears to be a true saying that regardless of where a person was born, their true roots will always remain there. It is a special place as it is the formation of how a person will progress in life. I am no exception to that rule. Born in a small mining village on the outskirts of Glasgow, I thought that all towns and villages were as compact and friendly as this, where everyone knew who stayed where and with whom. Looking back, it would appear that this was a stupid misconception in the "real world"; yet, as a small boy, I would have argued till I was blue in the face, a colour not widely referred to in this particular community.

The village, which was home to about two thousand residents, was a lively, friendly and welcoming place. One main thoroughfare linked the village with a nearby town. Off the main road were, in effect, two housing schemes. The new scheme was where I lived the majority of my life and the old scheme, where the housing was about fifty years old. A happy existence, albeit not the most conventional of family units!

Nonetheless, plenty of attention from female relatives, attempting to steer me along the path of life! I was born the youngest of four boys. It was a rough and tumble existence, as other kid siblings will no doubt agree. I bore the brunt of most of the fights. It would appear that the tradition of the wee yin being blamed for every fight and argument was par for the course in large families, I being no exception.

Tragically, my father, a miner, was killed in a mining accident. This was three months before I was born. His death meant that my mother had to cope with three sons, aged then 7, 5 and 3, as well as this six-month-old foetus growing inside her, soon to be me.

To all intents and purposes, I had a father figure in my papa. He was there to take care of me as I thought. I never did understand why I missed out in not having a dad as my papa was there. However, shortly after I started school, he died. I was only five. It was only then that I realised that I lacked the "dominant" male in my life. My eldest brother was there, but he seemed to have his own life from as far back as I could remember; he grew up quickly, not in the assuming father role as others no doubt did in similar circumstances, but personally for him, he was far beyond maturity for his tender years. He was living his own life even then, as he does now!

My upbringing was by no means affluent, as my mother had to survive on a widow's pension, as well as her pit pension, meagre as it was. I never really wanted for anything and presents were always there at birthdays and Christmas.

Perhaps they were hand-me-downs from the oldest of the pack, clearly expressed when I could hear one of my older brothers saying to my mum, "That was mine, I remember playing with that."

The retort would be "Shush, don't let on, he doesn't know." How many other families in the world had that? Plenty I'm sure and that is why I still take care of things now, "just in case", as my mother would say.

Life at school was quick from what I can recollect. I had many friends and enjoyed the rigors of school life. Education, I still believe, is one of the best gifts that a person could receive as it provides a purpose in life. I know obviously that others may not see it this way, but I bet that people look back and do genuinely wish that they had excelled academically. I do not just mean to be in possession of "paper" qualifications, but even sufficient educational attainments to have altered the path of their own lives.

I know that I am glad I was fortunate to be blessed with enough to create a good life for myself. That is what I believe most people aspire to. The only main stumbling block in my wee life was the fact that my mum suffered from poor health and seemed to spend long spells either in bed, or in hospital. Eventually, she received an operation on her spine that prevented her movement, but dispelled the pain, a fact she is eternally thankful for. The two-bedroomed house occupied by us was too much for mum to cope with, the stairs were a problem. We were given a four-bedroom downstairs flat in the older part of the village.

This meant us leaving the "posh" end of the village, if there was such a thing. I couldn't wait, as before this, I had to share not only the room but also my bed. In the room, we had two double beds side by side. I suppose in those days, this was quite normal, Catholics were invariably stuck for space due to their being an abundance of children in each family.

I often wonder if circumstances had been different, would my parents have continued to produce yet more children to add to their already growing brood of children! Contraception is against the Catholic faith. This was the reason for large families then. In my village, I knew of several families where it was not uncommon for there to be between eight and ten kids in the household.

It is difficult to believe that they did in fact have televisions then; whether they used them for its intended purpose or not remains to be seen! We were considered a close family, as were most of the village families, but as time went by, this changed—at least in my family it did. Having moved to our new house, I loved the idea that I shared a room now with one brother instead of three. It meant that I had more freedom and space within the sanctuary that was my room.

A downside of this was me having to walk further to see my pals up the "red ash fitba park" at the other end of the village. There was a good crowd of us who used to all play together—Pete, Alan, "Big Gaz", due to his height, and "Shmoo". For those of us who can recall, this was a cartoon character and as far as we were concerned, Jack resembled this character. God knows who came up with that one!

Jack and I were altar boys together and we were good mates as well. One night in May, me, Jack, his younger brother Philip and my wee cousin Paul all headed towards a nearby quarry to play around this forbidden area. We were aged about ten. I can't even remember whose idea it was to go there in the first place but suffice to say, we all knew that we shouldn't even be there.

The quarry was offset from the main road but it had originally been used as a working quarry, but over the years, it had been closed down and filled in to some degree with water. It was a dangerous exciting place in which to be, probably because we all knew that we should not be there.

We would run around playing like most ten-year-old kids. Kicking a ball about or throwing stones into the water. Dares also took place and normally involved walking along slippery stones to reach the other side of the island or even climbing the high rock faces that surrounded the water.

That particular night, it was dares, and we had already carried out the mundane walking over the slippery rocks. Jack suggested that we take it in turns to climb part of the rock face, albeit the generally easy section. Having done that too, it seemed all too easy.

Philip then decided that we should attempt to climb another section of the rocks, an area previously untouched by us but frequently climbed by "big boys". At first, it was a straightforward "no" from me as I was too afraid to do it. However, having been made to feel like a wimp, I reluctantly tried to climb the forbidden area. Having been successful, I then goaded the others to do it, including Paul.

He was smaller and weaker than the rest of us but he managed to make it most of the way. Suddenly, he lost his grip and fell to the base of the rocks with a crash. He landed on top of some huge rocks at the bottom, smashing his body in the process.

The look of horror on all of our faces was overshadowed by the screams we made on seeing Paul's broken body lying there, motionless. This happened in the time before mobile phones so therefore, the only other thing to do was to run to a nearby house to raise the alarm.

The nearest house was about half a mile away and I decided to go. Eventually, after what seemed like hours, an ambulance arrived and took Paul's broken body to hospital. Obviously, he was lucky as he could have been dead, but we knew that he was still alive, at least that was something. He was in a coma for two weeks; during that time, his broken bones had been set in plaster. Apparently, he was covered in white plaster from head to toe. He suffered broken arms, legs, ribs and vertebrae.

The cause for concern was his head injury. He had a fractured skull and his family had been told that he wouldn't pull through on several occasions, but each time, he continued to defy the doctors and battled on. I was not allowed to go near the hospital to see him as I was being considered the one who should have known better as I was the oldest, by about two months.

13

After three weeks, he slowly began to re-emerge from his coma and thankfully, he made a full recovery although it took about six months in total for him to do so. Obviously, I know that he could have died but in truth, I was just thankful that he didn't. It didn't make too much of an impact on his life and he is as fit now as any other man of his age is.

It had a significant impact on me as I felt as though I was to blame for it. I now know that it was a very unfortunate accident. Luckily, I was the one who managed to run the distance to raise the alarm, so I suppose at least I showed, even at that age, that I could do the right thing when it was deemed necessary.

Being Catholic and an altar boy, as were my three elder brothers, they used to laugh at me as I was forced to go to mass and serve, when they were all out drinking and having a laugh. Was it a strict childhood? Yes.

Several times, my mum asked me if I wanted to become a priest; if so, then I would be able to go to Blairs College (a formal training school for prospective priests) to be educated. No way, was my retort. Why would I want to do that? How proud would that have made my mum and gran plus all my relations! You must be mad, I used to say, I'll stick to the same school as my pals, thanks very much.

I was quickly beginning to change; although I was quiet, went to school and managed to have friends who were not trouble makers, I realised that I would have my own life to live and would make decisions for myself. The reason for that was due to me having watched my older brothers make mistakes, only to be chastised by my aunt as she considered herself the surrogate mother as my mum could not do household chores nor indeed look after us.

Auntie Cathy was the matriarch of the family. We all moved back to the new part of the village to my gran's three-bedroom house, to make things easier for them to look after my mum and all of us. Back to the old ways, two double beds in the same room for us. Not content with just us there, my oldest brother Matthew stayed the weekends at his girlfriend's house.

Next in line, Mark, who had previously left the house to live with his girlfriend and her family for about six years, had returned, like the prodigal son, to live again with us having fallen out with his "burd". He used the house, or our room, as a bedsit for his pals. After the discos finished in a nearby town, he would bring his pals up to stay at ours.

But the wide boy in me saw this as a business venture. I would make them food when they came in pissed, charging them a couple of quid each, to enable me to buy a carry out at the weekend. One of these carryouts was for the school Christmas party. Pete and I both had a half bottle of vodka each. We drank it with Irn-Bru before going to the disco.

He was really drunk whilst I, on the other hand, was just drunk. However, the school telephoned for his parents to collect him. His dad never spoke to him for days. Not for being drunk and bringing disgrace on the family; no, for drinking vodka, a woman's drink. Why did he not drink a man's drink, whiskey? Must be logic there somewhere.

What I thought about though was how liberal his parents were. My own mum would have gone mad. Just how mad she would go in these circumstances, I was to find out.

In May 1984, whilst still in fifth year at the nearby secondary school, I was selected to go on a residential outward-bound course in Ardrossan. I couldn't wait to go. The only drawback being that none of my pals had been selected to go. However, this was not going to deter me; I went for the week and had a ball. Bevy featured high on the list.

Although I did not look eighteen by any manner of means, I still managed to buy a carry out every night. We had a riot, and cider and I were buddies. When I returned after the course, I realised that I had been living in a bubble for my short seventeen years. I decided that I was not going to college; I wanted to be independent, get a job, maybe a car, more importantly, a flat of my own.

That week was the run-up to my oldest brother's wedding. My mum and Co were a nightmare, as things had not been going "their" way for the wedding. They were irate all of the time and I couldn't wait to get out of the house. The Thursday night was to be my official leaving night from school. This was an organised event by the school in a local hotel in the nearby town some three miles from my home.

I arrived there eager to get as drunk as I could despite not being old enough to buy alcohol. Buying alcohol at the hotel was difficult. They were aware that only a handful of the people there were of legal age. Off to the local shop for a cargo; the girls used their handbags to conceal the half bottles of vodka.

Towards the end of the night, I was caught by one of the bar staff swigging from the bottle. I was almost thrown out. More alarming was the fact that our cargo was confiscated. Still, a good night was had by all and off to a house for a party afterwards.

I eventually walked home about one am. I slipped my key in the front door. The lights were on the hall as I entered. Whack, there was my not too sprightly mother standing on the stairs inside the hall, with a telephone directory in her hand. I watched as it bounced off my head. Words about me being late rang in my ears as I struggled to cope with the feeling in my throbbing head. I went to bed to await the grilling in the morning. Why did I do it? Because at last, I was beginning to rebel, roll on being eighteen and able to do what I wanted to do.

I left high school with three highers and six "O" grades. I had been accepted to do accountancy at Glasgow College of Technology, now called Glasgow Caledonian University. Whilst I awaited the start of the term, I managed to get a job with the Royal Bank of Scotland as a trainee. The money was crap, but it meant I could enjoy life with my own money.

Pete was off to university, but had a part-time job, and Alan started an apprenticeship as a plasterer. We all had enough money to make it out on a Friday and Saturday night. En-route to the nearby hostelries, we would each buy a litre bottle of cider to drink before we arrived there. This saved us spending too much money in the pubs.

Another guy, who was part of the crowd, a good friend, Sammy, also joined us. The fortunate thing for us was that he didn't drink. The difference being, he had a car and would be our taxi, unless we managed to get a girl at the end of the night. He was tragically killed one night when his car collided with a tree; he was twenty years old. That was another turning point in my life, as I knew that there was more to life than what I was doing.

Time to make changes and change the path of my life and career. I had already moved on from my crowd of friends as they appeared to be stuck in the same routine. This was not my type of life. I started to branch out and became friends with a different crowd of guys who were older than I was. They were, in fact, friends of my older brother, Andy.

At this point, he was very close to me, but as the years passed us by, we drifted apart. Initially though, I had a ball with my new friends. They were older as well as being much more mature than the previous crowd I had run with. On hindsight, I now realise that this was the making of me; my confidence grew and I started to see that life was for the taking. I was going to grasp it with both hands, like a kid in a sweetie shop.

I enjoyed many holidays abroad; sometimes on occasions, about twenty-four guys set off on holiday to places like America, Portugal, Tenerife and Crete, to name but a few. There was never a dull moment with these guys, I can honestly say that this was one of the happiest periods of my life. A period I still recall with great laughter and fondness.

I still keep in touch with some of the crowd. The majority is by now all married with families of their own. I learned a great deal from these people. Mainly, how to speak to others, as well as how to treat others. The only problem I encountered was what to do with my life.

The new crowd made me feel unsettled. I wondered what to do. I doubted whether I would be able to spend the next forty years in a job I hated. I had passed all of my bank exams. Promotion was beckoning, albeit down in England somewhere as the Royal Bank had merged with Williams and Glynn's Bank.

I decided that I did not want this for myself. I did fancy the idea of moving away, just not as a bank employee. I completed two application forms for jobs advertised in a newspaper. One was the Royal Navy, the other being the Police. I passed the interview with the Navy, but I was becoming scared to make that transition.

The prospect of totally leaving friends and family behind whilst I left to pursue a new career terrified me. I received a letter from the Police asking me to attend for an initial entrance exam. On the day in question, I approached the police headquarters in Pitt Street, Glasgow. I walked around the outer perimeter twice. I felt sick at the thought of going into the building, sick at the prospect of being met by scary police officers, who no doubt would give me a hard time.

I was twenty-two, and I now know that I was naïve, although I was genuinely afraid to go in. After what seemed like hours, yet was probably only five minutes, I entered the building to sit the exam. Within two weeks, I received confirmation that I had been successful in passing the entrance exam, I felt that I had done well, yet at the same time the fear of actually becoming a police officer was way too frightening for me to fully contemplate. What a long drawn out process it was to be.

At that time, the police were short of funding for new recruits and it was estimated that I would not be starting, if successful, for about a year. After having passed two interviews, I told my mum, gran and aunt, who all still lived together with me, that I was trying to join.

They were flabbergasted at the very suggestion that I was going to leave a secure job in the bank to join the police. However, I asked that they support me, as I needed this to enable me to progress to the next stage. The police, you see, send out an inspector from a local office to ascertain your suitability through your own home environment, as well as to check on your family surroundings.

I later learned that my mum had told him of her reservations. As had my gran and aunt. Having spoken with him, he reassured them that the police was a secure job with excellent prospects, and no doubt I would have to make my up my own mind. This was the change in life I was seeking.

I eventually attended for a final interview and did very well. Well enough to be accepted as a police officer. Finally, my letter of acceptance was delivered to me in August 1990. In October of that year, I started seeing Carmen, she knew that it was my intention to join the police, as and when funds were in place.

In March 1991, the letter arrived; I was to start with Strathclyde Police in April 1991. I resigned from the bank, not bitter but content knowing that I had a career to fall back on should things go horribly wrong. One thing was for sure, I would always be good with money, the bank had taught me that much. Another reason for leaving the bank was my meeting with Carmen. Thanks to her help and guidance, I realised that for the first time in my life, I was getting settling-down pangs and the prospect of this on a bank salary was quite daunting, to say the least.

Obviously due to the lack of money in the bank, no pun intended. I am referring to salary, as my earnings doubled on joining the police. With Carmen's support, I was beginning to find out that I should really start thinking about my own future instead of taking care of everyone else.

My date to start my new life as a police officer was fast approaching; no way back, no regrets, time to move on with my life!

Chapter 2
The Point of a Gun

The day arrived, Monday, 15 April 1991. I left home, the pain clearly etched on my family's faces as they watched me leave home to begin my new adventure. I arrived at Pitt Street at the force headquarters in Glasgow, wearing a dark grey suit, perhaps reflecting my general mood that day, fearing the great unknown. This was my first step into the world of policing.

The large strained building was not welcoming at all. The officious concierge was also dull and uninterested in my presence there. I felt as though every time I opened my mouth, I squeaked. Proper conversation was not being emitted from my mouth. An alien feeling for me!

I was not able to say things in a normal tone, fear evident in not only my speech but also in the feelings I had in the pit of my stomach, I felt as though I had done something wrong and this was me going to account for my actions. Later, I would have these same feelings on various occasions throughout my career.

I was ushered into a waiting area, like a prisoner awaiting his sentence. I was about to receive mine. I took the oath that all police officers take yet I wasn't alone. I had twelve other colleagues to share the fear, twelve other people surely on my side and feeling the same way I felt! I learned from the Chief Superintendent that we were truly lucky to be there.

Privileged to be chosen, only thirteen new starts, money was not forthcoming to the police for new recruits, we were all told that we had to ensure commitment from here on in as we were now representatives of Strathclyde Police, both at work and play. Our lives were no longer our own. *What did he mean?* I thought. It was only in later years that I managed to grasp the reality of what this statement meant.

It seemed quite strange carrying an empty suitcase around with me. The reason for this was that I would receive my uniform—two pairs of woollen trousers, five crisp white shirts, two clip-on ties and two tunics (formal uniformed jackets). I thought that was it, but no, more to come. Baton, handcuffs, belt, keys, gloves, raincoat and two hats with badges. I was complete. Not quite; after we were kitted out, we were taken to the training office in another part of Glasgow.

Oxford Street was a large pink building near to the "Gorbals", an area synonymous with "flea-ridden markets", yet home to the training facility of Strathclyde Police. The guys, all eight of us, were taken for a visit to the barber;

yes, that's right—"you will have your hair cut" was the retort from the sergeant looking after us. After another short back and sides, we were treated to lunch.

Stodge more like—"this is similar to the type of food you will get at Tulliallan". This was the first time that day I had heard that name. This is the training facility for all Scottish police recruits in Kincardine. I had forgotten that I had eight weeks to look forward to.

I quickly put it to the back of my mind as the rest of the day, we were told what was expected of us, as well as what was not expected of us. It would appear that my life would no longer be my own, I had to conduct myself in a proper and fitting manner, as becoming of a police officer. Whatever that means I am not sure, as I have seen fellow officers conduct themselves far worse than members of the public. Already, the pretentious element was coming to the fore. It seems that cops think they are something in society, respected upstanding pillars of society! Some may be, the majority are not.

When I arrived home that day, I was met with a wall of eager relatives who wanted to see me in my uniform. I felt like I was entering an arena full of lions. I was to be the target of their attentions! I put on the full uniform.

I suppose if I really confess, I enjoyed the attention, as deep down I knew that I really suited it. The stares from my relatives clearly informed me that they too thought that I looked the part, despite the fact that I knew nothing of what a police officer was expected to do.

The first two weeks of my new job consisted of basic training at Oxford Street. During this time, I learned to listen without saying anything in return, fearing that I would make a fool of myself with my answer. The training sergeants were only too happy to make the recipient of his attentions appear dumb. The safest option was to sit quietly and take on board the constructive criticism.

The other twelve on the course were a good bunch. Eight males, five females, all ordinary people hoping for the chance to help the public! The previous occupations ranged from backgrounds such as banks, nursing, offices, navy and building sites. No posh people to contend with, just a couple who could speak more politely than the rest. We all shared a common bond of being totally unaware what lay ahead at Tulliallan Police College; bring it on!

The next trauma was the first day at the Scottish Police College at Tulliallan along with about another 40 new recruits from Tayside, Central Scotland Grampian and Lothian and Borders Police Forces. The first day walking across the Parade Square—so called as that was where the actual Final Parade would take place, it was daunting and exciting at the same time.

I was confronted with a Sergeant Major Army type person who shouted at every person as they walked through the door of the Police College for the first time. The police trainers shouted at everyone, despite not having told anyone in the first instance that a particular course of action was to be carried out.

I am referring to a guy who was walking through the door with me; I, as usual, was smartly dressed, but not Ian—he was wearing casual clothes and looked rather shabby compared with me. The Sergeant Major maniac bellowed down the corridor at Ian, words to the effect that he looked like a bag of shite.

Ian's retort was that if someone had told him how to dress then perhaps he would have carried this out. I was later made aware that Ian was an ex-Navy man and was well used to people shouting at him. Other mere mortals like me would perhaps have taken offence to the way that he had been spoken to, but as I was about to find out, that would be commonplace in the police.

I formed the opinion that it was more of a game within the college establishment. I decided that this is exactly the way that I would treat it in the future in order to see out my 8 weeks initial training. Some of the older guys on my course, by that I am referring to guys aged about 30 years, were quite annoyed at the way that they were being treated and at times were close to tears as they could not cope with the attitude of some of the instructors.

On occasions, it did test all of one's strength not to hit out at the instructors, as they appeared to continually annoy and intimidate us. All part of the learning process, I was told on several of these instances that I found myself in. This may account for the reason that even to this day, I still have no patience; I must have used it all during my training. I only hope Carmen believes me when I use this as the excuse for having no patience now.

In fairness, my time at the college did pass by very quickly. The run through the forest carrying ten-foot logs between six of us was actually very enjoyable, in an almost perverse way. The reason for this was the good laughs I had with colleagues at the college. Probably what kept us all going was the fact that we could enjoy a couple of pints at night within the complex.

Believe it or not, I definitely deserved this and I think that is what kept me sane during my time there. Soon, my training of eight weeks was almost at an end and life on the street as a police officer was beckoning. In July 1991, I began my police life with group 2 at Baird Street on the outskirts of Glasgow City centre.

The area covered the districts of Balornock, Barmulloch, Sighthill, Royston and Blackhill. To those of you who know these areas then it will be known that they are very deprived areas with a high instance of drug abuse, leading therefore to high crime rates. Undoubtedly, there is a lot of good people in these areas; the problem being the police only have occasion to meet them when they have reported crimes against them.

It was a pitiful existence for some of the residents, poverty and deprivation were evident all around. On reflection, I now see that I was totally naïve to this type of living. At times, I felt genuine sorrow towards the victims of crime, but as time passed, so too did these feelings. I learned quickly to switch off from each incident I dealt with.

My real training was gained here, thanks to the guys on the shift. I say guys as there were only two females on the shift and I never worked with them at this early point in my career. Thanks to the wide boys on the shift, namely, Cloherty, McIlvanney, Livsey, Murray and Baird, I quickly settled into the role of law enforcer and school-crossing patrol relief. My neddy boy colleagues gained my respect immediately. I liked them, as they never treated me any differently from themselves.

My own wide-boy retorts soon started as my skin began to toughen up due to the pretty boy image they taunted me with. I was quickly known as the cheeky wee bastard whose warrant card did not have dry ink on yet. I think that the reason I settled in as quickly was due to my age.

I wasn't straight out of school so I suppose I had seen a bit of life and I knew how to deal with people. I was always quick to answer back, as I do not believe in waiting until asked to give an opinion. This was the reason I was considered cheeky, but life is not about being told what to do and say…well, that's my philosophy anyhow.

My first call was to a house on the outskirts of Blackhill, it was a private estate and the occupant had reported that his clothes had been stolen from the washing line. My first reaction was: well, why even bother reporting it, but as I later learned, the philosophy of the hierarchy within the police is that crimes should be reported as it reflects a true image of what is happening in society. That was 1991. Now the reverse is true; the police do not want crimes reported as it reflects badly on them to the extent that crime is a problem, which quite clearly it is.

I noted all the relevant details from the complainer—I thought. When I arrived back at the office to complete my first crime report, alas, I had forgotten several important points. Like what clothing was stolen; however, at least Davie had been listening and he came to my rescue with the details. I realised that I have to listen to people more, a point I still have problems coming to terms with.

Four weeks after having arrived there, another new start came to work on my shift. Shona was older than I was but in police service terms, I was no longer the "new boy"; that title was now in possession of someone who had less street experience than I had. I was delighted that there was a new shift member. The heat was off me and on the new person.

In August of that year, with six weeks street experience, I had my first night shift to contend with. The actual working during the night was strange yet quite relaxing. This was my first time working with a real character called Mack, I felt as though I was his father having to give him advice on matters of the opposite sex. Not that I am professing to being extremely knowledgeable, but his apparent charisma towards members of the opposite sex would have me in stitches as I watched him in action during our tour of duty.

His attitude where women were concerned bewildered me, as I did not consider him to be a favourable candidate in the looks department. However, and I mean no disrespect to these ladies, but they themselves were no china dolls, so I suppose it's true when it is said that looks are not important. Well, that most certainly was the case with Mack.

On the Friday night of my night shift, I attended a call in the Balornock area, a disturbance in a house. On arrival, I could hear a man shouting from within the house. Mack told me to keep alert and watch what the guy was doing. I entered the house behind him, like a good probationer should do, only to be met by a six-foot-four giant of a man. He immediately attacked us both, resulting in Mack and I rolling about the carpet with the guy. My first fight had happened, unannounced and unwanted.

Eventually, having sustained a couple of punches to my face, as had Mack, we both managed to subdue the giant long enough to arrest him and place handcuffs on his wrists. I was sweating like mad, almost as mad as I was in temper. Livid at having not realised that members of the public do want to fight with the police. My lesson learned, my reputation intact, but my illusions shattered, we took the bleeding pig to Baird Street.

He had sustained a minor cut to his nose during the fracas. The duty inspector, who was responsible for processing the male, was not too happy to say the least when he saw that the prisoner was bleeding all over his desk. However, the prisoner was washed and he was found to be fit to be detained for court the following Monday morning. He was charged with assaulting the police and breach of the peace. He actually apologised for his behaviour when we escorted him to his cell. Did I feel sorry for him; no, not at all.

Walking about the office, some of the other guys on the shift were congratulating me on handling a violent situation so well, despite being the "new boy" on the shift. Mack was happy with me yet he seemed hesitant to make any great issue of what had happened. Sensing that something was wrong, I asked him what I had done; it appeared that he was wary of what to put in the report.

I was quite taken aback at this and my reply to him was simply to put in the report what had happened. He said that perhaps no one would believe that he just attacked us. I, obviously not used to this situation, suggested that the report be written as it happened and when it came to court, we would tell the same story— end of problem.

He explained that it would be suggested at court that perhaps the incident was complicated due our presence. I informed him that we would tell the story, and he laughed. As I would later learn, defence solicitors attempt to paint the picture that their clients are always the innocent parties. A storm that every police officer must ride, not always too well, I hasten to add.

My night's adventure was far from over; prior to leaving the office after having completed all the paperwork, I was instructed to go to the control room to receive another call. The control room is the nerve centre of the police office where all telephone calls reporting incidents are collated. The person in charge there, the controller, decides on the importance of each call and who should have the first available response unit. It is a difficult job and takes a certain type of police officer to do it.

Normally, a person who doesn't care what others say about them. When I went in, it was chaotic—phones ringing, others passing messages on air to other officers on duty. I asked what was required and I was told to attend Blackhill to assist senior officers there as there had been a shooting.

Being inquisitive, I asked who had been shot, not that I would have known that person as I knew no one from that area. "Arthur Thomson Junior" was the reply.

"All right, assign Alpha one to the call," I said as I walked out of the chaos. Alpha one being the call sign allocated to the car I was in. There were four cars covering the area, Alpha one, two, three and Delta Mike three. The latter was the car most officers wanted to work in as it was the car that received the cream of the calls, the opportunity to prove oneself as a good cop; I knew that I would work that particular car soon enough. I would have to be content at present.

Already I was becoming impatient, I was like a sponge, seeking to soak up as much experience as possible, and I was about to gain even more. I told Mack about the call. He was quite excited and proceeded to tell me that the man who had been shot was the son of a gangster and that no doubt it was over drugs. I was intrigued, as obviously I had never been to something as exciting as a shooting before. I had inadvertently forgotten to ask whether Thomson was alive or dead.

On arrival in Provanmill Road, I saw a wall of police cars, both marked and unmarked. Fluorescent jackets worn by the police to signify their presence were stopping people from going about their business. I spoke with an inspector who asked me to stand outside a large house next to a graveyard. This house was totally out of place as the area is run down and the majority of housing is council-owned.

This house as well as being large was well presented and obviously had a vast amount of money spent on it. This was the family home of the Thomsons and was apparently where Arthur junior had been gunned down. I say apparently as I was never given the full facts of what had happened; I was the probationer, you see. This did not stop me from asking another senior officer for more information as he walked past me.

All he did say was that the man had been murdered and that it was believed the shooting took place near to where I was asked to stand guard to preserve the area awaiting the attendance of forensic scientists. Fair play to him; at least he didn't just dismiss me in the same way as the other senior officer; a learning point for the future as I would soon realise that was how most of these ranking officers spoke and dealt with their staff—very poorly.

I felt quite important in the knowledge that I had been selected to stand guard. Yet, as the years went by, I soon realised that it was always junior officers who were left to do this type of job as it was considered menial. So, my idea that I was important was so wrong. I was told not to allow anyone past where I was. Only police personnel were to be allowed access as the area had been cordoned off with police tape, which had been placed around a lamp post on one side of the road and a fence on the other.

Although it was August, it was cold and damp. I probably would never have noticed the cold but when there is nothing much else to do whilst standing alone whilst the hustle of police officers concentrated on the other area of the cordon, about twenty yards further down the road, I was really cold.

Mack was being used elsewhere, so I had no one to keep me company. I was bored and had my first taste of the downside of the job—the preservation of a locus, albeit important where criminal investigations are concerned, but soul destroying for the officer concerned. It was only about two o'clock in the morning and I felt as though I had been there for hours, yet it was in real terms only about an hour into my task.

I was pacing up and down like an expectant father, impatience written all over my face, frustration evident in the stiffness of my aching bones. I suddenly looked towards the join of the road with the pavement adjacent to the Thomson house; the streetlight was shining down on a metal object; at a glance, I had no idea what the item was.

Curious, I walked over to it but was interrupted by some locals who were asking questions about what had happened; the main question was, "Is fat boy deed then?" A fact I now know was a reference to the now deceased Arthur Thomson Jnr due to his rather portly appearance. I did all I could to allay the residents' fears that everything was fine and there was no need to worry. Sounds like a statement from a police television series, but the fact remains that I thought they were caring residents—wrong, they were just nosey bastards.

They were just like most other human beings, nosey and consistent in their badgering of a young cop, hoping to learn a snippet of information. I was already feeling frustrated as the boredom was getting to me. I told them all to move or they would get the jail for interfering with a crime scene. I still don't know where I got that one from at that stage in my career. It was as though I was saying it in slow motion, like I was hovering above myself and someone else was making me say it.

They were quite taken aback at my cheek and I was met by a torrent of abuse involving several swear words, including the idea that they were questioning my parentage. They did move on though and I felt good again, good to the extent that I thought that I was coming to terms with the ability so say things and at least people obeyed my request. Albeit I did suffer verbal abuse; no more than I was used to and could handle though!

I had forgotten about the shiny object I had previously spotted and began my repeated pacing up and down. I saw an unmarked CID (Criminal Investigation Department) car entered the area and two suited detectives stepped out with an air of arrogance and casual flair. Out of the rear of the car stepped two scientists wearing white boiler suited overalls carrying what looked like medical bags that would not have been out of place in a horror film.

I thought to myself there and then, *One day I will do the job of a detective*, as it will mean I don't have to stand about here at a locus all night. I watched as the four of them spoke with the senior officers who were in charge and I could overhear the events of the shooting, as they knew them. It appears that the deceased guy had been on weekend prison leave and was walking across the street when a car pulled up and one of the occupants shouted, "Hey, fat boy."

As he turned to see who it was, he was shot twice. However, the Thomsons in those days had a reputation and Arthur senior, on hearing the shot, ran out of his house and found his son lying on the ground in a pool of blood. He put him in his car and took him to Glasgow Royal Hospital, hoping that the police would not find out about the shooting. Arthur Thomson Jnr died shortly after having arrived there.

The senior officer went on to say that the family was not cooperating with them and refused to say anything about the shooting and subsequent death of their family member. The occupants of the car had sped off prior to old Arthur leaving his house.

The scientists decided that they would have the area photographed as is normal in this type of crime, and then they began their search at the opposite end from where I was. I thought, *Oh well, an hour and this standing about doing nothing would be all over*. This was not the case, as I soon came to realise, as they were painstakingly going over the area with fine precision, looking for evidence. I suddenly remembered the shiny object.

I went to examine it myself and when I found it, I bent down to see what it was. It was, in my opinion, a bullet shell. I shouted over one of the detectives. Davie was about six foot two and to this day I have rarely seen him smile, let alone speak more than two words to anyone not connected with the CID. He reluctantly came over and I explained what I thought I had found. He seemed excited but on my sensing this, he played down my 'find'.

He told me keep an eye on it and he would fetch the scientist. They both quickly returned and the shiny object was gone. Photographed in situ and then placed in a plastic bag for examination. Both of them casually walked away to the opposite end of the police cordon and never even acknowledged my presence. I was fuming, to say the least.

I shouted Davie back to ask him what had happened and his retort to me was, "I think it was just a fag end, son, don't worry about it."

"Aye right, good one, big man," said I. "It was a bullet?"

He turned and told me to be quiet and he would speak to me later concerning it and with this, he walked away again. How pissed off was I! I felt like running over to him and punching him right on the chin.

About five o'clock, I was relieved from my post and someone else took over from me, allowing me to return to the office for my refreshment break. When I got there, I spoke to Mack and told him what had happened. He explained to me that I had lost my "speakey", as no doubt Davie would claim he had found the bullet.

I was bemused, I didn't understand what he meant and asked him to explain it to me. In effect, he suggested that the bullet was an important piece of evidence and the person who found it would be required to go to court to confirm its find. The reason I was being written out of the find, so to speak, was to enable someone else to say that they found it as no doubt this would be a high court case and the police witnesses would perhaps make a lot of money from having to attend there. I suppose he took possession of it so he could rightly claim to have found it.

If it occurred on days off, overtime could be claimed. I was beginning to understand that the purpose of our job was to present cases to the Procurator Fiscal and in return, if there was sufficient evidence then a citation to appear at court would be issued for those involved to attend. If that happened to be on one of my days off, then I could claim overtime for the inconvenience.

Sounds highly complex stuff but the reality is that a lot of officers would sign labels attached to productions hoping to be cited to appear at court, on the pretext of claiming money. This was what inspired the majority of police officers to arrest individuals—the prospect of making money out of someone else's misfortune!

Mack suggested that I leave it well alone and forget about it, so I did. On the day of the funeral of Arthur Thomson Jnr, a car containing the bodies of Paul Hanlon and Joe Glover was found in the Shettleston area of Glasgow. They had both been executed, shot through the head. Information suggests that Arthur Thomson organised this as revenge for his son's death. It would appear that they were also present in the car with whoever shot young Arthur the night of his death.

As a result of the investigation into the death of Arthur Jnr, Paul Ferris stood trial at Glasgow High Court and the charge of murder was found to be not proven; he walked free. The tit for tat style of shooting and evil conduct carried out by the gangster types in Glasgow has created many problems in the underworld circles. Yet this is still a problem as they all vie to take control of the lucrative drug market in the surrounding areas.

The following months from the murder were to be very lucrative for the police officers of Baird Street. This was partly due to the fact that there had been a murder in Blackhill, spelling calls of fear from the residents as the press laid constant siege around the area, continuing to publish news that made the respectable residents almost afraid to leave their own homes. The high-profile approach of uniformed officers was meant to allay those fears.

Cops were earning at least four hours overtime each shift, which if undertaken for the seven-day cycle in which the shifts operated, would amount to quite a lot of money. Even probationers like me took the opportunity to "fill our boots" whilst money was widely available. Even after the funeral, the patrols continued as speculation grew that underworld sources would attempt to desecrate Arthur Jnr's grave whenever the police stopped the patrols. Some of the older cops used to laugh about that possibility, saying that it was probably a cop working at Baird Street who leaked the story to ensure that the overtime continued. I don't know who made the call, but whoever it was—thanks, my bankbook was sure hefty after the hours I worked.

As well as working about twelve hours most days, I also had to keep up with the paperwork involved in my escapades with the different characters I was fortunate to work alongside. This was by no means easy as each cop has his/her own style of writing reports. I quickly developed a style of my own and managed very well; my only problem being that I just did not like report writing as I preferred to be out on patrol.

One afternoon, I was supposed to stay in and write as I had plenty to do. However, some of the lads were at court and the shift was short of officers to go out and man the cars. I joined up with one of the busier cops on the shift—Pat.

He considered himself to be funny, a bit of a joker, and was always into taking the piss out of people, both cops and members of the public. We were asked to attend the report of two males acting suspiciously at a nearby fruit market, which was one of the main distributors of fruit and flowers to the surrounding areas of Glasgow. Normally, petty thieves hung around trying to steal whatever they could.

The information was that two guys were loitering outside one of the banks. Pat and I attended and sure enough, when we arrived at the main entrance to the fruit market, there were two males who matched the descriptions given to us by the controller prior to leaving the office. Pat stopped the uniform marked car and approached the two of them. I was beside him.

General conversation followed and I learned that they were waiting on a female who was working there. The next thing, I saw one of them run away up a flight of stairs towards a carpark. Pat shouted at me to chase after him whilst he seized hold of the other one. My first chase on foot, not at all glamorous, as I had to run carrying about seven pounds of equipment! I used my personal radio to inform the control room of my location.

The only downside to this was that I was not that familiar with the area so I had to rely on Pat informing the controller of the street names as I continued my chase. I ran through a carpark up another flight of stairs towards another busy main road. I watched as the male ran across quickly followed by me. On running along a path towards a pub, I heard the guy shout back at me, "I'm gonna get you."

This sounded bizarre as I felt that I should have been shouting at him, as I was behind, chasing him. I could see that he was attempting to remove something from his right-hand jacket pocket. I was gaining on him all of the time until suddenly, he slowed down, turned around and pointed a gun right at me. I was terrified, as he was saying, "Come and get it then, prick." I stopped and could hear my control shouting through the radio at me to update them regarding my position.

I froze on the spot and my heart felt like it was going to burst, caused by running and trepidation. The guy laughed, turned away and ran towards the nearby pub. I instinctively gave chase again only this time as I grew closer, I managed to clip his heels and he fell to the ground with a thud, flat on his face, closely followed by me. I don't know if I fell or whether I threw myself on top of him as I obviously knew that I had been looking down the barrel of a gun.

I grabbed his arm and put it up around his back and there was the black monster in his right hand. Nerves most definitely took over as I also managed to radio my position. The problem being I didn't know the name of the street I was in. Just at that, Pat arrived with the car. I yelled at him to help me, although he was hesitant at leaving the other male locked in the police car. Pat could see that I was struggling with the guy and he came and assisted in putting handcuffs on him and he was placed in the back of the car.

In all of the excitement, I had managed to grab the gun and throw it to the side. I recounted the story to Pat and I found the gun. My concern was not about the gun, but what do we say happened. Pat laughed and told me not to worry; both males were detained under the Criminal Justice Scotland Act 1980 as it was suspected that they were about to commit a robbery. I was happy at this and although very shaken, I continued with the arrest procedure.

At Baird Street, the CID were told of the events by Pat; thankfully, the detective Davie was not there; he would no doubt have recounted the events to say that he had single-handedly wrestled with the guy and retrieved the gun! Found in the other guy's pocket was a Renault car key. The gun was not loaded but I did not know that at the time and I was genuinely terrified. A lot of 'what ifs' have gone through my mind since then—what if it was loaded, what if he had pulled the trigger?

Pat and I searched an area near to the fruit market and found that the Renault car key fitted a stolen car that was no doubt to be used in the robbery as a getaway car. Both males were interviewed by the CID; one of them stated that it was their intention to rob one of the banks and escape in the stolen car. They were charged with conspiracy to commit robbery and appeared at court the next day. I never received a citation for the case, and to this day, I still wonder whether the CID wrote me out of the case!

My own bosses on the shift complimented me on my good work. By now, the word was around the shift that I was a "gemme wee guy" who would try anything to get an arrest. I was considered a good neighbour (colleagues who work alongside each other) to work with. Yes, I was accepted as one of the guys; I could hold my head high and say I was a cop.

Chapter 3
Turning the Key

It wasn't long before my two-year probationary period was completed. I spent most of my time in patrol cars dealing with a variety of different cases. I was fluent in the necessary jargon to allow me to be able to complete reports for onward transmission to the PFs department. This truly was an individual thing as each police officer tends to develop their own skills as far as story-telling goes, as this is what writing cases is really about.

My own brand of humour tended to be inflicted within the reports, although I never received any complaints from the relevant departments. I learned from the various tutors I worked with that style may be created for each person as opposed to having bog-standard reports. I must confess that some of the reports written by my more experienced colleagues left a great deal to be desired and that was a trap I promised never to fall into. They would write such dull reports that they failed to tell the story of what actually happened. I'm not saying that they made things up, but perhaps they just saw or heard a version of events that I didn't.

However, by the time I realised this, I was about to go into court to give evidence! This used to freak me out as I tried to cope with the nervous trauma of having to give evidence. This was difficult enough, but coupled with Enid Blyton as a neighbour sometimes made life difficult when there was no need for it to have been.

It was always considered cushy to be in the patrol cars going to calls, as obviously those officers wouldn't have to walk around in the freezing cold. What those officers forgot was the fact that we were being sent to one call after another and at times, particularly during a busy late shift, I sometimes didn't have time for a pee, let alone have my dinner. Those on the beat would have managed to not only have dinner but also several cups of tea or coffee from their many "safe havens" away from the scrutiny of the gaffers.

Those driving around were being worked relentlessly by the control room staff, being sent from one call to another. Obviously, it makes better sense to send a patrol car as opposed to waiting on the beat cops getting to the call. There were about five other probationers now on my own shift so I was by no means the least experienced member of the shift.

Quite the opposite, in fact, I was considered to be experienced enough to get my ass out of the patrol car and I was given a beat all of my own. A nerve-racking experience as it meant that I was now responsible for a particular area and was expected to attend calls in that area, either alone or with another cop who was perhaps on an adjoining beat.

Probably my first experience of the beat cop lifestyle was during a winter night shift. I was allocated a beat and Shona, who had joined just a month after me, and she was given another beat. Rather than walk around on our own, we decided to team up. Without the gaffers knowing, as I think they were only trying us out to see if we could cope on our own. I didn't particularly like the idea of walking around Balornock on my own during the night.

We left the office together and made our way up to Balornock through the housing schemes of Springburn. In truth, we were both actually quite excited as it meant that the gaffers thought enough of us to trust us out on our own. That itself was quite reassuring as at least it meant that we were actually in a position to test our own abilities if faced with any criminal acts. The only downside to this aspect of the job was that it was a winter's night so therefore, it was bitterly cold.

However, wrapped up in waterproof trousers and coats meant that we were well protected against the biting winds. The first night was daunting to say the least. Two fresh-faced probationers eager to deal with any incident thrown at them. Well, not quite! We both knew that we could ad-lib our way around most situations. Neither of us were just out of school, we had both had enough experience of life to provide us with a basic instinct into how people react to situations. Even if we didn't know, neither of us was slow at asking for help if need be.

Walking up through the high-rise flats of Sighthill was intimidating as we were dwarfed by their enormous height. Normally though, most people tend to walk past police officers without even a glance. But obviously, there are occasions whereby young Neds would shout abuse as we went strolling past them. They were probably looking for a chase but I have to admit that neither of us was that desperate to jail anybody.

It wasn't uncommon for officers to just shout back at them "fuck off, ya wee prick". This may sound bad from the point of view that police officers shouldn't speak to members of the public like that, but my philosophy was that if it was okay for them to shout at me then it was fine for me to retort in the same manner! I'm not saying that it happened all the time, just most of the time!

We had only managed to get beyond Sighthill heading towards Springburn when a call came out over the radio that a male was attempting to break into a car. The locus was only about one hundred yards from where we were. Instant agitation crept in and before I knew it, Shona had answered the call saying that we were nearly there and to action us to the call. "Roger" came the response from the control room.

At last, it was our turn to prove to the shift that we were capable of getting a body of our own without their help. We both ran towards the locus and there before our eyes was a man inside a car trying to get it started. The engine was stuttering but would not kick in properly. I ran as fast as I could, closely followed by Shona, and I got to the driver's door of the car and she made her way to the passenger door. The man was caught red-handed.

He was about to try to get out of the car but I managed to grab hold of him by the arm and I threw him to the ground. Shona joined in and managed to grab his other wrist, forcing it up his back. I placed my handcuffs on him and that was it. We had secured our first arrest together. How did we know it was a car thief and not the owner? Well, his black gloves and woollen ski mask were a dead giveaway.

I shouted into the control room that we had arrested a man at the scene and requested a car to take us back to the office with our "body". When the car arrived, I placed I him in the back and Shona sat beside him whilst I spoke with the owner of the car who had been watching from the window of his house overlooking the carpark.

He was well impressed with the response by the police and gave me the necessary information to enable me to complete the crime report. I must confess that this was probably the best body I had captured and Shona and I did it without any help from other cops. I felt proud that we had managed to do this on our first night out on patrol together. Yes, it was luck that we just happened to be there but we still managed to arrest him.

Whilst in the car, one of the other cops knew who the guy was. Apparently, he was a prolific car thief and no doubt he had many other crimes to admit to. Back at the office, we did all the necessary paperwork and won great praise from the gaffers. More importantly, the CID were delighted that he had been captured and he went on to admit to twenty-five car thefts from our area.

This was considered to be a great apprehension as it managed to clear up a one-man crime wave that was running amok in our division. The CID kept him in custody and all that Shona and I had to do was leave statements of our involvement with them, as they would submit the report to the PF. Quite straightforward, as far as we were concerned.

That was just the start of a very eventful week for Shona and I; each night we left the office, we would be back in with an apprehension within the hour. The bodies we managed to bring in were due to our own observations and not because we had gone to assist others. I felt that I was finding out what it was really like to be a police officer.

Normally, what would happen on a night shift was that at least two people would be sent home about four in the morning if it were quiet. This would ensure that they would be able to get at least some sleep prior to having to attend court. This was a good deed by the gaffers and was not a universal solution to the terrible shift patterns. Some other shifts whose gaffers were bastards wouldn't allow any of their troops this afforded luxury.

We, however, were fortunate in that our own shift inspector was a real gentleman and liked his troops to feel that they were being rewarded for keeping the shift running in line with the way in which he wanted it. Quinn only had about two years left before he could retire and was probably one of the most approachable men I ever had occasion to meet. He had the respect of every member of his shift. A thing that most gaffers would love but due to their own failings, that is not the way other shifts were run!

For the second half of the shift, Shona and I would be split up in order to allow two cops to get home early. This was also good as it saved us from having to walk about all night in the freezing cold, plus it meant that we could catch up with the older cops on the shift and have a laugh with them.

One guy in particular, Gus, was such an outrageous character that no one ever believed a word he said as he was a bit of a jackanory. He told strange stories of things that had happened to him both at work and in his personal life. He relayed a story to me on one of the nights I was left to work with him during the second part of the night.

He loved Germany and all things German. His family holidays were to various parts of the country and he proclaimed that he was fluent in the language although I never did ask him to prove it. During one of his family holidays, he met Steve McQueen, the famous actor, who just happened to be there on holiday as well. They struck up a conversation about their love of hang-gliding and arranged to meet the following day to take part. When they arrived at their meeting point, they eventually set off over one of the mountain ranges.

But tragedy almost struck the actor and Gus had to manoeuvre his glider to save him from crashing into the mountain. Before he could get the chance to say anything else, I interrupted him, "Didn't see that in the news at any point about someone saving his life."

He was furious with me for doubting what he had told me and started to rant and rave at me. I knew that he did make it up because of the way he reacted, but I just laughed. He wasn't amused and refused to speak to me at all for the rest of the shift. When I made discreet inquires with the rest of the troops, they told me that he did this all the time and just to leave him as he was a bit eccentric. Bloody mad, you mean?

Deep down though, he was a really genuine guy who would have helped anyone out if they asked him. His baby was traffic offenders. I used to cringe at the stories about the way he spoke to members of the public about where and how they parked their cars. He was a frustrated traffic cop trapped in a shift cop's body.

That whole week was exciting for Shona and I as every night out on the beat, we managed to arrest at least one person each night; sometimes it was even more. On the Saturday, we were detailed the same as we had been all week. We walked up to our beat areas as normal, listening intently to the radio in case we happened to be near to a call.

Alas, the fights and domestic pleasures were in other areas of the division, being closely monitored by the area cars. The daunting thing about being on foot is that the closest car could have been several miles away should we happen to need assistance, although so far, neither of us had cause so far to request emergency assistance. As we walked along one of the many side streets in Balornock, an alarm bell could be heard in the distance.

This wasn't anything uncommon in that area, as there were many small shops there. As we approached a video shop, we knew that the alarm bell ringing was coming from it. On reaching the side of the shop turning the corner towards the shutter, there on his hands and knees crawling out of a wall was a housebreaker.

He caught sight of us as he jumped to his feet and took off down the road. I immediately gave chase after him, closely followed by Shona.

Quite clearly, he was a local guy, as he knew all of the streets and various alleyways to head to, in order to make good his escape. I was frantically shouting in through my radio that I was in pursuit of a housebreaker and gave my location to the control room staff. Luckily for me, I knew the street names thanks to my knowledge of the area having walked it all week.

Rather than relay my whereabouts to the other cops, who were in attendance, the control room decided to put me on "talk through". This meant that I was directly relaying my whereabouts to those coming to assist me. What was I saying about never having had to ask for assistance like this?

The guy had gone to hide in back gardens near to where the video shop had been, but he had in effect run around in circles, probably trying to outsmart me in the process. I could hear him moving about but I couldn't see him because of the darkness. However, as he tried to outsmart me, he went into a garden that had a security light.

This lit up the garden area like Blackpool illuminations, helping me once again find where he was. I informed those coming to help me that I was about to go into the garden to get him. By this point, Shona had managed to join me.

There was no real escape for him as that particular garden had a six-foot high fence all around it. He was trapped. As I approached where he was hiding, near to the bin cellar, I drew out my baton, as I knew that he would try to fight me to make good his escape. I shouted at him to come out but as I was shouting, he just lunged straight at me, probably hoping to knock me over.

I remained firm and grabbed hold of him and he started to punch and kick me in his attempts to beat capture. Shona approached him and warned him that if he didn't stop his nonsense (or a similar phrase to that using several swear words), she was going to hit him with her baton. Ignoring her request, he continued to wrestle with me and then I heard 'whack'.

True to her word, she hit him on the arm and he withdrew his grip from me. I managed to then cuff him and I walked him towards a waiting police car. We did it. We had managed to capture our first housebreaker. This is very uncommon as most of the times, crimes like these are reported and they have already taken place by the time the police arrives. Capturing one in the process of committing the crime is extremely rare.

He was taken back to the office by two of our colleagues as we made our way back to examine the scene of the housebreaking.

When the owner arrived, it was found that some money and videos had been stolen. He had managed to break into the premises by removing breezeblocks that formed the outer walls of the shop and he then crawled inside. Quite how he managed to do this alone I do not know, especially where the shop is—right next to a busy main road.

I still couldn't work out how no one saw him working away at gaining entry as I am quite sure it would have taken hours to do it. Some of the other cops searched the rear gardens and found some videotapes that he had obviously managed to throw away during the chase. I obtained all of the details necessary details from the owner and left him to sort out the mess within the shop and then we went back to the office to deal with yet more paperwork concerning the arrest of our housebreaker.

When we got back, the gaffers were waiting to congratulate us on our arrest. This was definitely our best body of the week and having carried out detailed checks on the man, it was discovered that he was already wanted in connection with various other thefts from the surrounding area.

It was decided by the duty officer that he was to be kept in custody pending his appearance at Glasgow Sheriff Court, on the Monday. This meant that I would have to do a custody case so that the PF would be able to read all the circumstances surrounding his arrest. I decided to stay in for the rest of the night to do the case. This was my first decent case and I knew that it would have to be written correctly. This was my opportunity to prove that I was competent enough to be left to get on with my job as a police officer. I completed the custody case and was then instructed to man up one of the patrol cars, as another cop was also to write a custody report concerning one of his cases.

It was about six o'clock in the morning and we were instructed to attend a report of a dangerous dog, terrorising neighbours. What the hell are they doing up at that time of the morning anyhow? Some people just don't know when to sleep. It was decided that I would just go to the house myself to deal with the call. This normally happens and really it is the best way to learn, I always believed.

I approached the house with trepidation fearing that the maniac dog would appear and rip me to shreds. I walked along the path and made my way to the back of the house to see if the dog was there. Sure enough, it was lying on the back doorstep, tied up. Or so I thought! I walked to the side of the house about to lift the letterbox to arouse the owner, when the demon dog came running at me, faster than the speed of light!

I still hadn't even managed to chap the door. It would appear that although I saw rope lying next to the dog, it wasn't tied up at all. It started to pounce on me, trying to bite me. I kicked it several times, attempting to frighten it off me. It didn't work. It kept on coming at me and eventually, I managed to grab hold of my baton and I hit it as hard as I could on the head. I was absolutely shitting myself.

At this point, the householder opened the door to see what was causing the commotion. I was furious and started to vent my anger at her, ranting and raving about her bloody dog.

Speaking of which, where was it? I had this vision of it lying beside the back door dead. The owner went around and saw that it was lying cowering in the corner. "Did you hit ma dog, ya bastard?"

"Pardon me, don't you dare swear at me or I'll lock you up, ya cow." The latter part of the sentence just appeared from nowhere. Obviously, I shouldn't have said that to her but I was incensed at what had happened.

Meanwhile, my colleague decided to get up off his fat arse and came to see what was taking me so long. When he reached us, all he could hear was this female shouting abuse at me. He quickly reminded her that she was close to being jailed so she calmed down but also told him of the 'ya cow' comment I had made. Obviously, I denied that allegation and changed the subject towards the demon dog and its attempts at mauling me.

There was no attempt. It had actually managed to bite me on the back of my leg and torn a hole in my trousers. I calmed the situation down and warned about the dog and told her to make sure that if it was going to be left outside at any time then it should be tied up. If she refused to do this then I was going to report her to the PF for keeping a dangerous dog.

She agreed with me and assured me that she would tie it up in future, apologising profusely about my leg. I left the house and returned to the police car, my dignity left somewhere between the front door and the gate! On examining my leg, it was decided that I would have to go to hospital for treatment.

I was totally embarrassed but nonetheless, I went to the casualty department where the nurses welcomed me with open arms. They took the piss right out of me when I relayed the entire story to them. As the bite was at the back of my knee, I had no option but to drop my ripped trousers. I received three sutures on the wound, but my embarrassment was about to become worse.

I was ordered to drop my pants to have a Tetanus injection on my ass. After my treatment, I was about to leave the hospital, thanking the staff for their help. I also said thanks for the jack on my ass when one of the smart doctors replied, "You know, you could have had the jag on your arm but seeing as how you were keen to bare your bum, it made sense to do it there!"

I was humiliated once more. Even the medical staff was laughing at my misfortune. Oh well, at least I could laugh at myself and my own pain; only the shift to face now.

By the time I managed to get back to the office, all of my colleagues had gone home. However, on walking into the muster room prior to starting my shift, I was met by the sound of almighty dog howls from all of the cops assembled there. Obviously, I knew that they were more than aware of what had happened to me at the end of my shift! I quickly dropped my trousers to show them my sutures, as I knew that they would go to immeasurable lengths to see the extent of my injury.

At that point, in walked Shona and another female colleague, whilst I stood there with my trousers at my ankles. They were taken aback as obviously they expected to see me standing quite like that in front of the whole shift. It seemed to work though as it was quickly forgotten by them and I was allowed to get on with my shift. It had been quite a memorable week in that we had managed to arrest quite an array of people during our shifts and I couldn't wait for my days off to come to unwind.

On returning to work that Wednesday after two very quick days off, I was informed by one of the sergeants that I was required to submit petition statements regarding the arrest of the housebreaker. This was my first reportable petition case and I was the reporting officer! I asked my colleagues at muster for their own statements so that this would enable me to send off the statements to the typist quickly. Petition is when someone who has repeatedly committed crimes, and because of the amount of charges, would need to appear before a Sheriff and Jury at trial.

They all laughed at me telling me to just make up statements for them and when it came to court, they would tell what had happened. I was shocked, as I had previously thought that everyone was responsible for his or her own statement. One of the wiser cops on the shift told me that technically, this is the usual way but realistically, cops don't have time to do statements like that every time they became involved in an incident.

Basically, what he told me was that I had to dictate all of the statements myself, telling the typist what each cop was responsible for seeing and carrying out in relation to the arrest. I did as I had been advised and submitted eight statements pertaining to those involved. All that I had to do now was wait three months until the trial by jury to see whether I had written them well enough to convince my colleagues that I was capable of doing a thorough job.

Several weeks later, I was summoned to see the inspector of my shift. He didn't take much to do with the running of the shift. He left that to the sergeants. This summons meant that perhaps I had fucked up along the way or I was to be moved from this shift to another.

I was very nervous when I went to see Quinn, but he must have seen this by the look on my face and he quickly told me that I was to relax, as I had nothing to worry about. It seemed that I had made an impression on the CID gaffers due to my thief-catching abilities and I had been selected to join about twenty others on a three-month attachment to plainclothes. The purpose of it was to crack down on housebreaking, and it was to be a Force-wide initiative called "Operation Turnkey". (Turning the key on housebreakers?)

It had been given a fancy name by those senior officers who worked at Pitt Street, the force headquarters, and it was going to be a high-profile campaign. I had never worked plainclothes before but I readily accepted the job. I had only two and a half years' service and I was told that I should feel proud to have been selected. I was excited yet at the same time nervous as I hardly knew anyone else who had been chosen as they had much more police service than I, but I couldn't wait to start the following week. I told a few of the shift what was to happen but I could sense that some of them were annoyed that I had been chosen instead of them.

I could now see that the job was one, which also displayed open jealousy towards younger service cops who had better potential than they themselves. I shrugged it off and prepared for my new challenge. No more night shifts for a while. Thank fuck for that.

My first day with Operation Turnkey (OT) was spent dealing mostly with the ethos behind the campaign and also meeting my other colleagues. There were ten cops and one sergeant to each team and a Detective Inspector (DI) was to be responsible for overseeing the two teams. I didn't know anyone else on my team as the cops had been chosen from Kirkintilloch, Easterhouse and Baird Street.

It would seem though that my own reputation had superseded me and two guys in particular had told me that they would ensure that I was well looked after. Ally was a great cop by all accounts and was well known in the criminal world as a good thief catcher.

Deek was the same, having learnt his own trade in Easterhouse. I decided that I would mix with these two guys, as the others on the team seemed more out for glory for themselves than having a laugh. I wanted to learn but I also wanted to ensure that I wasn't bored so Ally and Deek seemed a good compromise. The only downside to the team overall was the Detective Sergeant. (DS)

He was nothing but a gaffers' snitch who was out to enhance his career with this acting as a good reading addition to his otherwise dull CV. He had informed us all that everything was to be reported to him so that he could coordinate any possible searches as, after all, "he was in charge of us".

This quickly annoyed most of the team but at that point, I decided that I wasn't going to become involved in the politics of making statistics count. This was obviously my lack of experience as a cop showing through, as I knew nothing about what actually goes on behind the scenes where manipulation of statistics are concerned. I received a crash course on the etiquette attached to this from Ally and Deek.

They had spent most of their time in plainclothes and had about twenty-five years' service between them. This obviously dwarfed my own experience but they never at any time made any reference to this during our working relationship.

It didn't take me long to establish my own working way when dealing with neds. This was partly due to my shift experience, but mostly due to the fact that my two colleagues were fantastic when it came to spotting and catching criminals. Already, our three-man team had significant results when it came to capturing criminals responsible for housebreakings. Each time we caught someone, they would admit to numerous previously unsolved crimes.

However, behind the scenes, the not-to-be-trusted DS was telling the DI that he was responsible for the crime solving due to his expert interview technique. The truth being that Ally, Deek nor I were trained to interview under taped conditions so we were forced into asking him to assist as he was trained. When Ally found out about this, he was furious.

He wanted to punch the fuck out of the DS. I managed to calm him down so that he could just speak to him instead. This didn't work as the DS promptly told him that he was in charge and we would have to adhere to what he said and did. I was quickly beginning to realise just how desperate some people become in order to enhance their own careers. This DS was one of those characters and I didn't like it one little bit.

Between us, we decided to confront the DS and as he had no witnesses, he could virtually do nothing about it. We did speak to him. Deek and Ally told him that if he ever fucked us over again without ensuring we were at least acknowledged for our input, they would make sure that every criminal we brought in would refuse to be interviewed by him and therefore he would have no more pats on the back from the bosses.

He was livid but he saw that they meant business and he immediately backed down, telling them that he would do as they wished. It was to remain to be seen as to whether he felt threatened by them or whether he would grass them up to the bosses.

However, we never found out as shortly after that conversation took place, he was seconded away from the unit to work on a murder that had happened within the division. We, naturally enough, were delighted. This meant that the DS on the other team was to supervise the paperwork of both teams, but she took no active part in our daily routines, much to our delight.

Having not been long married myself, I was finding the long hours a tad difficult to deal with. What compensated though was the huge amount of money I earned in overtime. I was beginning to see the beauty of working long hours but my nearly new bride was extremely homesick. You see, she had moved from England to live up in this country.

My being out at work for anything up to fourteen hours a day was taking its toll. However, we decided that it was a short-term measure as this attachment was only for three months so the extra money would pay for a nice holiday in the sun once it was complete. Who says money can't help?

Although the remit of the squad was to combat the scourge of housebreaking, it was also meant as a way of leaning heavily on neds to ascertain just what exactly they had been up to. There was a huge database being compiled so that the police would be well aware of the various actions of those involved in crime. It meant that after having arrested an individual, a confidential report would also have to be completed by us to enable the computer operators to input all the information into the intelligence system.

What in actual fact we were doing was monitoring the movements of criminals and keeping it on computer so that if a crime was committed at a later date, the intelligence system would identify potential suspects. This would make the work of detectives easier as it should technically assist when trying to solve crime.

What I would say though is that the information is only as good as the accuracy of its content! This is because the police are well known for fabricating information. Well, what I mean is they made up a lot of things about people, which may not have been accurate. So therefore, the information contained on the computer may not be entirely true.

After a person is arrested, a form is completed detailing all of the information pertaining to the arrest of that person. Included in this would be the description of where the crime took place, what time of day/night, the modus operandi, which is the way the crime is committed. This is extremely relevant as it may track down would-be criminals at a later date.

What officers also tended to do was put other information down on the form so that it could be updated on the computer. Items such as descriptions were to be as accurate as possible as obviously criminals do give false details to the police in order to prevent them from being detected. If complete and accurate descriptions are already known, for example, a particular scar or tattoo, this could easily identify a culprit.

If a particular ned just happened to piss off the arresting officers, it wasn't uncommon for the officers involved to put in a false nickname or deformity just to annoy the person. An example of this could be saying that a person pisses his pants and by putting something like "pishy Nell" onto the form.

It has also been known for officers to have written "blatant homosexual" onto a form just so that when that person is arrested at a later date and his previous convictions record is printed out then the details are there in black and white for other officers to see, and obviously ridicule that particular individual. Sounds infantile, but it does happen. The police are probably more blameworthy of falsehoods than some of the criminals in our society!

It wasn't long before the majority of housebreakers were behind bars and the crime rate had dropped, although solved crime figures had dramatically risen due to the admissions made by those caught. There were even "gate arrests". This still happens today and involves a criminal being arrested when they have just been released from prison. This happens due to outstanding warrants for their arrest. This to me also appeared to be quite harsh, as often the criminals would have spent about six months to a year in jail only to be arrested on release.

I know that I would have hated cops for doing that to me but as the gaffers were only out to clear up as much crime and outstanding warrants as possible, then this seemed like a logical thing to do. The only real problem now facing the two ten-person team of officers involved in this operation was lack of things to do.

All of the problem criminals had been dealt with and that left the teams with too much time on their hands. The only exception to this rule was my own team. Well, by that I mean Ally, Deek and myself. We still tended to keep to ourselves and went off driving around the division seeking out criminals.

As I have already admitted, this was a real learning experience for me and I sat back and relied on the other two guys to keep me right. The only trouble was, the criminals we spoke to all wanted to give information about drug dealers and where the drugs were being kept. What we should have done was to submit the information to the intelligence officers who would then commit it to the computer system. Instead, I kept notes on a notepad of who was selling drugs and where they were stashing the drugs.

I had never been on a drug search so I was obviously keen to do one to see what it was like. The only thing stopping us was the DI. He was a grumpy arrogant bastard and he liked us all to think that he was calling the shots, so therefore everything was to be authorised by him. This made life difficult as he was not an approachable guy.

We decided that we would leave the searches until we had to work late shift. After all, it's not often that a DI stays at the office beyond five-thirty (1730) at night. They are normally off home, leaving the real workers to hold the fort. One particular late shift, there were only about five of us on duty and there was no supervisor due to the fact that he was still working on a murder investigation, much to our delight.

Ally, Deek and I were out scouring the streets when I suggested that we head to the Blackhill area. The reason for this was that a drug dealer called "Gramps" was supposed to be driving around in a Ford Granada selling heroin. This information had been given to us a couple of weeks before so at my request, we set off to find him. Obviously when patrolling the streets, officers must rely on luck as well. It doesn't always work out that arrests come through diligent police work. There is always that saying of being in the right place at the right time!

Lady luck shone brightly that evening as Ally drove into Hogganfield Street. There, about twenty yards in front of us, was the Granada. It came to a halt and as it did so, I quickly reminded the guys about "Gramps" and suggested that we stop him for a drug search. Ally stopped the unmarked car behind the Granada and before I knew it, Deek had done a 'bonnet role' over our car and grabbed hold of the male.

It was funny to watch, as it was so reminiscent of a Starsky and Hutch move. I stumbled out of the car to hear Deek informing the male of his rights and obviously showed him his police warrant card, leaving the man in no doubt as to our identity. Gramps pissed his pants. Yes, quite literally, he did. He had a huge wet patch all over his crotch area.

Obviously, he must have been quite surprised at seeing the police and hence his inability to hold onto his water. What was I saying about nicknames? Gramps wasn't that surprised though. He quickly realised what was going on and started to shout for help from nearby residents. Being Blackhill and all, it wouldn't have been the first time that the residents came to the assistance of one of its brothers.

I looked around and saw about six men approaching us. I turned and shouted at them that we were plainclothes police officers and the first person to try to come anywhere near us would get "battened tae fuck". I was shitting myself. We would have been pounded to hell with this crowd.

I also radioed for assistance, trying not to make too much of a drama out of it. In the circumstances, Deek handcuffed Gramps and placed him in our car, telling him that he was going to the office for a thorough drug search. The rest of the crowd was still circling around us; although, in fairness, they made no attempt to rescue our prisoner.

Due to the semi urgent nature of my radio message, a patrol car came driving at speed down the street towards us, and the crowd dispersed back to their rabbit warrens within the housing scheme. We left to take him to the office and Ally drove his car down, as it too would have to be thoroughly searched.

I sat beside Gramps and he was becoming quite cheeky. It wasn't long though before I reminded him that he was sitting in his own piss and I didn't think he had any cause to be like that. After all, we didn't ask for him to piss his pants! He was angry and started hurling abuse in my direction. He then said to me, "So you must be that cunt Dawson? You're the new Sheriff in town?"

I couldn't contain my amusement. I had been called many things in my brief career as a cop but never a Sheriff. I didn't directly answer him but he knew that I was Dawson, not that it made the slightest difference to me. He was, after all, still going to the office for a drug search and seemed quite calm about it. Obviously, he had nothing to fear.

By the time we arrived at the office, Ally was already there with the other car. We had to take Gramps to the charge area so that he could be processed as an arrested person. He was then taken into a side room where Deek and I started to strip-search him. He was really uncomfortable and attempted to fight with us.

Rubber gloves were the order of the day and we commenced the search. Found inside his jeans pocket was a plastic bag containing brown powder. My eyes almost jumped out of their sockets. I had never seen so much smack in my life! Gramps just looked at the floor. Deek handed the drugs to me and I placed them inside a larger plastic bag for safekeeping.

It was to be a full detailed body search, which meant that he had to strip naked, then bend over, and Deek had the ominous job of looking up his ass to see if he had concealed drugs in there. Nothing there, but also found in his socks were three smaller-sized plastic bags containing the same brown powder.

This was better than expected and confirmed my belief that sometimes cops just have to act on gut instinct in order to gain a result. Whilst Gramps was redressing, I came out of the room and informed Ally of what we had found. He was delighted and told me that what we had found was about five thousand pounds worth of heroin.

I was shocked. Deek re-emerged and told the duty officer what had been found and the only thing left to do was search his car. We also found two other smaller bags in the car. In truth, Gramps was well and truly caught. All that was left to do was search his house but there was still the small matter of a drug search warrant to be obtained.

As I have said before, obtaining a warrant to search for drugs is a long laborious system and requires a meeting with a PF and a Sheriff, all out of hours. Deek decided that we would cut out the middleman and just go for a Justice of the Peace search warrant and he would explain his actions at a later date.

We did just that and with the assistance of the other two guys from our team, we searched Gramps' family home but found no other drugs or paraphernalia. This tended to suggest, according to Ally, that the drugs were being stored elsewhere; we didn't know where.

One of the detectives on duty assisted Ally with a taped interview as none of us were trained in that way. Gramps refused to cooperate and refused to answer any questions. This ensured that he was not implicating anyone else in selling the drugs but he didn't admit that they were his either. I asked the guys if they would assist me in writing the report, as I had never reported anything on this scale before.

The report was completed and Gramps appeared at Glasgow Sheriff Court the following day. He was remanded in custody pending his appearance at court about three months later. He later received three years in prison having admitted being involved in the supply of heroin.

My first drug report and I was hooked from that moment on, as I loved the buzz of being involved in that type of police work. I knew that this was where my forte would lie in the future. Due to the nature of the allegation against Gramps, it was imperative that the case was completed properly. This meant having to incur overtime that particular evening.

In fact, we each made about four hours overtime by the time the custody case was reported after having taken the drugs to the forensic lab at Pitt Street so that they could be analysed. It was confirmed to be heroin and this ensures that the accused is charged with the correct offences. Having signed off and gone home, we all assumed that everything would be fine; we may even receive a pat on the back for our good work. Well, so we all thought!

On commencing work the following afternoon, we were asked to attend and see the DI within his office. We walked through his door and he began ranting and raving at us because we had claimed overtime. No mention about the reason for us having to work! Just the fact that we had the audacity to claim it in the first place.

Ally started to laugh at him and the DI was livid. Deek, being a little more patient, asked the DI why he was so angry with us. After all, we had managed to rid the streets of a large amount of heroin. Was that so wrong? The fact of the matter was that we had worked on without asking the permission of a supervisor. "How could we ask if there was no one on to supervise us?"

Again, the DI was angry because Deek had questioned him about our lack of supervision, or indeed, his lack of organising a supervisor to be there in the first place. "I don't care what you say, you will not be claiming that overtime!" We stood there open-mouthed at him asking us to work for nothing.

"I don't work for fuck all." Ally was pissed off with the DI and could back his temper no longer. "If you're not happy with it then take me off the squad and I'll go and see the commander about myself!"

"Me too," said Deek. Feeling sheepish, I went along with my colleagues as I realised that we had to make a stand together.

"Fuck off back to your room and I'll come back to you." We left without knowing what was going to happen. We had an anxious wait within the portacabin as we discussed what he would do. About half an hour later, the DI walked in with a bundle of papers in his hand. The commander (who is the main boss of the division) had sent down a handwritten note thanking us for the fantastic result the previous evening and said that we could claim as much overtime as was necessary to clear the paperwork related to the case.

The DI was fuming. "Although he says that you can claim OT, you will clear it with a supervisor first."

"So are we still a part of the team then?" I could just tell that Ally couldn't wait to be flippant with him.

"For now, you are. But step out of line and your arse will be back tae wherever the fuck you came from" The DI seemed more angry than ever. He then went on to tell us that our job was to alleviate the crime of housebreaking, not drug-taking. Again, a heated debate ensued with Deek, Ally and the DI, concerning our job. In truth, the crime figures were lower than they had ever been and all that we wanted to do was just jail as many bad people as possible. That was, after all, our job. Eventually, they all agreed to disagree. I just sat there listening, like all junior officers do!

He eventually left the room. Pissed off at the way he had been made to look a fool, thanks to the commander's note. He didn't even say well done to us for our work. I didn't know the DI that well but I detested the prick now. Deek even asked him about potential other drug searches. If we received other information about drugs, were we to act upon it?

Again, we were told that if we did then we would have to receive authorisation to remain on duty. What a farce! All that he was doing was making the point that he was in charge and we had to report to a supervisor. We still didn't know how we could do that, especially when we didn't have one. It was decided that if we were to incur OT, then we would speak to the CID boss who was on duty at that time and leave the decision up to them. They wouldn't knock us back, as they too earned plenty of money from being detained on duty.

A week passed and the DI had made himself scarce from our room within the rear yard of Baird Street. It was good being there; at least, it was away from the glare of the bosses. However, we knew that the DI was still about as each of us was allocated the crap crime reports to work on. This was his way of getting back at the three of us for answering him back. No one else was given the same amount of enquiries.

He was only trying to piss us off, and it was working. Between us, we worked hard so that we could clear up the crimes and we all kept our heads down, deciding to keep out of his way. About two weeks later, we were again late shift and driving around the Springburn area when Ally spotted a Ned who used to give him information about drugs in the past.

Deek stopped the car and Ally swung into action, depicting himself as a mate of the poor unsuspecting criminal. They seemed very comfortable with one another and it wasn't long before they were laughing and joking with one another. The guy volunteered some information to Ally, telling him that this was a certain piece of information. Ally thanked him for the information and bid him a fond farewell.

When Ally returned to the car, he told us that apparently an ounce of heroin had just been delivered to a house in the Springburn area and that it had been cut into deals on a mirror and was lying waiting to be bagged for sale from the house.

Ally knew all the details and it was decided that we would carry out a recce at the flat to confirm the name on the door.

I say we, but I meant to say me. I was to go there to the flat myself. I was apprehensive, as I had never done that sort of thing before. Undeterred, I set off on my mission and managed to gain entry to the secured front door, thanks to a woman leaving the close. I went to the flat and confirmed the name and as I left the close, I ensured that the front door was left unlocked so that we could gain entry later if necessary.

My heart was pounding. I felt like I had done something naughty. In fact, what I did was what all police officers should do prior to carrying a search, as the correct name must be on a warrant to make the search legal. I told the guys of my mission and we returned to the makeshift office to get ready for the job.

Deek decided that he would carry out the correct procedure and telephoned the on-call PF to ascertain whether he would sanction a Justice of the Peace search warrant. The information was given to the PF and it was agreed that a JP warrant would suffice, fearing that all of the evidence would be lost if we were to wait and obtain a Sheriff's warrant. After obtaining the warrant, we returned to the block of flats to begin our operation.

Deek also suggested that I should go to the front door of the flat and try to entice the occupant to open it. This would ensure that the evidence would not be lost. After about half an hour after having received the information, I was about to try to gain entry. My heart was pounding more than it ever had done before. I was sure that everyone around me could hear it.

I approached the front door of the flat whilst Ally and Deek remained hidden at the side. I knocked on the door, patiently awaiting a reply. "Who is it?"

"It's Paul, Joe-Joe sent me up." Slowly, the front door lock turned and the door opened about six inches. I seized the opportunity and threw my weight behind it, forcing it wide open. The female behind it was thrown against the wall and before I knew it, all three of us were within the living room, explaining who we were and why we were there. The six young occupants all sat there motionless and numb as Ally took over the proceedings. I was shaking with excitement. After dealing with the paperwork side of the events, it was then time to search all of the shaken occupants. We asked for uniformed officers to attend to assist and they conducted the strip searches of the males. Nothing was found and that only left the search of the one-bedroom flat to contend with.

Only plastic bags were found elsewhere and the bedroom was the last area to search. It wasn't looking good, as there was no trace of any drugs. Deek seemed quite cocky but I couldn't understand why. Until, that is, I saw him reach above a wardrobe and remove a three-foot square mirror. As he brought it down, I saw what was there. About thirty-odd cut lines of brown powder!

The informant had been right all along. The owners of the flat were brother and sister and they assumed full responsibility for the drugs. Never before had any of us seen this type of find before.

Normally, the drugs were already bagged and ready for sale, but here we had discovered them before they had been even packaged. Deek requested a police photographer to attend so that pictures could be obtained depicting the drugs in their original state. The reason for this was that prior to them being removed, the mirror would have to be placed inside a plastic bag and the actual way in which the drugs had been cut would have been lost. The evidential value of the pictures was important.

We even managed to obtain Polaroid snaps of the mirror and its contents. After the photographs were done, the mirror was placed inside a bag and we all left to go back to the police office. However, the actual mirror just looked as though it had dust splattered over it.

Thank goodness for Deek having had the foresight to photograph the evidence. The brother/sister combination admitted the drugs and being concerned in their supply, although the brother did try to keep his sister out of the frame by saying that it was him who was responsible and not her. I actually felt quite sorry for them both, as they were so young to have become mixed up in this type of crime.

He later pleaded guilty to supply charges, and received a three-year sentence at the High Court. Again, we incurred plenty of overtime and the DI ignored our good work and just explained that we were to work no more overtime again.

What he did was to piss us off and we all decided to work our stated hours and forget about jailing criminals as we seemed to be the only people bothering to lock Neds up. The rest of the squad just walked around doing basically nothing. The crime figures were low and it was nearing the end of our three-month attachment.

At last, our useless DS had returned from the murder investigation although we did our best to ignore him as he was of no interest to us by now! Behind the scenes of the two squads there was rivalry; well, not on our part but the other team of ten in particular seemed envious of our success. Deek, Ally and I had become a great team but we just did our job and didn't allow them to get to us.

However, one afternoon, I overheard a conversation about everyone going to a function that Thursday night. I hadn't heard anything about it so I asked the two guys involved. Duffy laughed and told me that it probably wasn't something I would like as it was only for a set crowd of guys to go to. I asked him to explain but he said that he couldn't.

I was becoming paranoid and needed answers. Deek and Ally were out at court and I had to wait until the next day to find out. When I explained to the guys about my conversation with Duffy, they too were none the wiser and knew nothing of the Thursday night out.

Later, our busybody DS revealed all. He knew everything that went on the office so it seemed only natural to ask him. It was a night out to celebrate the fact that one of the detectives on the other team was being made Grandmaster of his local Masonic order and the invites were only given to those who were Masonic members. It was to be a big bevy session and he would be buying all of the drink. Those of us not invited were clearly not in that particular Thursday night clique. Deek, Ally, two DS's and me were the only members out of twenty to be left out.

I knew nothing of these meetings although Deek soon told me all about their strange habits as he had friends who had become members of different orders. I was beginning to find out just how bigoted the police was and those Catholics employed there were in the minority.

Apparently, even senior management would be there too. If only we could get our hands on a picture of them all! The Monday after the secret night out was our last week in the squad and we were all ordered to complete all paperwork so that when we returned to our own shifts, we wouldn't be carrying work with us.

The three of us remained in the office alone and did as was asked. The rest of the team was nowhere to be found, although they didn't have any paperwork to complete as they hadn't done any work. Lying on the floor of the office was a picture of those who had been at the night out. It was a real eye-opener to me as I saw gaffers I never knew were of that ilk.

Detective Superintendents all the way down to constables from our division. These included several Catholics who had obviously sold their souls for the sake of a night on the bevy, although I am aware now of many Catholics who are members for business purposes. Each to their own, I know, but we were pissed off at not being asked to attend there in the first place.

The last I heard about that picture was that it had been photocopied and faxed to every subdivision within Strathclyde with a cheeky caption attached to it asking for those who knew of the identities of those in the picture, should contact the press office at Pitt Street. I don't know who did it but suffice to say, it annoyed several of those bosses in the picture. Thanks to the advances in modern technology, a happy night out could be shared by those who couldn't attend!

As the squad was coming to an end, the statistics were completed in respect of the arrests made. The reason for that being Pitt Street having to publish the results so that the local councillors could be appraised of how successful the operation was. Like all statistics compiled by multi-national companies, the content was somewhat made up. The reason for this was to create the impression that there had been huge arrests and that crime figures had dropped. This wasn't quite accurate.

It was true that arrests had risen, but the arrests also took into account those arrested on warrants as well as for drug-related offences. Those figures were merely added to create the impression that they were all housebreakers. In truth, these were the overall arrests for our division.

It wasn't only our division who was guilty of false reports. It was universally known in the Strathclyde Force that the figures were inflated to create the impression that there had been a huge rise in arrests thanks to the hard work of those involved in the operation. It was quite simple as to ascertain why the figures were 'doctored'. This would appease the local councillors that the police was value for money. That is what it all comes down to.

The police are hugely accountable to local government, as they after all are responsible for setting the annual budget given to the police. Therefore, it is politically correct to ensure that the work done by them is deemed to be value for money.

In defence of my own division at that time, it should be emphasised that our figures did reflect a huge upturn in arrests for housebreaking. But, although that particular crime had reduced, another crime had increased rapidly. Thefts from cars had risen by over two hundred percent. The reason for that was quite self-explanatory. The Neds had switched their attention from breaking into houses to now breaking into cars as a preferred option.

They were well aware of the high-profile police campaign to rid the areas of housebreakers so the astute criminals decided to turn their attentions to other areas of crime. Who says that the criminal mind is not active?

To finish off Operation Turnkey, there was an arranged press conference at Pitt Street so that the Chief could boast of the huge success of the elite squad of personnel who had rid the areas of the scourge of housebreaking. However, prior to this, those officers involved in the squads were assembled with the main hall of Pitt Street so that the Deputy Chief Constable could commend us all for our hard work.

Seated there alongside my other colleagues from the division seemed that yet another futile attempt by the bosses of showing us mere mortals at the lower end of the factory line that our efforts were greatly appreciated and that without our efforts, the results would have been unattainable.

So that was why we had to go to the headquarters to be told that? Just shows that the whole saga is orchestrated to create the illusion that the police are tackling the problems faced by the general public whilst at the same time high profile policing worked to rid areas of crime and the fear of crime.

Rubbish; it was yet again another stunt to bring to the fore the fact that senior bosses within the police were only attempting to boost their own egos in the hope that it would enhance their career paths, either within or outside the police in years to come!

Chapter 4
Try Not to Hit Yourself with It

The adaptation of returning to life within the confines of a stricter uniformed approach to life as a police officer was difficult. The total difference that life as an ordinary cop and that of a plainclothes one would-be detective was too much to comprehend. Although I had only been away from my shift for three months, it felt as though I didn't belong there anymore. Part of the reason for this was that I had gained far more confidence and I knew that I was destined to be a detective, even that early on in my police service.

Even the shift pattern was annoying me. I shouldn't have felt this way as I was barely out of my probation and already I had itchy feet and wanted away from uniform policing. The stark truth being that I still had more to learn about being a police officer and the only way that I could do that was to learn more through practical policing.

As I looked around, I saw that those attached to the CID were much older than me, as well as the fact that they had about fifteen to twenty years' service in the police. This brought me back down to earth with a crash. I now realised that I would have to gain more experience of life on the streets before that big move to a department would come at me!

I had no option but try to adapt to my life with the shift that had welcomed me from the beginning. Others on the shift also noticed the change in my mood and quickly told me that I would have to further prove myself as a cop before I would gain any real recognition.

Any officer who has completed two years' service may apply to sit the Police Scotland Examinations. I, however, had just missed that opportunity the previous year due to my start date with the police. I was now approaching the point where I was eligible to apply to sit the exams. I had watched others walking about like zombies whilst they attempted to work the arduous shift pattern, whilst at the same time study for all three exams.

I decided that I would do one at a time to ensure that I would pass. The three exams being crime, general police duties and road traffic were considered to be necessary if a person wished to be considered for promotion. An officer even had to possess these prior to becoming a detective, so therefore, I had no option but to at least attempt them.

I studied hard for the crime paper and eventually passed it in the first attempt. At least I had shown that I was willing to attempt the exams as many officers to this day still have yet to complete them, thereby preventing them from being promoted. I was settled doing my job now and I had the respect of those around me.

Occasionally, during spells of quieter night shifts, the sergeant would ensure that two of us would be in plainclothes working alongside our own shift and targeting whatever problems there were. I was again fortunate in that I had again been chosen to do this job along with another colleague who had just completed a stint in plainclothes within a crime unit who were targeting car thieves in our division.

Murray knew the area very well and had a great way with the criminal fraternity, albeit he was a sarcastic sod with a short fuse. Nonetheless, he was a great cop and his skills were never often challenged. I often thought that he would have been an asset to the CID but he didn't possess his exams so therefore he couldn't do the job.

Quite surprising really when I considered the calibre of some of the detectives already attached to that department. He would have outshone even the brightest but it wasn't politically correct to include him in the department due to the exam etiquette. I have to say that I learned a lot from Murray; although at that point, I wasn't aware how to manipulate a situation with criminals in order to create a story of events.

Whether they occurred the way that we told them remained to be seen. What was important was the fact that the gaffers saw a return for their trust in putting us out in plain clothes. So therefore, a certain amount of arrests was expected, by whatever means. During brief spells in and out of plainclothes, it merely reassessed my want to be a detective. Even during my spells of walking a beat accompanied by another colleague, I found that this was beneficial as it helped me get to know the area that was otherwise unknown.

The early shift was another shift that I detested. The reason for this was that I had to be up about five o'clock in the morning to be at work for around six-thirty. I am not a morning person at all so this was a particular hardship for me. Even at work, having to then walk around an area practically uninhabited on the streets as everyone was in bed at that miserable time of the day!

However, my neighbour during these early morning strolls was Mack. I have previously mentioned how he fancied himself as a bit of a hit with the ladies. His charms, however, ensured that we didn't go either hungry or cold. The police is well known for disappearing into places where they can doss and hide from the gaffers.

We were no exception to that rule, thanks to Mack and his contacts. There was a particular bakery situated within the leafy scheme of Balornock. The owner/occupier was a lovely middle-aged woman who had a fondness for the police and was happy to see them at all times. This probably ensured that she wouldn't be bothered by local criminals fearing that if they did anything to her, or her shop, then she would undoubtedly find out all about it and tell the police who was responsible. It also meant that if criminals decided to descend on her shop, there might have been a police officer hiding in the back shop!

The routine for us was to call there most mornings during the week when we were on early shift. Sandra would have the kettle on awaiting our attendance there. We would also have a couple of rolls to eat and possibly even a wee cookie. The banter was free and Sandra and her shop assistant daughter gave us much lip, which was fine as they were at ease with us. There would be much fluttering of eyes with Mack and the daughter, who was about thirty with three kids, all with different dads. But Mack was not adverse to 'any old port in a storm'!

Her best efforts to seduce him, at that point, fell on deaf ears as his mind was elsewhere. He had a love interest in another part of Springburn with whom he would try and arrange a dangerous liaison with, whenever he could. The only stumbling block for Mack was his wife.

The poor, unsuspecting and long-suffering wife was a likeable woman but was so trusting of her husband that he had quite a free reign when it came to having secret meetings out with his work hours, and indeed whilst working too! The Springburn love interest was single with an eight-year-old boy. They lived in a very rough area although she seemed quite a nice girl.

However, at that time, I was unaware that he was shagging her, as he decided to keep it to himself. Until, that is, he parked the patrol car outside her home and asked me to stay there as he had a message to deliver. This may have been the case but I was always suspicious of Mack and therefore knew that something was going on. After about ten minutes, he re-emerged from the close and came into the car.

His face was white. I couldn't help myself so I asked him if he was up to visit his burd. He calmly announced that he was seeing this female and had been doing so for about six months. His manner though was strange and I asked him if everything was all right. He told me that it was but something wasn't quite right about the situation. I asked if she was pregnant.

To my horror, he said she was. Yes, that's right, past tense. She had had an abortion the previous day and that was the purpose of his visit to her house that morning, to ensure that she was all right. I was horrified. Not at the fact that she had an abortion, but the very idea that he was having unprotected sex with this female. I wasn't being moralistic, just trying to educate him in the way of safe sex.

I suppose that was quite bizarre, as he was a forty-something man who should really have known better. I felt like a father chastising his own son and thereafter giving him a lecture on safe sex practice! It made no difference to him, as he was just relieved that she had gotten rid of the baby to spare him having to pay child support.

"Here's hoping you'll learn in the future to make sure you wear a condom then, Mack?"

"Don't believe in them so she'll just have to be sterilised then, I suppose."

This was obviously his idea of a solution. Several weeks later, Mack decided to have a party for those of his colleagues he worked alongside, as well as liked. About twelve of us were invited along with our partners. Included in this list was a female friend whose house we also used to frequent, although he assured me that he had never had any sexual relations with her. I must confess, however, I didn't believe him, as she was a bit of a police groupie!

She would sometimes appear at police nights out and stay there hanging on to whoever took her fancy. I stayed well clear, as I wasn't interested in anything that anyone else had to offer, apart from my wife! Although perhaps most men just like the attention given by another female, the only difference with Mack was that he preferred his to be ugly. So the party was arranged for our weekend off, which meant that no one would have to worry about work.

The last day before we finished for the weekend, Mack still had to clear up arrangements with his female friend, as she was only too willing to come along. He had a proposition for her. When we went into her house for a chat and a coffee, I had no idea what he would ask her to do.

Quite calmly, during conversation, he asked Kate if she would do him a favour. Ever the helper, she said yes. He then proceeded to ask her if she could bring his Springburn burd along to the party, pretending that she was a friend of Kate's. I burst out laughing, thinking that it was a joke. The harsh reality of it all sank in when he muttered that he fancied shagging this female in his own matrimonial home whilst his wife and friends were all downstairs, blissfully unaware. I was hysterical laughing at him but I sensed that he was being truly serious. Kate freaked out, calling him every name imaginable due to his lack of respect for his wife, as well as her. He expected her just to go along with the suggestion as though it was commonplace for people to do this.

He didn't bother to backtrack at any point to even hint that it was a joke. It wasn't meant to be a joke. Kate told him to fuck off and that she didn't want to be part of his lies and deception so his burd would have to remain at home all alone that Saturday evening. The party was all right, but nothing to brag about. The only reason I went was that I felt obliged to as we lived a short taxi ride from one another so it was difficult for me to say no. Kate surprisingly didn't turn up for the party. Perhaps she was washing her hair that night?

I never told anyone about Mack and his desire to bring a scheme chick out to his family home. Personally, I thought that it was so outrageous a suggestion that he was pretending; alas, I was wrong. Several weeks later, Mack and I were requested to attend the report of a housebreaking in the particular street where his burd lived. When we arrived there, other colleagues had beaten us to it so we turned to leave the area when a wee boy came running towards our car. Mack stopped it and I jumped out only to hear the wee boy shouting, "Uncle Mack, are you comin tae our house fur yer dinner?"

His face was scarlet and he quickly told me to get back into the car as he replied abruptly that he was too busy. Again, I couldn't believe my ears and found it hard to control my laughter. This was the turning point for him and he decided that after about nine months, he would have to finish with her.

This wasn't a straightforward break-up, as she had felt used by this particular police officer. However, she eventually saw sense and kept away from him. In the meantime, I was seconded onto another car to work with one of the other guys and I only saw Mack at the beginning and end of each shift. He never really spoke of his love life and I never asked. Yet another night out was planned with the shift but I couldn't manage on this occasion so I declined the acceptance of another major bevy session.

Mack, however, was up for it and even took his car. This was a strange thing to do, as he liked a good drink. The fact that he had his car with him meant nothing and he used to drink and drive frequently. This night out had other females there. One of them was the baker's daughter. That night, Mack drove her home and had a quick fumble with her in the car. At last she got what she wanted and he may have put to bed the ghost of his Springburn past.

About four months later, I was again out walking with Mack and during the early shift, we went into the baker's to see how they were. I almost fell over when I saw that the daughter had a little bun of her own in the oven. Mack's face fell a mile.

He managed to speak to her whilst I kept her mother talking so that she never noticed the conversation taking place between the other two. Sandra spoke of the fact that her single daughter was about to have baby number four to yet another unknown father, but she was standing by her daughter because she loved her.

I almost choked on my roll during this conversation, as I knew otherwise. It made me feel uncomfortable but I wasn't prepared to say who the father was. After all, it was none of my business. We made a hasty retreat from the shop and I quizzed Mack about his encounter but he refused to believe that he was the father! Despite the fact that he knew she had no boyfriend at that time. He just wanted to say nothing so he decided to keep well away from the shop.

I later heard through police circles that she had a baby boy and that Sandra had to be restrained when she found out who the father was. She did consider a complaint against Mack, for what I don't know but she decided to put it behind her. As for Mack, well, he had nothing to do with her or the baby. Everyone remains blissfully unaware, including his wife, that he has another child. What a tangled web of lies and deceit the police weave! No wonder the police receive such bad press.

There was to be another plainclothes operation set up within our area and yet again, I was chosen from my shift to do it. It was to be called the 'crime unit' and there were five of us along with a detective sergeant who would oversee the running of the unit. This was to combat car crime and drug problems in our division.

I only had three years' service and I was delighted to be given the chance to escape from the mundane role of an ordinary uniformed officer and I was desperate to prove myself as a suitable candidate for the CID. I hoped that this would help me gain more recognition with the gaffers. The team was well suited in that its range of police service was from the young (me), to those with about twenty years' service.

At least I would be able to learn more about what was required as part of a crime unit team. Having finished my last night shift, I relaxed knowing that I was about to embark on a three months' routine, hopefully filled with fun and excitement as that had been sadly lacking from my last few months in uniform.

It was also a chance to dress down by wearing jeans and T-shirts, as opposed to the thick woollen trousers and stiff collared shirts.

At long last, I had the chance to work with my new team. Peter was much older than I was and he had about fifteen years' service. Craig and Dooley were quite similar in service to me, as they too were still in single figures in years of police service. There was also a female on the team. Fiona was about thirty and seemed quite straight-laced, prim and proper. This was on the outside, but that false façade would soon be replaced by a great cop, who was competent and as ruthless as any other cop I had ever known.

Russell was the gaffer, but he was probably one of the nicest guys you could ever meet. He was very switched on and I knew that I was going to get along really well with him and the rest of the team. The first couple of weeks in any new environment is a time for getting to know each other's strengths and weaknesses. We were no exception to that.

It seemed that everyone was doing the job by the book and taking great care not to make any cock-ups. However, we all knew that it could not last indefinitely. By now, we were managing to amass a collection of information in order to start carrying out drug searches in houses. The only thing that we were legally required to do was ensure that there was enough evidence to obtain a search warrant.

As I have already said, obtaining a warrant could be a long process with the PF having to approve each and every application prior to going in front of a Sheriff and swearing on oath that the information was correct and accurate. The first time, I did it the proper way, I realised that it was in fact a time-consuming event and one that I was not wishing to be tied up in.

It was here I learned the art of waffle and decided that if I was called to question regarding why I hadn't obtained the warrant under the correct format, I would just say that the drugs were to be transported quickly from the house and that it was in the interests of justice that I obtain a warrant from a Justice of the Peace (JP).

Fiona was the best person to phone the duty fiscal out of normal work hours, as she had such a believable tone that we were never refused permission to go directly to a JP by any PF. The first search we carried out as part of the team was on a well-known junkie family in the Barmulloch area of Glasgow.

They sold jellies (Temazepam capsules) from their home. Even the mother was into selling them, but so far, no other crime unit had managed to nail them. We had been given information that they were busy between five and seven at night. It was decided that we would try our best to get them.

Fiona obtained a warrant from a local JP and off four of us set to conquer the family from hell. We had no real plan to carry out the raid, as it was difficult to access the house due to its location. We parked the car a few blocks away and Fiona and I walked towards the house, deciding to try to buy drugs for a laugh. This is frowned upon as the police use specially trained officers to do this type of thing.

Whilst we were at the front door, the other two would be making their way to the back door, in an effort to gain entry through there. One little discrepancy was that they also had a huge fuck-off Alsatian as well, but I had forgotten to tell them. The door opened and there was wee sweet mammy with a face like a bulldog chewing a wasp.

Perhaps this was the dog I had been told all about? I burst out laughing when I saw her and had to make a quick apology and told her that I was still high from the speed (Amphetamine Sulphate) I had taken earlier.

Fiona remained calm and asked her for five jellies, pushing a fiver towards her at the same time. "Don't stand there then, in ye come." As we walked into the house, I pretended to close over the front door but left it slightly ajar, hoping that the guys would see it and just come in at our back.

It worked; as the maw fumbled in her cardigan pocket to get the jellies, Peter and Craig walked in behind us. She started to shout like fuck at me for leaving the door open and told the other two to get the fuck out of her house. At this point, Fiona brought out her warrant card and told the demon that we were the police.

She went berserk and tried to get to her supply of jellies but we managed to handcuff her. It didn't stop her shouting on the real dog, trying to get it to attack us. By good luck, it was in the locked kitchen, although it was trying like hell to get out. Peter, being the old guy among us, said that he wasn't afraid of dogs and ventured into the kitchen to ensure that the back door was locked, to prevent anyone from coming in.

I still don't know how he managed it, but the dog was fine and he calmed it down. He always carried a handful of dog biscuits in his pocket so that probably helped him. Meanwhile, the old bulldog was still annoyed at us for taking the piss out of her. We started the house search and found several hundred pounds worth of jellies and knew that it had been a success, despite the shaky start.

The only problem with these types of searches is that there is always a large array of would-be buyers who attend at the house after we have entered. This makes the job more difficult as we have to take statements from them as it proves that the house had been frequently used for selling drugs. One of the callers to the house though was her son. He was raging at us for searching his mum's house. He was even madder when he discovered that it was she who had invited us in.

This was the first time I realised that four officers are not enough to search a house. What we were doing was putting our own lives at stake as there were not enough of us to cope with all of the tasks involved in the search. The number of callers kept growing and was becoming a pain in the ass to deal with. I'd had enough and set about scaring off the local junkies. I wrote on a piece of paper and attached it to the front door. "Police carrying out a search, enter and face the jail."

Surprisingly, no one else came to the door and that was what we decided to always do if we didn't have enough people to assist with the search. After we had finished with the house search, we only had the minor matter of the mother to deal with. I thought that we were going to have a fight on our hands when it was mentioned that we would be taking her to the office to be interviewed.

Her beloved son told us that he would take the blame for his mother, if only we would leave her at home. The caring side of Fiona told him that he was just being stupid and if he didn't shut his mouth then he too would be getting locked up. He did as he was told and sat back down, leaving the bulldog to face the music. It had been our first turn together and it was a learning experience for us all. Mostly for me, as I now had the added benefit that at least I wasn't turned away from buying drugs at a house. I knew that I would do that many more times in the future.

After having arrested a person suspected of supplying drugs, obviously the next stage would be to carry out a taped interview. This was a snag in the process as the only person trained to do this was our very own detective sergeant, Russell. The only other alternative was to carry out a question and answer written down in our very own notebooks.

Whilst this was good practice to do, the reality was that at court, we would have to produce our notebooks, which would then be open to scrutiny. I didn't particularly like this idea as it could mean that our actions could be criticised. However, as Russell wasn't on duty, Fiona decided that she would do the required interview in her notebook and I would just have to sign it to confirm that it was done properly. At least it would only be her notebook being looked at if it ever reached court.

The interview was conducted and the bulldog was now warming to both Fiona and I and she realised that we weren't really bad guys after all. When Russell returned to duty a couple of days later, he was pleased with the results we had obtained in his absence. The downside to him was that he was hardly ever there as he was always called upon to assist with other more serious matters, like murders!

He was seconded on to another one in our division, leaving the rest of us to get on with running the crime unit. Peter being the oldest assumed the mantle of leader and quite honestly, we were content with that arrangement. Craig and Dooley were great to work with, as there was never a dull moment when they were around. Coupled with the fact that we were each as keen as the other so this meant that there were going to be many other searches together.

One night, about a week after having searched the bulldog's house, an informant told us of another potential house to search as they too had started to sell jellies. It is quite true when the neds always told the police that when a drug dealer gets busted by the police, another house quickly steps in to fill the void left by the demise of the other seller.

The particular family, who started up their business, was horrible. They were well known to the police as housebreakers, thieves and drug addicts. Four sons, and a worse mother than the previous bulldog. They were dirty bastards and their houses were amongst the worse flea-ridden in the division. Cops used to dread going to the house fearing that they would catch something from them. Now, we were about to embark on a search for drugs, and I couldn't wait!

Dooley obtained a warrant in our usual manner by contacting a local JP to endorse our search. Getting to the house was going to be a problem as it was a top floor flat set within the bustling Barmulloch area. This was a densely populated local authority-owned area and was difficult for us to get to as they 'hung fae the windaes' looking for the police trawling the streets.

If they saw any sign of us, they would quickly dispose of any drugs down the toilet. Our plan this time was similar to the last search in that Fiona and this time, Craig would attempt to get into the house, followed by the rest of us. They pretended to be boyfriend/girlfriend so that it would increase their chances of getting to the door.

Whilst they did this, they would also be wearing a hidden radio so that we hear them and keep in touch, obviously for safety reasons. They set off towards the front of the block of flats. Dooley and I made our way via the opened back door of the close. Peter remained out of view with the car. Fiona and Craig surprisingly managed to walk right up to the front door and we remained on the stairwell waiting to see if they would get into the house.

The door opened after Craig wolf-whistled, an indication used by all drug clients when trying to score drugs. A man answered the door and on doing this, somehow, we all managed to pile into the house without as much as a sound being emitted from his mouth. There was only one other male in the house and we knew that there was no way that any drugs could have been disposed of.

After having taken control of the whole situation and declared our intentions to the men, it was time to commence a search of the house. I knew from other cops that the house was supposed to have been very smelly and dirty. What lay ahead of me was unknown, but already I felt nauseated by the smell.

Peter and Dooley had the pleasure of looking up the arses of these two particularly horrible junkies, a part of the search I always dreaded but one that was important as it wasn't uncommon for drug addicts to secrete drugs in places where the naked eye cannot see! The only thing that both brothers had on their possession was money, and not much of it.

My instincts told me that due to their calm demeanour, they had no drugs in the house but perhaps a delivery was due. As I was explaining this theory to Fiona, there was a knock at the front door. I looked through the spyhole and saw that the vision on the other side was yet another brother.

This was it, I knew that the drugs were on him. I managed to get Craig and together, we opened the door and grabbed the unsuspecting brother by the scruff of the neck and hauled him into the flat. He was shouting abuse at us as we did this and this caused a wee bit of unrest from the other two already cuffed brothers who were within the living room. (I use that term loosely as it more resembled a pigsty.)

Craig managed to cuff our guy and we took him into a bedroom to search him. He had five bags of jellies in his pockets, each containing one hundred yellow capsules. Whilst we found it difficult to hide our delight, he was really pissed off. We re-joined the others and asked them in the true manner whether they knew anything about the jellies and surprisingly, they were shocked to see the drugs.

In other words, they had decided that their poor brother would be left to take the flak on his own. No other drugs or other related paraphernalia was found so it looked like he was going to jail. The last room to be searched was the bathroom. Craig and I drew the short straw for this and I wasn't looking forward to it. On opening the door, firstly the stench was overwhelming but no wonder. Lying in the bath was a huge shit! I almost spewed.

I came back out and asked one of the brothers, "Who the fuck did that?"

He looked puzzled then after having looked at it himself, he calmly announced, "That wis the dug."

" You don't have a fucking dog!" Trying not to appear annoyed, I was looking for another explanation, but it appeared that that was it. An anonymous dog did it. No wonder other cops complained of a smell in the house when these dirty bastards left constant reminders of their own filth all over the house.

The search was over and again our trick of placing a sign on the door informing others that the police were within the house seemed to work, as there were no callers to the house looking for drugs. Due to the evidence all pointing at Jake, we took him back to the police office for further questioning. When Peter and Dooley were processing him as a prisoner at the charge area, the rest of us started to make coffee in celebration of another good result.

Shortly after that, Peter came hurtling into the room with news. Apparently, when Jake had asked for a lawyer, he gave the name of an infamous one who was hated by the police. This was the first time I had even heard of the guy but I had been assured that he was a right bastard. I couldn't see what all the fuss was about but apparently, the lawyer always took great pleasure out of ripping apart evidence presented in court by the police.

That didn't sound to me like a bastard; I would have thought that he was a very good lawyer and obviously good at his job. Much debate followed about how we would get a hard time at court but I tried to allay all fears by saying that we would be well prepared. I even agreed to submit the case and go into court first to face his wrath. This was agreed and I ensured that everything in my notebook was the way it should be.

The CID carried out the interview so that we could say that all procedures were adhered to regarding his arrest and interview. Jake made no comment regarding the drugs and due to his horrendous previous convictions, he was remanded in custody pending his trial. In the meantime, I submitted statements of all cops involved in the search in preparation for the trial.

Before long, a citation appeared for us all to attend court to face the dreaded lawyer. At court that day, I handed over the statements I had submitted on behalf of my colleagues and I noticed that some of them were corroboration statements.

This meant that on Fiona's and Craig's statement, there was only a few lines to say that they had read my statement and agreed with its content and they corroborated it in full. So, they too had to give the same evidence to support what I had written. This was commonplace for cops to do as it saved precious time, both report writing and at court. This was a huge issue for Peter, as he said that the correct way to submit statements was to write one after the event and each cop had to then give it to the reporting officer—in this case, me.

What I had done then was to cut out the middleman and simplify the evidence to assist the prosecution. I started to panic, as I knew that no doubt the lawyer would give me hell for not following procedures. I decided that I was just going to tell the others that I would say—

"PC Dawson please?" A voice came from around the corner and before I could tell the others my plan, I was to go into court to face the unknown.

I walked into the courtroom and saw the only familiar face I knew—Jake. The sheriff seemed okay, as did this badass lawyer. My evidence in chief, that is, the evidence given to the PF, was straightforward and seemed to pass by very quickly without a hitch. Then the lawyer stood up to begin his defence.

It was true what all cops had said. At that point, I knew he was a bastard! What a hard time he gave me in comparison to the PF. He questioned my every action and called into question which of us had even found the drugs. I was furious but tried not to show it. My own nervousness was replaced by arrogance. I was determined that he wasn't going to get the better of me. He even asked for my notebook to be produced and I was having none of it.

I knew of a stated case in law whereby a person doesn't have to produce his notebook if it has not been produced during the evidence in chief. As I knew that I hadn't produced mine, I became more confident. He barraged me time and again to produce it.

Eventually, the Sheriff asked me why I didn't want to produce it. Thinking quickly, I told him that I had nothing to hide but the stated case of "Hinshelwood v Auld" backed up my right not to produce it. There was a stunned silence over the courtroom and I was asked to leave as the defence lawyer jumped up to his feet to complain about this.

I was left standing in the corridor for about fifteen minutes whilst the legal team argued over what I had said. Meanwhile, my colleagues were eager to find out what was going on. In law, however, I was not supposed to convey any information to them about the trial, so I stuck to that. Well, maybe a little came out to allay their fears of the lawyer, although I knew that they would all be shit scared of going into the witness box.

Eventually, I was recalled to continue with my evidence. I knew that the lawyer was fucked off with me but I had won the argument over the notebook and I didn't have to produce it. I simply did not give in to his request and felt that I had won.

After another twenty minutes of questions, the lawyer stooped to his lowest ebb when he insinuated that we only carried out the search to get at his client, as like all police officers, I didn't like him. I retorted that I carried out the search because his client was involved in selling drugs and prior to that night, I had never even spoken to him. He was again angry with me, as it seemed that I had the upper hand.

The final straw came when he said that the search was a wind up. I was confused by his terminology and asked him to clarify what he meant by the comment. "Give me a definition of a wind up, Mr Dawson."

Thinking quickly, I replied, "You wind up a clock." He started shouting at me whilst banging on his desk, saying that I knew he didn't mean it that way. I remained calm although tried to control my laughter, as I knew that I had 'wound' him up.

The sheriff intervened and told the lawyer that he was asking out of order questions and he should get on with the job in hand. He threw down his papers and said that he had no further questions for me. The PF had nothing further for me either and I was at last free to go. I couldn't get out of the witness box quick enough to escape so that I could laugh my head off at what had happened. After an hour and a half, it was over, well, for me anyhow.

I left the courtroom thinking about what had taken place and formed the opinion that the lawyer was not a bastard. He was a good lawyer who had tried to do his job whilst representing his client! That is, after all, what he is paid to do. He went over the police procedures, but what other police officers fail to realise is that they are their own worst enemies and they always try to cut corners. This is what leads to fewer conviction rates and losing cases. He had my respect and I quite liked him despite my little verbal spat with him in the box. It was all good harmless fun. He did his job and I did mine!

After having given my evidence, I left the court building and went to the nearby Police Headquarters for lunch. The others joined me so that they too could find out what lay in store. Obviously, I am not supposed to talk to my colleagues about my evidence but I couldn't wait to tell them about the run in with the lawyer.

They were in fits of laughter when I recounted the latter part of my evidence, although Peter did comment that they would probably get a hard time thanks to my cheek. I briefly told them about what had taken place. I didn't tell them everything, but I did probably say enough to ensure that they did their homework prior to going back in to give their evidence.

Fiona was the only person who didn't seem that bothered about the grilling she would receive. She remained calm and focussed. I was highly impressed by her approach. The other 'men', by comparison, were terrified of what lay ahead. So much for the rufty tufty police in Glasgow!

After lunch, I decided that I would go back to court to listen to the evidence of my colleagues. This can be very off-putting but it didn't bother me in the slightest if any of my colleagues listened to my evidence. I wanted to know how strong my workmates were and this would be an ideal way to assess it.

Fiona entered the witness box and was still calm and focussed. She took the oath with a degree of honesty I had never quite seen before. She looked innocent and naïve. I knew that this would be fine for her. Initially, the PF led her through her evidence and she had no problem at all answering any of the questions. After about twenty minutes, the PF announced that he was finished. Over to the defence lawyer to begin his barrage of questions!

Again, Fiona remained calm and answered many of the questions asked of her in a similar way to my own answers. He asked her to produce her notebook and so began the same delays as previously experienced by me. The court was cleared to allow a legal debate and then after ten minutes, Fiona re-emerged to continue with her evidence. She stuck to her guns and was then asked by him to name the piece of legislation connected with her refusal to produce her notebook.

So as not to appear as though we had rehearsed it, she told him that it was the Hinshelwood case. He asked her to clarify but she stuck to the one name she could remember. After much ado, he gave in and moved on to other matters. Fiona looked content in the fact that she had stood her ground and won.

In truth, she didn't receive as difficult a time as I had experienced. Probably because she looked as though butter wouldn't melt in her mouth, let alone tell a lie. He was polite and courteous to her. Must have been because she was a soft tactile young lady, whereas I was a cheeky bastard.

I left after Fiona gave her evidence as I knew that we had done enough to ensure that the dealer got his just desserts for plying his trade in our territory. He eventually was found guilty and sentenced to one year in prison for being concerned in the supply of Temazepam. Meanwhile, we had all received our own baptism of fire with this particular lawyer. Not an event we were likely to forget in a while but if it made us more aware of being prepared for court then surely it was an event worthy of remembering.

We had been together for about three months as a team and had bonded very well. One afternoon, a DI (Detective Inspector) approached me in the corridor and told me that the team was to be disbanded. The reason for this was that another unit was about to be implemented as part of a force-wide initiative by Strathclyde Police, aimed at targeting drug dealers.

Operation Eagle was to become one of the most successful programmes ever to be introduced by any force. There were to be two teams in each division, made up of ten police officers in each team from all different backgrounds including CID, Community Policing and shift personnel. Our current team was to be split in order to spread our own experience with the new recruits.

However, I immediately thought of a new problem with the forthcoming teams. That of cops wishing to target the criminals in their own areas. You see, the police staff to be used were taken from offices from Baird Street, Easterhouse and Kirkintilloch, so this was a sure-fire way to cause problems among the teams. I could already feel the tension build as we waited on the start of Operation Eagle.

The DS in charge of the two teams was Russell. First impressions saw that he was laidback and jovial with a wicked sense of humour. I knew that I was going to get on well with him. As for the rest of the team, it seemed to me that there were too many egos to contend with and already the split was evident, as some of the officers from Easterhouse remained practically joined at the hip.

However, it also meant the return to a familiar partnership for me with Deek. It had been quite a while since our last successful encounters during Operation Turnkey, but I knew that we would probably just try to plod along without the interference of others. Fiona was taken from the team and transferred to work indoors in the administration department at our Divisional Headquarters. This was not a choice thing. She was told that she had to do it.

I knew that she would be a loss to the team but another female slotted in very well, although she was a flirt with all of the guys and a true attention seeker. I knew her from my pub days many years before and at first, I was very wary of her, as she only wanted to be the centre of attention. I couldn't be bothered with her false mannerisms and fluttering eyes, but I respected her as a cop!

Julie was a part of my team so I had to keep my mouth shut and just dig in with the task in hand. The first part of the operation was to gain as much information about criminals from all areas, so that we could create a list of those people who would be our targets. The officers from the various sub divisions all knew whom they wanted to target but what we had to do was create a package which would be presented to the bosses and they had the ultimate decision.

The word 'Eagle' was devised by bosses at Pitt Street and the operation was to be conducted by the terms laid out by them. **'E'**-Education, **'A'**-Awareness, **'G'**-Guidance, **'L'**-Legislation and **'E'**-Enforcement.

There was yet another major publicity campaign to make people aware that there was a major plainclothes operation in place and warned all drug dealers that they were to be targeted. This was supposed to scare off the dealers in the hope that they would just stop dealing drugs. It didn't work that way though, as there was always going to be a demand for drugs as the addicts were still in abundance.

I wasn't looking forward to the three-month long operation as I thought that there would be lots of rivalry. However, I was prepared to await the outcome, as I knew that this would be good experience for me. I was the kid on the block with only four years' service, although I was more than capable of doing the job.

By the time the enforcement period arrived, we were all like coiled springs waiting to pop. I had managed to put into place a package concerning a drug dealer from the Royston area. I regarded my information as spot on although there is always an element of doubt as far as criminals turned 'grass'. Everything was ready to be worked upon although the job required at least two days of watching his movements.

The reason for this was that he was supposed to have a safe house in the Sighthill area of Glasgow where he stored his drugs. I knew the block of flats but the actual flat number wasn't known. I also knew that he kept the drugs inside a double plug socket mounted on the wall. This was the sketchy part of the information but it was still good enough to be considered as a possible target.

One major problem was that none of the team was surveillance-trained so trying to follow him was going to be difficult. We decided that we would just do our best. The cars given to us to use during the operation were all well known by local criminals. I approached a major car seller and asked if he could give us an old heap of a car to use for our operation.

He agreed and gave us a Fiat Uno to use. It truly was a heap of shit and I even doubted as to whether there would be an existing MOT for it! However, I prevented the police workshop from seeing the car. It was left parked outside the police office. We had been moved to the Bishopbriggs sub-office during this operation, and the fact that it was free from bosses at all times was a godsend. It had plenty of facilities for us to use and was close to all of the surrounding criminal areas.

The day came for us to begin the operation against the Royston dealer. We were still unsure of how the surveillance would go but at least we had plenty of cops available to do it. Best of all was the fact that he wouldn't know most of them as they worked in different areas. I know that most criminals say that you can smell a cop a mile off.

Well, I would disagree as each of us dressed like Neds and acted like Neds. I remained in charge of the communications and kept regular contact with those involved in following the man. The first day was spent following him around Royston and Springburn, but he never made any attempt to go near the Sighthill address.

I had a brainwave. I knew his mobile number so I decided that the next day, I would ask Julie to phone him and pretend to make a drug arrangement with him. Perhaps this would entice him to go to the flat. Russell told me that we couldn't do it, but he did say that if he didn't know that it had been done then surely there would be no harm in it.

It was decided that this was probably the best way to do it and the following day, Julie made that nervous call to him. After much deliberation, he agreed that he would get her the 1/8th of an ounce of heroin and he would meet her near the graveyard a couple of hours later. We were now committed to the task and had to now organise who would do what. I agreed to drive the Fiat Uno and follow him to Sighthill and then Julie and Paul would grab him after he came out of the flats in Sighthill. It seemed straightforward, but the operation hadn't begun in earnest yet so no doubt time would tell.

The first operation with untested colleagues is never easy as each of us adopt different styles of policing ranging from aggressive to laidback. This was going to be our first test of whether we would be able to gel together as a team. After having worked out the teams, all that remained for us to do was lie in wait to see if he was going to show up. An observation point (OP) was set up near to his home so that we could see when he left to get the heroin.

As well as this, another OP was set up near to the block of flats in Sighthill where it was anticipated that he would attend to pick up the drugs. I remained in the Fiat Uno, near to his house in Royston.

About seven o'clock that night (1900), word reached me that he had just left his house. The game was on! I followed him at a distance in my heap of a car and watched as he drove along the busy area of Royston, heading towards Glasgow. As he came to a set of traffic lights, he managed to get through but by the time I reached them, they had changed to red.

I had no option but to go through the lights hoping that there were no traffic cops nearby to ruin my plan. I caught up with him near to Baird Street police office and continued heading towards the Sighthill area. I updated the controller of the position, failing to admit that I had just run a red light, as I would be penalised for doing this, despite the fact that I was a police officer.

He turned into Fountainwell Road and I knew that he was definitely heading to collect the drugs at his safe house. I told Julie and Paul that we were nearly at their position at the block of flats to be ready for him coming. They were to remain out of sight until he at least entered the block. He indicated as planned to turn into the block carpark and I could feel my heart ready to burst with excitement.

I told the others that it was a GO GO GO and they all knew that this was the moment we had planned for. He parked his car right outside the block and made his way inside towards the lifts inside the main foyer. I parked my car and started to make my way there. Julie and Paul rushed in behind him to see if they could work out which floor he was going to get off at. The lift display indicated 14. We knew that it was the 14th floor; only a matter now of ascertaining which flat out of the six on that floor was his?

After about ten minutes, the lift display again confirmed that it was stopping at the 14th floor. All we had to do was grab hold of him as he exited the lift on the ground floor. The bell sounded and the doors opened. Out stepped this insignificant wee guy and Julie and Paul grabbed him. They quickly told him that they were police officers and detained him under the Misuse of Drugs Act 1971, which allowed them the power to search him for controlled substances.

Paul stated that he was convinced the guy swallowed something so therefore he had nothing on him. But at that same time, he pissed himself. A good indication that he did have drugs. If not on him, then at his safe house? They took him away to the police office to have him searched thoroughly. This was the second time that a criminal had pissed himself within a few short weeks, the last guy being Gramps from Blackhill.

Meanwhile, Peter joined me and we set about doing a recce at the flats on the 14th floor to see if we could tie one to him. None of the doors corresponded with his name and we were left with a blank. I wrote down all of the names as they appeared on the doors and tried to eliminate them one by one. He didn't have any drugs on him and he denied having swallowed any. But he did have a set of keys so the next logical thing to do was to take the keys and see which door they fitted.

Peter and I did this and the second door we attempted unlocked the door to that house. The only difference was that we did not know the name and we couldn't contact the housing as their offices were closed for the night. Russell organised a warrant from a JP whilst Peter and I remained guarding the door to the flat.

Half an hour later, some of the team arrived with the guy we had detained, as well as the warrant allowing us to search the flat. He wasn't amused and kept swearing at us saying that he didn't know anything about the flat and if there was any drugs inside then they must have been planted by us. The information provided was that the drugs were kept within a double plug socket.

I arranged for a drug dog to assist us with the search and before long, in bounced a King Charles Spaniel. She set about her work and in true textbook style, she started to become excited at a wall socket. This was taken apart and inside was about five thousand pounds worth of heroin.

The Ned just about pissed his pants for the second time, only this time he collapsed onto the floor in a heap and started crying. Back at the office, we all congratulated one another for the way the operation had been handled by us. I was chuffed as it had been my turn and I had organised everyone from beginning to end.

I knew that the guy would get at least three years in prison for the drug offences and decided that this where my own forte lay within the police. I knew that I had the organisational skills required to be able to plan operations such as these. The first couple of weeks were spent trying to decide where we would concentrate our efforts as best to make an impact on the drug problem.

Russell had the overall say with the running of the unit but he did allow several of us to sway his decision. During the day shift, I found it difficult to apply myself, as I preferred the late shift to target criminals. However, information was received that in Easterhouse, most of the drug dealers operated during the day. I didn't know my way around there, as I had never been recruited there to work. I had to ensure that if I was going to work in that area I would work with someone from there.

Paul had worked in Easterhouse for about ten years and knew his way around. Others professed to know the area but I trusted Paul. Deek would have been my first choice but he tended to work with Julie all of the time and there seemed no sense in breaking up their partnership; at least I didn't have to listen to her talking about her hair or nails and that suited me fine. Another talking point she always mentioned was her PMT. Now I immediately thought she was referring to Pre-Menstrual but apparently it was he Pre-Maintenance Tension linked with the fact that her husband was divorced and was paying maintenance for his kids, and rightly so! However, as it was frequently pointed out, she should have thought about that before she had the affair with him when he was married.

One particular dealer was supposed to be selling about two hundred tenner bags a day from his flat and he was to be our priority target. It was decided that I would attend at the door and try to score two bags of heroin. The only downside was that I didn't look like a junkie; I was more your healthy living type of guy. However, not to be put off, I agreed that I would do it provided some of the others were within the close to assist should the shit hit the fan.

Off we set to make our way towards the flats, climbing over back gardens in order to get there unnoticed. I was however expected to walk in through the front door of the close. After all, I was going to buy the drugs. I was given the nod that the others were in position. I made my way into the close and walked past Peter who was carrying a garden spade.

I was puzzled at this but decided not to ask, as we had to ensure that no other junkies came to score at the same time as me. I got to the door and whistled the way all good Neds do when they attend a house of a mate. The door opened and this junked up addict appeared before my eyes, asking me what I wanted.

"Two TBs, mate." (2 ten-pound bags of heroin)

He produced a plastic bag normally used for putting cream cakes in, and I could see that it was crammed full of individual bags of heroin. The others on hearing that I was engaged in conversation decided that this was the time to call a strike and four of them piled into the house past me.

I grabbed hold of the guy at the door and also seized the bags of heroin. I quickly put handcuffs on him and made my way into the living room of the house. He was so wasted with drugs that I don't even think he knew what was going on.

Peter, meanwhile, was standing in the middle of the floor shouting at the occupants that we were the police and that this was a raid. Nothing unusual there, apart from the fact that he was holding onto the spade as though it were a rifle and threatening them.

When I saw this, I burst out laughing, as even I couldn't believe that the police would resort to measures such as these. He later defended his actions by saying that he had forgotten to take his police baton with him for protection so he just picked up a spade to help him in case anyone attacked him. I suppose it is logical in a way but he was making everyone shit scared to move, fearing that they may be beaten to a pulp with a spade. It did work however and four people were arrested from the house and charged with being concerned in the supply of 74 bags of heroin.

We were by now midway through the operational period and our success rate was fantastic. We worked hard and played hard too. During the last shift on a Friday and Saturday, we would take it in turn to cook dinner for the team of ten. Thanks to a large kitchen in the police office and a very understanding DS, this was the highlight of the previous week's work.

Not only that, it wasn't uncommon for us to open several bottles of wine to accompany the food already prepared. We were never drunk on duty or anything but after a couple of glasses of wine, it became more of a playtime and hobby than a job!

Also, some Saturday nights, we would finish early and go into a local pub across from the office and have a few beers before going home. All very civilised but we managed to get away with it because there was never any other bosses working from that office. Even our fridge was full of bottles of beer and wine although it was also padlocked so that others couldn't steal what was ours.

We had become a close group professionally and we managed to get the results for the bosses. The other team didn't appear to be as motivated as we were, and often we could hear squabbles among them. I suppose we were lucky that we all bonded very well. There were occasions where both teams would be targeting the same person and this meant that each team became quite secretive. As we were nearing the end of the operation, it was decided that we would arrange several hits together; that way we could pull all of our resources together.

With about a month to go before the whole thing was to be wound down, one of the packages in the Blackhill area was allocated to Peter and he arranged for the hit to take place early one morning. This was going to be a difficult turn to do as it was in the middle of a street and getting to the house was a problem as many people would have told the target that we were in the vicinity if he wasn't already aware.

The flat was an upper cottage type with four in the block. We were now becoming more organised with searches and knew that with this guy, he would flush the drugs down the toilet to get rid of them. So in order to alleviate that problem, we would just have to break his drainpipe before he got the chance to do this.

We hired a white transit van and drove into the street. About ten of us all piled out from the back of the van and ran to our designated posts. I went with Deek to the pipe and he quickly broke it off so that if anything were flushed, then it would come straight out towards us. I was hopeful that it would be drugs and not a pan full of human shite!

Peter was to be the man in charge of the 'rammit'. A device used by the police to force open doors by breaking the hinges used to support it. The rammit was a ten-pound piece of lead encased in black rubber with two handles that allowed the user to pick it up. It was already heavy and awkward without any other restraints used for security by Neds.

Peter tried to force open the door but it was more difficult than first thought as the door was reached by about five steps so therefore, height was also a very obstructive barrier. "Try not to hit yourself with it, Peter," came a voice from the side of the house.

I heard a thud and a crack but was more interested in the fact that the toilet had been flushed. I told the others of this but was aware of a commotion outside the door and thought that it was all of them trying to pile into the house. Deek and I waited and out plopped a brown leather bag containing a huge amount of powder wrapped in plastic.

I went to tell the others and saw that Peter was lying flat out on the footpath and one of the guys was tending to him. I asked what had happened and was told that when Peter hit the lower section of the door, the rammit bounced back and struck him on the cheekbone, leaving him unconscious on the path. The others managed to gain entry, leaving poor Peter out for the count!

An ambulance was called and he was taken to the hospital and CD went with him. The rest of us carried on with the search of the house that was probably one of the dirtiest houses I had ever been in. Obviously, we were all talking and laughing at Peter's expense due to his unfortunate accident. He had been warned to be careful but he was an accident-prone guy at the best of times.

After the search, the two brothers were arrested and charged with being concerned in the supply of Amphetamine Sulphate. Peter meanwhile was left at hospital waiting to go into surgery to have his elephant man face rebuilt. He had multiple fractures to his cheek and jaw that required metal plates to be inserted to realign his face. To say that it was horrific is an understatement.

There was also the problem that none of us had been properly trained in using that particular piece of equipment. Everyone one else could see pound signs with a claim against the Chief Constable, whilst poor Peter couldn't even move his eyes because one of them had socket damage. At least we got the result at the house for him. He would be pleased with that!

Having carried out the search at the house and with the two drug dealers locked up for court, the only other thing left to do now was to clear up our mess after the search of the house. The front door had been totally demolished in our attempts at gaining entry to the flat. The drainpipe used to flush away the toilet waste was halved in two. I contacted the local authority responsible for the area and the snotty cow preceded to tell me that she would ensure that Strathclyde Police picked up the tab for the damage to the property.

I was quick to retort to her that her manager had already authorised the damage, as he was more than happy to assist the police in ridding that street of the drug dealer. They were a hideous family and content with the belief that we may in fact provide the council with enough evidence in which to raise a civil action to have them evicted from their home.

She was so pissed off with my attitude that she demanded to speak with my supervisor, Russell. He spoke with her and she hung up on him due to his manner of putting her in her place and telling her bluntly that what we did was to assist the local authority in ridding them of a problem tenant. She should have eaten humble pie but she took the easy route and ended the call.

This got me thinking that what we were in effect doing was assisting all other agencies in tackling the problems they too faced when dealing with criminals. For the first time, I realised that plainclothes operations such as these were more motivated by political involvement than any other reason and this would account for the reason that these receive the highest possible advertisement campaigns in order to tell the public that the police really do care.

Nonsense; it is only politically motivated, as the police need to show value for money, the same as all other major multinational corporations. The police is a big business, and it is big business for local authority councillors and the Chief Constable, who must report to them with an annual report on what the police have achieved, or not, as the case may be. However, nowadays it is even worse with the Chief Constable reporting to the Scottish Government now that it is a Scotland wide service.

During the drug initiative, there were many searches carried out and our division was riding high on the overall success of the teams involved. We had managed to conduct in excess of one hundred searches and each time this was done, there was a report submitted to the PF regarding the circumstances as at least one person was reported for drug offences each time.

The split of resources was very evenly distributed throughout the division although at times it depended on who could shout the loudest to specify which area was targeted. I was used many times in the Easterhouse area to buy controlled drugs, or at least attempt to buy drugs in order that the dealers opened their doors. Once this was done, about four or five cops would pile into the house and start looking in nooks and crannies of the houses.

I was genuinely quite shocked at the number of dealers whose houses had a wide selection of porn lying under beds and mattresses. Even more alarming was the variety of sex aids also there. Obviously for a laugh, we would take them apart and switch them on. This was more to embarrass the occupants than the need to see them in operation!

I had one more target I wanted the team to raid as he had apparently been selling large amounts of heroin for about five years and there had never been a successful raid on him or his family in that time. I was determined that I would make sure we got the result as I was prepared to work my ass off in order to do it. He lived in Barmulloch in the middle of a housing scheme occupied by drug addicts, but most importantly, decent residents whose lives were being made a living hell because of him and his addict sons.

The Drug Squad and Scottish Crime Squad had all failed before; why would our team be any different?

At the time of these plainclothes operations, the Human Rights Act wasn't in force and the police were not as readily accountable as they now are. In truth, if you were to ask any police officer from the early days which era they preferred, the answer would always be the same. The early days made it easier to carry out surveillance operations without having to have express permission of senior bosses in the police, or even the Secretary of State.

It was a case of obtaining a warrant and searching a house based upon brief information. Now it is extremely difficult to do this as a log must be kept of the methods used to keep tabs on criminals. I was determined that we would keep proper records of the movements at the target houses. The current information then received was that one of the addict sons lived in another street near to his father and that he would only sell 'tenner' bags of heroin to other addicts known to him. However, the flat directly next door to him was lying empty and the council was awaiting new tenants taking over.

I decided to liaise with the local authority and formed a great working relationship with the staff there. I would say that we all helped one another in times of need. It was agreed that we could take over the flat for a couple of weeks to allow us to coordinate our search. I contacted the technical unit to see whether it would be possible to place a small camera there in order to tape the dealer in action.

Once I had everything in place I had to pass on the information to our own managers to decide on whether they would agree to the operation taking place. It was met with negativism due to the fact that other squads had tried and failed but it was decided to allow us to do it over a one-week period.

So began another task of watching the houses to see when the busy times were for the dealer to ply his trade. Rather than waste the chance of being seen at the safe flat already arranged, I decided that this time we would place two officers up on a roof of one of the multistorey buildings as it commanded a perfect view of the two target addresses.

All that was needed was for an operational log to be kept of the callers at the flats. Up on the 31st floor of a block of flats is not the easiest thing to do and can be quite cold even in the summer. I volunteered to go up there along with Paul and so began our watch on the addresses. It wasn't long before we realised that the operation was ready to proceed to the video camera stage, as the traffic at the son's house was chaotic.

There must have been about sixty callers within the first three hours. Normally, we would have arranged for other officers to arrest the buyers to find out if we could obtain statements against them but when that happens, word always gets back to the dealer of a police presence in the area. Russell decided that we would leave well alone for now.

Back at the office, Paul and I told Russell of the day's events and he agreed that we should move to the next phase of the plan. The following day, two cops dressed in working clothes and attended at our flat opposite the target house and closed the door behind them. Once there, they set up a spy camera in the door to watch the events opposite and record the details on tape. They left having set it up, hoping that they were unnoticed by the dealer.

The tape would record for 72 hours and would be replaced when the time was right. We left the observation post alone and concentrated on searching houses in other areas to keep away from the area altogether. After three days, yet another unknown cop attended there and changed over the tape.

When I sat down to view the recorded tape I wasn't prepared for the clarity of the footage. It was good enough to see the dealer sell drugs to some individuals already known to us. I recorded some of the footage in case it was required at a later date. Several days later, someone attended and removed the camera and video recorder. All that was needed now was time to conduct the searches.

Having obtained two warrants to search the target houses from a sheriff, we decided that a Friday would suit best in order to hit the houses. We assembled at the office about five o'clock in the morning and got organised to go. In all, there was seven of us and as we had hired a transit van, getting to the area unseen was going to be fine but actually getting into the house was more of a problem.

Having sneaked over back gardens with all of our equipment, one by one, we made our way in through the metal door of our flat to await movement. It was 0540. All police officers know that criminals do not get up before ten o'clock so we knew that we would just have to await the developments. At least we were in position and when time came to call a strike, we knew that access to the house would be okay as we would just climb in through the shared front balcony and gain access via his door leading to the living room.

We were well prepared and had brought sandwiches and coffee to keep us going. The only drawback being the fact that the call of nature may happen and if it did, then we couldn't use the toilet for fear of blowing our cover. Alas, several of them had to use the toilet and I can honestly say that the smell was almost enough for me to blow our cover by running from the flat for fresh air!

If we had flushed the toilet then the downstairs neighbours may have alerted the targets that there was movement from an empty flat! We all stood our ground and waited on "Operation Blobby" to commence in earnest. The name of the operation had been kept quiet until that morning and I had no need to explain why I had chosen that name. Quite simply, the targets were the fattest junkies I have ever seen in my life. Obviously due to the fact that they liked their grub too much!

Their mother was actually quite a nice wee woman and she obviously did what she did to protect her two golden boys. They, like their father, were grotesque and considered themselves gangsters. But they weren't, they were merely drug dealers who couldn't bear to see others doing well.

The fact that they were ruining so many lives by selling heroin and Temazepam to anyone who came to their door. The video evidence we had was overwhelming but the icing on the cake had to be a drug seizure to substantiate our claim that they were active drug dealers. The spyhole camera had again been repositioned so that we could monitor the movements at the house. About 0830 that day, the mother arrived at the door and the vision who answered it was enough to make most people spew at the sight.

He stood there in his boxers with his ever-expanding waist almost pushing his mother back down the stairs. She was up to take money from them. We assumed that this was to buy another consignment of drugs. As she left, however, she took their order for a delivery. A delivery of a huge fry-up, that is? First and foremost, these mutants needed food before they could start the day.

Of course, they also had their staple diet of Methadone (heroin substitute) prescribed by their GP. This was probably used to wash down the grease from their fry-ups. As the mother left the flat, I went into the living room area of the flat and watched as she entered the family car and made off from the Barmulloch area to uplift their drugs. This was the start of our operation in earnest, as we now had to get ready for the big push when necessary.

After about half an hour, the car returned. This time though, the father emerged from the driver's seat like Pavarotti getting out of a mini metro! Peter and Russell were in position. They gently raised the metal door and stepped out into the stairwell and quickly made their way down the stairs to seize hold of the target.

At this same time, some of the others climbed over the communal balcony and as lady luck shone from a great height, the target balcony door was unlocked, thereby allowing the police easy entry to the house of the other two 'blobbies'.

Russell and Peter carried out a cursory search on the father and recovered a large amount of heroin as well as Temazepam capsules. So far, the operation was a success as we had the seizure as well as detained the targets. Julie rushed into the street and detained the mother. It was decided that it would be easier to take the father to the police office and the mother would accompany Julie and I to search her home.

When we started our search we were already on a high as we had already achieved our objective; finding anything else would now be a bonus. However, having searched many drug houses before, it became quickly evident that we weren't going to find any drugs in that house, just plenty of money locked away within a safe in a cupboard.

It was quite funny to see that kept within a cupboard of a council house in the middle of Barmulloch was a safe! Not only were there thousands of pounds in cash but also thousands of pounds worth of tacky Ned's bling-bling jewellery!

We received further help from uniformed officers so that the search could be conducted quickly. There was even money found inside fur coats' pockets in the wardrobe and stuffed inside handbags. It was easy to see just how lucrative their drug business was. After completing the search, the mother was taken to Baird Street as she too was to be questioned regarding the drug activities of her family.

No drugs were found in the house apart from prescribed medication but we were still delighted that we had managed to remove so much money from them. The other house was busy with drug addicts attending to purchase heroin and the officers involved there had to take written statements from them at that time. The good thing being though was the fact that he had managed to identify more buyers from the already seized videotapes. Only small amounts of drugs were found in the house but it was enough to detain the two sons as well and take them to the police office. Not a bad morning's work and it was still not even mid-day!

Once all of the productions were processed, all that remained was to interview the "blobby' family. At first, they all denied anything to do with drugs and the father tried to pass off the drugs as personal for his sons, trying to convince us that they had horrendous habits.

However, having been told that they had been caught on tape selling drugs to other addicts, he admitted his part in the offence. The boys were more difficult nuts to crack but eventually, they too saw the error of their ways and confessed all. It was similar to a scene from *The Bill*, where it is depicted that all criminals admit their guilt.

This is definitely not always the case but at least for us that day, the fact they admitted their crimes was of great benefit to us. All that remained to do was report the custody case and ensure that everything was ready for the Monday morning for court.

What was most satisfying was that our little team with virtually no surveillance training had managed to do what other squads had tried and failed at. Several months later the father and his two sons pleaded guilty at the High Court and were sentenced to three years each. We always knew that we would get our men in the end!

Chapter 5
Bite Like a Pit Bull

It wasn't long before our reputation was preceding our attendance at houses, as it appeared that the majority of drug dealers had decided to stop. Not necessarily stop dealing, but change their ways of dealing so that there was no degree of consistency with their dealing habits. That was what normally trapped the dealers, as too many of the addicts were only too willing to tell the police who was selling what and where.

The dealers always thought that they would be able to get away with plying their trade but by this point, our team thrived on a challenge and set out to continue with the job. The operation itself had been a success and the Management decided that they would extend it for another four weeks. Although this would only deter the sellers for another short time pending the whole operation closing down, at least we were having the desired effect on the drug trade. As we had such a large area to cover, there was still more than enough 'jobs' to do in the areas.

One good thing to come out of the team was that I had gained many more new friendships and before, when I had been wary of working with these people, I was now ready to drop everything to help them out. Yes, there were wankers among the crew but I think it would be a fair assessment to say that this happens in all areas of life! As the Easterhouse contingent felt that we had neglected their own area somewhat, it was decided that we would 'hit' that area with a vengeance.

Julie had several targets she wished us to work on and so began another eventful time in the scheme. Deek was by now back in uniform and as he was a buddy of Julie's, we knew that there would be many good turns for us to go on. I must confess that I didn't like the area, probably because I didn't know it very well and it was way out of my own comfort zone.

The first target was a young couple who had three kids under the age of five, and both of them were addicts. As usual, because I wasn't known in the area, I was sent to the door in the hope that it would be opened. They then all virtually piled in right behind me. When we arrived in the house, it was only the female who was there and she was like a zombie, thanks to the cocktail of drugs she had taken.

She didn't seem bothered by the fact that we were there, usually an indication that there were no drugs within the house. The boyfriend was out, and we immediately suspected that he was away to uplift some drugs. When the phone rang, it was Julie who answered it and to her surprise, it was the target, Tam. She immediately told him that she was "Sharon" (another target drug dealer) who had just popped in to see Kelly. He asked to speak to Kelly, but Julie told him that she was in the toilet. "I'll be there in about five minutes wi the gear, let Kelly know for me, Shaz?"

This was like music to our ears, as we knew that he would have a large consignment of drugs on him. They only ever stocked up twice a week; well, that's what our information told us! We all kept guard at various points in the house; luckily, there were no kids at home so even if a scuffle broke out, at least we wouldn't have to worry about any kids at our feet.

Almost right on cue, he whistled as he walked up the stairwell, heading towards his flat. He opened the door and was pounced upon by two of the guys. They did say that they were the police but this didn't stop him from pulling out a six-inch blade. Peter saw it in time and immediately punched him right in the guts, causing him to fall to the floor. He was placed in handcuffs although he was screaming like a stuffed pig as they did this.

The next thing was a search, but he protested saying that they wouldn't be laying a hand on him. However, when these cuffs are put on, they can become very convincing when demands are made of you.

A brief cursory search of his pockets retrieved a large amount of Valium (blues) and Temazepam (jellies). This was a bonus as we had attended there to seize heroin. None was found, which tended to suggest that this was perhaps secreted somewhere else.

He was whisked off to the toilet and so began another screaming match. It wasn't long before Peter emerged with a large amount of heroin within a plastic bag. Apparently, it had been placed up his arse, quite literally. All that was on view was the knotted part of the bag, showing through enough to enable the 'carrier' to remove it by himself. However, the bag popped out itself saving us from having to get a police doctor to remove it once we obtained a warrant.

When I saw the size of the bag, it did make me wonder how the hell he got it up there in the first instance! Obviously, he was well used to 'carrying' drugs up there! All that remained was for a cursory search of the house and they were both carted off to the police office for interview. This was my first experience of Neds from a different area and culture.

Apparently, they all refuse to cooperate with the police in Easterhouse. I had never experienced this as I had always managed to use my persuasive charms in order to gain a confession. Not these two hard nuts; they were both committed to saying nothing to the police about their alleged drug dealing. However, the amount of drugs seized was more than enough to substantiate drug supply allegations.

It would have made the case simpler had they admitted their crime but they refused. All that remained was for them to be put to court the following day. Due to the amount of drugs involved, they were both remanded in custody pending a trial. The children were handed over to Kelly's mother, who would no doubt look after them far better than their drug abusing/dealing mother could.

I had only ever carried out a few searches in Easterhouse but I was beginning to warm to the area and I quite liked the array of criminals in the area. I hoped that I would be given the chance to work in that area full time someday, perhaps in the CID as I didn't fancy doing it whilst in uniform. Duffy had remained quite quiet during the previous few months and I had heard that he was supposed to be great with touts and providing information about local criminals. So far, he hadn't done so, apparently the reason for this was because he felt a bit 'put out' because of the good results already obtained by the unit. Alas, we decided that we would do one of his targets as he was beginning to get the hump about not listening to him.

One Friday night, I went with Duffy and a few others to a street in Easterhouse to search a house for Cannabis Resin (hash). Again, I was to be the guinea pig and was sent to the door to buy from the target. This time, it was a secured door system whereby I had to buzz the ground-floor flat and try to gain entry that way. I didn't know what to expect and must admit that I was very nervous.

When I buzzed the flat, a guy answered and I told him that was looking for a tenner bit. He asked who had sent me and again, as had been prearranged, I told him that "Tommy fae up the road" had sent me. He buzzed me into the close and I managed to unlock the close door so that the others could get in behind me. He opened the front door of his flat and invited me in.

I stood motionless in the kitchen and tried to engage in conversation but my stomach was heaving. The next thing I heard was a voice asking, "Dale, are you in yet?"

I had forgotten to switch off my radio and it was stuffed down the back of my jeans. I quickly managed to switch it off, but by now, I was sweating. The guy had gone into the living room to get a lighter so that he could heat the hash in order to cut it for me. Luckily, he never heard the voice, or so I thought.

He said to me, "Who were you speaking to?" I told him that I was speaking to him and had asked him if he was at his dinner as I could see plates lying on the table. He said that he had been and proceeded to cut the piece of hash for me. I was as nervous as hell and thought that by now the other troops would have been in the house. I was panicking but decided that I should just go through with my purchase and get the hell out of there as quick as possible.

Not that the guy was a maniac or anything but he was cutting the hash with a huge blade and I had visions of this being thrust into me. I was only in the house for a few minutes yet it felt much longer. He handed me the piece of hash and I in return gave him his tenner. He showed me to the door and on opening it for me, in piled the other cops to detain him. I ran from the house, making out that I was just another hash buyer. The guys all looked at me in disbelief as I ran past them. I couldn't stay there any longer, as I felt suffocated and needed to be elsewhere.

The smell of the fresh air was fantastic, as opposed to the smell of grease from the house. When I had composed myself I phoned Paul and asked him to meet me at the car and to bring the car keys as I had no intention of going back into the house. When Paul came outside, he was white as a sheet. I asked him what was wrong with him and he told me that he felt sorry for the family.

I was unaware that there were three young kids in the house as well as the fact that the mother was only about thirty and was suffering from MS and she also had cancer! I felt sick that we had rushed into the house to search for drugs and she was dying!

I know that it sounds strange and the husband was, after all, a drug dealer. We all felt a little compassion towards their plight. It transpired that he was selling the hash to pay to take his wife on a trip to Lourdes, in the hope that there would be a miracle and his wife wouldn't die after all. What a moral dilemma we faced with that household!

Paul went back into the house and about ten minutes later, all of the troop arrived, without the accused. I asked what had happened and Kevin informed me that the householder was given a warning to stop dealing in drugs and to make sure he looked after his wife!

I was quite taken aback as Kevin never struck me as a guy who gave a shit about anyone other than himself. The outcome of this search was that we were a tenner down, but had a nice bit of hash and no one would ever know that the police had at long last shown a little compassion towards a family whose only crime was to help their dying mother! The piece of hash was posted back through the letter box of the house as we had no need for it.

Easterhouse was flavour of the month with the squad as we targeted many known drug dealers. Temazepam capsules (jellies) were in abundance and almost every house we searched resulted in a recovery of jellies. These were just like jellybeans, and the liquid inside them was sometimes being injected out of them and then re-injected into the veins of desperate addicts. These were particularly dangerous and the addicts often had to have limbs amputated caused by the liquid contained within the jellies.

The police were keen to rid the streets of these and there were even attempts made by many GPs to the pharmaceutical companies to have them replaced with tablets as opposed to the liquid capsules, such was the effects on the addicts caused by these drugs.

Some addicts merely used them to 'top up' their heroin hell and swallowed them just like sweets. They caused the addicts to be in a trance-like state. The price ranged from one pound or two pounds, depending on where in the area the addicts went to buy them. The good thing about these was they were more difficult to disguise and the sellers would have about one hundred of them contained within plastic bank moneybags, so they could quite easily be kept in trouser pockets.

When we went to search the houses for drugs, quite often they would be thrown from the windows, so we had to ensure that there was enough of us to cover the front and rear windows to retrieve anything discarded from the houses. One Friday night, Julie had contacted us to say that a known target in the Wellhouse area was awaiting a large amount of heroin. We had already searched her house before and she had been released on bail from court but was as busy as ever.

We set up an observation point (OP) so that we could monitor the activity at the house. Getting to the house was easy on foot but we would be spotted a mile off if we were to have gone there by car. There was nothing else for it but to hide out in various back gardens and bin areas so that if the strike were called then we would be on hand to get there quickly. Paul and Peter were in the OP and watched the activity at the house for about an hour.

In that time, they noted that there had been about twenty callers to the flat. It was still not clear if they had drugs in the house or not so we had no option but to 'take out' a buyer to ascertain whether or not they had bought any heroin. However, just as we were about to do this, the target, Sharon, left the close and jumped into her car. The information given to us was that she would be getting a large amount of heroin delivered; perhaps she was going to get it herself.

The callers stopped coming to their house. An indication that there was no more heroin and they were awaiting a new supply. Two of the cops managed to make their way into the close and hid upstairs. We knew that the neighbours wouldn't mind us being there, as they wanted to get rid of the dealer from their close.

Sharon was a complete maniac. She hated the police and was always verbally and physically abusive towards any cop she came in contact with. She would hit first and ask questions later. I didn't know her that well and I had only met her once before when she came into another house whilst we were carrying out a search there. She and I rubbed each other up the wrong way and there was several spats of insults dished out by both of us then.

I wasn't looking forward to this search, as I knew that it would be mayhem in the house. After about an hour, Sharon returned to the close and looked all around the outside of the building before she entered. She also looked all around the back garden area, but apparently, this was always her routine; she was paranoid about being done again by the police.

The only way to get access to her flat was to force the door, but that would give her enough time to dispose of any drugs. We needed another way to get her to open the door. Peter decided to meet with Deek who was in uniform and asked if he could pretend to deliver a test address to her house in the hope that she would open the door. The test address is a common occurrence and involves the police confirming if a person stays at the address having been arrested. This must be done to confirm that the person lives there.

As Deek knew Sharon and all of her family, it sounded the ideal way to get the door opened. Deek drove the marked police car to her front door and he walked alone up the path towards the house. As usual, Sharon was watching from the window and stuck up her two fingers to Deek as he walked towards the close door.

Deek buzzed her flat and told her that he wanted to speak to her about her brother. She never thought anything of this as he was always in trouble and she always provided an address for him when he was arrested. Coupled with the fact that Deek was alone, she would never expect an ambush, would she?

Deek entered the close and luckily, Sharon answered the door and he engaged her in conversation. At this point, two cops walked down the stairs towards her flat and two others came from the back garden area. She shouted, "It's a trap, Jim, get rid of them."

She was overpowered by three of them and Deek along with Julie ran into the living room to find Jim sitting like a frustrated hamster. He couldn't speak as he had put the drugs into his mouth. After much persuasion by Deek, he handed over about ten thousand pounds worth of heroin that was wrapped inside plastic bags. There was never any chance of him swallowing that amount of drugs anyhow.

Sharon was placed in handcuffs and brought back into the house. She was like a rabid dog, spitting at the officers who were trying to hold her and kicking anyone who came into close contact with her. She was especially pissed off with Deek and told him that she was going to have him murdered for trapping her that way. He proclaimed his innocence and told her that he would leave her with the Drug Squad who would deal with her.

Everything appeared to be going well and we had recovered a large amount of cash and other drugs during the search. I had so far managed to avoid her seeing me until near the end of the search.

She spotted me standing in the hall and from her seated position on the settee, she lunged towards me. Luckily, Paul managed to rugby tackle her to the ground but this incensed her even more. I don't know why she despised me as we had only met once before. Perhaps she thought that I was responsible for the search of her house.

Jim and Sharon were taken to Easterhouse police office so that they could be interviewed regarding the drugs haul from the house. It was decided that I wouldn't have anything to do with interviewing Sharon or Jim fearing that I would set her off again. As they had both been charged before with supplying, they were kept in custody and we had to sit back and await the trial.

When the day of the trial came around, I was the first witness in the box at the high court. They had merged the offences of that night with the other charges already against them. As well as these cases, there were another two accused who were also linked in with selling heroin with them. In all, there were four accused and I was unfortunate enough to have been involved in all of the searches.

It was an absolute nightmare as I was shown different production schedules for each search and I was asked questions by the PF as well as four defence lawyers. To say that I had a hard time is a total understatement! I was being hung, drawn and quartered and the accused loved every minute of it. I had to grin and bear it and I tried hard to remain composed. It was the worst time I had ever encountered in a courtroom and I felt sick with the mental tiredness after it. In all, I was in the witness box for five hours, but at long last, I was excused by the judge.

The other cops had to endure a similar punishment as mine. Particularly Deek, as they were attempting to make out that he had duped Sharon into opening the door. He admitted that he had duped her but that didn't eradicate the fact that she was a drug dealer. The police do have to resort to using extreme measures to ensure that they can do a particular job and this was one of those occasions.

They were all found guilty of supply charges. Sharon received seven years in jail. Jim received five years. Donna and Steven each got three years. It was worth all of the hassle and abusive behaviour to ensure that they got what they deserved! Time was fast running out for the unit and it was coming to an end. By this point though, most of the drug dealers were wise to our methods of attack and more importantly, they knew the transport used by us.

There had been problems at the garage with the police cars and the cars used by us from the local car dealers had been returned. In truth, the momentum had gone from the squad and we couldn't wait until it was finished. I was still working long hours and as well as having to work either a day shift or late shift, the number of court appearances I had grew more and more frequent.

Some days, I would be away from home by about eight-thirty (0830) and I had to go to court, then straight back to work to begin a late shift. I was making a huge amount of money in overtime and being newly married, it would come in handy. I sometimes would be at court in the morning then another court appearance during the afternoon and then a late shift after that. Although tiring, I loved it!

One lunchtime, having finished court and whilst awaiting the afternoon appearance, I had a couple of hours to kill. Chick asked me to go with him in search of a drug dealer who was frequenting the Barmulloch area of Glasgow as he had information that this guy Robbie was supplying most of that area with heroin. He was already a convicted drug dealer, having served four years for various drug offences.

Chick and I are the type of guys who carry a lot of luck and usually, when we set out to look for someone, we end up catching them. This was to be no exception, although we weren't prepared for a search that day. The main purpose was to just locate the car he was using and perhaps where he lived. We had one radio between us and no handcuffs or batons, as I didn't want to become involved in anything due to the impending court appearance.

On driving past a petrol station in Barmulloch, Chick spotted Robbie putting petrol in his car at a garage forecourt with two other guys inside the car. He turned at the roundabout and made his way towards the garage. He asked me to radio for backup as no doubt there would be a little bit of a scene and as we were in plainclothes, I knew that what he said made sense.

I radioed and asked for a marked car to meet us in order to assist with a search. When Chick pulled up alongside Robbie's car, the front seat passenger opened his door and ran away towards a block of high-rise flats.

Chick went over to Robbie, who was like a non-green version of the incredible hulk; I had never seen him before. He, however, was fine and seemed to know Chick quite well judging by the way they spoke to one another.

I made my way towards the car and started to speak to the guy seated in the back. He was slurring his speech and I knew straight away that he was under the influence of drugs. I saw that Chick now had Robbie seated in the rear of our car. I was notified that the marked police car was about two minutes away.

I climbed into the back of the car and informed the man that he was to be detained for the purposes of a drug search and asked him to step out of the car. It was awkward as it was a two-door old-style BMW and there was hardly any room to move. He tried to place his right hand down into his pants and refused to step out of the car.

I jumped into the back of the car in order to prevent him from getting the drugs I immediately thought he had down there. As I grabbed his hand, he leant forward and bit me on the forearm. It was sore as fuck and I immediately retaliated by punching him on the side of the face, hoping that he would let go.

This annoyed him even more and he maintained his bite, he was like a pit bull dog! I held onto his right arm but he still held onto my arm with his clamp-like bite. I tried to poke his eye and this made him loosen the grip on my arm. I still had hold of his right arm but now, he began to punch at my face.

Chick only saw a brief struggle but he was in the process of dealing with Robbie so he couldn't come to my assistance. I managed to radio in to my control again and told them that I required urgent assistance. Meanwhile, this guy is now trying to put his left hand down into his pants. I grabbed hold of his two hands and tried to force them out of there.

When I did this, he again leant his head forward and sank his teeth into my right arm and again refused to let go. I was shouting like a maniac at him and I could feel the blood trickling down my arm. I let go of my grip of his left hand and started to punch into him like he was a punch bag. He remained committed to biting on my arm and still refused to let go despite my protestations.

At this point, I saw the marked police car arrive in the forecourt and both officers made their way to assist me. The only way that we could force him into letting go of my arm with his teeth was by forcing one of his own hands into a wrist lock. This involves forcing pressure onto the wrist tendons and, when applied properly, is extremely painful.

Having correctly applied the wristlock, he was deemed almost helpless and complied with our request to let go his vice-like grip with his teeth. He was eventually dragged from the car and placed in handcuffs, with his hands behind his back so that he couldn't get to whatever he had concealed in his pants.

I couldn't believe the mess my arm was in. It was swollen and had two huge teeth marks and the blood was flowing from my forearm. I had to put a temporary bandage on it from the first-aid box in the police car so that I could take the prisoner back to the office for a thorough search.

He never spoke to the uniformed officers whilst en route to the police office. Once there, Chick and I took over so that we could explain to the duty officer the reason for his detention. I was quite hesitant about removing his handcuffs due to his earlier behaviour. He began to apologise profusely and said that he would comply with our every request. Still not entirely convinced, we decided to start the search of him by going through his outer body clothing. This merely provided identification and a small amount of cash.

Then I decided to remove his jeans so that I could get to his pants where I believed he was obviously concealing drugs. He again started to lash out at us although it was easy for us to control him due to his cuffs. He was thrown onto the floor and as I removed his pants, I saw a plastic bag containing a quantity of paper wraps. Experience taught me that there would probably be heroin within them.

There were about ten paper wraps within that bag and a closer inspection at his back passage was another bag with similar paper wraps there. When he realised that we had recovered the drugs, he relaxed and said that we had retrieved all of the drugs he had. Not entirely convinced of this, we continued in our search and again found another ten paper wraps secreted at the entrance of his back passage.

I allowed Chick to remove these as I had removed the other wraps found. This was definitely the worst part of being a police officer—having to look up a man's arse for drugs. This is a very popular area to hide drugs and no matter how often I had to be involved in something of this magnitude, it never became any easier. "When you've seen up one arse, you've seen up them all!"

When I reported back to the duty officer about our 'findings', he was happy to inform us that he would be remanded in custody pending his court appearance the following morning on drug supply charges as well as the police assaults on me. I still had the minor matter of the bite to deal with and off I went to Glasgow Royal Infirmary in order to have my wounds dressed properly.

I never thought much of it at the time, as I had never been in this position before. When I informed the casualty desk of the purpose of my visit, I was taken straight away into a waiting room and a nurse removed my bandage. The bite didn't appear to be too bad but once it had been cleaned, I could see just how badly bruised I was around the bite area. It was a particularly nasty bite and there were clear teeth marks and the blood was still dripping from it.

It was redressed by the nurse and I awaited a doctor for his advice. I couldn't believe what he told me as he was so matter-of-fact about the injury. He told me that I wouldn't be able to have unprotected sex for six months until the blood results confirmed that I was clear of Hepatitis B and HIV.

It had never even crossed my mind and now I was being told to be careful over the coming months in case I caught these diseases. I had blood taken from me in order to scan it for these diseases and I would again have to do this at three- and six-monthly intervals. I forgot that drug addicts are really quite infectious and now I would be monitored for the next six months. I felt dirty and betrayed by the criminal who had subjected me to this.

Having left the casualty department, I felt numb and worried what I would tell my wife in order to ensure that she too wouldn't be at risk. Not only that, I had provided a blood sample for comparison against potentially fatal diseases. Never once was I offered counselling by either the police or the hospital staff regarding the analysis of my blood, yet drug addicts must receive this prior to having their blood examined for the diseases.

I knew that I would have to put it to the back of my own mind and get on with my life as best I could without dwelling on what may happen. Back at the office, we still had the case to write and the wraps of heroin examined. It was going to be another long day and I was supposed to have been at court that afternoon. I had to contact the District Court and inform them that I wouldn't be there.

Luckily, I was excused, a very rare occurrence as normally when a person is cited, they must attend as it was also a common situation whereby warrants would be issued for those not in attendance. At least I didn't have that to worry about.

When it came to writing the case, I knew that I would have to be accurate with the information in case the accused decided to raise a complaint against me for assault. It was quite a straightforward case for me to report and I rattled through it in no time. The only difference being, I would have to ask for the Sheriff to order a blood analysis from the accused so that it could be checked for any disease. I wanted to find out if I had anything to worry over. The following morning, I spoke with the PF who dealt with the custody cases and explained my predicament.

She was very sympathetic and assured me that she would speak with the Sheriff and ask that my request is granted, and it was. The results of his blood analysis confirmed that he was disease-free, thus making my six months wait seem less dark and worrying. He pled guilty at court and was sentenced to eighteen months in prison and when sentenced, his lawyer asked that his client be noted as being extremely sorry for the upset he had caused. This gave me a little hope that perhaps Neds do have feelings.

I was given the all-clear after six months and decided that I would have a course of treatment to ensure that I wouldn't have to worry about Hepatitis and I received inoculations against it. The moral of the story that day was I shouldn't attempt to become involved in matters when I have other arrangements. This proved that I had such a lust for the job I would drop everything in order to join in the pursuit in arresting criminals.

I think at that point in my career I would have stopped at nothing in order to prove myself as being completely ruthless at my job and throwing myself in at the deep end at all costs. I was working myself ragged and perhaps this was the reality check I needed to make me aware that perhaps I was becoming too involved in being a police officer. It was time for me to break free from the dirty end and try to succeed doing the job I loved whilst in more comfortable surroundings.

Chapter 6
Like an Apprentice

Whilst I had enjoyed my time working with the team targeting the drug dealers of the division, I needed to get back to concentrating on the criminals in my area and perhaps even to resume a life more ordinary than it had been over the previous months. I initially thought that I would have to return to my old shift working again in uniform, although I didn't look forward to that prospect.

During my days off prior to returning there, I received a phone call from the DI telling me that I would remain in plainclothes with the others from my area for the foreseeable future. This meant that we were to remain under the watchful eye of Russell, our previous DS. I was quite pleased; as the time had drawn nearer for me to look out my old uniform, I realised that I didn't want to do that line of work anymore.

However, with about four years' police service, I had managed to be involved in cases that most people do not even see in their lifetime as a police officer. I knew that I was lucky, but I was also a great plainclothes cop.

On returning to work, I met the team. It had been decided that the team would change slightly as Peter was still off work due to the horrendous injury he sustained with the rammit. We needed another replacement for him and we got Davy or "Circus", as he was referred to. The reason for this was that he should have been in a circus because of his freaky appearance and his height.

He was a decent enough guy although I didn't know him that well. Craig and Dooley were also there so pretty much the main structure of the team remained the same. I don't know what it was but I was losing my interest in the line of work and developed a minor 'couldn't be arsed' attitude. Not that it was totally apparent as I tried to hide my feelings, until one day I decided to speak to Russell about what I wanted to do in the future.

The CID was always the way forward as far as I was concerned and now that I had completed two of my promotion exams, I thought that this would be the ideal opportunity to apply for the six-month traineeship. Russell supported me fully and he suggested for me to submit an application form for consideration by the bosses.

With Russell's endorsement, I knew that I would stand a great chance of being accepted. I regained my enthusiasm as I thought that I would have no problem in being accepted. The bosses gave consideration to my application and I was informed that I would start with Baird Street CID in March 1996. I only had a couple of months to wait before that time and I knew that I would have to make sure I remained focussed and committed to my current job.

The DI of the CID was an arrogant and domineering man who belittled all of his staff and if any person stepped out of line, he would come down on them like a ton of bricks. Everyone who knew him despised him and lived in fear of stepping out of line. He would stop at nothing in order to further his own career and he couldn't care less who or what stood in the way, he was a complete arsehole and he knew it but he didn't care what others thought of him.

I always tried to keep on his good side and avoided having any contact with him, preferring to leave the team's contact to be conducted via Russell. It made our life an awful lot easier that way. One afternoon whilst walking along the CID corridor, I was summoned into his room as he wanted a quick chat. Fearing that I had perhaps done something wrong, I walked sheepishly into his lair.

It turned out that he was very complimentary towards my work with the plainclothes team and acknowledged the fact that I was to undertake my traineeship soon. Eventually, he arrived at his point; he wanted me to work with the CID for two weeks, as they were short-staffed and he suggested that this would be ideal training for me prior to commencing officially with the department. Naturally, I was chuffed to bits and duly accepted his offer. I was to begin my new role in two days' time and I couldn't wait.

When I reported for duty on the Monday morning, I looked like something out of the Next directory wearing a new suit, shirt and tie with highly polished shoes. Not that I looked much different from the usual slick bunch of detectives who also worked in the department!

I was chosen to work with Brian and John. Although I knew them to see, it was more their reputations as excellent thief catchers that I knew of. Both possessed different styles of policing but were equally effective. I assisted them as far as I could but did mostly what they asked as I didn't really know exactly how a detective worked. They both had many on-going enquiries including rape and robberies.

I felt confident as they appeared to know what they were doing and going along with them to interview witnesses was good for me to find out how to take concise statements. At that particular time, there had been several robberies in the Springburn area with the premises off sales and bookmakers appearing to be the main seats of victims being targeted.

One afternoon whilst out on patrol with them both, a call came over the radio that the Springburn branch of the TSB Bank had just been robbed. We attended the scene and so began my first insight into the job of a detective.

Having obtained statements from some of the staff and customers, I looked on as the crime scene officers also attended and did their job to try to find a clue as to who had carried out the crime. About ten thousand pounds had been stolen but at least no one was hurt or injured.

Back at the office, the DI took all of the statements away so that he could read through them to ensure that we had done a good job at the scene. Shortly after having taken them, he returned and congratulated me on having taken concise and detailed statements at the scene. I felt invincible and knew that I wouldn't have any problem with the DI who was despised by so many.

Working in that environment for three days, I instinctively knew that this was definitely where I wanted to work. The buzz around the place was incredible and there appeared to be so much going on in the division with specialised teams of detectives working on so many different enquiries.

On the Thursday afternoon, John and I were summoned into the DI's room, as he wanted a "chat" with us. Obviously, we were immediately suspicious of his intentions although both of us knew that we hadn't done anything wrong. He slammed the door shut when we entered his room. I started to feel really uneasy. So began his plan for the three of us the following day.

A female from the Balornock area had been involved in a fight with her neighbour, resulting in her having a miscarriage. She had been eight months pregnant and during the scuffle with the neighbour, she fell to the ground. Later that night, she was rushed to hospital and lost her baby, a boy.

By law, a baby is not considered to be a human being until it is born. In other words, a person cannot be accused of killing a foetus whilst it remains in the womb. This particular case was to be investigated as the assault may have resulted in the miscarriage. Not any more of a crime but nonetheless, the woman was assaulted and her injury was the death of her foetus.

It sounded complicated but I still didn't know how it would affect John and I. Then the DI made his revelation to us. We were to attend a post-mortem (PM) of the baby on the Friday morning. It was to be my first one and I was apprehensive, as I didn't know how I would be. Bad enough having to attend one in the first place but what made matters worse was the very idea that it was a tiny baby who was the victim in this.

We both agreed and were then told to get on with what we had been doing. As we left the room, we both looked at one another and John said, "Fucking hell, could he not have given us a better job to do?" I knew then that he too didn't relish the prospect of having to endure that particular spectacle. However, John did try to allay my fears about the actual post-mortem as he had been to one before so at least he didn't have that added worry of what to expect.

We didn't have long to dwell on it as Brian had a lead on one of his robberies and he wanted us to assist him. What Brian had on his side was local knowledge as he grew up in the very area he was now policing so he knew all of the local criminals as he went to school with most of them. Personally, I wouldn't have liked to be in that position and preferred the fact that I was unknown to the criminal fraternity in the area and wanted it to remain that way for as long as possible!

I tried not to think too much about what I would see the next day and on driving home that night, I focussed on what I would be doing that evening and what I would have for my dinner. The only way a cop can switch off from events of that day or what might lie in store is to put the events to the back of the mind. It is sometimes better to purposely forget than to purposely remember.

I did manage to forget about what I might see the following day and spent time with Carmen. At least working a day shift meant that we could catch up with the world together as opposed to being on completely different places. She was well used to my shifts and accepted it as a part of the job. Despite not seeing one another for days on end, we always made sure that we could spend as much time together as possible and the only easy way to do that was to go away for the weekend or a week abroad, as we frequently did three of four times a year. I suppose a perk of the job was the overtime and the ability to spend it!

No breakfast for me that Friday morning as I felt too anxious about the post-mortem. When I arrived at the office, I sat down to a cup of coffee with John when in bounced the DI summoning us to leave straight away. Before I knew it, I was walking towards the Mortuary at Yorkhill Hospital (Children's Hospital) in Glasgow and felt as though I was walking to a funeral.

Prior to going into the theatre, the DI gave John and I a pep talk and told us that if we wanted to leave at any point, we could and not to feel obliged to remain inside if it was too stressful. This actually made me feel slightly better as at least he was giving us permission to leave if the going was too tough. I decided that I would stick around for the entire duration and try not to look too closely at what was going on.

We all put on our gowns and looked the same as the staff in the room. The nurse, who was preparing the baby for the post-mortem, handled him with care and dignity as though he was merely asleep. She was gentle and even spoke to him as she removed the sheet he was wrapped in. I couldn't help myself and looked straight at his lifeless body lying there on the table.

When the pathologist arrived, he just got on with what he had to do. Although it seemed cruel, he too was gentle yet thorough enough to do what was required under the circumstances. The main reason that we were there was to obtain various samples from the baby so that further tests could be done. The nature of the post-mortem was to ascertain whether he had died as a result of the assault or perhaps due to another reason.

This other reason was due to a weak low-lying placenta and could have caused the mother to have a miscarriage at any time during her pregnancy. This ruled out any foul play and meant that the accused would be charged with assault as opposed to serious assault. At the end of the post-mortem, the baby looked the same as he did before any intrusion into his little body. The staff was remarkable and it was probably one of the most poignant moments of my police career.

Afterwards, the three of us all spoke in depth about the events of that morning and reached the conclusion that the staff involved in that line of work were dedicated and courteous and had treated the baby as though it was still alive. We had so much respect for them and their profession. I was grateful for the opportunity of attending a post-mortem and thanked the DI for including me.

I knew that I could undertake any task asked of me as a police officer having endured the events of that morning. I quickly tried to put the events to the back of my mind and I concentrated on the workload given to me. I was an inexperienced detective but I was being treated as an equal. My enquiries were growing but I still managed to keep on top of them with the help of John and Brian.

Between us, we had worked tirelessly on the robberies in the Springburn area and eventually managed to lock up two guys in connection with them. Although no money was recovered, at least the two Neds were off the street. It was kind of strange actually, arresting them, as it was more of a hunch than actual evidence.

The difference being, they both incriminated each other as being the person responsible for the crime. All we needed was a hint of forensic evidence from the crime scenes and that would be their downfall. Whilst they were both locked up in a cell, Brian contacted the fingerprint specialists at Pitt Street asking them to compare the prints of the two accused to see if there was a match.

As luck would have it, there was enough to secure a conviction against them both, as there was fingerprint evidence of them both at some of the crime scenes. In truth, the two accused were quite sloppy and would have avoided being arrested if they had worn gloves. I settled into the role and loved the thrill of being bogged down with a huge volume of enquiries. I struggled at times as I was at a loss as to how to deal with frauds, robberies and serious assaults.

John and Brian ensured that their own work wasn't being neglected yet at the same time they made sure that all of my cases were dealt with. I was working long hours but I enjoyed every minute of it. My scheduled two weeks was nearing an end and the DI took me into the office on the Friday. He thanked me for my efforts and told me that I had worked extremely well during my time there.

However, there was a slight catch. Apparently, my own shift bosses had complained that they were short of troops and asked that I be returned as soon as possible. I was to begin with my shift again the following Monday morning. I was gutted as I had hoped that I would be allowed to remain in situ with the CID. I left his office absolutely gutted at the prospect of returning to the shift.

The only thing that kept me going was the fact that I knew that I would begin my "Aid" to the CID within a month. I just had to grit my teeth and get on with it. Back on the shift, my first task was a school crossing patrol. I knew that the gaffers meant this as a joke, as it was to bring me back down to the harsh realities of life as a cop.

I did the duty as required and never complained but deep down, I was fuming as there was plenty other probationers who should have done the job. After all, I had done that type of thing when I was a probationer. I bit my tongue and carried on as though it didn't matter, but it did!

Having been paired up with the oldest guy on the shift, I knew that I would have to do most of the work as he was due to retire. Gordon had only six months left before he retired and he really couldn't give a shit! He had asked on several occasions to be allowed to walk a beat. However, the sergeants on the shift at that time were bastards. When a cop asked them for something, they would simply order them to do the opposite and laughed at the cop concerned.

Gordon was no exception and he was ordered to drive one of the cars. He told me that he would do what was required but nothing more. He refused to stop drug addicts to search them and he would only do a basic job to get through the day. This made matters worse for me, as he was not in any way a conversationalist.

I had to drag anything out of him and he felt that the whole world was against him. I tried my best but decided that I would just sit back and wait until he spoke to me. After about five days together, he mellowed and I grew to like him. I respected him anyhow as he had almost completed thirty years in a job that wasn't particularly good to its staff.

One late shift after having attended the briefing, I knew that I would have to work with Gordon for the next seven days. I had again been allocated a school crossing patrol, leaving Gordon to attend any outstanding calls. The first call of the day was a sudden death. Police officers must attend these to ensure that there are no suspicious circumstances. It takes few hours, as the deceased must have their GP attend to decide as to whether they will issue a death certificate.

However, if the deceased has not been to their GP for a while, it is more than likely that the Police Casualty Surgeon must thereafter attend. They never give out death certificates so that means a wait for the mortuary attendants to call to remove the body. That means a long wait, sometimes trying to make idle chit-chat with bereaved relatives.

In this case, the lady was eighty years old; she had been found slumped on a chair within her home. The home help phoned the police to say that she was dead and Gordon was to attend to obtain the particulars for a sudden death report. He dropped me off at my school crossing and he left to attend the death. After my school crossing, I walked all the way back to the scene of the sudden death in Sighthill. When I got into the house, I met Gordon who said that he was still awaiting the arrival of the GP.

The next-door neighbour was there and seemed upset at the death of the old lady. The house was very clean and tidy and there was no sign of a break-in or a disturbance. All good signs, as at least there was no suspicion of foul play. Shortly after I arrived, the phone rang and Gordon waltzed over to answer it. It was a nephew of the deceased and Gordon started to tell him that he had bad news for him as his aunt had died.

"Oh no, wait a minute, hold on tae a check something." Puzzled, I wondered what he was doing and watched as Gordon went over to the old lady and declared that she wasn't dead at all. He could feel a pulse. He went back over to the phone and told the relieved nephew that his aunt wasn't dead at all, she was maybe in a wee coma or had suffered a stroke and she would be going to Stobhill hospital!

I walked out of the room and burst out laughing. There was this poor wee woman lying there unconscious and everyone around her assumed she was dead but didn't take the time to feel for a pulse or even to check whether she was breathing. Gordon had been in the house for nearly two hours and didn't think to check out for himself whether she was dead or not! He just assumed she was dead because she hadn't moved.

He was frantic when he discovered that she was alive and immediately contacted the control room to request an ambulance rather than for the mortuary attendants. I could hear the laughter from the control room as they relayed the message. I couldn't look at Gordon fearing that I was going to erupt into laughter myself.

Shortly afterwards, the ambulance crew arrived and said that she probably had suffered a stroke. She was taken to hospital and was eventually discharged back to her home. Meanwhile, back at the office, the gaffers were furious and tried to give me a hard time. I was quick to point out that I wasn't there as I had been carrying out a school crossing patrol and Gordon had gone there himself. He was looking for a scapegoat and I was to be that person.

However, I reminded him that as sergeant, he should have attended the death himself as that is what the procedures manual state on action regarding what to do at sudden deaths. He was pissed off at me for arguing back with him but I just wasn't going to be blamed for the error. I suppose Gordon should have done more at the time but he didn't.

It was simply a mistake and now our bosses would have to explain what happened to senior bosses. I knew who would get his ass kicked for the error. The sergeant because he failed to attend the death! This made me smile, as it was no more than the prick deserved.

The confirmation that I was to become a CID aid arrived and my own shift inspector took me aside and told me that I was due to finish with the shift and he didn't want me leaving with any outstanding reports. The last three days of my life in uniform was spent in the office report writing. In truth, it only took me a couple of hours but I walked around the office getting to know my soon-to-be new colleagues in the CID and drank gallons of coffee whilst chatting to the troops. It was bliss.

Knowing that I was soon about to leave for at least six months was great. I had been told that after six months, I would probably have to return to the shift again pending a full-time position becoming available. The previous guys who had been in the same position, however, were kept on and remained there until they became full time without having to return to uniform duty. I hoped that I would be the same.

My first day as an apprentice felt like my first day at school. I had butterflies in my tummy and I felt really excited. When I walked into the room, I met my shift colleague Drew. He was a few years older than I was but had been in the police since he left school, therefore he had a wealth of experience in how to do the job.

My DS was Ross. A real gentleman but took no shit from anyone and he was competent at his job. I couldn't have wished for a better team. Drew and I knew each other to say hello to but we didn't know anything much about the other and immediately upon speaking with him I knew that I was going to enjoy myself. I never got the chance to get my jacket off as Drew had stuff to do and he wanted me to accompany him.

I left the office not knowing where we were going. I eventually asked him as we approached Glasgow City centre and he told me that he "was going to buy me the best cup of coffee there was to be had in Glasgow".

We arrived at a café/bar in the Merchant City called Café Gandolfi and stayed there for the next hour drinking coffee and chatting. It was probably the best way ever to break the ice with a new colleague. The DS wasn't there. He remained at the office, as he wasn't the 'coffee' type of guy. Obviously, he wasn't aware of our whereabouts, as he trusted Drew to be out there fighting crime, as opposed to receiving a caffeine fix. So began our almost daily ritual of going for a coffee at the start of the day.

On reflection, I would say that it was a much more relaxed way of life and it also meant that we didn't have to hang around the office waiting on the senior bosses plying us with additional work. What I found very strange was the fact that the majority of on-duty detectives from our division could be found within the four walls of "Café Gandolfi".

It was also a sort of social gathering and gave all of us the opportunity to catch up with the rest of the team of detectives we probably only ever saw at either court or spoke to via the telephone. I, being the newcomer, felt very much at home and soon became accepted as part of the team of detectives who descended upon the café culture of the City of Glasgow. I soon found out that being a detective wasn't all it was cracked up to be.

In particular, there was the small matter of having to work a late shift. The difference was that now there was only two of us to cover the whole division. Not only was it a busy area but it was also a huge area to cover. It seemed that the police management was of the opinion that there was little or no crime took place at night hence the reason that most detectives were left to work a day shift.

I found this quite a strange approach although Drew was quick to point out that we would only be able to deal with one serious crime at a time. I would have to learn to prioritise my workload. For example, if a murder occurred then obviously that would come before a serious assault or rape. I knew that I would be fine as long as Drew was there, but what would I do if he weren't?

My first late shift came and went without anything of significance taking place. In general, the CID was experiencing one of its less busy periods and this meant that Drew and I could get out onto the streets and jail a few criminals of our own. Ross meanwhile remained within the office, choosing not to get involved in that aspect of policing he found to be very mundane.

One afternoon, an anonymous call was received at the CID and Drew took the necessary details. It was to the effect that a male called Currie had uplifted a supply of drugs and was heading back to his house in Balornock to 'cut them up'. Drew asked me if I knew who the guy was and I told him yes.

We both set off towards where the suspect may be and on driving towards a high-rise block of flats, there was Currie walking down the waste ground. Drew got out of the car and decided to approach him and I would get to him from another direction. Currie stopped and chatted to Drew and then when I arrived, he was detained for a drug search. Sure enough, he was found in possession of a large amount of heroin. He was arrested and taken to the police office. Having been interviewed and charged, he was then detained pending his appearance at court the following morning. He was a particularly nasty and violent individual yet that day, he was fine with us.

As it was a custody case, it meant that Drew and I would have to remain after our normal day shift hours to do the custody case. Ross authorised the overtime for us and we were happy at earning a few extra bucks for what was a straightforward case. The following morning when I arrived for work, the DI asked me to come into his office. This particular DI was not liked as he had his own little clique of detectives who received all of the overtime available.

Drew wasn't a part of that clique and I had no idea just how vindictive this DI could be at that time. He asked me about the overtime worked and I told him that Ross had authorised it. His reply was that he was to be consulted regarding overtime.

I quickly pointed out that he had in fact gone home early that day and therefore it wasn't possible to ask him if he wasn't there. So began his little outburst about respect and doing as I was told, etc. He then told me that I would claim only two hours overtime instead of four hours and I wasn't to tell anyone!

I laughed at him and politely told him that if I worked four hours then I would be claiming four hours and I walked out of the room, laughing. Five minutes later, he entered the CID room and scored through the four hours I had written and replaced it with a two. He looked at me and walked out back to his own room.

At that point, Drew walked into the CID to begin his shift and saw what Murphy had done. He about-turned and went to see him. I heard raised voices and then Drew re-emerged and told me that we had to go out. En route to Gandolfi's, he told about the conversation with the DI who told Drew the same as he had told me about claiming two hours.

Drew told him that he would be claiming the four hours and that was it. When he learned that I had told him the same thing, he laughed but told me to be on my guard, as the DI would make our lives a misery in the future. Both of us laughed at the way in which I had told him that I wouldn't be claiming for anything less than that worked. After all, it's not as though Strathclyde Police can't afford to pay a little overtime.

Not once had Murphy even said well done in recovering the drugs. He was more concerned with the idea that Drew and I had made money without his say-so. Within a month, Drew and I had been working like maniacs and had locked up several criminals, as well having managed to deal with our own heavy allocated workload.

Then one day, a citation arrived for us both to attend court during our day off, case against Currie. This meant that he had obviously been remanded in custody pending a court appearance. We both knew who his lawyer was. It was the same one I had the verbal spat with during the case when he asked me to produce my police notebook and I had cited the Hinshelwood v Auld to prevent me from doing it!

Yes, he was one of the dreaded few who truly has a grudge against the police having been an ex-cop himself, well, for a 3 or 4-month period, that is. Although

I had personally been in the box several times against him, Drew hadn't. This time, I would have to follow Drew in the box and therefore I knew that I would get a hard time, having to remember my own movements and those of Drew.

The day of the trial came and initially, we both thought that we would not have to give evidence as he would probably plead guilty. Next thing we know, Drew is called into the box to give his evidence and we haven't prepared properly. I sat anxiously outside, awaiting my call.

After about twenty minutes, I was called in. I took the oath as normal and began my evidence in chief with the PF, all straightforward so far really! Then the other lawyer started his questions about how I had prepared and asked me what I had read and spoke about with Drew. In truth, I told him that we hadn't really discussed the case as we both saw it as being straightforward. I told him I had read a statement and he asked me whose. I wasn't really aware of where it was leading but was immediately suspicious of him asking me.

I said that I had read Drew's statement, as I had not submitted a statement, as it was a corroborated statement that had been submitted. I knew what he was getting at, as technically, I should have submitted my own written statement to Drew for the case. I quickly retorted that yes, that should happen but as it doesn't always happen like that. I was now best placed to speak the truth in person, in court.

He began to shout at me saying that I had obviously been lazy and neglected my duty. I again had to think on my feet and told him that it was no more of an oversight, as clearly his precognition agent must have made. He looked puzzled and asked me to go on and I told him that she (precognition agent who takes statements on behalf of solicitors) should have spoken to us both individually yet she chose to accept the same corroborated statement when she called at the office.

He was furious and again shouted at me accusing me of neglecting my duty. The Sheriff stopped him and told him to get on with the proceedings. I had won again and I liked it. He was technically correct, of course, but it never happens that way and merely pointed out that even his staff cut corners! We got a guilty and Currie received six months in prison. Not a bad day's work as we earned a lot of money for appearing at court on our day off.

Having returned to duty after our days off, Drew, Ross and I decided that being Friday, we would descend on Glasgow for a few beers that night after work. All that was required was to take our cars home during the shift so that we could enjoy a drink without having to worry about taking the car. Having done this during the day, we went to a few bars and had a good night. The downside to this was that one of us was to start at seven the following morning so that we could compile the crime figures for the bosses.

This was a daily routine and I always wondered why they couldn't just look at the computer like the rest of us mere detectives had to do. Obviously, they weren't capable of this type of thing. I had the short straw and headed off home early as I had to be at work early the following day. I arrived at the office just after seven to find the DI already there. I felt like shit but couldn't show it as I knew I had to put on a brave face in front of him.

He told me to get ready with my clipboard as there had been a murder in Kirkintilloch (still part of our division then) and that I was to be the 'productions' officer. This meant that I had to log all productions seized in connection with the murder. I had never done that job before but nonetheless I was up for it. Then came the bombshell—"Head to the mortuary as you will also have to attend the post-mortem." I could feel the sick in my guts rising up towards my gullet. The thought of a post-mortem at any time of the day was bad enough, but with a hangover?

It was the first time that I had dreaded an event so much but the combination of alcohol mixed with blood and guts was almost enough to put me right off. I went to the toilet to gather my thoughts and on looking in the mirror I told myself that I would just go along with the request and just to concentrate on dealing with productions as opposed to dealing with the fact that there was a dead carcass on the table being carved up.

I made my way to the mortuary as requested and met up with the detective who was to be my 'mentor' for the course of the investigation. "Trigger", as he was known, was not much older than I was but by fuck he had had a hard life. He looked and acted at least twenty years my senior and he had the most atrocious eating habits and mannerisms I had ever come across in my life. He had about twenty-odd years' service and was very experienced.

The only downside at this time was that we didn't know each other and I felt that I was too long in the tooth to have to listen to an old ogre like him. However, I had no idea what was expected of me at the PM (post-mortem) that I would have to do as I was told.

When we entered the PM room, I saw a male lying on the slab with several bullet holes in his body and he was pretty roughed up. He was still semi-clothed but from what I could see, he was extremely athletic. I asked Trigger what the story about his death was and he told me that apparently he had been tied up and beaten within his home in the Kirkintilloch area.

Afterwards, he was dragged into the toilet area and shot in the head and body. I knew that this would be a long drawn out investigation but I didn't know just how long it would last. Clearly, this had been a gangland slaying. Probably as payback for edging into someone else's area to claim drug clientele.

The two pathologists entered the room and so began their documenting the injuries on his body and the exact size of the holes and scratches. When they turned him over onto his front, I could see just how badly beaten he had been as his back was a mass of bruises and scratches. His hands and feet had been tied together with thick rope and that too had cut into his wrists and ankles.

After about an hour of documenting the injuries and having them photographed for court purposes, the pathologists began their PM. It lasted about six hours, by which point I knew that I wouldn't eat again for a few days thanks to the extent of the process of cutting and sawing. It was official. He had been killed by a single shot to the head. At least, that would be the final blow that caused his death. Not taking into account the other injuries sustained by him.

For the next three weeks, Trigger and I remained within a room of the office, bagging and labelling the productions and taking them to the lab at Pitt Street. During that time, we both got to know one another very well. We had several fall-outs along the way but on the whole, we were good buddies. It was a hard and thankless job but I made a fortune in overtime whilst working there.

The story of the murder was very slow at coming through but eventually, the team of detectives managed to find out that it was a team of Neds from the Southside of Glasgow who had carried out the hit on the male. It was in retribution for him commanding a lucrative share of the drugs market.

The information also suggested that when his mother found the body lying in the toilet, she allegedly contacted one of his friends prior to contacting the police so that they could remove all traces of drugs and money from inside the house.

A trace of the telephones confirmed that there was a lapse of about an hour before the police were eventually contacted, thereby giving them sufficient time in which to dispose of whatever they wished. His mother claimed to be a medium and was trying to assist with the investigation. If I had been in charge, I would have told her to fuck off but Murphy, who was the senior investigating officer, took the piss out of the woman by asking her to look at various pieces of jewellery to see if she could 'get a feel' for what may have taken place.

The DI was really bugging the hell out of me but I couldn't say anything as I was only working there for a short time and had little or no police service. After about two months, the productions fazed off as there was nothing much else to do but take statements of witnesses but with no productions to be seized, this meant that Trigger and I no longer had a definite job to do and so we became a part of the investigation team.

I would have much preferred to be sent back to work with Drew and Ross but I was told by the DI that the experience would be good for me. I vowed to stick it out for one more month then ask to get back to learning basic detective skills. I was given one of the crime unit guys as a work colleague and Trigger was given another.

The idea was that I was like any other detective and was therefore capable of doing the same role. It didn't bother me in the slightest and my new colleague was Mike. He was a nice guy who was everyone's pal and he wanted to swan around wearing a nice suit but he didn't want to do any work. This was probably why I was given him as a neighbour as no one else wanted him.

We were given all of the rubbish to do whilst everyone else received good interesting actions. We could do about between six and ten actions per day as opposed to the others doing one. I wasn't happy and asked why I was being given all of the crap but I was asked to speak to the DI to get the answer to that!

I immediately thought that perhaps he was getting back at me because of the overtime problem I had with him a couple of months ago. I went to his room and before I could knock on the door, I listened and could hear familiar voices from within room, including Trigger's.

I decided to wait and ask Trigger what was going on later that day. True to my word, I saw Trigger in the office and managed to grab his attention long enough to find out what was going on. He told me that there was another side to the investigation that only a select handful of detectives knew about and that I shouldn't rock the boat. Not content with this, I asked him to explain further and I swore that I wouldn't tell a soul.

Trigger told me that there was a team of eight who were looking deeper into the actions of Chick and it had led them to a seedy sauna in Glasgow where Chick and other major criminals went to discuss their business, as well as to have sex with the girls who worked there. But there was a major problem.

Some of the sauna girls had told of two police officers who also used the same sauna. They referred to the cops as "Tan and Teeth". They were trying to ascertain who the cops were and that was why the investigation was being kept quiet. I trusted what Trigger had told me and I decided to keep to myself that information and I never told Mike anything about the other team. One afternoon, Mike asked if we could go and meet one of his friends who worked in Kirkintilloch police office.

I went along with him as I was pissed off with the crappy actions we were expected to do. Whilst there, Mike met up with an Asian cop, Stevie. They went into a room and started to talk in private. The only thing being, they left the door open and I could hear the general conversation. It was about a sauna and the girls who worked there and the murder investigation and how it was looking likely that the police would soon find out they too frequented that sauna.

The penny dropped; this was "Tan and Teeth" the girls were speaking about. "Tan" referred to the Asian cop and "Teeth" referred to Mike because of the row of capped white teeth he had. I was livid. I walked into the room and told Mike that I would have to get back to the office, as there was other things I had to do. He begged me to wait but I was annoyed at what I had just heard. I understand that this reference to "tan" and the fact that it referred to ethnicity, but it should be remembered that this is the mid '90s and this type of conversation did take place. It wouldn't be tolerated today.

Back at the office, I made my way to the DI's office and asked to speak to him. He told me to close the door and I just blurted out something about trying to find out why I was being treated like a 'dafty' and being given all the rubbish enquiries. He fobbed me off by telling me that I would just have to get on with it. I told him that I wanted to know what other investigation was being carried on behind everyone else's back. He was furious and told me to get the fuck out of his room. I stood my ground and said that if I was being used to keep someone else at bay then I had a right to know.

He stopped and asked me to explain what I meant but I refused. "Do you know something you are not telling me?"

"No, do you?"

He laughed and told me that I reminded him of himself, when he had been young in service and then he completely changed his manner towards me. I knew that he was trying to get me to tell him what I knew but again, I refused to budge. He said, "Dale, fuck off out of my room and I'll get back to you in an hour, ya wee prick."

I met up with Trigger and told him about the earlier events and he laughed saying that they too were now aware of the two cops involved although the DI and others had known about a week earlier. I was well fucked off. I knew that I had been made a scapegoat and left to babysit Mike whilst the police carried out their investigation.

The DI was taking the murder investigation off onto a different tangent in an attempt to make a name for himself. He was wrong as he should have concentrated his efforts on the murder and not on the drug side of things. It seemed that this was becoming a very personal enquiry to him and he was letting his own personal judgement cloud what the main issue was. That of catching the murderers.

True to his word, the DI called me to his office and the DCI was also there. They told me that they had only found out that very day who the cops were referred to as "Tan and Teeth", and that they were going to clear up the matter now. I had nothing to worry about and was to continue working on the case.

I had never mentioned who the cops were but they were trying to get me to tell them. I told them that I wanted to know who the cops were. I only wanted them to tell me and they did. They confirmed that it was Mike and Stevie but they still wondered how I knew. I told them that it was because I was a good detective but I also told them that I had been made a fool of by being left with Mike whilst they had been snooping behind our backs. The DCI asked me not to say anything and assured me that I would have a new neighbour by the end of the day.

After the evening briefing, I was told that I would be working with Trigger for the rest of the enquiry. Mike was sent back to uniform and Stevie was moved to another sub-office to work but neither of them told anyone the reason why. They should have been disciplined for frequenting a brothel as it is against police regulations to be in the company of known criminals.

However, nothing happened as apparently at that time, the problem with another Asian police officer was a political hot potato and had resulted in a high-profile court case accusing Strathclyde Police of being racist. The last thing needed was for another Asian officer to complain of discrimination at this time too.

However, what if both the officers had been white, would that have had the same outcome? The full story about why they had been frequenting the sauna never ever surfaced although many cops think that these same two officers moved in very dodgy circles and were frequently seen in the company of many high-profile criminals. Nothing was ever done about it as Murphy and Co were too busy trying to lock up those involved in the murder of Chick.

After about three months on the investigation, I asked the DCI if I could be returned to work with Ross and Drew as I felt that I wasn't learning anything about the actual art of being a detective. He assured me that I would return within two weeks and said that he admired my ability to confront senior officers without feeling pressured into going along with their requests at all times.

I knew that he was referring to the fact that I had tackled them head-on regarding the Mike situation and refused to believe what they had told me. I knew that I couldn't last two more weeks on the investigation.

Prior to leaving the team, I was sent down to London with Trigger to take items of clothing seized from several accused men who had been locked up in connection with Chick's murder. They had little or, in fact, no evidence against them and they needed a specific type of forensic test to be carried out. It was to see if there were any traces of firearms residue on the clothing already seized.

When a gun is fired, there are millions of particles spread over a certain area of the body of the person firing the gun. This is an expensive test and can only be carried out in Birmingham or London at the met Lab. Trigger and I went there with the clothing in the hope that a match for the firearm evidence already seized. Having flown down there with these items, we had to remain there for three days.

This meant that we had nothing to do except explore London and live it up at night. We stayed in a lovely hotel but because of Trigger's inability to drink much, he ended up in bed the worse for drink, about nine o'clock at night. Leaving me alone with no company other than the hotel bar. Not exactly a great introduction to the life of a detective when my neighbour was pissed and in bed!

I didn't venture too far; knowing my sense of direction, I would get lost and probably end up in another country, let alone another part of the city!

The murder investigation had so many twists and turns throughout its course that at times even those of us working on it were aghast at how far the DI was prepared to go to deviate from the actual fact in hand, i.e., to find the deceased's killers. Information pointed to the fact that at least four people were involved although there was no specific name coming to the fore.

Until one day, one of the detectives managed to 'burst' a story previously given by a sauna girl. She had lied through her teeth in order to protect herself and of course, her children. She told the story about four men coming to the sauna the afternoon after the murder and Eddie, who was a notorious criminal from the Govan area, was splashing cash around and drinking heavily.

He spoke of a 'hit' that he had carried out and how he was spending his money received from it. The female was afraid and that was why she told lies to the police the first time. Apart from this information, the DI centred on getting at the deceased's best friend who was also supposed to be heavily involved in the drug scene. Then there was the sauna crew and again they were being harassed by the team of detectives in order to "noise them up".

I was glad to be bailing out and the London trip for me was a great way of winding down. I couldn't give a fuck about what work was still to be done on the investigation, I just wanted out. The only real reason I was with Trigger was that as production keeper I had to be involved so that there could be no suggestion of too many people dealing with the items seized and thereby avoiding cross contamination.

At least, there was only Trigger and I who had dealt with the items seized. Some defence lawyers grab every opportunity to discredit the handling of productions and try to infer that there could be other sources of DNA evidence on clothing due to them having been passed around like a porno magazine amongst cops!

Trigger and I had managed to ensure that the items seized had been dealt with properly. One thing the investigation had taught me was how to deal with productions and bag and label them correctly. This was the best thing that could be taught to any good detective, as it is an imperative part of the investigation process.

The news from the lab wasn't exactly what had been expected but may prove to be vital. At least it confirmed that one of the jackets had traces of firearms residue material and the specialist was prepared to give evidence to that effect. Having spent thousands of pounds on the lab process, I doubted as to whether it would be good, but Trigger was more upbeat and painted a better picture of the overall scenario. He thought that there would be enough to convict the team concerned.

The three days with Trigger was an enjoyable experience and I truly found out just what type of larger-than-life character he was. He was funny and argumentative but great company nonetheless. We had met up with some of his many friends in London and I had enjoyed plenty bottles of wine listening to them reminisce about their early years in the job. But after three days, I was desperate to get home and back to normality. I missed my wife and I have to confess she is much prettier than Trigger!

On returning to Glasgow with the news of the lab tests, the bosses weren't happy. They had been relying heavily on a better result and they didn't get one. The four accused had been remanded in custody and now Crown Office was demanding to know the extent of evidence at hand.

After all, they couldn't hold on to four accused men and deprive them of their liberty based upon the information provided by the DI. Eventually, the trial day arrived and all of the detectives involved in the case were called to court. One by one, we were reduced to about six who were to be used as witnesses.

Trigger and I sat there for days on end and eventually, I too was excused, much to Trigger's annoyance. He was called and asked to account for his handling of the productions and surprisingly, he didn't receive a hard time from the defence team. They were quietly confident that they would get the right verdict. They did. The case against all four was found to be not proven. They walked free from court smirking at the DI and Co standing around the court foyer. They weren't the only one smirking; half of the team did the same thing.

Again, justice wasn't seen to be done, as the deceased's family was left knowing that the right men had appeared in court but when it came to the witnesses telling the true version of events, they appeared to have temporary amnesia. It was the fault of those witnesses who were too afraid to speak out against a group of evil, twisted, sadistic murderers. Given the choice, what would any other ordinary person do? I meanwhile had re-established myself within the CID and enjoyed working with Drew and Ross.

I was beginning to learn the laidback way to policing and I enjoyed it immensely. I'm not saying that we didn't work hard, we did. But for the first time in my career I was actually spending less time out in street and more time report writing as I was inundated with huge volumes of statements for serious assaults, robberies, frauds and other serious crimes. I loved it.

The downside was that I only had about a month to go before my attachment to the department was coming to a close. I stayed out of the way of the DI as far as possible and exchanged pleasantries with him when I had to. I had a new DI and though I detested the previous DI, this other guy was ten times worse.

Bert was opinionated, disrespectful and he loved himself. He would walk into the CID office, walk past all of the detectives and stop at my desk. "Dale, my boy, get me a coffee." He never liked saying please or thank you so I thought I'd better teach him a lesson.

One afternoon after he sauntered up to my desk, he again asked for his coffee. I sat there and didn't even lift my head. "Did you hear me, Dale?"

I looked up at him and said, "Yes, I heard you but I'm too busy to make you a coffee, get it yourself."

He looked at me and said, "I'm the DI and I asked you to get me a coffee."

"Boss, I told you I'm too busy. Anyhow, perhaps if all DIs had manners and could say please and thank you, it wouldn't be such an arduous task for mere trainees like me."

He stormed out of the room and slammed the door behind him. There were five other detectives there and after he had gone, they laughed like hyenas at me for being so cheeky. "Fuck him. My days of running after bosses have finished, I'm a detective like the rest of you, not a fucking tea boy!"

I knew that I had been accepted as one of the team as the DI never answered me back. Perhaps he would see that I wasn't there to keep him going on coffee but to detect crime. I knew that I would perhaps suffer but I was prepared to face that if I had to. In the meantime, I would keep my head down and get on with my job.

In fairness, I think it was his way, old-school bosses who thought that others had to run around after them but I wasn't like most people. As time progressed, I got to know him better and respected him as he did his job very well, which wasn't always the case with people of his rank. I found Bert to be really down to earth and hard working. It did surprise me as I had let my initial dealings with him cloud my judgement. That was quite a learning curve as I knew then that really there was no harm in him asking the junior to make him a coffee. I still sometimes do this myself – albeit, I also make others sometimes!

The late shift came and I was teamed up with a cop from a shift, as there were no other detectives available to work with me. Quite a scary prospect when you consider that I was only a trainee! Ross and Drew were night shift. This meant that I was virtually on my own covering the north part of the city out towards Kirkintilloch accompanied by a cop with no CID experience.

Alan was a decent guy and he was a great cop so this could perhaps make matters easier for me. This was one of the quietest weeks I had ever experienced which meant I could catch up on my paperwork as well as leaving enough time to get out and cruise the streets looking for criminals with Alan.

About ten o'clock one night, a call came over the radio about a robbery taking place at McDonald's in Springburn. Alan and I were the first to arrive at the scene and the masked gunman had left with a three-figure sum of money and in the process had hit a sixteen-year-old girl on the side of the head with a handgun.

She was distraught and all attempts at calming her down were proving to be useless. She was taken by ambulance to a nearby hospital suffering from shock. I felt really sorry for the girl as she had only been doing her job when this idiot walked into the place and after striking her on the head with the gun, he pointed it at her face. No wonder she was in a state of shock! Two cops arrived and assisted us in taking statements from the twenty-odd staff and customers who had witnessed the crime.

During this time, there was a call over the radio about an off-duty cop requiring urgent assistance in Sighthill only about 2 miles away from where I was. By the sound of the night air, I could hear police sirens coming from all around the area. We continued with our job but I kept thinking about the fact that an off-duty cop was in Sighthill at that time of night.

No disrespect to anyone from that area but it is a rough area and not someplace cops frequent unless working. "Whoever it was must have been up to no good," I commented to Alan. He laughed and said something about the guy (assuming it was a guy) must have been up at a whorehouse for a shag. We laughed and carried on with our task.

After completing the statements, I arranged for the forensic team to attend the following day to dust for fingerprints. When we arrived at the back foyer of the office, the place was awash with bodies waiting to be processed. There was one particular cop who pulled me aside and asked me why I hadn't turned up at the assistance call. Before I got a chance to answer, he then said that the whole shift was pissed off with me. I told him it was none of his fucking business and I walked away. I was angry with him but vowed to speak with him later to clear the air.

When I arrived in the CID room, there was the on-duty DI. Because of the size of our area, we actually had 4 DIs altogether who covered the whole area and they had a rotation of being on-duty DI. This particular DI had been called out because of the Sighthill incident.

He was the same DI who had taken me to the baby PM several months before and although no one liked him, I always found him to be fine with me so that was good enough for me to be pleasant towards him. I told him what had happened at McDonald's and what we had carried out at the scene.

He was pleased with the work and then began straight away by briefing me about the other incident. It would appear that an off-duty cop from our division had been at a night out in Glasgow and went down to the area known as "the drag". This is an area frequented and policed through tolerated zones, of prostitutes. This guy had paid the girl fifty quid for sex and went with her back to her flat in Sighthill to do his "business".

The girl's boyfriend had returned and tried to get the guy out of the flat but ended up fighting with him. The cop was now at the hospital and the guy and his girlfriend were in custody. I was shocked, but what annoyed me was the fact that this other cop had accused me of neglecting this other call. He didn't even know that I had been dealing with the robbery.

I stormed past the DI and walked up to the cop who was standing with a prisoner in the back custody area. I pulled him aside and told him to let the shift know that I was dealing with a robbery at the time the assistance call came out where a sixteen-year-old was struck on the head with a handgun. Meanwhile, they were trying to help a married cop escape from the claws of a prostitute.

He was flabbergasted and tried to make light of his earlier comment. I left him knowing that he had made an arse of himself and never try to do that with me again. I knew that the shift would have had their questions well and truly answered as to where I was at the time of the assistance call.

The DI had a lot of work to do with his case and I was happy to let him carry on with it. Ross and Drew had arrived for their night shift and I knew that they would have a busy night ahead of them. I too had plenty to keep me occupied and phoned Carmen to let her know that I would be late home, not uncommon in the CID. As the night wore on, I gathered all of the statements together so that I could leave the package for the day shift to carry on with. I would have been delighted to receive a package like this one as it was very well organised and all that was left to do was the forensic tests, oh and also to catch the perpetrator!

I was also kept up to date with the story as it unfolded by the night shift troops. However, as I had completed my paperwork for the robbery, Ross asked me if I wanted to stay on a few hours to help them with this other enquiry. Me being a good soul and wishing to help my colleagues, agreed to help!

In truth, I did it because I liked working with Ross and Drew and I would also be able to claim even more overtime. So Drew and I went to the nearby hospital to speak to the poor cop who was himself that evening, the victim of a bad crime? On arrival, I met a staff nurse whom I knew from many other previous visits to A & E dealing with other crimes; she smiled at me and immediately asked us to come into a cubicle as she wanted to speak to her.

The nurse was about 60 years old and looked like the bird lady out of *Home Alone 2*. The only thing missing was her coat, hat and birds sitting on top of her. However, she was a fantastic lady, superb at her job and very police-friendly!

Apparently, when Stevie, the off duty cop, had arrived at the hospital, he still had a spent condom on his dick and this was thrown into a bin by this very nurse. However, being a stickler for attention to detail, she was now wary that, in fact, this patient—the cop—had been up to no good. Especially when she saw two detectives hot on his trail!

Stevie had denied that any sexual contact had taken place between him and the girl and he said that when he got to the flat, he changed his mind and tried to leave but the boyfriend beat him up and threw him down some stairs. I couldn't believe this guy; bad enough having gone with a prostitute, but the thought of the potential diseases he may have contracted, and might pass on to his wife!.

This particular prostitute looked like 'Zelda' from the *Terrahawks*. Not only that, she was a raving junkie who had sores all over her body from the ravages of drugs and abuse she had inflicted upon her body over the years. I knew Issy as she was local to our police area and I had searched her with other colleagues during drug busts we had been involved in. I felt sorry for Steve's wife and two children and things were about to take a turn for the worse.

Later that morning, Stevie was interviewed at the hospital concerning the events of that night by the DI and a female detective. He denied having had sex with the prostitute and he said that he was up at the house as he was being a Good Samaritan to the female. He told of how he had met her in Glasgow City Centre and fallen for her tale of woe and that she needed money to get home. He did even better than her request for cash; he paid for a taxi to her home and to make sure that she got home okay, he walked her to her door. I think it is a fair assumption that he was telling blatant lies!

However, the DI and DS knew all about the spent condom. They even seized it as a production, should it be required for court purposes. They told him that he was lying but that they would be back at a later stage to speak with him further.

Meanwhile, a member of the concierge staff at the flats had contacted a tabloid newspaper and sold his version of events. When the police were contacted and asked to comment on the fact that a police officer had been caught having sex with a prostitute, they naturally declined to say anything. But this raised a major issue concerning the leaking of the story. What about the guy's wife and family?

They were only told that he had broken his leg in a fall, yet now a different story was about to reach the press! The DI and DS had no option but to go to Steve's wife and tell her that there may be an allegation appearing in the newspaper naming her husband and that there was a sexual element to his injuries.

Naturally, she was annoyed and humiliated at the very idea that this type of story was going to appear in the news and perhaps her children would suffer also because of its nature. Meanwhile, Drew and Ross were tasked with interviewing the suspects in the case, Paul and Issy. He was also a drug user and a known criminal in the area, as well as being well known to the police. They both told the same story about that night.

Paul and Issy had gone down the 'drag' (area in Glasgow where prostitutes plied their trade), hoping that she could make enough money to buy them heroin. Often, he would go down with her and keep out of the way, lurking in the shadows. When she went with a punter for sex, he would remain close by fearing that she would be harmed.

Sounds very caring, but the downside to this story is that Paul was prepared to allow his girlfriend to perform sexual favours to buy him drugs. Not exactly a modern-day story of Romeo and Juliet, more a realistic version of events depicting drug addicts and the lengths they would go to for drugs.

That night, Issy had been approached by Stevie asking her for sex. She had agreed the fifty pounds for sex at her flat in Sighthill. They were going to get a taxi there. They made their way back to the flat and did what they did! Paul meanwhile walked back from Glasgow to Sighthill, hoping that the punter would be gone when he returned.

When Paul arrived back at the flat he heard Steve shouting at Issy about her lack of sex as he thought he was to receive more. Paul entered the flat and told Stevie to get out. However, a fight ensued and Paul threatened to give him a hiding so Stevie ran out of the flat and fell on the stairwell, knocking himself unconscious and thereby injuring his leg. Paul and Issy then rummaged through his pockets and obviously found his wallet containing cash and, more importantly, his police identification (warrant card), which they stole. They walked out of the flats and dumped the wallet contents, keeping the money. In fairness to them though, they did phone an ambulance for the 'victim'.

Paul and Issy refused to tell Ross where the warrant card and other contents were. They were both arrested and charged with attempted murder of a police officer and were to appear at court the next day. Steve had stuck to his story and he said that Issy and Paul had assaulted him, hence the reason they were charged.

There was also video surveillance around the flats so their steps were monitored. I returned to work the next afternoon for my late shift and was asked to speak to the DI. This meant that no doubt I would have work to do regarding the incident. As Paul was known very well to me, I was asked to try to persuade him to tell us where the warrant card was as the police didn't want it to fall into the wrong hands.

I agreed and set off to the cell area with some fags so that I could chat to Paul. I actually did like him and had never had any problems with him in the past. I openly told him what the gaffers wanted but before he got the chance to tell me, I explained that the reason he had been charged with attempted murder was due to the injuries as well as the fact that Steve was a cop.

Paul was angry as he said that Stevie was telling lies about what had happened with his injuries. Stevie declared that Paul beat him with a baseball bat, although nothing like that had been found at the scene. I actually believed Paul and told him that at trial, he would be able to plead guilty to common assault and it would definitely be accepted.

The reason for this was simple. Under no circumstances would Strathclyde Police want the full extent of the events to be made public as it was bad for their image. Any PF dealing with that case would be asked to accept a guilty plea rather than have a full trial. Obviously, the police and PF liaise very closely regarding high-profile cases and it is well known that deals are struck by all parties in these types of cases at least that is what is known in police circles and is openly discussed about deals being done.

Paul seemed a little more upbeat about the charge after I explained what to do. Of course, I did tell him not to tell anyone about the advice I had given him and I knew that I could trust him not to say anything. I also advised him about the warrant card and other items. I told him that I would tell the gaffers that he said he would only tell us where the stuff was if Issy was released and that the police would state in their report that he cooperated fully with the police during the investigation.

He laughed and said that it would never work but he was prepared to trust me to at least try. This type of bargaining tool was always used by police in order to obtain evidence or information. I had quickly learned that sometimes slight manipulation of the facts are required to get the result—albeit I wasn't exactly bending the law!

When I told the DI about his demands, he was livid and began ranting and raving about Paul. I was told to tell Paul that the police would not be held to ransom. Paul stuck by his guns and with my advice sat back to await the police backing down, which they did. I took Paul from the office and he led me to the drain where he had dumped the items from Steve's wallet.

I returned to the office and although the bosses were delighted to have the warrant card back, I feared that they would withdraw the conditions already agreed. Much to even my surprise, the police released Issy and submitted the report saying that he had cooperated fully.

Paul was delighted and it proved that criminals and police officers sometimes do have a reasonable relationship at times. I knew that Paul would come good for me if I ever needed his help and vice versa. Paul appeared at court and was remanded in custody for seven days to allow the police to carry out an identification parade.

Stevie had to ensure that he knew who had assaulted him. I was asked by the DI to collect Paul from prison on the Saturday morning and he was going to arrange for the ID parade to be held at another police office. When I arrived at work on the Saturday morning, the same DI who was conducting the investigation as he had done from the start was waiting on me.

He took me into his office and asked me to obtain a photograph of Paul from the intelligence section. I naturally asked why he needed it and he told me that he wanted to show it to Steve before the parade to ensure that he picked him out.

I was shocked and annoyed that basically, the DI wanted me to help him pervert the course of justice. I told him that I wanted nothing to do with it and suggested that if he wanted a photo of Paul, he should get it himself. I turned and walked out of his office and he followed behind. "That was an order I gave you!"

"I don't care, boss, if you want to discipline me for that then go ahead but I will also say what you wanted me to do."

He told me to "get to fuck out of my sight" and he would speak to me later.

"You know where to find me if you're looking for me."

I walked into the CID room and told Drew what had happened. He laughed and advised me to keep out of his way, but I had done the right thing by not going along with his plan. I felt a little better knowing that another detective agreed with my actions.

Time came for me to collect Paul from prison. Drew volunteered to come with me and after picking Paul up we went to the police office where the parade was to be held. Prior to it starting, Drew spoke to Stevie and asked him if he would be able to identify the guy who assaulted him. He said that it was fine as someone had allegedly shown him a photograph. When Drew told me this, I was ready to tell the defence lawyer all about this as I was so pissed off with the way the investigation had been conducted.

Drew told me to mind my own business and keep quiet about what had taken place. After all, it was only alleged. Reluctantly, I agreed and let the parade continue. Stevie positively identified Paul as the man who assaulted him, despite Paul changing his top with a stand-in who was also in the same parade.

Having returned him to jail, I felt annoyed with myself for allowing myself to be drawn into that situation with the DI. He never spoke to me for about three weeks and when he did, it was only to chastise me for being late one morning. I put it to the back of my mind and tried to keep a low profile as far as the DI was concerned.

Paul appeared in court and pled guilty to common assault, which was accepted by the PF. He received three months in prison, backdated to when he was arrested. He walked free from court that day, satisfied that my advice to him was correct. Justice was done.

Stevie eventually returned to work after a while but eventually received a medical discharge. Nothing ever happened to him about his actions with the prostitute by the police. Rules for one and rules for another!

Having established myself within the department, all that remained for me was to receive a good appraisal and then be appointed full-time. I knew that Ross would write a fair assessment of my time there, although I was absent from his team for three months because of the Kirkintilloch murder investigation.

He submitted a great appraisal and I was delighted with it. The only thing left for me to do was have my interview with the DI, who was the main line manager at that time. He called me into his office and spoke briefly about the appraisal and admitted that it was very good and asked me to sign it so that it could be sent away to Pitt Street.

I thought that the interview was over, but as I got up to leave, he told me to sit down. I duly obliged and then he began to question my loyalty both to my colleagues and senior officers. I told him that I was loyal to those who deserved loyalty but I wasn't playing anyone's game, just doing my job!

"Do you think I play games?"

"Of course, you do."

"Do you think I have a clique?"

I just burst out laughing and told him that I wasn't going to even merit that question with a reply. He seemed quite annoyed that I wouldn't play his games but I didn't want to be a part of his infantile ways. He laughed but this time he seemed more anxious for me to commit to an answer. "Who do you think is in my clique then?"

"Don't know and don't care, boss. All I know is that I'm not in this job to be in a clique."

He then had the audacity to tell me that within the coming months, he would be promoted to DCI and that I would do well to remember this. After all, I may need his assistance in the future and it would be better for me to keep on his side as opposed to falling out with him.

I laughed. A nervous laugh, as I knew that he believed in his own self-importance and bosses like him do hold grudges. I told him that I would remember what he said and if I ever needed anything, I knew that I could rely on him. This gave his rather growing ego a huge boost and he told me that I could leave his room.

I had played the game with him and unbeknown to him, I was actually massaging his ego but I really wanted to punch his fucking smug face. I bet he thought that he had recruited another member of his fan club! Well, he hadn't.

This type of behaviour by bosses was not uncommon. I was being true to myself and didn't allow myself to be drawn into these situations. My upbringing taught me to be true and follow your instincts. This wasn't something my brothers or anyone in my family had taught me; it was my true self. My own beliefs and I always tried to be open with comments and give my opinion.

My gran had advised me of this many years before and I still stand by that advice to this day. I still miss her to this very day, some 20 years after her death, and know that all of her advice was real and made me the way I am today!

My appraisal was sent to Pitt Street and the recommendation was that I should be appointed to the post of detective constable. Meanwhile, I received good news from the appraisal DI. I was to remain in the temporary post until I was wanted back to my uniformed shift. I was pleased, as this meant that I could continue working with Drew and Ross and perhaps gain even more experience in the ways of the job.

Due to annual leave, they both were off at almost the same time, leaving me alone for about a week doing the job of the three of us. I was busy, as there had been more robberies and housebreakings than before. I was inundated with paperwork but I still managed to go out on patrol, alone.

The other teams were short-staffed and felt the same pressure I did so I wasn't alone. One morning, having left the office to get another statement, driving along Springburn Road, I saw a Ned running towards his house, looking rather guilty. As I was alone, I couldn't do much about it so I just let him go. Within about five minutes, there was a call over the radio about a robbery that had taken place in a nearby dry cleaning shop. I was virtually about fifty yards from the shop, so I responded and told the control room that I was single-manned and wished backup.

I arrived at the shop to find the male member of staff cowering in a corner, crying. I identified myself and tried to help him. He was shaking uncontrollably and I found it difficult to find out the story of what had happened. I locked the shop and calmed him down as much as possible. Eventually, he told me that a guy had come into the shop, threatened him with a knife and demanded money.

At first, he had panicked but then he told him to "fuck off". The guy jumped over the counter and the shop assistant made his way into a lockable cupboard area in the back of the shop and closed the door. The Ned then started to stab through the door with his knife and was desperately trying to get at the poor guy. No one else was in the shop. The Ned then emptied the till and ran away.

About five minutes later, when the shop assistant thought that it was clear, he emerged from the cupboard and contacted the police. The description of the accused matched the same guy "Tony" I had seen earlier. The uniformed guys arrived and carried out door-to-door enquiries in the area and got two statements from witnesses who saw the same described male near to the shop premises.

I knew that if I showed a picture of the male to the shop assistant, he would be able to identify him. I arranged for a forensic examination at the shop hoping to get fingerprint evidence. I took the witness to the police office and showed him a selection of twelve pictures—this is the correct process to follow when showing possible suspects. They are chosen randomly by the computer and you add in the one suspect you have; the witness positively identified "Tony" as the man responsible for the robbery. I knew that I could not show the picture to the other witness as this is against protocol. If there happens to be more witnesses then an identification parade would need to be arranged once the person is in custody.

Later that day along with a colleague, I detained Tony, despite his protestations regarding his innocence. Once detained, he was interviewed and denied any involvement despite the fact that I had a witness who had positively identified him from a photograph and I had also seen him entering his house minutes after the crime wearing the same clothes he was still wearing and matched the descriptions given by witnesses.

He was arrested and appeared at Glasgow Sheriff court the next day. The PF ordered me to carry out an identification parade and the three witnesses identified him during the parade. The parade consisted of 6 similar build and looking males standing alongside the accused. All that remained was for the fingerprint evidence.

After having submitted the results of the ID parade to the PF, I awaited the decision as to whether Tony would be remanded in custody pending his trial at the High Court, or whether he would be released on bail. I hoped that he would be remanded but it was in the capable hands of the PF. On the day that Tony was due to reappear at court, I received a phone call from the lab saying that the fingerprints found at the scene of the robbery were Tony's.

I immediately contacted the PF with the news and as a result, he was remanded in custody. Great news as it meant that the case had all come together and this had been all of my own work. I knew then that I could tackle any job thrown at me as a detective.

The guy who worked in the dry cleaners wasn't so lucky. He was having flashbacks to the event and was receiving counselling for the trauma. He decided that he didn't want to give evidence in court, as he couldn't face seeing the accused. I tried to allay his fears but he was too afraid. It looked like it was going to go down the toilet if I couldn't persuade him to give evidence.

I knew that I would just have to leave it until nearer the trial. The statements had all been submitted and eventually the citations arrived to attend at the High Court. I spoke with the main witness and he confirmed that he would attend. On the day of the trial, the witness from the shop was a nervous wreck. He went into court and I was pacing up and down the corridor outside. I heard raised voices and feared the worst.

Later that day, I spoke with him and he told me how the defence lawyer tried to say that he had made up the whole story and painted the story that he was a liar and was mistaken with his identity of the accused. The witness started to shout at him then stated that his client had tried to stab him through the locked door and as a result, he was unable to return to his work because of the nightmares he suffered. He was in no doubt that his client was guilty. I felt proud of the guy for sticking up for himself and having the courage to tell the truth.

Luckily, the jury believed the evidence of the witnesses and as a result, Tony was sentenced to three years in prison for the robbery. At last the witness could move on with his life as the accused was out of his way for a long time. I, meanwhile, felt pleased that my first case as a detective was a success.

I was called to Pitt Street for an interview at personnel regarding my application to become a full-time detective. The inspector interviewing me was about the same age as me and was really quite negative about the CID in general and kept reminding me that I stood a better chance of promotion by remaining in uniform.

I told him that it was my intention to join the CID and didn't care much about promotion at present. I left that interview feeling dejected. All I could do now was wait on a suitable vacancy. About three weeks later, I got my wish. I was appointed Detective Constable at Baird Street in June. Nine months after starting my initial "apprenticeship". I was delighted and knew that I had the chance to show the bosses that I was as capable as they were of doing the job!

Chapter 7
God Rest Albie

Monday, 24 August 1998, late shift CID at Baird Street along with my colleague Jas. He was only recently appointed to join the CID as a trainee for a period of six months. This is a type of probation working alongside other experienced detectives, the same as I had previously. The trainee period is used to assess the suitability of that person with the ultimate aim being the opportunity of becoming a full time detective.

Jas worked out of Kirkintilloch office and this was a sub-office of the divisional headquarters of Baird Street where I was stationed. The late shift tour of duty was from 1630 until 0030. The night shift commenced at 2300 until 0700.

The police philosophy is that crime does not invariably happen during these times, therefore, it makes sense to reduce the detective manpower when it is not necessarily required. I always thought that it was a ludicrous thing to do, having only two detectives on duty when the reality is that nothing in life can ever be assumed. So the assumption that crime does not happen at that particular time of the day is nonsense.

Another point to dwell on is the idea that two detectives can spread themselves over a radius of about ten miles, quite a task at times. Arriving to start duty at that time of the day resulted in the chance of being lumbered with other detectives' ongoing work to do.

It was not uncommon for late shift officers to have to arrange identification parades (referred to as ID parades) during a tour of duty. This type of work may take up to an hour to do, followed by the necessary paperwork at the termination of it to also carry out. Tedious as it may sound, I have conducted many ID parades, and they can be quite good for the officer to do but extremely nerve-wracking for witnesses to have to endure.

I have actually had to take part in one when I witnessed a robbery whilst off duty. I can identify with the anxiety of witnesses having had to go through one myself, it is not a pleasant experience. As well as this type of work, it may have been the case that as a result of other investigations, some witnesses may only be available at night-time, hence the late shift would have to proceed with the enquiry on behalf of colleagues.

Probably the main bone of contention was that on commencing a shift at this time, the possibility of meeting senior officers was also prevalent and they would also have tasks to be carried out. So as one can imagine, to commence a shift with other work to do and not knowing what was around the corner was off-putting to say the least.

That particular day when I arrived for work, Jas was already there, keen to get going. The strange thing about a person carrying out a trainee period such as this, that person always tries to impress and will work much harder than those already in the department. Jas was no different. Six foot three and slim build, wearing a suit, he looked every inch a detective.

Although I was smaller at five foot eleven, my immaculate appearance always overshadowed that of my colleagues. The reason was quite simple—my suits were nonconformist, i.e., not bought from Ralph Slaters in Glasgow City centre.

I suppose one could say that I was sharply dressed and looked more like a catwalk mannequin rather than a detective. On entering the CID room, there were about five other detectives there, enjoying yet another cup of coffee. The usual banter thereafter ensued and along with Jas, I sat down to have a cup with the troops. After about twenty minutes and several requests from the lazy so and so's to do some of their work, I announced to Jas that I wanted to get out of the office before being handed more work to do.

Jas laughed, agreeing wholeheartedly, so I grabbed a set of car keys for the pride of the CID fleet, a Rover 214si, which incidentally did not have the power to pull you out of bed let alone go fast whilst on patrol. Off we set in possession of two personal radios to monitor the calls from the control room as we drove around the area. We left the office at five o'clock.

Not being the keenest person to drive, I delighted in handing the keys to Jas as I did most nights whilst working together. I just like to watch what's happening in the streets around me than drive. Jas left the office yard and made his way up Springburn Road, which is one of the main thoroughfares in the sub division. This road links the M8 motorway heading towards both Edinburgh as well as Glasgow Airport and Glasgow City centre.

In the direction that Jas was heading leads to other districts in the vicinity of Springburn and Balornock. Approaching the first set of traffic signals, Jas indicated to turn right and he made our way towards Barmulloch, an area famed for its drug problems and home to about ten multistorey flats.

These contain about twelve hundred flats and large proportions of residents there are drug abusers. About two hundred yards after the lights, a dark grey Rover Metro passed our unmarked car, travelling in the opposite direction. I knew the driver. Wullie was a prolific car thief as well as being a disqualified driver. I informed Jas of this and he quickly carried out a U-turn in our car and made our way towards the Metro driven by Wullie.

I did not think that he had noticed as we passed, but I was about to find out. On approaching the traffic lights, I saw that Wullie was in the inside lane indicating to turn left. This is a filter lane and leads on to Springburn Road, the same road we had travelled on having left the police office.

I asked Jas to draw parallel to the other car so that I could speak with the driver. On doing so, I rolled down the window of my car and spoke to Wullie through his already opened window. "All right, Wullie, how's tricks with you?"

His face was a picture. "Fuck's sake, Mr Dawson, you gave me a fright, I never noticed you there."

It was all quite amicable and I noticed that there was also a front seat passenger in his car, although I didn't know who the guy was. I asked Wullie to pull into the bus bay once he had negotiated the filter lane. He told me to fuck off and I watched as he started to drive but instead of turning left, he turned right, heading towards the path of oncoming traffic.

I called into my control via my radio asking for the assistance of a marked traffic car as we attempted to pursue him through rush hour traffic. Jas was fortunate not to crash our car on several occasions as he gave chase after Wullie.

Perhaps I would be asked why I didn't get out of the car at the traffic lights; well, I knew who the driver was and thought that I would ask him to comply with my request to pull over—alas, he never; you win some, you lose some. I knew Wullie and vice-versa so I saw no need to be heavy-handed with him.

I continued to update the control room via the radio in the hope that a marked police car would be in a position to assist. Jas was encountering difficulty driving through the traffic due to our car not having any siren or flashing lights summoning other cars to move to allow us a clear passage. The official line is that we had to await traffic lights changing to green prior to negotiating the junctions. Although whether that happened or not remains unknown to those not involved in the car chase. Suffice to say that Jas managed to keep within a reasonable distance of Wullie who was enjoying taking the piss out of the CID, no doubt.

The Metro turned into a small council estate, an area known to me but not Jas. I instructed him to head towards Gourlay Street in the Springburn area and watched as the Metro started to descend a flight of wooden stairs that leads to a dead end.

We allowed him to go, as the damage to the police car would have been too much if we had followed. I know that for sure as years earlier, I had occasion to be involved in another car chase, only that time, my colleague who was driving had carried on down the stairs after the offending car; my life had flashed before me as we had careered down. We never got that driver either so we decided not to tell anyone about the chase, as there was damage to the underside of the police car. I never did hear anything about that one.

In order to get to the dead end, we had to go around several streets and by that time, the Metro had been abandoned, crashed into a tree, with no occupants on board. This did not surprise me in any way, as Wullie would have been off like a rabbit out of its burrow.

About five minutes later, the uniformed station that had acknowledged the call arrived. Where is the police when you need them? You see, even the CID can't get a cop when they need one! On closer examination of the Metro, it was decided that it would require a removal vehicle to uplift it due to the extensive damage.

I informed the control room of the current condition of the car and they ascertained that the owner was a nurse who worked at Glasgow Royal Infirmary; she had already reported the car as having been stolen. She was contacted as was the removal company and when the owner arrived, she was happy that at least her car was recovered. The only other annoying problem was Wullie; he was due the jail for stealing the car as well as endangering the public with his manner of driving, oh and taking the piss out of the police.

By the time we arrived back at Baird Street having awaited the contractor to remove the Metro, it was about a quarter to seven in the evening (1845). Luckily, there were no other calls of importance for us to attend so I decided that I would attempt to locate and arrest Wullie. Back at the office, I entered the divisional intelligence office (DIU), so called as this is where officers who deal with all information relating to the criminals of the Baird Street area collate and disseminate the data, which is put on computer.

But as it was late in the evening, again there was only one officer on duty carrying out the same tour of duty as the late shift CID officers. The person working that night was a good friend of mine, Chick. He is always happy to help when asked. I had to ask him to investigate the computer system for me, as he was the only person able to do so that evening. Information suggested that Wullie was staying with a known drug dealer in the nearby Sighthill area. I asked Chick if he would assist Jas and I to arrest Wullie, having informed him of the events of earlier.

The reason for asking him was simple; we were going to a known drug dealer's house so I expected there to be a few people in the house and wanted backup with me prior to going there. Keen and enthusiastic as he is, he duly obliged and about seven pm (1900), three plainclothes officers left Baird Street to arrest Wullie.

Events to happen would totally change the lives of the three of us. Jas drove the short journey to the multistorey block in Sighthill; the three of us entered the lift and I pressed the button for the fifteenth floor. I decided, as the senior officer there, that we would just knock on the door of flat 15/1 and hope to ad-lib our way into the house to look for Wullie.

As the lift doors opened on the 15th floor, Jas and Chick left the lift followed by me. I saw a guy at the door engaged in conversation with a female, who from my experience was trying to purchase drugs. Although information was to the effect that heroin was being sold from the house, it was never a consideration to obtain a drug search warrant for the premises as the information was old and had not been directly received by any of us that day.

This is a prerequisite prior to obtaining a warrant in these circumstances so I would not have been allocated a warrant for the house anyhow. The male at the door immediately shouted "police" as he ran into the flat, followed by Jas and Chick, leaving me to speak with the female on the landing outside. She told me that her name was Andrea and that she was there to buy a bag of heroin for ten pounds. I knew Andrea as a drug addict from the area so trying to identify her was not a problem. After a very brief conversation, I heard shouts from inside the house of "spit it out, spit it out". I quickly made my way into the flat to find out what was happening.

As I entered, I was met with the vision of Jas and Chick wrestling with a man. Standing near to them was two other men, Joe and Frankie, as well as a female, Sally, who was having difficulty zipping up her trousers and duly asked me to assist, which I did. You see, all of the occupants were drug addicts and apparently Sally had been attempting to inject heroin into her groin when we arrived, hence the request to zip up her trousers.

I saw that my two colleagues were struggling with the other man, Albie. He appeared to be choking but no one in the room would tell us what he had done. Jas had said that he saw him place something in his mouth. His condition deteriorated so rapidly that I was genuinely concerned as to what was happening. Jas and Chick were frantically trying to retrieve the item that he had swallowed.

I at first thought he was pretending so that they would leave him alone. However, no sooner had we arrived in the house than Albie had swallowed something and he collapsed onto the living room carpet. I started to shout at the other three people who had been with him, pleading with them to tell me what he had swallowed.

Jas and Chick were by now trying to place Albie in the recovery position, as his breathing was erratic. Chick suggested that I radio the control room to ask for an ambulance. I went into the hall and used the radio asking for an ambulance to attend as a male had taken an overdose of drugs. I didn't know the truth at this time but felt that at least if I said an overdose then the ambulance would come quickly.

I returned to the living room and saw that Joe, Frankie and Sally were just sitting talking between themselves yet they kept a watchful eye on Albie's condition. I asked Sally to accompany me into the bedroom where I spoke to her about what had happened. Sally and I both knew each other from the area and previously, when I had occasion to search her for drugs, we had always had good banter between us. I knew that Sally trusted me.

She said that they all thought we were the drug squad and that we had gone there to search the house for drugs and they had all panicked. I told her that we were there purely to arrest Wullie for stealing a car.

Sally then told me that when Jas and Chick ran into the house after Albie, he grabbed a solid piece of heroin the size of an oxo cube and he must have swallowed it. I was flabbergasted, as I immediately knew that Albie's condition was caused by him swallowing the drugs. No doubt they were stuck in his throat.

I went in and told Jas and Chick what I had learned. Albie was getting worse by the second. I walked over towards where he was lying and saw that he was grey and could not hear him breathing. I tried to check his pulse but I was having no luck at his wrist. By this time, the others were shouting that we had murdered Albie.

This wasn't helping the situation at all, here I was trying to feel for a pulse and all hell was breaking out. The only way to stop it was to tell them all to "shut the fuck up". It did have the desired effect and I informed them that I was trying to find a pulse and needed them all to be quiet. I eventually found a very faint pulse in his neck, very faint. I contacted my control room requesting that they re-contact the ambulance to find out how long it would be as it already felt as though we had been waiting such a long time for them to arrive.

The message was that the ambulance was en-route. The only thing was Albie's condition appeared to be deteriorating right before our very eyes. I felt totally helpless. My first aid skills, you see, are basic, whereas Jas who previously worked with the Army was better trained to assist in circumstances like these.

In effect, Chick and I left the first aid treatment to Jas as we were both more than confident that he could cope with Albie. I again told the other occupants of the house that the purpose of our visit was to arrest another guy called Wullie; they weren't interested in anything I had to say.

At periodic intervals, either Joe or Frankie would shout that we had murdered Albie as his motionless body lay on the floor. For the first time in my career, I was really afraid. The reason though was clear in my mind, I was afraid of someone dying and I could do nothing to prevent it. I was cradling him in my arms. At this point, the ambulance crew arrived at the flat. About 20 minutes after the police control room had called on their assistance.

I briefly explained to them the sequence of events and led them both into the living room area. Joe, Frankie, Sally and Chick all went into the bedroom to allow the ambulance crew to do their job. Just at that though, one of the crew reappeared and said that they had forgotten to bring resuscitation equipment with them. I accompanied the guy down in the lift to help him carry it back to the flat. En-route to the flat, the ambulance man told me that it wasn't looking good for Albie as he had the appearance of thick mucus coming from his mouth, an indication that the heroin had mixed with his own saliva; he didn't expect him to survive.

On returning to the flat, I met Jas who was the same colour as Albie. He was shaking his head. The two-ambulance crew worked on Albie and then placed him into a stretcher so that they could take him to hospital. I shall never forget the look on his face as they wheeled him out of the flat. He looked as though he was dead, although I am not sure if he was as the ambulance men did not say anything to me as they left.

Chick decided to go along with Albie in the ambulance in order that we could be updated as soon as possible regarding Albie's condition. I, meanwhile, had to arrange for someone to convey the others to Baird Street, as they would be required to provide statements regarding what had happened.

We informed them that he was away to hospital and would hopefully be all right; however, I knew deep down and from experience that he was already dead. In the circumstances, I decided to lie to them and say that he was going to be all right, fearing that they would start fighting with us, blaming us for what had happened.

I contacted my control room and requested the assistance of other officers. I also requested that a uniformed officer be left at the locus in order that it is preserved should Albie die; it may be treated as a suspicious death, police protocol taught me that.

One of the detectives who was seconded to another murder investigation from Baird Street was also late shift. He arrived with other colleagues to assist in conveying the witnesses to the office. When Allan arrived and saw my face, he burst out laughing. "What the fuck has happened here, you look like shit!"

I briefly told him what had happened and he was shocked to say the least. "What you gonna do, wee man?"

I laughed and told him that I hadn't a fucking clue what to do. Neither did he so he was no help to me either. My mind was racing and I tried everything I could to remain composed, but I was struggling to remain in control. Allan ferried the witnesses to the police office whilst I made arrangements to secure the house.

It seemed everything was taken care of and the door of the flat was locked, the key being left with the officer who had the short straw of having to stand there awaiting further instructions. I quickly followed the ambulance, Jas driving like a maniac in order to catch up with Chick who was alone with Albie, and he had no radio or mobile phone so communication was going to be a problem.

On arrival at the Royal Infirmary, Jas abandoned the car at the casualty area and the two of us ran in looking for Chick, eager to find out what had happened. On entering the patients' area within the casualty department, there was Chick sitting alone, ashen face, with a worried look about him, and rightly so. He looked up at us and smiled, glad to see a friendly face; he walked towards us, but I instinctively knew what had happened. Albie was DOA (dead on arrival).

My stomach heaved, I needed air. I looked around and saw Jas and Chick beside me. What the fuck happened? Chick shrugged his shoulders, don't know, they couldn't do anything for him, he must have suffocated. What were we going to do? Jas too was feeling the strain.

I told them that the first thing to do was to get the fuck away from the hospital so we could gather our thoughts. Not for any reason other than to regain our composure prior to going back to the office, I knew that the bosses would be out in force for this, due to the fact that this was now technically a death in police custody. Despite the fact that we did nothing wrong, it was my own instincts that made me fearful. The very idea that the witnesses had previously been shouting "murderers" in the flat obviously made me feel uneasy.

I knew that they might perhaps bend the story of how we had dealt with Albie so that it could look as though we were to blame for his death. I never confided in Jas or Chick about my concerns at this point; they were worried enough as it was. Jas drove to a small carpark near to Baird Street and pulled over.

Silence. No one knew what to say, or for that matter what to do. I contacted the control room to inform them that Albie had died. I asked for another uniformed officer to be dispatched to the hospital as in circumstances such as these, someone should remain with the deceased to ensure that all evidence is preserved.

Why is Chick still not there, came the response from the control room. "We have to return to the office" was my stern reply. I looked at my two mates and said, "Fuck."

I had also been informed that the Detective Superintendent, Divisional Commander (person in charge of all police in this area), had been informed of the circumstances and that they would be at the office to see us. I decided that I would speak to them, leaving the other two to chill out and have a coffee.

What if they split us up, what will we tell them? Chick was beginning to frighten me with that one. They won't; even if they do, submit a brief operational statement to them but tell nothing of what happened in the house. After all, they have three witnesses.

I also told them that a post-mortem would be carried out right away as it was a suspicious death. Although we did nothing wrong, instinct told us all that the police would no doubt point the finger at us, insinuating that we went there for drugs and should have obtained a warrant.

"Don't worry, guys, we won't be doing anything that is not fair, or that we do not wish to do."

I hoped that this would allay their fears as they were panicking me now. In truth, I didn't have a clue as what we should do apart from running away from the situation! On arrival at the office, we were met by the usual police ghouls who wanted to know every gory detail of how the guy had died—"fuck off" was as good a retort I could muster at this point.

I spoke with one of the detectives who were to obtain statements from the witnesses from the flat. He was speaking to Frankie, who apparently was shouting his mouth off saying that the police had murdered Albie.

He still did not know that his friend was dead, and I was not going to tell him. I asked that this information be kept from him until the bosses arrived and they could make that decision. I made a telephone call to one of my mates in the police to see if he could advise me on how to deal with the incident as far as the bosses were concerned.

His advice was to the effect that I would have to see how they reacted and how they would progress with it. Not much help at this stage. I met up with Jas and Chick who were having a coffee and talking over the events. However, I had only just sat down when I was asked to attend and speak with the bosses who had arrived at the office.

I walked the long walk to the other end of the office and entered a room. I was gobsmacked when I saw that no fewer than six bosses of various ranks were seated around a table awaiting my arrival.

Included in this group were my Detective Chief inspector, (DCI) as well as my Detective Superintendent (DS). This was the first time that I had met the latter person as he had only recently been promoted to our division some two weeks prior. I knew all of the others present.

I was asked to account for my movements and how I managed to be up at the flat in the first instance. I recounted the events of the car chase and how it was decided to attempt to arrest the driver of the stolen car, Wullie. I went on to tell them that it was suspected that he resided at the flat we had gone to in Sighthill. I continued, without interruption, that Albie swallowed a piece of heroin and I believed that he had died due to this having obstructed his airway.

"The witnesses say that he was murdered, what do you have to say to that then?" The DS, new as he was, didn't waste any time in coming out with it.

The DS was not on my side, I immediately thought. I retorted that on putting it that way, perhaps he should obtain tapes and caution me under taped conditions rather than expect me to give an answer in the presence of a room full of bosses.

"Oh, I hope you didn't mean it like that!" was his response.

"Well, whatever the witnesses say is wrong; we administered first aid and tried in vain to help him."

He swallowed the drugs himself, me and my colleagues did not force him to do that, they continued with a barrage of questions. I did my best to answer them until I had enough. I said that I needed a cup of coffee to settle my nerves as I had been through a traumatic experience and asked that I return to see my colleagues. I reminded them all that not once did they inquire as to how we were feeling.

The look of horror on their faces, horror at the idea that I had questioned their actions! They were attempting to piece together a jigsaw for themselves, basing it upon what they assumed and presupposed. I knew that there was more to come. I walked out of that office and was angry at what had taken place.

They were only interested at showing that we had acted wrongly. I made my way back to the guys, convinced that we would have to stick together and be strong, to stand up against them. I met up with Jas and Chick and told them what had happened. Suspicion ran through our minds, suspicions of the bosses' actions, the reason being the witnesses were neds who could twist things around and they would perhaps paint a bad image of the events.

The fact was that we had tried to help him but these efforts may be misconstrued as hindering his ability to breathe as opposed to assisting him. A knock at the door of the room we were using and we all just about jumped out of our skins, it was the DS. He walked in and made his way towards a seat. He sat down and started by introducing himself as the new DS.

He then jumped straight into the standard police jargon of how everyone was here to help and support us throughout this time and we would be given every form of guidance if required. He went on to ask each of us individually how we were coping. Police mentality is however to say that everything was fine and that everything was all right. Deep down though, we were petrified.

He told us that the death was not suspicious and that we had nothing to worry about. I quickly reminded him of the definition of a suspicious death according to the police procedure manual, as I had already looked it up on returning to the office. This quite clearly was a death that fulfilled the criteria. He reassured us, badly though, that it was not suspicious and that we weren't to worry, they (the bosses) were all on our side!

He left us having requested that we each submit a written operational statement for him to peruse. (This is a statement of events during a tour of duty.) After having closed the door, Chick was the first to air his views, that of the bosses being insincere and that they probably had a hidden agenda.

He was right; you see, any cop with a bit of experience at the sharp end of policing knows when bosses are trying to pull the wool over their eyes; this was such an instance right here. The only difference with us was we had experienced this style of management before and we were determined not to lie down to them.

In particular, Chick and I had several years of police experience and were not afraid to speak out. Jas, although he had less police experience, he had been in the army and had served in Ireland as well as the Gulf, so dealing with cocky bosses was not going to be a major problem to him either. Sticking together would be enough to prevent them from bullying us, or so we thought.

We decided to make a start on the statement. I had only just begun when there was another knock at the door. Jas opened it and in walked the DS again. "I just thought that I would clarify your status, you are all witnesses and have nothing to worry about."

I had forgotten to ask that very important question when he had previously been in the room with us. However, he continued, "To prevent anyone from saying that the police tried to cover anything up, I have decided that I will arrange for you all to be medically examined, have your photographs taken and also seize your clothes, just to protect you."

I almost fell off my seat; here we were, not dealing with a suspicious death according to the DS, yet he wanted to treat us as suspects? "We all know how suspects are dealt with, boss, and this is exactly what you are doing with us yet you say we are witnesses."

"I know how it sounds, Dale, but it's to protect you all."

"My arse, if that is the case then you do not treat witnesses that way, you are most certainly not treating us like this."

He was fuming. His face was literally like a cartoon picture in front of me. It was as though he had steam coming from his ears. Only after I said it did I realise that I sounded cheeky, but I did not care.

At that, Chick calmly informed him that he would not be treated in this manner unless he was a suspect, but as far as he could see, no crime had been committed and it was not a suspicious death so he would not submit to his request. I felt almost like laughing as Chick was saying this so calmly yet he looked as though he was going to burst into tears.

Before the DS had a chance to say anything, Jas confirmed that he too would not submit to the requests made. The DS was fuming and said that he could order us to do it, but he did not want to do it that way.

"What is our status?"

"You are witnesses, Dale, I told you that."

"Then I will not be treated as anything else so your request is denied, sorry boss." I told him that he could not order me to do anything; at the end of the day, I have rights too and so do Chick and Jas. It is quite impossible to describe just how he looked and sounded at this time; angry is not even close to the description. He stormed out of the office, his face ready to burst.

We initially laughed it off until the realisation of what he was inferring dawned on me. Those bastards think that we did have something to do with his death! He is hinting that we are suspects yet he will not confirm it. Chick decided to contact the police federation to ask for advice. The on-call representative informed us that he would be at the office within the hour. Perhaps at long last, we will be able to get the correct advice.

The call of nature was upon me due to the gallons of coffee I had consumed. I left the room and on reaching the corridor, I turned to close the door. I couldn't believe it. There was a wall of people on both sides of the corridor, at least twelve of them. It was like a scene from a western whereby upon my presence, they all stopped talking and stared at me at first then lost their stare only to gaze at the floor in a fit of ignorance.

I glanced up and down the line of poker-straight faces in an attempt to learn the identity of at least one of them. I recognised two guys, so I asked what was going on. It transpired that they were late shift detectives from the Serious Crime Squad who had been informed to attend our office regarding a "suspicious death".

I almost keeled over from the phrase "suspicious death". I had, only five or ten minutes before this, been told by a DS that this was not a suspicious death and it would not be treated as such. I was so fucking angry. We were being treated like idiots, expected to comply with the senior management's line of thinking.

I retrieved more information from the group as I started to recognise some of them having worked on various murder investigations in the area. The Serious Crime Squad is a group of experienced detectives who assist divisions when there are serious crimes to be investigated, e.g., murder, robberies or long investigations into child abuse, etc.

My own division has had its fair share of serious crimes and the majority of them have involved the squad. They had not been informed which officers were involved. The information was merely to the effect that they were required to assist with a suspicious death. When they realised that I was involved, they told me that they would find out more information and keep me posted as they couldn't believe what they were trying to do to us.

I left them to visit the toilet although by now I was fuming about what was happening. I re-emerged and spoke with a couple of the detectives who told me that they were to carry out the interviews of Joe, Frankie and Sally, who were Albie's friends. It appeared that Joe was shouting about the police murdering Albie.

This may explain the bosses conducting the investigation as a suspicious death, or were they just suspicious of our actions? I returned to the room and spoke with Jas and Chick. They immediately knew something was wrong as my face was grey. I informed them of what was going on behind the scenes and they too were annoyed.

It would seem that the police yet again had decided to carry out an investigation without being truthful to those involved. At that, yet another knock at the door, this time I opened it and in walked the DS again.

He was there to tell us that the doctor was en-route to the office to carry out the medical examination on the three of us. I was livid and began shouting at him. "Have you not been listening, we will not be treated like this by anyone, least of all someone who is lying to us about what is going on, just get out and leave us to continue with our statements. We will not be submitting to your bully tactics, Sir."

My insides were churning as I watched the expression on his face change to one of rage. I was told to mind my position and not to speak to him like that. "Well, don't think you can swan in here and tell us what to do when we all know that you are treating this as a suspicious death and you believe we have something to hide; we have nothing to hide. If you wish to speak to us again, it will be with either a lawyer present or a federation rep, so get out, Sir." Chick was pointing right into the DS's face as he said this.

The DS didn't know what to say or do, he turned around and walked out of the door, slamming it closed as he rushed away to regain his thoughts. I laughed, probably due to a combination of nerves and fear, Jas and Chick laughed too and we began ridiculing the DS because of the way he was handling the investigation.

In our opinion, he had no idea on how either to treat staff or deal with this type of incident, preferring to ridicule and bully others in to achieving what he thought was the correct outcome. The only blessing to his behaviour was the fact that he never entered the room accompanied. He was always alone. Therefore, he had no corroboration of what we had said to him. This proved how inexperienced and naïve he was!

Shortly after this, the DS returned to our room and he was now trying a different approach by telling us that we had suffered a major trauma and were clearly upset. He was there to help us and had our best interests at heart. I listened, as did the others.

At the end of his speech, I felt like standing up and applauding then telling him to "fuck off", but I also tried a different approach. I asked him again to confirm our status. "Witnesses" was the reply.

Right then, I wondered whether he would assist us so I put it to the test by asking him to arrange for a post-mortem; this would allay all our fears and would answer all questions regarding our conduct and it would prove we did nothing wrong.

He told me that he would contact the duty Procurator Fiscal (PF) for advice on this. I then asked why all of the detectives were at the office; he simply said that it was to help with the interviews of the witnesses. The DS returned and informed us that the PF had said that it was not a suspicious death and that a post-mortem would not be conducted until the following day, and anyhow, it would cost too much money to have one arranged at short notice.

I was reeling. I told the DS that cost should not come into it. I also played on the fact that it was clearly a welfare issue as this will affect our families and us. What are we going to do until then? "Well, you will just have to carry on as normal until then and if it doesn't happen tomorrow, then just come into work as though nothing has happened."

I couldn't believe he said that; a guy had died in my arms a few hours ago and here he was telling us to continue as though nothing had happened. *What planet is he from*? I wondered.

Again, he left the room and we praised him highly, not. More like cursed at one another concerning the way we were being treated. I felt like running home and staying there, fuck them all! I also decided to ask the DS what would be the worst possible scenario for the three of us should any adverse marks on his body show up at the post-mortem.

The reason for asking him this question was quite simple; when we had struggled with him during his choking spell, hands had been placed over his mouth and at the tip of his throat to try to retrieve the heroin. These marks may be misconstrued although I never told the DS about our hands at his mouth area.

After a few seconds, he told us that if it could be proved foul play on our part, then we would be charged with murder. However, he knew that that wouldn't happen! We sat there in horror at what he was telling us. The bastard did believe that we had something to do with Albie's death! He went on further to say that the very least would probably being charged with careless driving if it was ascertained that during the car chase, Jas had not followed correct road procedures.

At this, he left the room without clarification of any of the points raised. Jas was livid. In other words, the DS said that he would find something to charge us with if we failed to comply with his requests. Is that proper policing or bullying?

We were again left in limbo, fearing to write anything down as we may be adding to our own court case; this was not a pleasant experience! It wasn't long before our representative arrived from the federation and he was briefed about the sequence of events of that evening. He was very supportive and reassured us that he would keep the bosses at bay.

I informed him of the DS' request for the medical, etc. He said that under no circumstances were we to submit to anything like that unless our status was clarified. Just then, the door was knocked and on opening, I was confronted by the DS and he brushed past me. He appeared to be furious at the presence of the federation rep.

He said that it had been decided to have the police casualty surgeon attend to view the body at the mortuary to ascertain whether there were any adverse marks on his neck or body. I asked him what would happen if there were any adverse marks. He told me that we would have to wait and see.

The Fed rep told him that we would all be keeping our statements brief, as at that moment we did not trust anyone due to the way the situation was being handled. Flashbacks of his comment concerning the worst situation we may find ourselves in could be that if it was found that during the car chase we had driven through a red light then we could face prosecution for that.

Jas was near breaking point again and said that he too would be wording his statement very carefully. The DS left the room and we again spoke with the federation rep and he was, like us, annoyed at such an insensitive and unwarranted comment regarding the possibility of a driving offence. This confirmed just how far removed from reality the DS was.

I was really annoyed at his arrogance and insensitivity towards our situation. This meant that we all had to word our statements very carefully fearing that we would write something down that could be used against us.

It sounds all very like an episode of *The Bill* but the reality is that we had to ensure we weren't going to admit to having broken the law, regardless of the fact that perhaps Jas may have driven through a red light. Only him and I were aware of that.

We began our epic statement and all conversed throughout, composing it in order that the content was much the same for each of us. After about an hour, the DS returned to the room to confirm that there were no adverse marks on Albie's body so it was decided that a post-mortem would be conducted the following day (Tuesday). He then left the room without saying anything else.

We were again left just to get on with it; not once did the bosses ask how we felt or whether we were coping. Deep down and on reflection, we were quite clearly not coping with the situation. We were all dealing with an incident way beyond any training we had ever experienced. This is not something that is taught in any practical situation by the police. Yet here we were being lambasted by the bosses of a truly draconian establishment who were in dire need of change. I decided that I had better telephone my wife as time was getting on so I left the room to call Carmen from elsewhere.

Again on reaching the corridor, I met the wall of stony faces, albeit on this occasion, they at least wanted to speak to me. One of the guys told me that two of the witnesses were still sticking to the idea that we had tried to murder Albie, despite the fact that they were unaware that he was dead—they still believed that he was just ill at hospital.

Sally appeared to be the only one telling the true version of events. I'm not too sure whether the bosses believed her or not, choosing instead to believe Joe and Frankie. I suggested telling them that Albie was dead, but apparently the bosses decided not to tell them just yet, I have no idea why though.

I was also informed that the bosses were trying to arrange for the house to be searched thoroughly for evidence. I just accepted this, as I am aware of how the police operate so it did not come as any surprise to me. I made my phone call to Carmen and tried hard not to let on that something was wrong.

However, Carmen is very perceptive and knew things were not right from the tone of my voice. I attempted to soothe things by saying that I was just busy and could not speak, as there were too many people around. I even tried to end the phone call but she was persistent. In effect, for the first time that evening, I almost fell apart. I just blurted out brief details of what had happened and that I would be late home as I would have to wait and see what happened with the incident. I told her not to worry and that things would be fine. I am not sure whom I was trying to convince, her or me.

Obviously, I never told her the whole story, but I know that she got the impression that it was not going well; after all, she knows me better than I do! It must have been difficult for her. Not being in the police and being left at home knowing that there was a bad situation at work for me, as well as trying to cope with a four-month-old baby for hours on end without the support of her husband.

These ideas are now clear in my mind but at that time, I was too wrapped up in my career to consider that side of things. I returned to the room of discontent and continued with the statement, listening to the instruction given by the federation rep. Jas and Chick, like me, were pissed off and really wanted nothing else but to get away from the whole sordid saga.

After about two hours, our statements were complete and the DS obviously wanted to read over them to ensure we had submitted the correct information, although how would he know as he wasn't there at the flat, was he? He wished to speak to each of us separately although we refused and compromised with him by having the rep with us.

Jas was first and returned after about fifteen minutes. He was swearing like mad when he came in as he felt that the DS was dismissive of the content of his statement and ordered him to put more detail in it. Jas had refused and walked out in disgust. The rep followed shortly and told him that it was all right and his statement would not have to be altered in any way.

I don't know what he told the DS but it had the desired effect as he never interviewed either Chick or me. The DS spoke to us all again to inform us that someone would contact us at home on Tuesday and that we should return to work as normal the following day and "just get on with things".

Just before we went home, we were told by one of the guys from the Serious Crime Squad that they had been ordered to inform the witnesses that Albie was dead. All we could do was wait and listen. Joe and Frankie were furious and shouted, "Murdering police bastards, they murdered our pal!"

Not what we wanted to hear but I could accept the fact that they were upset; after all, their friend was dead. Sally, on the other hand, said, "It was his own fault, he shouldn't have swallowed the kit." (Kit is a slang word for heroin)

At least her response was a little more realistic of what had truly happened. The three of us left to go home about three-thirty in the morning, having just worked three hours overtime because of the incident—did I claim payment for it, you better believe I did.

When I arrived home about four o'clock that morning (Tuesday, 25 August), my wife was awake, patiently waiting for me. At first I spoke about the car chase and tried again to play down what had happened but she instinctively knew that I was hiding things from her. Just at that, the sound of my four-month-old daughter distracted us both as it was feeding time.

I started to feed her and at the same time discussed the events of the previous evening with Carmen who sat listening intently as I went through the chain of events. I could see that she was livid and extremely anxious about the way things had occurred and in particular about the way in which the DS had treated us all. We eventually went to bed and I tossed and turned all night, going over and over the events leading up to Albie's death and wondering if there I could have done more to assist him.

I formed the opinion that I probably would not have carried out any other approach if, God forbid, it were to happen again. Still not asleep and it was again almost time to feed the baby again. Watching her lying there so peaceful helped me immensely. It certainly puts a lot of things into perspective when considering life and death issues. Here I was worried about a dead man I didn't know that well, yet on the other hand, worried, as all new parents do about their own children. The difference was that my daughter was there and she was a tremendous deterrent to the reality of what was going on around me. I also felt great pity for my wife, as she would have to endure this with me. A fact that is overlooked by police officers when they are involved in incidents such as this, particularly when my own wife is not a police officer.

She thankfully did not know the possibility of what may happen, and I certainly was not about to tell her that I may be arrested for murder if the police have their way and the post-mortem shows up anything contradictory to what I have submitted in my statement!

About ten o'clock that morning, the phone rang, it was a detective inspector (DI) asking how I was. Brief chit-chat ensued, thereby the content of the call emerged. He was contacting me to say that it was decided not to hold the post-mortem until Wednesday as it was feared that Albie may have HIV or another drug-related illness, thereby putting the attending pathologists at risk from infection. What the hospital had decided to do was analyse Albie's blood to find out what infections he had, if any, and if any were present, the pathologists would have to wear fully protected clothes to reduce any risk of infection.

I was mad. "Why then don't they just wear the fucking clothes and do it today to prevent us having to wait another day for the result; this is a disgrace." The line was silent and I was told not to be upset. "Patronising cunt, of course, I'm upset, the police think we had something to do with this guy's death and we are being left to wait whilst protocol is adhered to. Protocol that can be changed when it suits!"

The DI probably wished he had never phoned me as I ranted and raved like a madman. At least he didn't interrupt me, he allowed me go on and on at him until he said to me, "Right, I will see you at half four when you come in for work."

With these words, he hung up. I had forgotten all about work and wondered how I would manage to go. Carmen tried to calm me down but it was all getting too much for me to cope with. I was so tired and this was the final straw. I cried for what seemed like hours and fell asleep with Carmen cradling both her husband and baby.

I contacted Chick and Jas to see if they had been told the same story concerning the post-mortem. They had and they too were equally pissed off by the lack of concern shown towards us. The most angering thing was that we were totally unable to speed the process up. We would just have to endure the chain of events. Chick was particularly anxious and this was evident in his tone of voice. He seemed ready to break but we were all in the same situation so hopefully by sticking together, I knew we would be able to cope somehow.

Waiting to go to work that day was a nightmare and every minute seemed like an eternity. Before long, it was time to start preparing to leave the house. As we left the house that day, I placed my daughter in the back of the car. I made my way to lock the front door of the house and said to Carmen, "This could be the last time I lock this door for a while if I get locked up for murder."

She freaked out! I don't think the realisation of it all had dawned on either of us and a throwaway comment was enough to almost break us both. After being suitably chastised by Carmen, I apologised and told her that no more thoughts like that would enter my head and that we would be fine.

I left to go to work earlier than normal that day as I had prearranged to meet Jas and Chick so that we could have a meeting regarding what was happening. It was decided at a local hotel that we would not cooperate in any way with the bosses and if they wished to question us at all then it would be in the presence of a lawyer. Not that we had anything to hide but I felt that the police were attempting to intimidate us and it was working, so we all decided not to play at their games by not cooperating.

The three of us formed a pact that we would help each other through this and that we would play along with what the bosses ordered. On arrival at the police office, the three of us walked into the CID room and again, it all went quiet. About half a dozen or so faces looked at us, then one guy said, "Oh, here comes the Sighthill stranglers."

Obviously a reference to what had happened at the flat the previous evening. I looked at him, trying hard not to laugh as police humour had taught me to laugh at things when they were bad; all police officers do this to alleviate the stress involved in the job. Jas and Chick walked out, mad as hell at the inference that we had perhaps strangled poor Albie. "This is what the bosses think we did," said Chick, his eyes almost bulging out of his head as he tried hard to remain focussed.

But at that, a DI came into the room we were now in and asked us to follow him to his room for a chat. This was the same guy who had phoned us all earlier that day with the news of the post-mortem, which was, as far as we knew, still scheduled for the Wednesday morning.

On arriving at his room, we were confronted with four bosses who all took it in turn to shake our hands and tell us that they were there to help us. Before we could say anything, the DI handed us the statements submitted the previous night and told us to redo them, only this time they were to contain more information, as the Procurator Fiscal wanted it.

"Tell the Fiscal to kiss my arse, I'm doing nothing else to assist!" Chick had that mad look about him again as he said this. I meanwhile burst out laughing, not the correct thing to do. I was quick to apologise saying that he was tired and could do with not working because of the incident. Jas stood saying nothing.

It wasn't finished there as the DI then had the audacity to accuse us of trying to hide the facts of what had actually happened. I told him that the bottom line was that we had been there in the flat and he hadn't, so until he knew the true facts of what had actually happened, he should just keep out of it. This, as you would imagine, did not go down well with him. "It is clear to us that you all have something to hide about last night, tell us now and we will help you get out of it."

I looked at the DI as he said this; clearly, he was now trying the soft approach hoping that we would fall for that. "I appreciate your concern, Sir, but really we have nothing else to say to you on the matter."

I tried my best to be polite as I said this to him. Again, before I got a chance to say anything further, Chick piped up, "Good criminals get off at court because of advice from lawyers, it's high time we did just that; if you wish to ask any of us any more questions about what happened, do it in the presence of my lawyer."

"The police don't have a good reputation of managing to secure convictions at court, the reason for this is due to a lack of knowledge of the events by the police and having a good lawyer at court. I'll take my chance with a lawyer." It seemed that Chick had hit a raw nerve, as the DI was mad and about to start shouting.

The reason for his actions was due to a high-profile murder that had happened several months before when a man was brutally beaten to death in broad daylight in the Royston area. The trial had only just been completed and a not proven verdict was reached. This meant that the accused walked free.

You've guessed it; the reporting officer was the DI. Part of the reason for the verdict was due to his lack of detailed evidence he had overlooked. I know this to be a highly accurate thing to say, as I was one of the frustrated detectives who had worked on the investigation. This invoked a huge grin on my face, as I knew that the DI would be furious at Chick's outburst. At this stage I told him that if we were witnesses then we have fulfilled our obligation with providing the original statement. If we were suspects then get it sorted and detain us in line with what criminal law states. Either way, we need and deserve clarification.

He and Chick were about to walk out of the room when the Deputy Divisional Commander (second in charge of the area) walked through the door. He asked if everything was all right as he had heard raised voices whilst coming along the corridor towards our room. The DI's face was scarlet with rage, but he ensured the boss that everything was fine, "just a little difference of opinion".

The Superintendent started to tell us how well we had coped with the events of the previous evening and told us all to take the night off and enjoy our days off so that we could be refreshed for returning to work that Friday.

Well, I have to say that we needed no second telling, off out the door like a shot, barely thanking the boss for allowing us to go home. We drove home, agreeing to meet in my local pub for a beer, copious amounts of it after all the heartache that we had to endure. It was the least we deserved.

When I arrived home, my wife was not in so I quickly changed out of my suit into jeans and a T-shirt and left for the short walk to the pub. I called her to tell her of my intentions and she was happy in the knowledge that at least we were given the night off and a couple of pints would calm us down a bit. The police tend to turn to alcohol when times are tough due to stressful events at work. It is a great escape from things when the going gets tough.

I knew though that the topic of conversation that evening would be all about Albie and what happened. I walked over to the pub. Jas and Chick were already there and had started on pints and spirits. I think it was to be a get-drunk-quick night and I had no objections at all. The first thing discussed was the subject of the post-mortem and whether it would totally clear us of any blame. We did guess that the pathologists would find that Albie had died from choking due to the drugs lodging in his throat.

What we all didn't approve of was the way in which the bosses decided to listen to the version of events as told by the witnesses in the flat. This confirmed the suspicion that it is better to believe known drug addicts than believe anything the police say! Not exactly reassuring when the bosses believed that their own colleagues might be trying to cover up a murder! If they had even told us that this was to ensure that there was no suggestion that they hadn't carried out their role properly but they didn't. Instead they were genuinely treating us like idiots. Obviously from a legal perspective this would have been laughed out of court. The alarming thing was that senior managers know nothing about how to deal with this situation.

I say murder as whilst sitting in the pub, my mobile phone rang. I left the pub so that I could hear what was being said; it was another colleague who was working on this incident earlier that day. He started to tell me that he had overheard a conversation with senior bosses who said that they did believe Albie was murdered, or at the very least had been choked by us during the struggle and that the post-mortem would probably confirm what two of the witnesses had said.

I didn't know what to say to him. I just kept listening as he went on to say that apparently that day (Tuesday), Joe, Frankie and Sally were re-interviewed to find out whether they wished to change the stories they had given the previous evening. Sally was the only one on our side and insisted that all our efforts had been an attempt to save him. Joe and Frankie on the other hand were even more adamant that we had murdered their friend.

I couldn't think straight, I felt sick at the thought of what the result of the post-mortem may bring. The guy continued to tell me that apparently the bosses, in particular the DS, was livid at us for not complying with his requests for the medical and photographs. The caller further told me that if there was the slightest hint that foul play could be proved, we would all be arrested and possibly charged with murder.

The words rang loudly in my ear, echoing the fear already felt by us all. Momentarily, I was oblivious to his continued talking to me on the phone. I regained my composure and apologised for missing the latter part of the conversation and asked him to repeat it. He said that it was the bosses' intention to perhaps interview us the following day (Wednesday) to find out if one of us would admit that we did something wrong.

Although I was grateful to him for contacting me, I felt as though it was a bad dream. This would suggest that the reason they wished us to be medically examined after Albie's death was to secure evidence against us.

The whole situation was bizarre and extremely frightening. "What else did they do today?" At last I could ask a question, my mouth dry and quivering. I was told that a team of detectives had searched the house where Albie had been and had found only traces of drugs on foil that had been smoked by them, as well as used syringes lying on the table in the living room.

Nothing to suggest any form of fight or anything so at least that would go in our favour. I must have been on the phone for ages as Chick came out to see what was taking so long. I told him that it was my wife and just to go back in, as I would only be a couple of minutes.

My heart was racing and I could feel the sweat running down my forehead. I thanked the caller for letting me know what had happened and I asked that he contact me should he hear anything else.

Before I walked back into the pub, I had to make the decision of whether or not I should tell the guys what I had just learned. I made the decision not to say anything but trying to make out that things were fine was going to be difficult. I suppose the reason for the deceit was to avoid them having to worry more as we had enough to deal with. As well as the fact that Chick was already near to breaking point. I thought that this would push him over the edge. I genuinely did have everyone's best interests at heart.

On returning to my marked position at the bar, I desperately tried to hide my news. I just said that my wife had been boring me with the events of that day with our daughter and laughed it off. It appeared to work as we continued with our alcohol frenzy. The highlight of the night and probably the funniest situation came as Chick was becoming more drunk!

Out of the blue, he suggested, "When we were up at the flat and realised that Albie was dead, or almost dead, we should have thrown the three witnesses from the flat window, thereby preventing them from telling a pack of lies."

I was hysterical at the thought of it. After all, we had been fifteen floors up! The idea, although outrageous, would have saved us from having to endure the accusations being made by the bosses. We left the pub very late and, of course, very drunk, still not having managed to alleviate the fear of what Wednesday would bring. It was decided that we would all refuse to cooperate if the worst scenario became a reality; only time would tell!

"Happy anniversary!" Not a day I will forget for a long time for all the wrong reasons. Carmen had been up for most of the night with our baby daughter, leaving me in a motionless sleep, thanks to the alcohol. Not a good feeling though as my head ached and I felt as though I was dying. No food for two days but plenty of fluids.

Again, a phone call from another friend, telling me that he would be present at the PM and would contact me as soon as he possibly could with the result. I was apprehensive and paced up and down the house, trying to pass my time until hearing the result. The phone rang again.

I jumped to answer it. He told me that the PM was going well and so far, there were no adverse marks on Albie's body to suggest foul play. I would know for certain within the next half-hour, as the pathologists were about to retrieve the item from his throat. I immediately rang Jas and Chick to update them. They too had huge hangovers so I didn't feel as bad.

This was the longest period, sitting waiting for the phone to ring. At last he rang with the news. Asphyxiation caused by a foreign object lodged in his trachea, no foul play suspected. We were in the clear! I could hardly speak as all my emotions poured out. I was sobbing from the sheer relief of the result. Carmen had to take the phone from me as I cried oceans of tears.

It was about ten minutes before I could gather my thoughts and regain my composure. I phoned Chick to tell him the good news. Not much response from him as he quickly handed the phone to his wife who informed me that he would phone me later; I could hear his own wails of relief.

Jas, on the other hand, was polite and courteous thanking me for contacting him and promised to call me later. It is true when it is said that the police each deal with situations differently; stress affects each of us in a different way! My phone was red hot that day with many of the calls being from friends at work who were probably as anxious as us to find out what the result was.

As this was now my wedding anniversary, I decided that perhaps the best thing to do in the circumstances was to leave the house and get out for a while. We were almost ready to leave and had packed the usual twenty bags to take the baby with us when the phone rang.

It was Colin, one of the guys from work. He too had been at the PM and had just returned to the office with some bosses. He was calling to tell me that apparently two of the bosses were on their way to our houses to tell us in person the result. I was glad in a way that he had called, as I would definitely have left the house rather than be forced to speak with them. A point I did think of at the time was what if I did not know the result and two bosses turned up at my door? I would have freaked, run out the back door and hidden in a back garden somewhere.

The reason I say this is because the only reason bosses come to your house is to deliver bad news, or to arrest you. For the first time in ages, I felt like an ordinary member of the public, as it is a well-known fact that people detest the police coming to their house. I was no exception on this occasion, as I would have to listen to patronising comments from them concerning their handling of the situation. The best thing to do was to get away from the house as quickly as possible, so we did. I contacted Chick and Jas to let them know and to give them the opportunity to fuck off out the house before they arrived.

Trying to gain light of what had happened was difficult for me as I am quite headstrong and if someone does something against me, I want answers. This situation was no exception and I couldn't wait to get back to work to speak with the DS so that he could explain to me why he had treated us the way he did. I tried hard to put it to the back of my mind as it were my days off and I intended to enjoy them.

My days off passed quickly and before I knew it, I was parking my car in the police yard at Baird Street on Friday morning (28 Aug). On walking into the CID room, again there was stony silence until McMurdo announced, "It's the Sighthill strangler, he's already got away wi one murder; he could do it again!"

I know that it should have been a joke but I wasn't in a joking mood, especially when I had unfinished matters to attend to with bosses. I walked over to him and said, "If you say that again, I'll not strangle you, I'll kick your fucking cunt in, ya prick."

He knew by my attitude that I was not taking his comment as a joke. He apologised and said that he had tried to make light of an awkward situation. Perhaps it was just a timing thing, and his timing was crap.

I stormed out of the room as I felt as though I was going to hit him. I would have been able to vent my anger and perhaps feel better but it wasn't his fault! I met the ashen face of Chick coming towards me who said that he hadn't slept since Monday. He looked like it too. I actually felt sorry for him and I have to admit that I burst out laughing at how bad he looked.

He also had been subjected to one-line comments from some of the troops but it was too soon to hear colleagues lambaste us for the incident, we were still too raw. Both of us decided to go and see the DS to find out why we were treated so badly.

When we arrived at his office, it was empty. We both sat down patiently awaiting his return. About ten minutes later, the DCI passed the room and told us that the DS was out all day and he wouldn't be back until Monday. "It's just that I have some things I want to say to him, boss, that's all."

He looked at me and said, "I can imagine, Dale." Chick and I followed the DCI to his room and he made a feeble attempt at explaining their actions that night.

It would appear that all instructions came from the Deputy Chief Constable and that they were only trying to carry out his orders. I, obviously, was livid and was ranting and raving like a lunatic about being treated as suspects when all along we were witnesses and how we were being bullied to do things, which quite frankly were way out of order.

The DCI sat back and listened to me, then he put his hand up, signalling me to stop. He explained that regardless what I said about fairness or anything else concerning our treatment, it would only fall on deaf ears as the matter was closed and should remain so. Basically, he was telling me in the nicest way that I had to just accept it as part of the job.

Chick and I both stood up and left the office with the DCI running after us, asking us to wait. For the first time in my service, I was out of order with a boss. "Fuck off, you patronising bastard, don't tell me what I have to accept and not accept. If you had stood up to them on our behalf, I wouldn't feel the way I do now." He looked stunned but in fairness to him, he just turned and walked away towards his office.

That day at work was hard going. Not because it was busy, just from the way in which every corner I turned, colleagues asked what had happened and how I felt. They were just being nosey or perhaps even sympathetic. The bottom line was that I was in no mood to be pleasant with anyone. I decided enough was enough and spoke with Chick. We decided that the pub was the order of the day and about one o'clock that afternoon, we headed home to go to my local to get drunk. Not a very grown up thing to do but hey, it helped in the short term.

At last, on Tuesday, 1 September, Jas, Chick and I were afforded the pleasure of an audience with the DS. Obviously, us mere mortals were not important enough for him to concern himself with our welfare until then. He talked at length about how the decisions were out of his hands and he was only acting on instructions from others. It came to the point in his conversation that he told us that if we didn't like the way we were treated then we could get other jobs outside the police.

I was livid, as were the others. He also reminded us that perhaps we would struggle to find other jobs that paid as well as the police. "Money is not the issue here, the issue is the way you tried to treat us as suspects despite the fact we were witnesses."

He glared at Jas for having the audacity to even speak out of turn. His retort was mainly to reaffirm the idea that if we weren't happy with the job, then leave. In truth, he was lucky not to have been beaten to a pulp by us due to his arrogance and ignorance. He then told us to just get on with the job as many other stressful incidents would come our way and no doubt we would be better prepared in the future.

Not bad for a guy who hasn't even seen, let alone arrested, a bad man in his service and he had the audacity to say these things to us! The harsh reality of our audience with the prick was that when the shit hits the fan in the police, the bosses would do nothing to assist, only hinder the good guys!

Chapter 8
Nepotism

It may seem strange to even consider this as at times, we may all forget that we are living in the 21st century, to suggest for one moment that senior officers "take care of" other senior officers' offspring in the job. These senior officers stem right to the top of the ladder. The Chief Constable serving at this time was well known for this. Obviously these are my views learned from many other police colleagues and no doubt, they would be denied. But at this time, it did happen according to what people said but I will leave that hanging in the air for now.

Soon after he was made Chief of Strathclyde, officers who thought that their careers were over suddenly took off again. It was not uncommon for them to be quickly promoted thanks to one of the "Ayrshire Mafia", yes, the godfather himself—"The Chief". The term "Ayrshire Mafia" comprised of ranking officers of at least superintendent rank who had all served at one point in the Ayrshire area.

They were also at one point part of the clique who stuck by each other through thick and thin. This goes back to the days when there was the great divide within the City of Glasgow police, which amalgamated with Strathclyde, to form one of the largest forces in Britain. The Chief is known to have promoted his pals in order to keep them on his side as they all surrounded him in "cowards castle" at Pitt Street. This is the term used by the police to speak of those officers who work there on a Monday to Friday basis, normal office hours apply.

These officers are not required to work the arduous shifts, which had been implemented many years before. The reason for the promotions was quite simple, to keep his allies close to him. This would help him if the shit hit the fan for any reason and they would all stick up for one another, as well as their pal, "the chief".

Now they could all sit back and watch their pensions grow as they had become greatly enhanced thanks to their additional promotions. This was all down to their pal. He had promoted them and enhanced their already substantive salaries, as well as enhancing their positions within the realms of the police.

The Chief even promoted his own son on three occasions during the time he was in charge! Although some would say that his son was in fact a very nice guy, the official party line being obviously that he is good at his job. Perhaps this would account for his promotions during Daddy's reign? The standing joke in police circles was the Christmas dinner within the Chief's house when a conversation between father and son may have run something like:

Q What would you like for Christmas, son?

A I quite fancy a sergeant's job, say in a city centre area as long as it's not too dangerous, Daddy!

Three or four years later, the same "present" question was uttered:

Q What would you like this year, son?

A How about the Detective Inspector's job at the Serious, Daddy? (Serious Crime Squad, who deal with murder investigations although the DI post only oversees the investigation!)

Never to refuse his wee boy, he was duly on the promotion list before you could manage to eat the Christmas pudding!

This may appear to sound like jealousy, thereby asking the question why not me? I could offer several analogies to this, ranging from the straightforward approach in that my father is and never was in the police, therefore no one knew me. The more mundane response would be for me to say that I was not good enough.

However, the harsh reality is that the majority of the promotions were of people who were not good enough and could not lace my boots when it came to practical policing. Not only me, there was many outstanding cops who were and never have been considered for promotion as they have no senior figures banging a drum for them! I could be really controversial and say that it is because I am catholic? Oh shock horror I hear you say, that would never happen in a force, which is known for its fairness, and with the recently re-accredited Investors in People, at that time this could not possibly be the case. Let me dispel all rumours. The Catholic serving officers were like ethnic officers—in the minority.

We are placed and paraded to make us think that we are there because we have earned the right to be there. Be under no illusion, the great religious divide is there for all to see. The only reason that Catholic's were employed is to ensure that the police cannot be seen to be discriminating against the religious minorities. "What school did you go tae then, Son?"

It does exist, at least it was certainly alive and well during my time serving as a police officer. I am quite sure the Chief would be reeling if he happened to read! No doubt it will be the topic of conversation at the Thursday night Masonic meeting. He would no doubt refute this allegation but let me tell a story about this actual allegation.

Picture the scene: a drab afternoon in November at Baird Street in the north of Glasgow when an Australian comes into the office wishing to speak to the CID about something. I was alone as my colleague who should have been working along with me was at the other end of the City watching football, we all know crime waits till the fitba has finished on a Saturday!

So me being of a cheery disposition, attends the front office to speak with him. I introduced myself to him and shook his hand, as one does. However, there was a strange grip during this intimate man bond. Let me clarify, I mean that he did the Masonic handshake to me. I just gripped his hand in the normal man way!

To those of you who have no idea what I am referring to, then I shall briefly explain. Whilst I have no issue with this ritual and it should also be noted that there are many different people attend the various Masonic Orders around the world and it is also not uncommon for a Catholic to be admitted to these orders, but there is a particular way in which one can identify if another person is in an order.

The first sign being linked to a handshake whereby the person places his thumb on the middle knuckle of his friend and rubs it. Sometimes the other hand comes over and covers the action of the rubbing so as to disguise this fact! All harmless man fun, I suppose!

Anyhow, as it turns out, the Australian visitor was in fact at the wrong office but explained to me about his stolen car from Glasgow city centre. For geography purposes, Baird Street is about 2 miles from the city centre. I obtained the details, as I am a decent guy, and engaged in casual conversation with him. He was over here working for a year as a bouncer (minder) to the stars at concerts.

He had to ensure nothing happened to them and his job was to protect them. He asked if I wanted a job but I was quick to explain that we were not allowed to take on other jobs, plus I worked shifts etc. Yes I continued to do the decent thing and was pleasant as normal. He said that he could clear it with the Chief for me.

A bit puzzled, I asked how he knew him and so his tale began. He had met him on several times at his father-in-law's (well, future in-laws, that is) Thursday Masonic meeting at which the Chief was well respected as it was his particular order. Hey, each to their own, I say; it did however confirm my worst suspicions, that of the Chief being a "Brother".

So it pays to be part of the scene as it helps in business and work. My Australian friend was more than happy to discuss the events of the meetings and so grew my fascination. What surprised me more than anything was the fact that he openly discussed it without quizzing me first about my own "meetings". This is normally done by asking various questions of new friends to ascertain whether that person is in fact within a masonic order.

It is alleged these questions could vary but an example could be when someone asks how old your grandmother is, it actually means what lodge number are you from. It is not actually asking how old your granny is—in actual fact, they couldn't give a crap about that. Sounds far-fetched but hey, we do live in a strange world! Perhaps this is where I went wrong right enough, perhaps I should have tried to join a local lodge!

I refused his gesture and accepted his business card, just in case I changed my mind! I asked him to pass on my best wishes to the Chief and jokingly said to tell him about the wonderful job I was doing by taking reports for other police offices!

It would appear that the Thursday night ritual of going to a Masonic meeting does not rest solely with the male senior management. Allegedly yes, even the women do it, albeit they would attend their own meeting with other like-minded ladies.

On one particular Thursday night, it would appear that a certain Deputy Chief Constable who was having an affair with a female officer, who was Assistant

Chief Constable of a particular department within Pitt Street, attended for their meetings at "The Neptune" in the Govan area of Glasgow.

After having dropped his mistress off at her meeting, they apparently agreed to meet up afterwards. Oh, how I wish I was a professional photographer and not an ex-copper! To all of you attendees on a Thursday night in the Govan area, beware, a camera never lies!

I seem to have lost my point here; I think it was about nepotism in the police. There have been too many promotions to speak of whereby young in service officers suddenly become fine officers to such an extent that they were promoted. Really, it was all to do with the fact that daddy was a chief superintendent or even assistant chief constable? It has even been known for the deputy chief constable to be included in this, as a wee thank you for their numerous years of dedicated service and backstabbing, sorry, I mean, support and hard work! The result was that their siblings were promoted. Not fiction, but fact.

At "E" division alone (London Road), a female was promoted in December 2000 thanks to daddy having been a chief superintendent. In February 2001, another female was promoted with 6 years' service thanks to daddy having been a recently retired former deputy chief constable. A senior officer had forecast the latter example here to me some six months before. I was told that this female would be promoted as a "thank you" to her dad for his years of hard work. The Chief would do this as a favour to his deputy, prior to his own retiral in 2001.

How spooky is that! Was she a good cop? Average, not any better that most other cops, in fact, less experienced, but who needs that when there are other things on the horizon for you? I know this as I actually worked with her, let me rephrase that. She worked for me as part of a plainclothes team as it was decided that she needed some plainclothes experience before she could be promoted, you see.

Although, initially when she was placed in my team under my lead, this was not explained to me. We both had similar service in years but I had a wealth of experience already under my belt but she had only worked in administrative departments after her probation period. I was quite shocked when I was advised that she would be joining my team as she had shown no signs of wanting to do the job before.

Don't get me wrong, I actually got on really well with her, She settled in well to the plainclothes team albeit out of her depth but she quickly became used to the ways of working and was liked within the team. However, several months into her attachment with us, I was instructed to speak with the Divisional Commander.

In fairness, him and I got on well and I had a great relationship with him and we would meet every 2 weeks to discuss results and forward plans for the unit. He wanted to discuss my career with me and advised that I would soon be given the opportunity to try for promotion with an interview panel as he felt that I was capable of this and he heaped praise on me telling me how wonderful I was. This wasn't uncommon for him to do this as we were a very good unit and the results were outstanding.

However, when I thought the conversation was over as he advised that the panel interview would be in the next 6 months, he said he had other news for me. He advised that the female in my team with less service than me and less experience but with a father as an ex-deputy chief constable was to be given an acting sergeant role before me. Without an interview!

I was furious and told him so; he tried to calm me down and said he understood but that was the way it was to be. In fairness, I knew that he had no real control over this type of decision and I had to accept it. Obviously, it was rather strained within the unit over the coming weeks pending her departure.

I suppose it is one of those situations in that she was well aware as to why she was being given the acting rank—due to her father. But to others, her party line was that she had a great deal of experience and had earned it. No, she hadn't, but that was the way it was!

Another example is that of a cop whose father was a chief superintendent; he was given the rank of acting sergeant on the same shift he worked on as a cop, which was unheard of. After 6 months, a report was completed saying obviously how wonderful he was. He received an interview at Pitt Street to assess his suitability for promotion to the rank of sergeant. However, he failed. "Oh, all is not lost, son, don't worry, we'll make sure that you'll just do your acting rank somewhere else and then you can have another interview."

Again, this is not standard procedure; if you fail this type of interview, you have to start again, and wait about 2 years. He was promoted within 6 months. You would think that this is made-up nonsense to cover for my jealousy but in fact this seemed to be commonplace within the force and I was not alone in my frustrations at not being able to control it.

Another controversial appointment and indeed outrageous situation surrounded that of a serving deputy chief constable, Mr Mac. His devoted daughter joined the police only to find out that she was six months pregnant whilst doing her initial training. She was allowed to continue, because who would argue with her daddy?

If that had happened to an ordinary member of the public, you can bet that his or her career would have been short-lived!

Perhaps I am being too hard on the police; there have been genuine cases whereby officers have not been promoted despite their father's high rank. One cop whose father was in charge at Tulliallan Police College, he never was promoted. He is a really nice guy but more to the point, the fact remains that his father is not a part of the "Ayrshire Mafia" clan. Perhaps he is the exception to the rule.

A point to touch on is that you will notice I have referred to all of these people as "daddy"; the reason is clear, at the time during my service, there was no high-ranking woman in the police who had any siblings of their own as their career paths have resulted in the choice between family or promotion. Although many of the high-ranking women officers may be more "man-like" than other male officers are, they have bigger balls when it comes to dealing with staff!

It has nothing to do with the fact that women just did not reach the same levels within the police, as they could not do the same job; could it be due to their sex? You decide! However, at this time, there was one female who was high-ranking but all other posts were filled by…men! It was also alleged that she got to that position by having an affair with a deputy chief constable—all speculation, of course.

One of the last instances of nepotism occurred prior to me leaving the job. A good friend of mine was working as a detective sergeant in a busy division when he saw an advertisement for the post of DI at the Witness Liaison Unit based at Pitt Street, the Force Headquarters in Glasgow. This would have meant a promotion for the guy concerned.

However, the police maintain that they have a policy of equal rights and advocate that those suitably qualified may apply for positions above their current rank. It was his intention to apply, as he knew that the job would be high profile plus it would be a good career opportunity at the same time.

Unfortunately, he was not supported at his own division. But he decided to apply anyhow, albeit this is frowned upon and invariably leads to refusal, as one's own division must support the application. Undeterred, he submitted it anyway and patiently awaited a response. Two weeks later, he received a letter from the personnel department stating that his application was unsuccessful.

This meant nothing to him; in fact, it made him more determined to gain promotion sooner rather than later. However, he heard that three men had been lined up for interviews for the job. Two of them were DIs already and the other, being a good crony of another detective chief inspector; this guy was a detective sergeant. He had worked within different departments of Pitt Street over the past five years. He was considered to be hot favourite for the job. The reason for this was that he was very much a "gaffer's snitch" and would keep them well abreast of who was doing what within the job.

Although, in his defence, he was very much fluent in the necessary "wank speak" (police jargon). This is a prerequisite for all interviews and no doubt he would shine during this, the fact that he had never arrested nor seen an angry man in his fourteen years as a cop was neither here nor there. The decision was made. The job was awarded to one of the DIs as he had previous experience within the department and would need practically no training for the post. So on the whole, perhaps the right decision was made, for this job.

But what about the golden boy detective sergeant? At the same time, another job, for the position of DI in the Scottish Drug Enforcement Agency (SDEA), had been advertised. But like a bolt from the blue, none of those applicants were suitable and now the job lies with the golden boy himself, having been promoted into the rank to get the job.

Well, the fact remains that he actually learned he had the job before the job was advertised.

The reason for it being advertised was to discount any suggestion of discrimination. At least he didn't have to go through the stress of an interview. He was just too good. No, he doesn't have a daddy who is a gaffer. He just walks the walk and talks the talk the way all good boys should do! Horror of horrors, it would appear that even senior officers manage to skip through their service and despite being the subject of complaints against them, they still manage to be promoted, which is contrary to police promotion policy. Allow me to explain.

A major demonstration took place in the Govanhill area of Glasgow. Local residents were complaining about the closure of a local swimming pool. The demonstration was anything but peaceful with so many residents turning out in force that large groups of police officers were recruited to assist with the large crowds.

Some of the protestors decided to stage a demonstration in the premises, having gained entry through previously locked doors. They refused to leave and eventually, the attending police personnel forced them out. Some of the officers were injured due to the clash between all concerned.

Afterwards, there was a debriefing session by the bosses with the officers involved. Tempers flared between both sets although the police officers lost, the bosses walked out and refused to answer any questions. Some of the officers complained regarding the actions of the Chief Superintendent (CS) from that division and the Assistant Chief Constable (ACC). Both were responsible for the decisions made to have the officers carry out particular duties and actions.

As a result of the atrocious behaviour towards them by the public, several of the police personnel involved lodged official complaints against these two high-ranking officers. The investigation into their actions was carried out by another police force. It is normal policy that when an officer is the subject of a complaint then that person cannot be promoted.

Well, surprise, surprise! The usual rules didn't apply to these people. The CS was promoted to the position of ACC and the ACC was promoted to the position of Deputy Chief Constable. This again shows that the rules do not apply to those close to the top. I still cannot say what the outcome of the complaint was as the investigation seemed to disappear.

Ladies and gentlemen of the jury, nepotism and Masonic bigotry was alive and well in Strathclyde Police!

Chapter 9
The Janitor

The events concerning Albie, I have to concur, affected me greatly. I was genuinely deeply saddened by his death and often felt that perhaps if I had been suitably medically trained by the police, then perhaps he may have survived. You see, guilt is a thing that I never felt before his death!

Now here I was left to ponder the whys and what ifs concerning his death. I do appreciate the position of his friends who were present in the flat the night he died, but I also feel that they were too quick to point the finger at us. They blamed the police for the death of their friend when deep down I knew that he had died as a result of his own stupidity. However, that did not shift the blame away from me, I felt that in some way I was to blame for his death. Had I not forced my colleagues into going to that flat then he may have been alive today. Yet there are days that I convinced myself that such was Albie's downward spiral in the drug culture he had become attached to, he possibly may have succumbed to death by way of an overdose, albeit we will never know.

Although, in real terms, the mental scars remained during that time and I still frequently recall the events as the timescale is after all linked to an important time of my life—wedding anniversary! The event wasn't over and a Fatal Accident Inquiry was to be held due to the fact it was a death in police custody and these are quite uncommon so a FAI is needed to establish facts about the events.

Not that we had anything to hide at all but it was just something else that needed to be dealt with. It was bad enough that things were strained on the work front with a pending FAI but I also had personal issues with in-fighting between my own side of the family resulting in a significant break in relationships between me and my brothers.

I suppose it is one of those situations that is difficult to control and sometimes control is left in one person's hands and nothing gets resolved. I felt like I was being ostracised and ignored but I had my beautiful wife and daughter and great support from my in-laws, which was a great comfort. At a time when I needed my own family, I had to rely on others and dear friends to do that.

Probably one of the strange things to come out of the Albie incident was my trust and belief in the two guys I was involved with. A certain bond now exists with them and to this day, I still keep in touch with Chick and would regard him as one of the real few people in my life I genuinely trust and would trust him with my life!

On the lead-up to the FAI, it became apparent that we were in for a bumpy ride during the process and having contacted the Police Federation, I fought to engage the services of a lawyer to represent the 3 of us during the FAI. This was again more about protection and also to allay our fears as we genuinely wanted and needed someone to be on our side.

During the FAI, it was a very traumatic experience as it all centred around our actions and behaviour during those fateful minutes within that house. The fact we were there for an unrelated matter did not make any difference as the family lawyers were out for blood and we were easy victims. Having spent a full day in the witness box going over and over the events, I felt genuinely drained.

We all endured a similar anguish during the evidence and recounting of the events but we were hopeful of a good outcome with no direct blame being passed our way. Our lawyer Anne was excellent and did her best to protect us during the events and came to our defence several times. Anne lived a few doors away from me, I only knew her to smile and wave at and I never knew what she did as an occupation until one day in court when she defended a ned from Blackhill.

He had been caught by me in possession of a knife. She was an absolute bitch in court—direct, antagonistic and ferocious! Just what every ned needs, and every cop despises. After that, I was actually pleased that she was to represent us and I was comfortable with her presence during the FAI.

It took another 14 months before the FAI outcome was published. I hadn't forgotten about it by any means but I needed to park it and get on with my own work and life, pending the outcome. In fairness, it was an accidental death but to have it confirmed by a Sheriff seemed to help too.

We were praised for some of our actions but definitely condemned for our lack of first aid assistance that may have prevented his death. But until someone is in that position, I would ask people not to judge us. We did our best and not being in possession of full facts at the time didn't help. It took a while to prise out the information about Albie swallowing a rock piece of heroin!

I think there was more criticism of the ambulance crew who attended that evening to a high-rise block to treat someone who was unconscious, without bringing resuscitation equipment. Regardless of the outcome, it was finished as far as the paperwork was concerned but it will never be over for Albie's family.

Trying to focus on life after the events was difficult but I did try. I was still attached to the CID, having been moved to Easterhouse where I was plying my trade against the criminal fraternity. Even on routine patrols during my tour of duty, I still thrived on the buzz of arresting those found breaking the law.

One afternoon, whilst patrolling the Blackhill area of Glasgow along with a fellow detective, I stopped a female who had just left the house of a drug dealer. I waited to pounce on her some distance away from the house and on doing so watched as she placed a small paper wrap into her mouth. It was gone! Just another hazard of the job!

The female addict, trying to avoid being found with drugs, did the next best thing by getting rid of the evidence. I was incensed at her as I wanted to arrest her for possession of heroin and hopefully, she would give me information in place of her being sent to court the following morning. All part of the way of life in "Neds world".

As it happened, on this occasion, I did not even have the opportunity to detain her under terms of the Misuse of Drugs Act 1971 for a search. (That is the legislation in place to assist with her detention.) But I failed to detain her and inform her of her rights so I couldn't charge her with obstructing me! Alas, all was not lost as I could at least get her details to carry out a PNC (Police National Computer) check on her.

This would inform me whether she had any warrants to arrest her. What normally happens though is that invariably she would provide a false name if she thought that there were any outstanding issues to deal with. The harsh reality here was that in order to buy drugs, the addicts have to either steal or even prostitute themselves in order to get money. This female was no exception and I knew who she was.

She gave me the correct details informing me that when she was working the previous night, she'd had a warrant check "Doon the drag?" the tolerated zone where she could ply her trade as a prostitute in Glasgow city centre.

True enough, it came back negative, much to my surprise, as I still carried out the check choosing to ignore her pleas to let her go, but trusting these people can be hazardous. I thought that all was well and had a brief chat with her about her whereabouts to buy the drugs but she refused to tell me anything and even denied having been in possession of any heroin that day.

Whether I believed her or not made no difference but I tied to have a little banter with her as on previous occasions; she was more than up for a bit of a laugh with the CID. However, she was rather subdued and was itching to get out of the car. When I asked her as to why she wanted away so quick, she blurted out, "Cos you murdered ma mate Albie, Mr Dawson!"

I reeled in shock at what she had just said to me. Tom was also taken by surprise but he burst out laughing and said to her, "Away ye go, ya daft cow, Albie swallowed smack and killed himself."

She was furious and a little tête-à-tête ensued between them both. This took the heat off me as I tried to come to terms with what she had just said. I eventually calmed things down and she went on to say that the rumours going around the whole area was to the effect that Dawson fae the CID had murdered poor Albie and he had managed to get away with it.

I was livid and put her right as to what had actually happened in an effort to clear my name. I felt that she did believe me as at times she even said that she couldn't believe I would do such a thing, as I was "an awright guy".

She left the car and was polite and respectful. Whether she believed me or not made no difference at all. What she said had hit me like a brick and I felt quite sorry for myself. Tom laughed it off and tried to make me feel better but it didn't help. I was now beginning to think that everyone was out to get me because of Albie. I was letting the job get to me for the first time in eight years. I had to snap out of it.

That was the first time anyone had mentioned this to me since his death and I decided that it was time to lay it to rest and forget about it. It wasn't the last as on several occasions criminals said something of that ilk to me but I made sure that they never saw how his death affected me! I was also feeling the toll of the long hours at work coupled with the death of Albie.

I decided to take matters into my own hands and requested a change of duties. The other reason for this was that I was required to work night shifts and the late shift sometimes led in to a night shift such was the enormous workload, thanks to the criminal fraternity of the East End of Glasgow. There had been a shooting in the Garthamlock area and the witnesses were at risk from being executed themselves for cooperating with the police.

This meant that the witnesses were to be cared for by a specialist team of officers who formed part of the Witness Protection Unit at Pitt Street. However, as the witnesses were drug addicts and horrible bastards that preyed on the elderly to feed their habits by stealing from them, it was decided that they would be cared for by officers without any specialist training in Witness Protection. The CID was going to have to provide the cover to do this.

As the incident happened in the Easterhouse area then they would be responsible to carry this out. What was being kept a secret was the fact that the threat to the witnesses was that of being shot by those they had grassed on. A colleague of mine was given the initial task of doing the job. He was to look after two drug addicts who were also boy/girlfriend as well as another couple who had met in a psychiatric unit in Coatbridge. All in all, Peter had to contend with four loonies.

Peter knew all four of them and he dreaded every day doing the job. I felt so sorry for him that I volunteered to assist as it meant working a day shift and as I stated to the DI at the time, how difficult can it be? How wrong I was.

I became a wreck working with these people as I found it difficult dealing with them. I genuinely did not know what kind of existence these people had until I spent about three months with them, five days a week. It eventually involved me having to relocate two of them to England, without any help from the specialist teams at Pitt Street as they had washed their hands of them completely.

What I have to stress is though, it was one of the most fun-filled times in the job. I did things that only criminals do, but it was a necessary evil in order to assist these sorry people. I have purposely decided to leave these events out. Perhaps it will be a book in itself regarding how the police deal with the sensitive issue of witness protection. I certainly saw a different side of the criminal world and how ordinary people try to get by from day to day!

After having finished with the witness protection, I resumed my work again with the CID. One brisk summer's morning in July 1999, I arrived as normal at work, bleary-eyed from yet another disturbed sleep thanks to my precious daughter!

I spoke to someone coming off the night shift as our paths met in the back yard of the office as I closed my car door. "Christ, Dale, you look like shit, mate, been on the bevy then?"

"No, just a teething wean all fucking night!"

He laughed telling me that his days of all that were long gone as his kids were at high school. Not content with telling me that I looked like shit, he told me that I could expect a long day, as there had been another murder. I thanked him for cheering me up, not, and made my way up to the warm cosy CID room. When I got in the door, no sooner had I my jacket off than I was told to report to Baird Street to assist with a murder.

"Whose dead then, boss?"

"Mick the janitor from Baird Street!"

His words dropped like a bomb. He briefly told me that Mick had left his house to get to work and he was stabbed at a bus stop in the Riddrie area of Glasgow, not far from our own office in Easterhouse. I couldn't understand why anyone would want to kill Mick, as he was a really quiet guy who worked hard.

The offices at Baird Street and Easterhouse each had a janitor that was responsible for the cleaning staff. Mick had been there for about three years. I had never heard anyone say a bad thing about him before. Now he was dead!

Along with John, I made my way to Baird Street to await the nine o'clock briefing about the murder. This is commonplace as all senior CID management meets with the officers involved in the investigation and within the confines of that room, privileged information will be divulged concerning the crime. It is always reiterated that under no circumstances should the details of the crime be divulged to those not working with the investigation team.

We arrived at Baird Street and spoke with some of the other CID officers and tried to find out what had happened to Mick. The brief story was that he was standing at a bus stop in Riddrie when a man approached him and stabbed him, in broad daylight!

All that was known was a Ford Mondeo car had driven off at speed away from the scene. He died at the scene shortly afterwards. Some of the cleaners were hanging around the CID corridor as well as in the CID office, ear-wigging. This is not uncommon as they are horrid gossips at the best of times but now their supervisor had been murdered so they would have to be extra vigilant to find out the gory details.

Nothing else was known to us mere detectives so we just sat there together having a coffee and a natter. The briefing was to be at 0930 in the conference room. Before long, the grim-faced detectives who are the Serious Crime Squad arrived.

I knew that this would be a long investigation as already the services of the 'alleged elite squad' had been requested. About thirty officers piled into the conference room awaiting the arrival of the senior CID management.

In walked the (DS) and (DCI). A hush went around the room as the DS took centre stage to tell us the story. The opening gambit was that under no circumstances were the events to be discussed with anyone, as this was a particularly sensitive enquiry. It's not every day that the police have a murder investigation with the deceased being a police employee!

The DS told us that Mick had been approached at the bus stop by another male who then punched him and kicked him as he lay on the ground. Mick managed to get up and shouted at the man, he then returned and stabbed him. The male made off in a waiting car. There was only a handful of witnesses so far and a partial registration of the car had been obtained but this was incorrect. The only other vital piece of information was that the car might have been a taxi. This was the briefing.

No other information was available at this time and it was again reiterated to us that this was an extremely volatile situation and to avoid speaking about it other than within the conference room and under no circumstances give the cleaners any information concerning his death.

After this, we all left to await the announcement of who the teams would be and what we were required to do. This can be very boring as the setting up of a Major Incident room is time consuming and everything was to be documented on computer through the Holmes system. This meant that there would be an audit trail for every action allocated to officers.

One of the most important jobs would be the door-to-door enquiries that would be undertaken to ascertain whether any of the local residents saw or heard anything. This is a soul destroying job and a thankless task, yet it is so important at the same time.

I hoped that I wouldn't be lumbered with it, and I wasn't. It was allocated to Peter, my buddy who had been working with me on the witness protection. He was gutted as he too finds that particular job boring. Nonetheless, someone had to do it so at least they had a good coordinator to do it!

I was to team up with another friend of mine from Easterhouse, John. I knew that at least we would have a laugh together. Another aspect of this investigation was that undoubtedly, there would be loads of overtime. This is always the best part for the CID officers, as they would all ensure that they could earn as much from the investigation as was feasibly possible.

I was no exception to that rule and decided that I would 'fill my boots' with as many hours as I could get. This would pay for a holiday for my family and me later in the year! Sounds harsh, but there is a price to pay for good detective skills, after all! There was no work to be done straight away as it was too early and the office manager had not allocated any actions as yet.

John and I decided to go back to Easterhouse office in order to tidy up paperwork. That is the only downside to these murder investigations, the work-in-progress already in my queue would still have to be dealt with. We both decided to speak with the DI and ask that the other serious crimes we were previously dealing with be allocated to those officers not involved in this investigation.

Our colleagues who inherited the outstanding enquiries would be eternally grateful, not! The only plus to this was both John and I were similar in that our paperwork was excellent and there would be no problems in receiving our enquiries.

When we arrived at Easterhouse, we were pounced on from all directions concerning the death of the janny. We, of course, said nothing, informing them that we had been told not to discuss the investigation with anyone and therefore managed to avoid telling anyone that we too knew nothing. As I reached the CID office, the janitor approached me. In truth, I never did have any time for him as I found him to be a loud mouth with too much to say. However, I don't know why he chose me, but he told me that he wanted to speak with me in private. He was tearful and I felt genuine sympathy for him. Perhaps he thought that there was a hit taken out on all janitors employed by the police.

I took him into an interview room and so began his own tale of woe concerning Mick's death. He was friendly with Mick and went on to tell me that Mick had told him the previous week that it was a known fact that he had a run in with one of the cleaners at Baird Street as she refused to do as she was asked.

Apparently, Mick knew that she was leaving work early and failed to do her job properly. This 'rift' had been going on for about a month and Wilma had verbally threatened Mick that if he didn't stop picking on her, he would be sorry. Although as we all know, this can be just office tittle-tattle and that people do tend to say things for effect so I tried to dismiss Joe's concerns.

He refused to be put off and went on to tell me that Mick said to him that he was afraid that the cleaner Wilma would get her sons to sort him out. He was afraid. Again, I tried to reason with Joe but he insisted by saying that Mick genuinely believed that Wilma was serious and he wanted to tell Joe what was happening so as to get some advice. Joe had told him to approach the cleaning company bosses and let them handle it. Mick decided to do this and informed Wilma of this.

Joe was extremely upset and cried uncontrollably. He said that it was his belief that what had happened to Mick was as a result of his feud with Wilma. I told Joe I would come back to him and I would make discreet enquiries. What surprised me about Joe was he never asked me anything about the murder. He was too upset and genuinely concerned. I felt straightaway that what he had told me might carry some truth and that this may be the only explanation for Mick's death. Perhaps Wilma did have something to do with it?

I left Joe and spoke to John. When I told him the story, he too said that it was a possibility and that I should at least speak to the DS and let her make the decision as to what to do. I told Joe of my intention and he was relieved that I had believed him enough to take the matter to the gaffers.

What surprised me was the fact that there was a uniformed superintendent working from Easterhouse office; why had Joe not gone to him with the information? His response was that he knew I would believe him and the boss wouldn't! Not exactly a happy indictment on Strathclyde Police when the staff feel that they cannot approach bosses to speak with them.

If there were any form of truth in what Joe had told me then this would completely blow the whole investigation up in the air! Although I believed Joe,

I still had things to do at Easterhouse. I wasn't going to simply run away and speak with the DS. Anyhow, I knew that she would probably not even speak to me, as she would be too busy trying to work out her strategy of how to deal with the investigation.

John and I sat back and cleared our paperwork. Managing to allocate it all to our pissed off colleagues. They would probably have little or no time in which to carry out the necessary investigations of their own work, let alone ours! They would be inundated with other crimes in which to investigate.

During these Major Investigations (MI), some detectives are kept working at the sub-divisions in order to keep on top of the on-going crime in that particular area. This meant that they would be working at least twelve-hour shifts in order to keep on top of their work, and that they too would be financially better off by working plenty of overtime. Detectives relished this prospect as it meant financial security for their families. Eventually, after about two hours, John and I headed back to Baird Street to speak with the DS. Before that though, we still had to do some 'digging' about the female cleaner, Wilma!

The first port of call was to speak to some other colleagues who were familiar with the cleaners from that office. I knew Wilma but I couldn't say what her surname was. She worked for a short time on my shift when I had been an uniformed officer in my earlier years. She was the female turnkey. This meant that she was responsible for the female prisoners brought into the office. It was her responsibility to ensure the well-being of the females during her tour of duty. Cooking them their meals if required and generally making sure that they were being treated in accordance with the Police Procedures.

I actually quite liked her and she was always very pleasant, at least to my face. Having ascertained her surname, I went to the incident room in an attempt to glean more information from the operatives responsible for inputting the data on computer. Imagine my horror when I walked into the room and saw Wilma hanging around speaking to some of the police officers there.

She was supposed to be emptying bins and cleaning the room. I thought immediately that this would be an ideal opportunity for her to find out just how much the police knew concerning Mick's death. I was beginning to assume her guilt. This is the wrong thing to do, as one should never presuppose anything about a person because I had been told that she might have had something to do with his death!

I politely asked her to leave the room and advised that all bins would be left outside in the future during this investigation. Others around looked at me disapprovingly but I didn't care; I knew something was wrong and didn't want any cleaners in there at all.

However, I had a gut feeling that she did have something to do with Mick's death. I spoke quietly with another officer and he told me that apparently a Ford Mondeo car was spotted near the scene of the murder and that local taxi companies had already supplied the names of the drivers who were working at that time. I asked to see the list of names and smirked when I saw the name at the bottom–it was Wilma's son, Jason. Even more of a surprise was that his car was a Ford Mondeo!

I thanked the officer for the information and told him that I would speak to him later. As I walked outside of the room, Wilma said to me, "HI Dale, how are you, that was terrible about Mick, eh?"

I struggled to be pleasant to her as her comment sent a chill down my spine. I can honestly say that I hadn't had that feeling very often during my police service but on this occasion, it felt so creepy.

I exchanged pleasantries with her and made my way downstairs to find John. He was in the general CID office talking to some of the others who were also working on the inquiry. I motioned for him to follow me to an interview room where I updated him on what I had found out. He too was of the belief that Wilma did have something to do with the murder, especially the fact that her son was the owner of a Mondeo, too many coincidences?

It was time to speak to the DS, never an approachable person at the best of times, particularly in times of stress. John came with me so that we could put the story to her about the possibility of the cleaner having something to do with a murder! When I entered the room, the DS was engrossed in paperwork. "Can I have a word with you, boss, it's important?"

"No, I'm too busy. If it's to do with the murder, stick it on an information sheet."

I was quite angry with her, as she didn't even raise her head to acknowledge our presence. "I don't want to do that, boss, as what I have to tell you I don't want anyone else to read it, particularly the cleaners."

At last, I had her attention, she threw down the papers and sat back in her seat. "Right then, jackanory, get on wi it then." This was her undivided attention so I just rushed straight into the events of that morning concerning what I had found out.

When I finished, she laughed. "You think she might have something to do wi Mick's murder?"

"Yes, we do." I think when I said "we" she only just then realised that John was there too.

"Do you have a motive then?" Her face fell a mile. Here, I was questioning her about the murder.

"No, do you?"

"Yes, revenge for having to do work when she got away with doing nothing for years!"

The DS sat quietly and told me to write out what I had just told her and to hand it to her. We were told not to discuss it with anyone and that the information was to be treated as confidential. We left her room and made our way back into the interview room. I closed the door and John and I laughed. "She believes you, Dale?"

"Yes, I think she does." I wrote out the information and placed into an envelope. I walked towards the DS' office and could hear raised voices from within. I knocked on the door and walked in. There was the DCI and DS standing beside each other, both of them red from shouting.

I handed the envelope to the DS and she walked over to the door, slamming it shut. "Right Dale, tell the DCI what you told me earlier."

After having recounted the story, I could tell that he was shocked at the accusations I made against Wilma. He too was of the opinion that it was a possibility, but the DS was becoming more focussed. She stated that the case was solved. All we needed now was the evidence to secure Wilma's guilt.

I had managed to at least get an audience with the female DS, which was more than most did. In real terms, she was a formidable character—bully, terrified men, reduced grown men to tears and ruined many careers. Not one to fall out with although during this particular event, she was pleasant to me but even I would eventually fall foul of her inappropriate conduct!

Although it is never quite as clear cut as the DS was attempting to portray, it wasn't going to be an easy task as there was still plenty of work to be done before hitting those responsible. All that we had to go on was the fact that there may have been bad blood between the cleaning staff. The first thing to be done was to speak with those taxi drivers who had been working the morning of the murder.

When dealing with taxi companies, it is always prudent to find out who actually owns them. The reason for this is that these private hire businesses earn the owners of the firm vast amounts of money as the drivers in effect hire out the use of the radio equipment per week and also have to pay for the radio controllers. This means that literally thousands of pounds go to the owners of the firm.

In this particular area of Glasgow, it is well recognised that the owners are criminals who use this type of business as a front for perhaps putting other "criminal money" through their books thereby making them "legitimate" business men.

This particular taxi firm was no exception and experienced CID officers know that there would be no great help from those involved with that business. Therefore it takes a great deal of persuasive skills to ascertain the information required. John and I were tasked with this role and we set off to obtain as much information as possible from the taxi firm.

Behind the scenes it wasn't going too great for the DS as she was encountering problems from Pitt Street as the Chief wanted answers quickly as it was embarrassing to have the media report on the fact that a member of the Police cleaning staff had been murdered in broad daylight. As yet there was information to assist in catching his killers. So in effect, the police couldn't even solve a case involving one of its' staff. What type of message was that sending out to the public?

The DS had nothing much to go on with this case, as so far, there was no witnesses who could assist with the investigation. All that she had was the suggestion that it was a Ford Mondeo car, the colour and fact that there was a verbal dispute between the deceased and another cleaner. The DS wanted answers. She set about carrying out door to door enquiries and she wanted every person who stayed within the surrounding streets interviewed.

This is a huge job, as it requires meticulous planning and forms must be completed as well as obtaining statements from the occupants of the houses. However, one problem existed: this could take about a week to compile and she was not happy at this prospect. Another guy from the CID at Easterhouse was given this to organise. This is a real shitty job and normally the detectives involved in this type of investigation try to steer clear of this job.

Peter was landed with it and had to arrange the house to house with the assistance of about eight uniformed cops. He knew that it would take ages but he was also aware that he would make plenty of overtime out of it so he rolled his sleeves up and got on with the job!

John and I prearranged our visit to the taxi company by phone so that they could prepare the necessary information for us prior to attending there. What was needed was a list of who was working and where they were at the time of the murder. Specifically, if anyone was working in a taxi then the fare would be confirmed from the computer records held at the controller's office. I knew that they wouldn't be keen to help but whenever I mentioned that it was a murder investigation, the woman who was in charge at the office was pleasant and asked that I leave it for a couple of hours and she would get the information required.

I couldn't have asked for any better a response and I knew that she wanted the CID in and out of her office as quickly as possible, suits me, I thought. Having telephoned the DS to inform her what was to happen at the taxi office, she was pleased that at least we would be able to find out the information soon.

John and I sat back and enjoyed lunch as we decided not to do anything else, as this was a priority so all we could do was wait. Joe appeared at the CID asked to speak to me. I had no hesitation as I could sense that he was anxious. He told me that he was to be interviewed about what Mick had spoken to him about and he was worried that it would perhaps affect his position with the other cleaning staff. I think he was more concerned about word getting out and he may end up like Mick! I tried to reassure him that he was doing the right thing and that if what he says can be confirmed, then the important thing was to find out who killed Mick and have them arrested. He was still afraid but decided that he would tell all.

The time came for John and I to obtain the information from the taxi office. When we arrived, the waiting taxi drivers jumped into their cars and drove off. We both laughed. This is normally the case when the CID appears on the scene. I spoke to Maggie who was very helpful and provided me with a printout of the hires undertaken by the drivers the morning of the murder. Included in that list were the details of the Mondeo car driven by Jason. At or near the time of the murder, according to the taxi records, he had no hires.

The reason was simple. He was off duty at that time. This was good news as it proved that at least he wasn't out on hire so therefore, he would have to account for his whereabouts. No doubt he would have an alibi though!

We drove to see the DS and gave her the information. She smiled and looked quite smug. I was sure she had other information but she had no intention of sharing it with us. We were told to attend a briefing at four o'clock that afternoon and she would explain more to us then.

As is normal with all major investigations, there are always briefings. Sometimes these can be as much as three or four times a day. It all depends on the information obtained by the many detectives attached to the case. At these briefings, each pair of detectives must share with the room the information obtained from the witnesses and who said what. Basically, it allows each of those involved to find out at what stage the investigation is.

However, I had always heard that in these murder investigations, there is always a 'team within the team'. This means that some privileged information is not shared with everyone. Only those entrusted with vital pieces of the remaining jigsaw. It sounds very SAS style but in actual fact, I would describe more as a "clique".

The DS arrived into the briefing room accompanied by the DCI who scuttled behind her like a rabid dog. She seemed to be, yet again, smug in her appearance and manner. The event started with the DS telling everyone that there had been significant progress and she thereafter started to make her way around the room in order to obtain the information from the detectives present. It may seem strange that there would appear to be only detectives working on the investigation.

This is quite normal as usually the more mundane jobs are allocated to uniformed constables to deal with. Or even perhaps to those detectives who fall out with the DS. When she asked Peter to explain what information he had gained from coordinating the door to door enquiries, he started to ramble on about some "dotty old spinster" who was a resident of the street where Mick had been murdered.

His ramblings included details of how this spinster who was only in her mid-forties had probably never seen an angry man in her life. He went on to say that she was also nosey and her manner and appearance was due to the fact that she had lived with her mother all of her life. The only time she left her home was to go to work or the local shop. There was a stunned silence in the room and the DS started to egg him on to see whether he would continue with his abusive assessment of this woman.

He duly obliged and continued poking fun at the "spinster". All of a sudden, he stopped dead in his tracks. This was thanks to the scribbled note from one of his colleagues that was beside him. It read, "You're describing the DS, ya tit."

You see, our very own DS could almost have fitted that same description, with the exception of the fact that she was more manly than most of the men in the room. He went crimson red. Meanwhile, everyone in the room started laughing. Until, that is, the DS went ballistic at the audience before her.

Peter was so embarrassed that he hadn't even thought of the DS when he began his torrent of abuse regarding the witness. The DS told everyone to leave the room and to return at five o'clock as she wished to "go over a few things of significance". Peter was asked to remain behind as the DS wished to speak with him!

On returning for the briefing at five o'clock, the room was buzzing with the previous banter started by the unsuspecting Peter. He blushed and said that she had read him the riot act and he decided that in future he would just tell facts as opposed to his opinion. It may seem strange that grown men accept what people like the DS tell them. It really is quite simple, he really was quite scared of her. She had that effect and this was certainly one of those occasions. She was, quite bluntly put, a bully and aggressive with it.

It is easier to listen than to make an awkward life for yourself as police bosses do carry grudges, they are control freaks, or on occasions, just freaks, who like to hear the sound of their own voices and no one else's. The DS was no different. The only thing different with her was that she was horrid to those who tried to belittle her position. I did say control freaks, didn't I?

We awaited the audience with the DS and she walked into the room without the smug look on her face. She got straight down to business and started to tell the gathered detectives that the case was becoming somewhat more interesting but that she was not at this point going to divulge any further information as it was "secret". All that she asked again was that the details of the case remain private and any person found speaking about it to anyone not connected with the investigation would be booted off the inquiry and transferred to another division.

This wasn't so much of a request as a veiled threat by the boss! Everyone nodded, as it was clear she meant business. Before we left, about six of us were asked to remain, as she wanted to speak with us. Included in this group were John, Peter and a few others, as well as myself. I automatically thought that with Peter there, it must mean that we too were going to get a verbal doing from the DS. I tried to muffle my laughter as I relived in my head what Peter had said earlier. This was brought to a sudden halt as the DS began by telling us that what we were about to hear was for our ears only and would not be discussed with the others involved in the investigation.

I was at last about to experience the "inquiry within the inquiry" I had so often heard about. She went on to say that it would appear that the information I had given to the DS had some truth. She discussed the events of my discussions with her and how this actually could have been the breakthrough with the investigation that was needed. It had been decided that the investigation was to be centred upon Wilma and her son, as there was a witness who saw a Mondeo taxi at the locus of the murder.

This was too much of a coincidence as the witness saw that it was a taxi plate on the car, albeit no registration number had been noted by this person. The only downside to the investigation was that Wilma was still working as a cleaner within the very office where the heart of the inquiry was operating so therefore, it was of vital importance that she be left to think that there was nothing to concern her and that she could just continue to come to work as normal. This seemed quite bizarre to me as surely the investigation had reached another level as far as Wilma was concerned. She was now a suspect.

However, this was the DS' decision to keep quiet about what was going on as there was still a lot of work to do before anything could be done. All of the taxi drivers were to be interviewed, including Jason. At least this way it would seem that there was no finger being pointed at any particular person, so far! I suppose this would account for the secrecy surrounding the investigation.

The cleaners were now barred from entering the main room where the computers containing the information on the investigation was being stored. This should have aroused suspicion as normally, they would still be allowed access to the room in order to have it cleaned.

However, Wilma was one of the cleaners whose responsibility was to clean that particular area so it was important that she should remain outside the room. They were instructed to leave bags for the rubbish and those working in the room were to empty the bins for the foreseeable future. There was also the problem of the ground floor of the building, in particular one of the CID rooms as this was used as a manual paper room where paper documents were being sorted. These paper documents were of great importance and therefore, the cleaners were told to leave this area alone and concentrate on the other areas of the office.

The reason for this was Wilma had friends who were cleaners and it was their job to tidy the ground floor area. It was vital that no one leaked any information to anyone. As the Serious Crime Squad had also been drafted in to help with the investigation and they were given the task of obtaining the taxi drivers' statements. They had not been told about the link with Jason and the murder. It was decided by the DS to ask them to obtain statements to see what the witnesses were prepared to tell.

Jason gave a statement to the effect that he was off duty at the time of the murder and he provided an alibi. At least the police knew what steps they had to take to prove what Jason had told the CID when they obtained the statement. It was decided that the people he said could back up his story would also be interviewed, as it was a crucial part of the case.

Meanwhile, the door to door wasn't going too well as no significant information had been received from the mostly elderly residents. It was decided to stretch the boundaries of the door to door enquiries to see if perhaps anyone else saw or heard anything the morning of the murder. Peter, who was organising the door to door, was at the end of his tether, as he was receiving virtually no assistance with the job.

He had a showdown with the DS telling her that he needed help or the job wouldn't be done properly. He didn't want to have any evidence missed because the uniformed officers didn't want to assist with the inquiry? She requested assistance and twenty support unit officers were used to blitz the area in order to seek out potential witnesses. It wasn't long before it paid off!

A witness came forward to say that she saw a Ford Mondeo taxi in the street with three males on board. She noted a registration number down on a piece of paper at the time as she thought that they were perhaps housebreakers on the prowl. However, the registration number was incorrect. The last digits were wrong, although it was still similar to the taxi owned by Jason. This was hugely significant as it at least put his taxi at the location that particular morning. Albeit Jason had stated that he was elsewhere at the time.

The only downside was the fact that his alibi was family members and another friend. The alibi witnesses had been spoken to but one of them had mentioned about another friend who was also there, a guy called Todd! Prior to speaking with witnesses, sometimes there are computer checks carried out to see if there are any previous convictions. This means that a person has been in trouble with the police and has gone to court accused of having committed a crime, or indeed crimes.

The computer record for Todd gave significant information concerning this man and his associates. It made interesting reading as it proved that he was not of good character and his associates were of the same background. The main information was that he lived in another area of Glasgow and there didn't appear to be a link as to how Jason knew this man. The family had provided various stories about how they knew this other man and how he came to be at their house around the time of the murder. However, at this point, the identity of the other male remained unclear.

Yet again, a secret briefing was called involving the chosen six detectives who were to be used for the investigation. John and I attended and were again briefed by the DS concerning the new evidence. There was still work to be done but the DS didn't want to arise suspicion, hence the reason for the cloak and dagger approach to inquiry. It would appear that there was cracks appearing in the statements from Jason's alibi and these required further work to be done on them.

These were to be left with the Serious Crime Squad officers to deal with as they had already built up a rapport with the witnesses. Often, this is always done, as witnesses tend to prefer to speak with the same detectives. It doesn't always work like clockwork but this is normally the stance adopted during protracted investigations.

John and I were like the others in the 'secret team'; we were still carrying out routine inquiries but we were never given anything too time consuming as it was decided that we would all be kept clear in case we had to do vital inquiries at short notice. Word was circulating amongst the cleaning staff that Wilma might have had something to do with the investigation due to her having had a fallout with Mick.

Many of them were her friends, so obviously they would stick up for her. Perhaps one of the sickest stories was that some of the cleaners, including Wilma, had a party to celebrate Mick's death! This was quite a shock, even for detectives who are used to dealing with death and horror, but this was really quite disgusting to think that people could react in such a way to another human being's death! Perhaps this just proved the calibre of people employed by the cleaning company.

Personally, when I heard the names of those involved, I was quite shocked as I got on well with most of them. That was about to change, as there was no room in my life for those who treat death with such contempt! We were by now almost two weeks into the investigation and rumours were going around the office that we were making no significant headway and that there was no suspects in the frame. This was good news as it allowed Wilma to continue coming to work whilst also leading her into a false sense of security.

The truth was however that Jason's alibi had so many flaws that he would now be well in the frame for being involved in the murder. The identity of two friends of his, Humphrey and Todd, added significant flames to the already burning embers that there appeared to have been a friendship between all three. How they all knew each other wasn't known but they did, and that was very significant as Humphrey had a criminal record which certainly could have fitted in with the offender profile of the would-be murderer.

The DS was also being hassled by Pitt Street, as this was a very sensitive murder due to the nature of the relationship between the deceased and his employers! The end was in sight, although even we didn't know that then.

Statements were noted from Wilma's family concerning their movements on the day of Mick's murder. This was not out of place as other cleaning staff had also been interviewed in a similar manner. The only difference was that the discrepancies would be enough to interview each of the family members in turn, at length if required. The guys from the Serious Crime Squad were still being given the best actions to concentrate on.

This wasn't going down too well with some of the other detectives at the division as they assumed that they should have the best actions. In truth, it would appear that the DS was ensuring that no one was going to know about the general direction the enquiry was headed, i.e., after Wilma as prime suspect. Another significant breakthrough came when it was discovered from local police intelligence that Humphrey's association was with Todd, so therefore it was assumed that it must have been Todd who organised the meeting for Jason.

It was becoming more and more sinister as at this point, it was still unclear why Wilma wanted Mick dead! It was also ludicrous that someone was go to such lengths in order to get back a person because of a fallout over cleaning responsibilities.

The Friday afternoon briefing was very vague concerning evidence and who perhaps did what. However, the usual six were ushered into a small room to speak with the DS as she had something to tell us. In she walked with the DCI and she slammed the door shut. It was clear that she was in a mood yet again about something, or perhaps someone, who knows what was going on in that crazy head of hers.

She immediately started ranting and raving about rumours circulating in the office about the secret six and how they were being fed with confidential information. She didn't know who was spreading the story but she was going to castrate the man responsible if she found out who it was. John and I knew who it was. We knew it was Davy, being a bit of gaffers' pet, he couldn't keep his big arrogant mouth shut.

He had been bragging to his other Masonic mates at their usual Thursday meeting that he was part of the chosen few who were being taken into the DS's confidence. The difference being, one of them told John and I that Friday morning. A part of me wanted him caught due to his arrogant ways. But under no circumstances was I going to be the one to tell the DS.

She again warned us that the information was to remain secret and that we should expect a phone call early on the Saturday morning as we might be going to arrest/detain those responsible. Nothing else was said to us other than to be available. We all left to go home that night unaware of what was about to happen.

About four o'clock on the Saturday morning, my phone rang. Assuming that perhaps something was wrong with a relative as this is normally the time of day that death phone calls are received, I jumped to answer it. It was the DCI asking me to be at the office for as close to five o'clock as possible as we were urgently required. Although I thought that my services would be required, I didn't imagine that I would be called upon so early. I told Carmen that I had to go to work and quickly got myself ready.

I reached work about five, as had been requested. John was already there and we sat and had coffee with the DCI awaiting the others to arrive. He told us that those involved would be detained that morning. They included Wilma, her twin sons Jason and Derek, Todd and Humphrey. The others arrived, including Davy who was pontificating as soon as he came through the door about how much money he would make out of being called to work so early.

He was rubbing his hands in glee at the prospect of earning an extra one hundred pounds for that day. John and I both laughed, not with him but at him. He infuriated a lot of other cops as he was always bragging about how much he earned. In truth, what he didn't realise was that John and I earned about the same as him, despite the fact his basic salary was more than ours due to him having more police service. The difference was we didn't discuss money, as it was part of the job. Also a necessary luxury to make up for the lost time spent at home with our wives and family.

I would much prefer to have quality time at home than a few extra hundred quid in my pocket. I didn't really need money that desperately. This was however a hazard of the job, long hours away from home!

By about five-fifteen (0515), everyone was present and the DS began her briefing of what was required and who was expected to do what. We were split into teams and assigned different people to detain. John and I were a team and we had to assist Laidlaw and Shona to detain Wilma, then we had to go around the corner to Derek's house to detain him. The DS still refused to use any other detectives other than those she entrusted to get the job done.

However, she reluctantly had to request the assistance of uniformed officers to accompany us as we would be unable to do it all ourselves without additional help. Prior to ending the briefing, the DS told us that she knew for sure that the targets were all at home as she had commissioned one of the surveillance squads who work from Pitt Street to follow the targets the previous day.

It was ascertained that there had been a family meeting up at Jason's house on the Friday night where Wilma and Derek had gone.

"How do we know that Jason is at home just now, boss?"

She looked at Davy in disgust as she replied. "Because I've got someone hiding under a car at his house watching his every movement. He has been there all night."

We were all looking at one another. Then the DS told us that a guy who was working at Easterhouse used to be in the Royal Marines and he had volunteered to 'stake out' Jason's house if required. The poor sod had been there out in the cold all night hiding under a car. He had vast experience in surveillance so this was nothing to him. This showed us all how committed the DS was about arresting those involved.

I'm just glad it wasn't me she asked to hide under a car, as I would have told her to fuck off. The strike at the targets houses were to be orchestrated at the same time so that no one could contact any other member of the family to let them know that we were coming. With everyone in place, we all attended at the relevant house in order to detain the necessary individual. Wilma answered the door. She was already up to get ready to go to work at Baird Street.

Laidlaw, being the senior ranking officer, informed Wilma of the nature of our visit and detained her in accordance with the legislation required to make it legal. She was shaking like a leaf, telling us all that this was a mistake and that she had nothing to do with Mick's death. "Shona hen, you know me, ah widnae dae anything like that."

Shona looked right through her and calmly told her to get her clothes on and it would all be discussed at the office. "But Dale, you're too nice tae dae this tae me, ah liked you?"

"Wilma, I'm only doing my job, just get your gear on and we can get to the office, okay?"

Her pleas fell on deaf ears and we all knew that she was behind Mick's death. The stark reality was that we all did feel quite attached to the enquiry, as Mick had been a really nice guy. Too nice to die at the hands of maniacs!

John and I left that house and made our way to Derek's house to detain him. It seemed quite strange detaining all members of the same family for a murder, Wilma, her partner as well as her beloved twin sons. We took uniformed officers along to Derek's house but it wasn't really that necessary as he came along quietly and without any hassle. His girlfriend was left in the house with their small daughter.

When we arrived at Baird Street, Wilma was already at the charge bar being processed. It seemed strange taking her to the very office she worked from, but this was to show to the other cleaners that Wilma was implicated in the murder. The shock on all of the cleaner's faces was evident.

These were the very cleaners who all celebrated Mick's death. Therefore, they were all incapable of emotion as far as I could see. To laugh at someone else's misfortune is no joke. I despised all of them. The only difference being, I couldn't hide my feelings and chose to ignore them. John was as bad, but he would just tell them, "Don't speak to me, just clean the floor like you're supposed to." This was just John's nature, a spade's a spade!

When Derek saw his mother, he freaked. Up to this point, he had been quite calm but seeing that his mother was also detained and his twin Jason just enraged him. John and I took him into a side room and he was told in a polite manner that he was detained regarding a murder, as were his mother and Jason.

After all, why else would the police come to your house at this time in the morning? "Time to wake up, sunshine, and start thinking about what you are going to tell us to save your ass." He went quiet. I don't think he realised that he was going to be questioned about the murder.

He went a deathly grey colour. John and I looked at each other, smirking. We knew he had a story to tell and we would get it! Once all the paperwork was processed, yet another briefing was called by the DS so that those involved in the interviews could be spoken to regarding what to ask of the suspects. As there were three suspects, there would have to be three teams of two to conduct the interviews. It was decided that those who detained each party would conduct the interviews.

Therefore, John and I would have Derek. Laidlaw and Shona would have Wilma, Davy and Peter would have Jason. Before the DS could speak, Davy being the loud mouth decided that John and I needed expert advice on this type of interview as we were young (ish) in service. Davy started to tell us how we should conduct our interview.

I was mad. "Excuse me a minute, Davy, you concentrate on your interview and John and I will concentrate on ours. We don't need you to tell us how to conduct an interview. Furthermore, shut the fuck up and let the DS advise us, she's in charge, not you."

He was about to reply when the DS said, "Thanks Dale, sometimes people like Davy lose sight of that fact."

He was livid and his face went crimson. I tried hard not to laugh, but I really wanted to just punch his pretentious face. The DS told us to do our best and get as much information as possible and if necessary we could break up the interview to discuss what we had been told.

John and I left the room, followed by Davy. Before he got a chance to say anything to us, John grabbed him by the collar and pinned him against the wall. He said something to him about where he was going to stick his boot if he ever interfered in that way again. He let him go and we both walked away, laughing. I didn't feel as bad as I knew that John was also furious with Davy.

The police are one organisation, it is fiercely competitive. Davy was perhaps afraid that John and I were well respected by senior management as well as other colleagues, something Davy didn't have and in truth, he was jealous. At that particular time, John and I were considered high fliers as we both only had about nine years' service and were more than capable of doing our job.

Davy, on the other hand, had about twenty years' service and thought he knew it all. The only difference being, he had a shady past and had only just managed to redeem himself after about ten years! In police terms, experience is based upon how long you have been in the job as opposed to actual criminal case handing, which is rubbish as I had covered far more aspects of policing than most people had with more service. The fact that Shona was also involved in this process was equally welcomed by me. Having worked together as beat cops we had the same sense of humour and willingness to learn. As well as being good at what we did. Shona worked within the Female and Child Unit (FACU) dealing with sexual crimes against men and women as well as children. That isn't an easy job and Shona was well respected at what she too did.

We organised ourselves and decided that we would play good cop bad cop, me being the former and John the latter. Derek was taken into the interview room and without discussing how we would conduct the interview we began. The reason we did this was because John and I both knew that we were comfortable working alongside one another and we would ad-lib with the questions, but we would be fine.

The interview commenced with John doing all the talking whilst I took notes. It was clear from Derek's responses that this was a pre-planned response he gave us. I knew this as did John but surprisingly, I let John continue, as he appeared to be forming a bond with Derek.

This is sometimes good as it leads the suspect into a form of trust and usually they then open up with the information required. I was becoming quite frustrated and I had had enough of his lies. I started shouting at him that it was about time he realised that he was in deep shit over this and that he was covering up to protect his mother.

Either way, he was looking at going to jail for perverting the course of justice. I asked him, "What will your burd do when you're inside, and your wean, who'll be a father to her?" He looked right at me. I seriously don't think he realised just how much shit he was in until I mentioned his daughter. I told him that we were going to begin again only this time, I wanted the truth. So began the interview in earnest.

He answered both our questions only this time, he answered them truthfully. After a few more minutes, he described how his mum, Wilma, had come to his house the afternoon of Mick's death. She was upset and kept saying that she was responsible. However, at this point, Derek clammed up saying that he couldn't tell us any more as he couldn't remember.

"Tell me why she felt responsible," I shouted at him furiously.

"Because she paid two hunner quid tae get him done in." I almost fell off my chair. I still to this day do not know how I managed to remain composed. I started to ask him question after question about what had happened and he answered each in turn, with no hesitation. After about another ten minutes, I stopped the interview. John and I spoke outside and we were high-fiving ourselves as we had at last managed to expose the story behind Mick's death. I left to find the DS but couldn't find her anywhere.

I found Laidlaw and Davy, telling them to go to the DS' room as I had something to tell them. Davy pestered me to tell him what it was but I refused, looking smug as I searched for the DS. Within the confines of her room, I told the DS, DCI and the others about the interview with Derek.

The story being that Wilma had confided in her sons about her dislike for the janitor. Jason said that he could arrange for him to "get done in" as he knew someone who could do it. Jason contacted Todd who knew the guy Humphrey who would do him in for two hundred pounds. However, all was not well as poor Mick got up after the first attack by Humphrey and stumbled after him down the street.

The alleged attacker, Humphrey, then turned on Mick and stabbed him, resulting in his death. The room was deathly quiet. The DS was ecstatic that we had at last found out the truth (well, John and I did that part).

"Excellent work, Dale, excellent." However, Wilma was a tough nut to crack and she was stringing Laidlaw and Shona along by refusing to admit to anything. They both knew she was lying but she refused to admit her involvement. Davy was also having the same problem with Jason. My, how good I felt, there was the expert trying to tell John and I how to interview and he couldn't do it himself, how ironic!

The interviews recommenced, although this time, they were armed with more information to assist with the questioning of Wilma and Jason. John and I could glean no more information from Derek. I don't think he knew the full facts of what had happened!

After our interview with him, he was put back into a detention room awaiting the outcome of the other two interviews. Wilma and Jason kept up the pretence that they knew nothing of the death. Wilma was asked about providing two hundred pounds in order to have Mick 'roughed up'; she denied this also.

However, when Laidlaw explained that perhaps they would check her bank account to see if that sum of money had been withdrawn, she even had that angle covered too. She boldly said that it was given to Jason to help him pay his mortgage as he was having difficulty paying it.

This quite clearly was the action of a cold, calculating orchestrator who had organised the murder of her boss! Although this was a murder investigation, Wilma had only paid to have him roughed up enough to be off his work and not murdered. That fault lay solely on Humphrey who took it too far. Despite their best attempts, Laidlaw and Shona had no option but to terminate the interview and await further instructions from the DS. It was decided that the Wilma's family would be interrogated so see if any more evidence could be obtained.

Derek's partner told a similar story to her boyfriend, obviously fearing for their daughter. After all, what would happen to her if they were both jailed for perverting the course of justice? Jason's girlfriend also provided corroborating evidence to assist with the investigation. Wilma's boyfriend, on the other hand, was as adept at lying as she had been.

Nothing of great significance was learned from him either. It wasn't the best case in the world and without any other witnesses coming forward, it was looking pretty grim for gaining a conviction; that was a long way off.

The DS called a briefing to inform those not in the know what had happened. She informed everyone that there was still a lot of work to be done. She calmly announced, "We've got the arrest, let's get the evidence."

This wasn't exactly encouraging for those of us involved in the investigation as it was always drummed into us that prior to an arrest, there should be evidence; she appeared to be doing the opposite. Still, I'm sure she knew what she was doing.

The Serious Crime Squad was enlisted to detain the other two men involved in the murder, at least alleged to have been involved. Several hours later, Todd and Humphrey were brought to the office, the latter being the person responsible for knifing Mick to death.

The interview with Todd showed him to be terrified of Humphrey and he initially refused to cooperate. However, he did admit to enough to tie him to Jason and Wilma but then went quiet, refusing to say anything further. Humphrey, on the other hand, being a seasoned criminal sat and made no comment throughout the interview. Eventually, the only thing he did was to provide an alibi for his whereabouts on the day of the murder.

At least there was something to work on, perhaps a glimmer of hope for the police! The DS decided to tell Jason that the other two had been arrested. The police had seized Jason's car and blood had been found under the front passenger seat. This was significant evidence as this blood was confirmed to have been Mick's. Therefore, whoever stabbed him must have been in Jason's car.

Eventually, Jason changed his mind about what had happened that morning, insisting that it was Humphrey who murdered Mick, albeit paid for by Wilma. He confirmed that Wilma only paid for Mick to be 'roughed up' as was earlier indicated. He said that he didn't know that Humphrey had a knife until he came back into the car after having stabbed Mick. He placed the knife under the passenger seat.

This was a major breakthrough, although Humphrey refused to comment about his alleged actions during yet another interview. The knife was never recovered, therefore making the police job more frustrating and difficult. Todd, on the other hand, became more withdrawn and difficult to interview, fear played a major part in this. Fear of what Humphrey would do to him if he grassed him.

I had been working since about five that morning and it was now seven at night. I was like a zombie and looked forward to going home. I had barely seen my wife and daughter for about a week and I missed them.

The night wasn't over though as the DS had another special job for John and I to do. We were sent to a council scheme in Easterhouse to interview, rather burst the alibi given by Humphrey regarding his whereabouts on the morning of the murder. When we arrived at the house, I met a young guy who was quite clearly shitting himself when he saw us walk through his front door. I took him to the nearby police office and began taking a statement off him about his movements with Humphrey.

After about five minutes, I stood up and walked towards the window in the cramped office. I looked at him and went ballistic at him for lying to me. Deep down, I was venting my frustration at not being allowed to go home because I had to interview him. All he was doing was lying. I had plenty of experience to tell me that. I walked towards him and he stood up. "Okay, I'll come clean, don't hit me."

I sat back down and he told me the story of that morning. He didn't know what had happened concerning Humphrey, except that he had been asked by him to say that he was with him all morning. He was also terrified of Humphrey and feared for his own life. This was enough for me. We had managed to burst open his alibi at last. The ironic thing about that interview was that I had no intention of hitting him. Not my style, you see. I have never found any need to do that sort of thing.

That poor guy had confused my actions with perhaps someone who had had a bad experience with other police officers in his time. I am of the belief that I would rather gain a confession the proper way, by allowing the person to tell the truth. Not that I have never shouted at witnesses or those accused of a crime, I have. But that has always been enough to get their attention and ensure that they tell me the truth, although it doesn't always happen like that!

We took the guy home and headed back to Baird Street to tell the DS the news. When John and I walked into the room, she looked up at us and said, "If you've no burst his alibi, I'm gonnae burst your balls!"

We both burst out laughing. She was in no laughing mood and John quickly told her, "Hey relax, boss, here's his burst alibi, are our balls safe?" She read the statement and sighed, a smile answered John's question. We left the room with our balls intact.

Thinking that the day was over, we sat down finishing off the paperwork associated with the last interview. I heard voices from the corridor and I looked out to see Todd being escorted into an interview room. Shortly, two senior officers went into the room after him. The door was slammed shut and it appeared that two detectives were standing guard on either side of the CID corridor. It was their job to ensure that no one came up near the interview room.

I shouted on John to come to the door. We were about ten feet away from the interview room. All that could be heard was raised voices of a particular senior officer. As well as "stop it" and "get tae fuck".

After about ten minutes or so, the two senior officers left the interview room and headed off to another room. One of them told a detective who was standing nearby to "get rid of that bin out of there".

When he returned with the bin, it was severely dented in half. Something like a crushed can of juice. Meanwhile, Todd was sitting there in the corner of the room holding his head in his hands. Suffice to say that that method of interrogation is not one I would consider, perhaps that is why that particular senior ranking officer is of a particular rank today, through beating people to a pulp. Todd was interviewed but provided no other information so the assault he had to endure was to no avail. It merely ruined the rapport previously built up with the interviewing officers earlier.

He never made any formal complaint regarding that incident. This was quite a scary thing that happened. Even other experienced detectives were appalled at what had taken place. The bin was taken away and is still in safe hands to this day! Eventually after Todd was placed back in his cell, another briefing was called and it was decided that those arrested would now be charged. Humphrey with murder, Wilma, Todd and Jason were all charged with conspiracy to commit murder.

Derek was released, as he was merely a helpful witness. The next day was going to be paperwork, as the case was to be prepared for the Monday morning. That was a job for the DS whilst we all had to write out summaries of the interviews we had been involved in. It was now midnight and I had been working for nineteen hours. I was physically and emotionally drained. Yet the assault of Todd was still fresh on my mind. I couldn't believe that in our modern-day policing, that type of thing would actually happen.

What was most difficult to comprehend was the very idea that the person responsible was a high-ranking officer. I wonder what would have happened to me if I had resorted to that sort of drastic action in order to gain a confession?

I can answer that quite freely. I would have been charged with assault, as well as being disciplined under the Police Regulations and booted right out of the CID and possibly lose my job altogether. It proves my point that there are rules for some and rules for others within this type of establishment.

The following day, I returned to work to complete the mountain of paperwork. The DS was in a foul mood, probably aggrieved at the idea of having to report a man for murder without much evidence against him. It was clear that there was still a lot of work to be done on this investigation. The first priority was to have the case reported to the PF. Even once this had been carried out, there would have to be more door to door enquiries at the scene, in the hope of gaining a witness to the murder.

It was known that Wilma and the others would not incriminate Humphrey in any way, fearing for their own safety. The case was complete and ready for onward transmission to the PF on the Monday morning. "Fingers crossed they get remanded, that will show them we mean business!"

This was quite a sweeping statement from the DS, I thought. I knew that there was no way they would be remanded in custody based upon the evidence obtained. That Monday morning, the PF contacted the DS to discuss the evidence of the case, or lack of it. It was decided that at a push they would be able to remand Wilma and Humphrey for seven days to give the police more time to collate evidence.

Humphrey was to stand in an identification parade with residents from the street where the attack had taken place. They were brought along in the hope that one of them would identify him as a murderer. Suffice to say that the parade was a shambles and no one picked Humphrey out. The case was looking dire, to say the least. After the seven days given by the PF, Humphrey was released on bail and Wilma was remanded for her part of the conspiracy. After a few weeks, Wilma's lawyer managed to get her bailed too.

In effect, Mick was dead and no one was being held responsible for it. Goes to show just how poor the policing skills were. Perhaps more could have been done to prevent it, but it wasn't. After about a year, the case was called to court.

All four accused stood side by side in the dock. Humphrey was accused of murder, Wilma, Todd and Jason on trial for conspiracy to commit murder.

No sooner had the trial started than the cases against Todd and Jason collapsed. Leaving the prosecution with the opportunity of using them as witnesses against the other two. However, even this did no good as eventually, a jury returned a not proven verdict against Humphrey. He was a free man. He laughed as he was led down from the dock. He had escaped without true justice.

Wilma, on the other hand, was found guilty of her crime of conspiracy to commit murder and ordered to spend eighteen months in prison. She was released after nine months. Meanwhile, Mick's beloved partner had been sentenced to a life without the man she loved.

In truth, the events portrayed here did happen. The detail is my recollection but more alarming is the fact that yet again as a Divisional HQ for the Police we failed to see justice served. It's frustrating for those involved in the investigation but the odds are certainly stacked in favour of criminals. A reality check for us all when we consider that another human being was killed because of the hatred felt towards him. I do not believe that Wilma intended for that to happen to Mick. She did wish him roughed up a little.

However, sometimes events take a horrid turn for the worst when we least expect them to. This was one incident where that did happen and the only person who truly paid for it was the partner of the deceased. Our judicial system let her down badly. In addition, perhaps the female DS could have done more during the initial part of the case as opposed to failing to obtain more robust evidence in order to secure a conviction for murder.

Rest in peace, Mick!

Chapter 10
Volvo

Having attempted to move on due to the various events, I managed to put on a brave front at work. Only Carmen knew how I felt regarding the way in which the police had treated me during the Albie case. I was struggling to deal with the betrayal felt against those involved within the police but I put it to the back of my mind and made myself busier than ever at work. This was a good distraction, but I was beginning to wonder why I remained in the profession.

I was still working at Baird Street at this point and I had a DI I didn't get on with as I never did become part of his clique, but he was still my boss. I detested the way he used to speak to those of us not in his clique.

However, I wasn't afraid of him, nor did I give a shit what he thought about me as I was a good worker and no one could take that away from me. I had been moved onto another group away from Drew and Ross, due in part to the huge sums of money we had earned whilst in partnership. Although this wasn't the reason given by the DI as to why I was being moved. It was merely supposed to be for career development, but alas, the 'old boys' network was far too big for me to argue with!

The guys on the other shift were good to work with and I already knew Trigger from the Kirkintilloch murder. I decided that I would do what was required of me but secretly, I hated the new team and wasn't happy there. Within one month of my move to the new shift, I was taken into the DI's room, as he wanted to speak to me.

He told me that I was being moved back to Easterhouse police office in order to facilitate another guy who had just been appointed as a detective. Sometimes that happened and detectives were often moved around but I just had to accept it. Ian had completed his Aid to the CID several years before me but had never been appointed due to the lack of help and guidance he received during his traineeship. His boss at that time another DI and he detested Ian.

The job is so fickle when it comes to these types of situations and in all honesty, if a boss takes exception to a cop then it's a no-win situation. Now that the DI had moved on, Ian had managed to get what he wanted, a full-time position.

In fairness, I was delighted for him but at the same time I was annoyed that I had to move to a new area to suit the current DI. He had won, as he always wanted to get rid of me because of his dislike of me. I bit my tongue and didn't show my annoyance and just laughed.

When he asked me why I was laughing, I told him that I couldn't wait to move to another office to get away from the area I had been in for most of my service. He never said anything else to me and just told me to get out of his office. We both knew that I was saying that I couldn't wait to get away from his self-adoring conceited way.

I settled in well into my new role although whilst there, I was busier than I had ever been dealing with a range of robberies and serious assaults which were happening on a daily basis. I was becoming a master at these types of investigations and nothing shocked me. The team of colleagues there was mixed, Catholic and Protestant. This was the first time I had never experienced the continuous barrage of jibes regarding the great Celtic-Rangers divide and how the "Tims" were in the minority in that particular office and the reason for that was quite simple, we were in the minority because that was the way it should be.

Quite dismayed at this clearly outrageous attitude by my new colleagues, I didn't rise to the bait and took it upon myself to ridicule the fact that the main reason they were working out of Easterhouse police office was down to the reason of their incompetence as police officers. Although this was a bit of contradiction in terms as I was now working out of that office too but for different reasons—because the DI didn't like me! This didn't go down well and I was being ostracised because of my comments.

I really didn't give a shit, as I had to listen to the half-wits walking around the office whistling the 'sash' and 'follow follow'. To add insult to injury, I also had to listen to them whispering behind my back about their usual Thursday night Masonic meeting. I felt so alone, isolated and annoyed but there was no way I was going to give in to the bad element in my new workplace.

I kept my head down and worked as hard as I could and put to the back of my mind that I was now working with a crowd of religious bigots. Within a couple of months there was a huge difference in the office and finally, several other Detectives had been transferred there. Some of the masonic bigots had been moved onto different offices as part of a major amalgamation with Glasgow East, or "E" division as it was known.

The shake-up was part of the reshuffle of the police and was intended to make the areas 'super divisions' that could provide a better service to the public. The real story was that the detective superintendents were now responsible for larger areas, thereby piling more pressure onto the rest of us mere mortals as they would become more stressed and take their frustrations out on their staff.

There was at last real harmony within the CID office and the environment was a more relaxed place to be in. The morning routine at work consisted of having coffee and toast or even a proper breakfast courtesy of the terrific cleaning staff who looked after us very well. All in all, it was a totally different office and was now one where all of the detectives working there were happier than they had been in a long time.

Even the DI was approachable, coupled with the arrival of Ross; he was to be my DS again. There was also a female there called Carole whom I had worked with off and on during other investigations and in real terms, we actually got on really well.

One Tuesday morning, I started work as normal at Easterhouse. I had just sat down to my usual tea and toast when I was instructed to head down to Baird Street with Carole, as there had been a murder. The victim was a thirty-year-old female who had been thrown from an eleventh floor window in the Royston area and a male was already in custody. Our job was to be productions officers and as I had previous experience in that field, it was thought that I would be the ideal person to do it again.

I was pleased to be given the responsibility and the idea that Carole would be my partner was also great. Off we went down to Baird Street to speak with the DCI to be informed of the circumstances of Liz's death. Only brief details were known and Carole and I were told that we had to keep the information private, due to the nature of the death.

The information suggested that Liz, who was allegedly lesbian, had invited two men into her house for a drinking party involving the three of them. The party had gone on most of the night resulting in one of the men falling asleep.

Liz felt safe in their company as they were homosexuals and one of them was her friend. The other guy became aggressive and all that was known at this point was that neighbours had heard shouting coming from the flat, but this had died down as the evening progressed. In a fit of rage, Liz had been assaulted and eventually, she fell from the eleventh-floor window. No other details concerning injuries were known, but the two men who had been at her house walked past her body in order to make a quick exit from the scene.

An observant member of the concierge, who was night shift, saw them walking towards a nearby car and noted the registration number. After the body had been discovered and the police attended the scene, all police officers in the area started to look for the car. Night shift officers from Cranhill found the car in an industrial estate and when they went to investigate, found that both male occupants were having anal sex.

Both of them were arrested for a Breach of the Peace, which meant that if one of the men had murdered Liz, then they were already in custody. At least there could be no doubting any of the forensic evidence, which could be obtained, as this was only about an hour after the discovery of Liz's body.

Obviously, there was a huge amount of work to be done regarding the case. In particular there was still the small matter of how she had died. The only visible injury noted by ambulance staff was that her ankle was badly broken on the fall and her anklebone had burst through her skin. The only mark on her face was a slight bruise and a scratch.

Quite surprising really when one considers that she fell about one hundred feet to her death. As Carole and I had been allocated the production task, this meant that we would be required to be present at the PM.

Not a nice prospect, but nonetheless, I had already been experienced in that department, but much to my surprise, this was to be Carole's first one. She had more police service than I, but perhaps I was just the unfortunate one who had been chosen on several occasions to be a regular Dr Death and attend PMs!

Having organised ourselves with the array of bags and labels required for our task at the mortuary, we left the office to make our way down into Glasgow City Centre where the mortuary is situated. From the outside, it looks just like any other building in the Saltmarket area, although it is eerily chilling inside. There is even a smell of cleaning fluid, not unlike that noticed in hospitals, although it seems more unpleasant, or perhaps that is a psychological thing!

Knowing that we had about an hour to kill before the PM was about to begin, I decided that in the interests of our tummies, we would go to Café Gandolfi in the Merchant City. Carole assured me that she couldn't face the prospect of coffee!

I told her that it would probably be the last thing she would eat that day. And so we settled into our regular seats in the café, as this was a favoured haunt of the CID both during and after work hours. As we consumed the toasted scone and sipped the delicious coffee, Carole opened her heart about her fears of the PM.

Trying to persuade her that it would be fine was proving a difficult task, such were her misgivings. "Dale, I should tell you though, I'm wearing a black bra and red knickers today. Trust me not to be colour-coordinated today!"

Looking bemused, I thanked her very kindly for sharing that fact with me and told her that I would be thinking fondly of that during the PM. I couldn't contain my laughter though, as I wondered why she had told me that piece of information in the first place!

With a look of pure innocence, she told me that no doubt I would have found that out during the PM when she slipped on her gown and mask. My laughter was now uncontrollable and tears flowed down my face. I couldn't speak to her for what seemed like ages and by now, her face was crimson with rage. I eventually calmed down sufficiently enough to inform her that when she put on the gown, which tied at the back, she could keep her own clothes on as that is what the doctors would be doing.

She burst out laughing on realising that she had shared her intimate wardrobe malfunction with me for nothing. After all, I wouldn't be taking my clothes off, only putting a gown on top of my work clothes. At least the mood was lightened, but every time I looked at her, I imagined her taking her clothes off and walking out into the PM area with her underwear on view. Perhaps I should have let her carry on without telling her the truth! I'm sure she would have seen the funny side of things and I promised never to tell any of the troops about Carole's Freudian slip!

Liz had been formerly identified by her family members, which meant that at least the PM could commence. We gathered in the room awaiting the arrival of the two female pathologists to begin the job. The DS, DCI, Carole and I all stood back to allow the pathologists to do their job, assisted by the mortician assistant.

Seeing the naked body of Liz lying there was a sobering thought; only the day before she was enjoying her life, now she was the subject of a murder investigation, only problem was, she was the subject of the scrutiny. At first, the pathologists noted and measured the injuries on her body and the attending photographer then photographed these. He was as close as the doctors were. He had to ensure that for court purposes, he had sufficient photographic evidence to prove to the court that what was being spoken about was in fact the truth.

Carole and I stood well back preparing some of the labels, as I knew in advance what would be seized for evidential purposes. The worst part of the PM process for me is the cutting of the body like the ribcage or skull and when some of the organs are moved or handled, that is when the smell appears. It is not pleasant, to say the least, but at least I was used to it; Carole still had that to face. The main part of the PM involving the body and internal organ area passed quite quickly and it was looking fine for us, as we were well prepared for the productions.

One of the pathologists had mentioned early on that she had grave concerns about the privates of the deceased and was of the opinion that there had been severe sexual activity prior to death. Not-consented sex but more like a case of deep painful torture. For at least 2 hours both, pathologists examined the vagina and anal areas of the deceased.

Such were her injuries it was suspected that items possibly resembling juice bottles or even pool cues had been inserted in these regions. She had been raped and sodomised by the murderer. What seemed like a fall or push from a flat was now turning into a very gory grisly death.

The extent of the injuries sustained by Liz meant that the pathologists were hoping to have her examined by a sex expert, specialising in crimes of a sexual nature. I knew that what had happened in that flat must have been horrific for the poor victim. In essence, perhaps, she actually opened the window to flee from her attacker.

Jumping to her death must have been the only other option available to her. Or indeed, there was still the possibility that she had been thrown out of the window. Either way, I'm sure that her death was a blessing to her, due to the extent of the abuse she suffered at his hands. The bosses were dismayed at the injuries and were adamant that they would do everything in their power to lock up the man, or men responsible. At least they had the two men who had been with her prior to her death. Surely they would be able to provide answers to the questions. There was more than enough DNA evidence, so that would be a start.

After ten hours at the PM, we were all shattered and that was without even having lodged any of the productions seized. Meanwhile, the detectives carrying out the investigation at the office had other news for the bosses. Apparently, whilst Liz lay dead at the bottom of the block of flats, as well as the two arrested suspects having walked past her, so did a local resident who was in fact a doctor at a nearby hospital.

Doesn't really say much about any care a sick person would receive from him if he could walk past a dead body without noticing it. One of the men who had been arrested was Liz's friend and he stuck to his story that he didn't know anything about what had taken place as he was sleeping. This tended to contradict the evidence of the pathologists who stated that the extent of the injuries were such that the victim would have been screaming in pain due to the horrendous injuries inflicted on her. Unless, of course, she had been gagged.

This guy had also told detectives that after they had left the flat, they walked past Liz's body and the other guy, John, had told him that she had jumped out of the window. He stated that he had no reason to doubt the story given by his boyfriend. They drove away from the Royston area and were making their way to Easterhouse when John told him to drive to an industrial estate so that they could have sex. John couldn't wait to have sex, hence the suggestion about doing it outside.

They had full penetrative sex in the rear of the van and when this guy was medically examined, he was found to have extensive anal ruptures caused by the sex and gave the doctor an indication of the type of monster they were dealing with. Even the doctor examining both men was aghast at the injuries Paul had sustained as a result of anal sex, although Paul was a practicing homosexual, according to what the doctor had witnessed, he stressed that his anus was severely damaged.

Even when John was examined, being such a deviant, he had an erection and seemed genuinely pleased to have swabs taken from his penis and other internal areas. He maintained his innocence and refused to be drawn into the idea that Liz had been sexually abused and thrown from the window. Indeed, he was a cold calculating manipulative man who would stop at nothing to be released from police custody.

A decision had to be made regarding his status. Was he to be released or was he to be kept in custody with Paul? Further information came to light that dramatically changed the format of the case. It would seem that over twenty years prior to this incident, John had been an outpatient at Gartloch Mental Hospital; he had befriended a female who was also a patient there.

She disappeared and to this date, her body has never been found and the assumption being she was murdered by this man. Without a body, it was difficult to pursue the matter in those days and as he had been found to be insane, nothing could happen to him. Many years later, here he was now in a similar situation in that he was a suspect in another murder.

What was required was a DNA link identifying John as having had sexual relations with Liz. He had denied that they had sex so this was a very important fact. Awaiting forensic test results could take at least two days so, therefore, the police needed more time to investigate the murder. A decision was made to charge John and Paul with Liz's death and keep them in custody based on a circumstantial case. The DS was going to have to plead with the PF to keep them both in custody for at least seven days to await the other vital results.

Luckily, that was what happened and the police awaited with avid anticipation the results. The forensic team worked tirelessly to ascertain what took place and luckily they found traces of Liz's DNA on the window, as well as John's which suggested that they were at the window together, another fact denied by him. DNA evidence was found on various bottles and a piece of wooden pole, confirming that these objects had been inserted inside her.

John's fingerprints were also on these objects, although that wasn't conclusive as he could have said that he touched them during his time in the house. At last the DNA results confirmed that John did have sexual relations with Liz, the case was looking better.

Meanwhile, Paul and John had been kept on remand for seven days to allow the police to do further investigation and they were kept in different jails. John had been kept on the same wing as other guys awaiting trial on charges of theft and perhaps housebreaking. It didn't seem right that they had to share the same facilities as a murderer.

However, this was the way it had to be and John shared a cell with another guy, Gary who was a car thief. After two days of sharing, Gary contacted the prison bosses requesting to be moved, as he was fearful for his safety. He asked to speak to detectives working on the murder investigation as he had "something to tell".

Two detectives arrived at the prison and Gary burst into tears as he told them what had happened. During their first night together alone in the cell, John had told Gary that he was going to shag him as he liked his men young. The twenty-year-old was terrified and tried to remain awake all night to prevent falling into his clutches.

John told him about the murder allegations and how he abused Liz and forced her out of the window to her death. Gary was terrified and wanted as far away from him as possible. I cannot divulge the extent of the sickening acts carried out by him but it was truly the work of a sex-depraved animal.

Gary attempted to stay awake in the bottom bunk and eventually had to give in to tiredness. He fell asleep and hoped that he would be okay. When he awoke a short time later, John was performing a sex act on him and John had blocked the spy hole in the cell door used for viewing by the prison staff, with paper. Gary was shouting at John and pushing him away, yet John still tried to force Gary to lie there whilst he performed the sex act.

Gary managed to press the alarm within the cell and eventually, the prison staff arrived, much to the amusement of John. Gary never told the prison staff anything about what had taken place. He just said that John had threatened to kill him and he believed this could take place.

The staff knew that there was perhaps another reason and indulged Gary in his feeble excuse for a move. He was removed from that cell and placed onto another wing within the prison. At last the police had the statement of a witness who was prepared to tell the truth about Liz's death.

The seven-day deadline approached and armed with the new evidence, the bosses went to the PF and eventually it was decided to keep Paul and John in custody until the trial within one hundred and ten days, the normal time scale for petition cases.

A sigh of relief went around the police office and everyone was delighted that we had enough evidence in which to pursue John for the murder. Not long afterwards a lawyer's letter was received on John's behalf stating that he was being treated by psychiatrists and it was looking likely that he would be found to be unfit to plead at court.

It was generally felt by all those attached to the case that John was utilising the mental issues as his get out of jail card. About three months later, the trial date arrived and John's legal team argued the case that he was unfit to plead but the trial nonetheless went ahead and he was found guilty of Liz's murder. However, due to the extensive psychiatric reports received by the judge, he had no option but to sentence him to be detained without limit of time within Carstairs Mental Institution.

Although Liz's family was pleased, what they didn't realise was that he could technically be released after several years if he is found to be "cured", or at least sane. Not exactly a great outcome as opposed to being kept incarcerated for life within a mainstream prison. But I suppose that is what the legal system is all about, ensuring that justice is done!

What about justice for Liz, did she get that? The murder of Liz was probably one of the most horrific cases I ever worked and having endured the PM only to find that the murderer managed to have himself admitted to a psychiatric unit seemed unfair although his actions that night were not normal behaviour so I guess the right conclusion was reached.

Meanwhile, it was business as usual on crime-street and the crimes committed, in the schemes continued. Murder after murder, attempted murder, serious assaults and robberies were commonplace in a society doomed for failure. The bosses were asking questions about how we as an organisation could integrate with the communities to prevent serious crime from escalating.

The only way in which that would happen would have been to build a twenty-foot wall around 'E' division to keep the criminals in and allow the decent members of society to live their lives in peace. However, we all know that that was never going to happen and so the bosses in their infinite wisdom decided that the best way to tackle these problems was to have pro-active units tackle the criminals.

All they needed now was experienced detectives to run these units and take the political heat off the bosses as the Chief Constable was attempting to reduce the fear element among members of the public. Local councillors were putting pressure on the police hierarchy to reduce the fear of crime and this seemed like a good, reasonable response. Whether it worked or not would remain to be seen!

I managed to avoid the confrontational approaches the bosses made to some of the cops to try to get them to go into the unit in the first place. However, after about a week, the plug was pulled and it was decided that this wasn't the best time to commence a high profile operation. There was a huge sigh of relief and us mere detectives got on with doing the job as best we could.

We were being inundated with enquiries and staff morale was at an all-time low due to the lack of cover during the shifts. It was still very common for detectives to be taken away from the different sub-divisions so that they could provide other cover to areas outside our own.

One morning I was taken into the office by the DCI and told that I was to head up a new proactive unit. I was to be answerable to the DI and account for the running of the unit and ensure that we got the required results. I turned it down telling him that I didn't want to do that role again as I was still struggling with the Albie incident. I didn't know if I wanted this extra burden on me at this time.

He casually told me that the FAI was nothing to be annoyed about and that this was my stepping stone to promotion and with nine years' service. I asked him if I could think about it and he told me that it wasn't open to any suggestion from me, I would simply be ordered to do it if I refused. In other words, I was being forced into running this unit against my will. I was to be responsible for five staff but I didn't outrank any of them.

I had less service than two of them and I knew that I would be resented for trying to play the "I'm a gaffer" card. I knew that it wouldn't have made the least bit of difference whether I stamped my feet and cried that I wasn't going to do it, as the reality of it was I had no option. I was being bullied into accepting this shite job no one else wanted.

I did tell the DCI my feelings but I agreed that, if I were being forced to do it I would have no option but to get on with it. He was genuinely sorry for my predicament but sympathised and told me that it was the Divisional Commander who had requested I do it. Not that it made the slightest bit of difference. I knew that this was my last day at Easterhouse for a while.

I commenced my new role within about three days of being told. The only plus side to the role was that I had good shifts, no night shift, plenty of overtime and I was back at my old base within Baird Street. The rest of the team I had never worked with before. I knew that it would be a challenge as the oldest and most senior in service was a guy called Eddy.

I knew he resented the fact that I was young in service, and a detective. He viewed this opportunity for me as being a stepping stone although I had never publicly told anyone about the DCI's comments to me to that effect. Sean was a transferee from another Force and had more service also but I seemed to get on well with him as the weeks progressed.

The female cops included Caroline and although I didn't know her then, I would gradually learn that she was a very good cop and capable of doing a good job, despite her three years' police service. Then lastly, there was Mandy. I still, to this day, have no idea how she managed to even get into the police. She was scatty and unknown to me at that time, had serious mental health issues. I suppose on the whole, the team showed a range of experience and ability. No doubt time would be our test!

Within our first month, we were inundated with requests for help by different departments within the police as they all tried their best to get us work to concentrate on. Not that we needed any help as already there had been a steady stream of arrests through the back door of the office by the team. The DI asked that we concentrate on car crime as it was a major problem in the Springburn area. Within a few days, we had locked up the main man responsible and he admitted to twenty thefts from cars as well as several thefts of cars form our area.

The bosses were delighted and the very idea that we, as a team, had done it all ourselves was great for our morale. I interviewed Bud, Eddy wanted to do the case and this showed me that I needed someone with his conviction to help me out with complex cases. Compiling reports of that nature requires the type of dedication to fact that normally detectives have, although Eddy wasn't a detective, he would have been a great one.

After having interviewed Bud, he told me that there was another guy who was also as busy as him and if I let him out, he would tell me his name. I wouldn't normally do the dirty on criminals in this way by agreeing to false promises; however, on this occasion I knew that it would be out of my hands as the decision to keep him custody would rest with the DI.

I allowed Bud to tell me the name of the other guy and then the DI told him that he was going into custody due to the high number of crimes involved. We all felt sorry for him but knew the boss was right. If we allowed him the chance of leaving the office, he would simply keep stealing and this would mean the crime figures would hit the roof again. To think that all Bud wanted was to sell the goods on to buy heroin, I suppose we did him a favour by keeping him in custody.

Once we had cleared up the paperwork relating to Bud, we set out to arrest the other target, Wullie. This was the same guy I had previously chased in a stolen car on the night of the Albie death. I knew who he was and decided it best to keep out of the way; fearing if he saw me, I would scare him off. Within an hour of leaving the office, Eddy and Sean phoned me to say that they had arrested Wullie at his home. We would never have found him without the help and cooperation of the local housing department who kept us informed of the whereabouts of criminals when we requested it.

Also within his house was a whole cache of stolen goods from a housebreaking, which had not even been reported to the police yet. The poor householder was on holiday and had no idea that her house had been broken into. This was a significant capture as Wullie turned his hand to anything, in order to feed his one hundred-pound a day heroin habit. He admitted to about ten thefts from cars, ten thefts of cars and about six housebreakings.

Obviously, he assumed that by admitting to these crimes, he would be allowed free, but we had to do the same with him and boy, was he pissed off! Sean grabbed the chance of reporting this case and I was happy with my team of cops doing a great job. Obviously, this also meant that the bosses were delighted with the team and heaped praise on us at every opportunity. I was on first-name terms with the uniformed superintendent and his deputy, the chief inspector. They knew that it would cost a lot of money in overtime, but it was worth it to decrease the crime figures and this was what they wanted.

Meanwhile, we were alienating ourselves from the rest of the proactive teams in the division as we had done remarkably well so early on. They were still playing catch up but we didn't care; we just worked as hard as we could. The measure of a good cop is based upon his ability to cope under pressure. So far, we had limited scope to test these levels as we were merely kicking in doors and attempting to obtain good results to keep the bosses happy.

Our specific remit was to reduce the supply of drugs in and around our whole division, which meant that on occasion, we would have to help out the other units should our services be required. London Road unit was the first to call upon the services of all of the units in order to carry out a drug operation in the East End of Glasgow.

We all turned up for duty, all fifteen of us and along with other uniformed cops, we carried out various house searches. We didn't actually seize any drugs but the unit had worked hard and secured evidence through the use of "Test Purchasers".

These were specially trained officers from the Strathclyde area whose remit was to infiltrate known drug dealers and each time they scored drugs, this would count as a charge against the individual drug dealer. On paper it is a very good option, but personally, our team wasn't interested in that particular way of getting results.

The London Road team had good charges against several dealers so I suppose it worked for them. What I thought about was the very idea that we had assisted them so they in turn would have to render assistance to us when we needed it. I already had the ideal location in mind but all that was needed was the opportunity of do some digging of our own to create enough information to convince the bosses that it would be worthwhile.

I knew that it would take us a while to do, but it would be worth it just to close down the particular operation. Going back to the ability to cope under pressure, we had done a fair amount of varied work but so far we remained untested. This was always on our minds and I felt that the unit lacked some commitment.

There was a strange split appearing early on in the team due to Eddy's resentment at me calling the shots for the team. He did say on several occasions that I "flew by the seat of my pants".

A term used to project the idea that I craved danger and didn't exactly carry out the plainclothes job according to the police guidelines. My argument was that we didn't need rules and regulations to tell us how to search a house, we needed luck and good judgement to decide when and where a search should take place.

One night, whilst patrolling the Royston area of Glasgow, Sean, who was driving our unmarked police car, noticed a brown Volvo going through a red traffic light and almost collided with an oncoming car. Sean decided in his infinite wisdom to follow the car and so began a car chase through Royston and then along the M80 in the Stirling direction. What was I saying about ability to cope under pressure?

The Volvo car had four occupants inside and the driver drove at speeds in excess of one hundred miles per hour. The reason I know this is that Sean was driving at between eighty and ninety miles per hour and we were still not even remotely close to him. To be able to drive in a car chase is difficult enough but when one doesn't know the roads being driven on, it makes that task much scarier for the driver.

I updated the control room via the radio, as I knew where we were going as well as knowing the roads so the attending traffic cars were being kept updated of our whereabouts. The Volvo took us along back roads leading to the Lenzie area and these roads are especially tricky as they run alongside farmer's fields with some particularly bad slopes alongside them.

My heart was in my mouth as Sean tried his utmost to keep up with offending car and we watched as it eventually turned into a side road in Lenzie and came to a halt at the dead end leading on to a huge field. Sean had truly done a remarkable job and I knew then that he was a calm individual as he had managed well under difficult conditions.

The driver of the car made off, as did the occupants but the attending dog van managed to capture three of them within a short time. The driver made good his escape through the field and into the night. The Volvo was owned by a man from the East End of Glasgow and the occupants identified him as being the driver.

He was disqualified from driving and therefore had no driving documents, hence the reason for him driving like a bat out of hell to get away from us as it would have meant that he would have been kept in custody for these offences. The other occupants gave us detailed statements and a warrant was craved for his arrest.

The Volvo meanwhile was taken back to Baird Street awaiting its owner to reclaim it. After about a week, he still didn't show up at the office and we remained in charge of it pending its removal. The duty officer asked us to lodge the car through the property books in the normal manner and as there was no room for it in the locked area within the police car park, it remained parked in a bay with the keys being easily accessible by us if required.

It gave me an idea that perhaps the car could be used by us when doing searches as it would enable us to drive it closer to these target houses without being recognised. This however should not have been done and the bosses would have thrown us out of the unit had we been caught. Within a couple of weeks, it was decided that the car would be used on one particular operation as Caroline and Mandy had set up a meeting with a drug dealer, to buy an eighth of an ounce of heroin to keep us all legal and above board, I spoke with the DI we reported to and he said that we could use it for undercover work. Although I knew he would deny telling us this, we all noted it in our police notebooks "just in case".

Mandy had phoned the guy telling him that another friend, a drug addict from one of the schemes, had recommended him and the guy agreed to meet them. As it was raining, we decided that we would try and use the Volvo to drop the girls off, as using one of the unmarked cars would have ruined the operation completely.

Having managed to obtain the keys from the duty officer, one of the team drove the girls towards the area for the meet but at the last minute, the girls backed out, as they were concerned for their safety. On returning to the office and telling me that they had changed their minds, I accepted this and told them that he would come again.

The Volvo had come in handy though and we decided that it could be used again later that night if necessary. Shortly after they returned to the office, a telephone call was received form an anonymous caller that a target of ours was selling heroin and that his house was busier than it had ever been. We had a dedicated phone line that we passed to informants to leave messages on the answer machine. Our office was always locked and we were the only ones with the door code to enter as we had changed it not long after the unit started. We even cleaned the office ourselves and emptied the bins as we didn't want the cleaners rummaging around the area.

It was decided that we should hit the house as soon as possible and off we all set to try to get our man. Being within the Volvo seemed so wrong but it was a good compromise. It worked a treat and remained parked right outside the house during the search.

Mandy and Eddy had managed to gain access to the controlled entry door system and even bought a bag of Heroin from the dealer. Whilst they were engaged in the deal at his door, the rest of us piled in and grabbed all of the evidence out of his hand. He was locked up in possession of a large amount of heroin and appeared in custody the next day on drug supply offences.

The Volvo meanwhile was returned to its normal position in the carpark of the police yard and the keys were returned to the safe. All bosses blissfully unaware of its use to the proactive unit!

What shocked me the next day was that the drug dealer was released on bail from court and went straight back to selling heroin that very night! When I heard this, I was livid and set out to arrest him again. This was quite a common occurrence and annoyed us immensely. We worked very hard to lock up the dealers and the Procurator Fiscal would let them out the next day. It was so frustrating and we always felt that the criminals would be laughing their asses off at us.

That night, using the Volvo as our transport, I called at the house in question with Sean and managed to gain access to the close, as the front door was lying open. I knocked on the door and a female answered it and asked me what I wanted. I barged into the house and entered the living room.

There was the dealer rolling up a joint of cannabis and he pissed himself when he saw me standing in the middle of his floor. I kid you not; the dirty bastard pissed his pants right on the spot. I laughed my head off at him and engaged him in trivial conversation. The female was ranting and raving at me for walking into the house without a warrant but she was soon silenced when I reminded her that it was in her best interests to shut the fuck up or else she would be arrested for obstructing me.

All was calm and quiet and I could sense the Ned was nervous. Always a good indication that there was drugs in the house. I decided to ask him if there were any drugs in the house but he assured me that there was none and he had seen the error of his ways. I looked over at the fireplace and there, in its resplendent glory was a large bag of uncut heroin as well as about twenty smaller bags of wrapped Heroin sitting beside it.

This was a volatile situation to be in as there was only Sean and I in the house with this mad drug dealer and his obnoxious girlfriend. I wasn't sure if Sean had seen the drugs but I just let my instincts take over and grabbed hold of the Ned and cuffed him. He tried to lash out at me with his feet but I was too strong for him. The guy started to shout at his burd to get rid of the drugs and immediately, she lunged forwards to grab them only for Sean to cuff her and throw her on the floor.

We had them under control and using my mobile, I contacted the rest of the team asking them to assist us. The first thing needed was a retrospective warrant to search the house. What we had done was unconventional, but not out with our police power. This warrant would cover us to carry out the search legally. All in all, it was a good show of solidarity and again I knew that Sean was a cop I could rely on in any situation. The fact that the door was open allowed us to gain entry and as soon as I saw the Ned rolling the joint of cannabis I immediately cautioned him as normal and that allowed me to place him under arrest. The real reason for the visit was to warm him that he shouldn't be dealing but here he was ignoring the fact that he was already on bail for dealing.

I was happy with this and knew that we had coped very well under the circumstances. Eddy was furious and again reiterated his feelings that we were not doing the job properly. I bit my tongue and put it down to his moods. After all, it was Sean and I who had been in the situation and we were happy with the outcome and knew that it had probably brought us closer together in understanding terms as a result of the incident.

It wasn't for Eddy to voice his distrust of how we should conduct searches. After all, regardless of what happened within that house, the Ned ended up receiving five years in prison for drug offences so at least the night was a success!

After that night, Eddy's whole attitude started to change and he was alienating himself from the rest of the team. I tried to speak to him about it but he didn't want to discuss anything with me and I suggested that he speak to the Superintendent if he wasn't happy with the way in which the unit was being operated.

Mandy meanwhile started turning up late for work and her appearance became very shabby and dirty. I spoke to the others about her time-keeping and they laughed saying something about her lack of interest in life and perhaps she would try and do away with herself again.

I was puzzled about that comment and so began a long conversation with the rest of the team who told me that about one year prior to the unit coming together, Mandy had attempted suicide. I was furious as I felt that she should never have been put forward for the role within the unit due to its demanding nature.

They all assumed that the bosses had told me before we started working together. I stormed off to speak with one of the bosses and managed to grab hold of the Chief Inspector who told me the story behind her illness.

I asked why she had been put into the unit and was told that the bosses thought that the unit would be good for her recovery. I disagreed and told him that I wanted her and Eddy out as they were turning the unit against me.

The next week, I got my request and in return I received Ian as Eddy's replacement and Pauline as a replacement for Mandy. The latter replacement I wasn't too happy about as she was the daughter of the deputy chief constable and had very little practical experience to do the job.

However, when I voiced my concerns about her ability, I was told by the boss that this was a stepping stone for her and was necessary for her own police CV. In effect, I had to train her and her reward would be a promotion. I knew I was being used but could do nothing about it, as it was what the bosses wanted. Anyhow, who could argue with the Deputy Chief Constable? I previously mentioned this during the Nepotism chapter and briefly spoke about her in that.

I had mentioned this earlier when I discussed nepotism within the police. The new make-up of the unit was relaxed and felt more comfortable than it had done in ages. The addition of Ian was a breath of fresh air and despite my initial reservations, Pauline was proving to be an asset to the team. We decided that we would use the Volvo only when it was desperately needed.

This day arrived soon after their arrival and we used it to try to get access to another area in Springburn. Whilst en route there, the Volvo broke down next to a notorious gangster pub. The driver phoned me right away and we had to tow the Volvo back to the office using one of our unmarked cars and a towrope.

Luckily, no one saw us from the police office and the car was parked for the last time in its parking bay. The car had done its job and perhaps this was the final push we needed to do the job using whatever tools the police gave us as opposed to having to improvise!

The unit went from strength from strength and our success was well known throughout the division. I never felt that there was ever any animosity between any of the other teams and we all had our own way of doing the job. I knew that I would have to call on their services as we had done all of the groundwork to enable us to obtain a search warrant for a public house premises, where it was known that heroin was being sold in large quantities.

Having spoken to the boss about the search, he was keen to assist as far as possible. All that I needed now was for additional troops to help with the search. Having enlisted the help of the other units, I knew that I needed more assistance. I contacted the Support Unit, who agreed to provide twenty officers to do the search.

I was delighted and arranged for them to attend at the office on the day of the search so that I could carry out a briefing of what was expected. In all, there was forty officers involved in the search and after I conducted the briefing, all that we had to do was wait on Sean giving us the okay to start the search.

He was pitched about two hundred feet above the ground on top of a multistorey block of flats, which afforded him a direct view of the pub. About half past two in the afternoon, Sean phoned to say that the target had arrived at the pub.

We all left the office and sped towards the pub and I stood back whilst the uniformed Support Unit arrived and ran into the pub. By the time I got in there, they had all twelve patrons of the pub cuffed and ready to start the search. One particular male standing at the bar had pissed himself when the police arrived through the door. A search of his jacket revealed an ounce of heroin worth about three and a half thousand pounds. I know that I have mentioned on numerous occasions about people pissing themselves. These are genuine cases where it has happened. It is obviously a clear indication that they have something to hide. It is more commonplace that you would even care to imagine and almost every case I say, it was a man.

We got our result, but this guy wasn't the target. The target stood smirking, knowing that he was clean. The search took about an hour thanks to the excellent job the support officers did. This was reassuring as it proved how well various sections within the police could come together and work as part of a bigger team.

It helped that I knew some of the officers from the support unit and they were only too pleased to help! The main target was arrested and taken to the office as well as the other guy whose jacket contained the drugs. On being interviewed, the guy made no comment in relation to the drugs and he was charged with supplying a class 'A' substance.

However, he told me off tape that the drugs belonged to our target and that he had to sell them for him as he owed him money and he was frightened that if he refused, he would have been beaten to a pulp. The sad thing being, I believed him.

The target was released, as we had nothing to pin on him. The poor guy who owed the money ended up serving three years in prison. And what of the main target? He still sells drugs for a living and lives in a shithole he calls home.

During our many tours of duty, we collated plenty of information regarding the movements of many drug dealers in our area. Sometimes the information would be accurate, other times we would receive information that was just rubbish. We had to make a judgement call in relation to what we treated as correct and what we disregarded.

One particular piece of information came from a female addict who was so disgusted with her life that she was determined to go on the straight and narrow road to a healthy lifestyle. She was waiting on a placement at a drug rehabilitation centre and promised to keep us updated of drug dealers in our area.

She liaised with Caroline and Pauline and gave us many pieces of information regarding drug dealers that led to significant arrests for our team. On one occasion, she told Caroline about a man who lived in the Springburn area who would sell large amounts of heroin from inside a local bookmakers. He would carry the drugs around secreted in his underpants. As he was a fat bastard, there wasn't much notice given to his bulging packet, as he was too fat for anyone to care.

This was one of the times that we thought the information was crap, but what stopped us from this thought was the very fact that her information was normally accurate. So began a six-week expedition for us to try to identify the man. Having made enquiries with other addicts in the area, we learned that he stayed in a new housing estate and he was called "RFC".

Those remotely interested in football in the Glasgow area can testify that he was obviously a Rangers fan. Still, we had to try and ascertain who he was without knowing his name. Even police records proved negative which tended to suggest that he had never been in trouble with the police, or at least our records showed nothing about a man's nickname with those initials.

Again, another addict told us that he worked in a nearby factory during the day and that he also stashed drugs there. Armed with this piece of advice, I took it upon myself to arrange an interview with the managing director of the company.

The day of the interview came and I still didn't know how I was going to ask if the manager knew whom this employee could be, but I decided that I would just tell him what I knew to see if he could help. Midway through me explaining what I knew, he laughed and told me that he had suspicions about two members of his staff. He told me who they were and then I asked him for their addresses, as I knew that he lived across the road from the factory.

He found out the information and sure enough, one of the men who the manager suspected, stayed in the estate opposite. I was delighted at the responsible way in which the company had dealt with this sensitive issue, and I was assured that they would leave me to do my job, without letting on that they knew what he was up to.

One week later, armed with a search warrant, I ascertained from the company that "RFC" was day shift and due to finish at two-thirty that afternoon. Due to court commitments, there were only three of us on duty at that time although I knew that the other two would join us soon enough. We parked near to the factory and having never seen the man before. I knew that we would have to act on our instincts. Just after the due finish time, about thirty factory employees left the premises to go home.

Only one fat man walked the few hundred yards towards his house and crossed the busy main road. We patiently waited to see where he would go and sure enough, he jumped over a wall and headed into the estate. Ian and Sean made off from the car and detained him before he got much further.

He was shocked but calm, a bad indicator as far as we were concerned but we were too late to worry. A marked police car took him to the police office and we made our way to the target's house.

His wife seemed surprised to see us and played the dutiful wife and protested their innocence regarding drugs. The arrival of the other two members from the unit meant that we could continue with the search and get it done quicker. Within two minutes of searching the kitchen area, Sean drew my attention to of a large clear plastic bag with a huge amount of brown powder inside (about five ounces).

The wife made no comment and maintained her innocence about the drugs. In the upstairs main bedroom, found underneath the mattress was another three ounces of heroin and several hundred Temazepam capsules and several hundred Valium tablets. Hardly items that a normal person would know nothing about! At the end of the search, I detained the target's wife and took her to the police office to interview her.

Back at the office, I prepared to conduct the interviews and estimated that the heroin alone was worth about twenty-five thousand pounds, and the tablets were worth about seven hundred pounds. Quite a lot of drugs for someone who was still declaring that he knew nothing about them. No drugs had been found at his workplace and his employers were keen to sack him if it was ascertained that he was using their premises to hide drugs.

I knew that they were disappointed that none were found there but I was relieved, as it would have meant more work for me to do. The interview started very badly in that "RFC" refused to say anything during it. This eventually changed as I reminded him that if he didn't admit to the drugs, I would have no option but to charge both him and his wife and that they would both go custody to court the following day.

He quickly changed his mind and admitted the drug offences and how long he had been selling them. I was well chuffed with the result, as were the bosses. He appeared at court the next day and was remanded in custody pending a trial at the High Court.

Once there, he pled guilty and was sentenced to three years in prison, as it was his first offence. He was released after eighteen months. Since his initial arrest by my team, having served his sentence, he was again caught with a substantial amount of heroin and drug supply charges and recently received a twenty-five-year sentence. At last, he got his just reward for making the lives of hundreds of people in and around the Springburn area of Glasgow a misery.

Chapter 11
You're Gonnae Get It

After the success in arresting RFC, we were being given 'high-fives' from every boss in the division, with the exception of the DI who was responsible for us. He seemed very unappreciative of the idea that we were doing a great job with little or no help from anyone. It seemed logical to us that perhaps another swap was in the pipeline. No sooner had this idea been put into our heads than I was summoned to speak to the boss.

He told me that he wanted to change some of the personnel and I had to choose who was to be ejected, as well as choosing who was to be the replacement. Sean had been with the unit from the beginning and as much as I liked him, I knew that he would be the one to go. I asked to have another guy I knew and had previously worked alongside him so I knew his strengths.

I gave the boss the guy's name and within an hour I was told that the swap would commence the next week. All that remained was to tell Sean. He took it well and was glad that he was leaving on a high!

The new boy, Jake, knew Caroline and Ian, so it meant that he would settle in really well. There was no time to gauge how he would fit into the team as I had another target that I was keen to get hold of. I knew that in order to get this particular Barmulloch dealer, I would have to organise a good location in which to watch the activity at his home. I knew that the only place in which to do this was on top of a multistorey block of flats. Luckily, this afforded a view of the target house.

Ian volunteered to be the one on top of the roof and would keep a log of the activity. The rest of the team would be in cars nearby so that they could detain anyone seen leaving the close. The day of the operation was the very day that Jake started with us. The downside to this operation was that the Human Rights Act had just came into play and as a result, I had to apply to the boss for permission to watch over this target.

We had to ensure that all operations were now watertight from a paperwork perspective, otherwise we could lose the case on a technicality, should it be found that we didn't do everything according to the letter of the law! Ian remained in position and we remained on the ground awaiting his command.

It wasn't long before the first addict appeared and left the house shortly thereafter. We followed the girl and eventually stopped her, finding her to be in possession of an eighth of an ounce of heroin. This was worth about three hundred pounds street value. She was arrested and charged as well as obtaining a statement from her regarding whom had sold her the drugs in the first place.

Having arrested the female, we left well alone for a few days, as we didn't want the target becoming suspicious. He was out on bail, having already been arrested by me for supplying heroin and he had a three-year conviction already served in relation to this. (Operation OJ – overweight junkie was the previous case discussed).

New information had been received that he hid the drugs within the common close, inside an electricity metre box. On the Friday of that week, we decided that this was to be the day that we would try and get him. "Blobby", as we had referred to him, was a rather slimy slippery character and would blame his own mother if he thought that he would get away with anything.

He ruled his house like a dictator and his long-suffering wife would do as he directed. I also hated searching his house, as it was an Aladdin's cave of bric-a-brac and tacky ornaments. However, I decided that we would just give it a try to see if we could get him. About ten o'clock that morning, we were all in position, only this time I was on the roof doing the observing and keeping a log. It wasn't long before we struck gold, and we had caught yet another dealer at the home and another statement was obtained regarding who had sold the drugs.

It seemed that even his son was also selling the heroin. This meant that we would get two of them at once if all was well. I called a strike and the team all set off to attempt to search the house. They managed to secure the house very quickly and set about the job of locating the drugs. I arrived well into the search due to where I had been previously and when I entered the house, all hell broke loose.

The reason for this was that 'Blobby' detested me, as I was responsible for his previous sentence. Having managed to calm things down, he protested his innocence and informed us that it was only prescription drugs that we would find within the house. A search of the kitchen found an eighth of an ounce of heroin.

We were delighted, as at least there was enough to arrest him and send him to court. A search of the house found no other drugs and we were hugely disappointed. A search of the common close also drew a blank. We knew that there must be some drugs there but we could still find no trace. In the corner of the close, there was a metre box but this was also searched and was found to be empty. Or so we thought.

The box hadn't been searched and had been missed, although we all thought that it had been done by another member of the team. It was decided that a second search of the close would be done as we had a gut feeling there were more drugs.

Jake searched the corner area and found seven other bags of heroin within the metre box. We were all absolutely delighted but Blobby denied any knowledge buy I could tell by the look on his face that he was gutted at us for finding his secret stash. Blobby and his son were detained and taken to the police office. He was even more surprised to find that his beloved wife had also been detained, as I wanted him to know that I meant business.

During the interview, he denied anything to do with the drugs found and refused to answer questions. I even told him about the statements already obtained by us but still he denied any involvement. I told him that it was my intention to arrest all three of them, including his wife and send them to court.

Eventually, he saw sense and admitted that he was selling heroin from his home and that his son was doing likewise. They were both arrested and appeared at court the next day on drug offence charges. His wife was released, with no charges against her.

Several months passed and eventually, we were summoned to appear at court as witnesses. We had ensured that the paperwork was impeccable and accurate in case we were required to give evidence. In fairness, I was slightly disappointed when we were advised on the day that the trial was about to start that they had both pled guilty to being concerned in the supply of a class 'A' drug—heroin. As they had both a previous conviction for the same charge, we all knew that they would receive lengthy custodial sentences.

Sitting in the court during the sentencing was strangely rewarding. Not only had we managed to secure the conviction by them pleading guilty, but we had done what other major crime squads had failed to do—that of securing first-class evidence against these notorious drug dealers.

Despite all of the fancy training given to those in the drug squad, it was basic police work and teamwork that actually secured the conviction. Coupled with using our imagination about how and where we could watch the premises and having the patience to wait and hit the house at the right time.

They both received five years in jail for their crime and both smiled and nodded their heads as they were taken down from the dock. A final acknowledgement from them indicating a degree of respect as they were caught red-handed. What they didn't realise was that there had been historical information on the police intelligence files that the drugs were stashed within the common close at the address given.

This had previously been totally missed as we had not been given full access to the historical data. But on this occasion, I had requested the opportunity to read all of the data to see if we had missed anything. In fairness, my gut instinct was right but it wasn't me who found it. I asked Chick who worked as part of the intelligence team to research it and as he sometimes worked with us to provide an extra pair of hands occasionally, it was him who found the information—all 2 lines on a report. No wonder it was missed but at least it was there for us to use if required.

Overall, the conviction of the Blobby family was an outstanding achievement for the team. Actually, the drugs were only worth a couple of thousand pounds but more important was the fact that the area was rid of another dealer and the decent residents of Barmulloch could walk free about the streets without having to look over their shoulders fearing that drug addicts were going to attack them for money to buy drugs.

However, like most schemes, the problem shifted to another area as the addicts tried to buy drugs to feed their habit. It was such a vicious circle and not one that we would ever be able to totally eradicate.

Not long after this, I was asked to attend and speak with the Chief Inspector as he had something he wanted to discuss with me. When I entered his room, he got up and closed the door. I knew that it wasn't good news, as he had never done this before. He told me that it had been decided that Pauline who had only been with the team for about three months was to be replaced.

I asked why and he went on to tell me that she was being given an acting sergeant position within the division. I was furious and told him so, as I was the one who had been left to train her in this line of work and here she was being plucked for promotion before me.

He was sympathetic and stressed that I would be next. In truth, that wasn't good enough for me as I knew that I was being made to look a fool. I had single-handedly run the unit and now a female with about five years' police service was being chosen over me? He knew that I was angry and I told him that I wanted back to the CID with immediate effect, as I wasn't going to be made to look a fool any longer. He tried to calm me down, but sensing I was livid, he decided to let me share a little secret concerning her.

This was supposed to make me feel better, but in fact, it only made me angrier as he confirmed why she was being semi-promoted, linked to her father. I told him that I wanted out and that was my final decision on the matter as I had done enough to help the police manipulate their crime figures and I wouldn't do any more. He told me to leave it for a couple of days and that he would make enquiries to find out why I hadn't been chosen for promotion.

The next day he called me back to his office and told me that I would be given a panel Interview to assess whether I would be given an acting sergeant rank as well. In the meantime, I was told not to discuss what he had told me and to just 'bide my time'.

Being very impatient, I went to speak to the superintendent regarding the fact that a less experienced officer was being considered before me. I entered his office and he immediately became very defensive and told me that he knew why I had come to speak to him and that he had already found out for me that I was to be given a panel interview within two weeks.

He conceded that it was a disgrace that Pauline was being considered but that was just a fact of life in the police when the officer concerned had a father who was very well connected with those who could make or break careers. I accepted what he had told me as I knew that it wouldn't really have made any difference anyhow and I agreed to remain with the unit for the time being. I was dying to tell the others in the team and when Pauline left the room, I did just that.

I knew that Pauline was well aware of what was going to happen to her as far as her career was concerned. The others weren't that surprised as they knew that this was merely a stepping stone in her career path. Two other females who were keen to join the unit had already approached me, so replacing Pauline would be easy. By now, we were keen to be rid of her, as we all felt that she had been two-faced as she never once told any of us that she was only going to be there for a short time. Not only that, once all of the other cops in the division heard that it was now official—she was to begin as Acting Sergeant at Baird Street—they too were furious as they all knew that this was blatant nepotism.

Pauline left the unit and we were delighted to have Linda as a replacement. She was a very quiet innocent type, but a great cop nonetheless. She settled in well and in no time had been accepted in the criminal community as "the new burd who worked wae Dawson".

True to the boss's word, I was told a week after Pauline left that I had a panel interview the following week and I was told that I would have to read up on all of the police procedures so that I was prepared for the interview. There would be two superintendents and the chief superintendent (Divisional Commander). This didn't faze me in any way, as I knew that I would be fine. Although I was at work, I wasn't really working per se. I studied within one of the upper floor offices so that I could become more accustomed to the police jargon.

One morning, Mandy approached me and asked if the team could assist her to search a house for drugs. She had already obtained a warrant and although now back working in uniform, her own bosses had told her that if the unit could assist her then they would allow her to be absent from the shift and she could use a couple of cops from her shift to assist.

I asked her all the questions about who the target was, etc. and having asked the team if they would assist, they agreed, reluctantly. The next day, the team all left and carried out the search whilst I remained in the office studying. After a few hours, they returned with their haul of drugs including a half-ounce of heroin and some Cannabis Resin.

I saw the productions and told them that when the items were all placed within bags with labels attached, I would interview the accused so that they could wrap up the case. Prior to the interview, I looked at all of the productions to ensure that they were in order. On looking at the piece of cannabis, I thought that someone was having a laugh as the piece had allegedly reduced to almost half its normal size.

I asked my team about this and they confirmed that as far as they could remember, the cannabis seized was much bigger than the current piece. I didn't know what to do but I immediately had my suspicions about what had happened but I don't wish to speculate further about that. I then looked at the production schedule and found that the heroin seized had originally been five bags but this had changed to four. Again, I asked my team about this and they told me that they only saw four, so I accepted this and went ahead with the interview.

During the interview with the main accused, I showed her the productions seized and in particular when I showed her the cannabis, she laughed and said that she thought it had been bigger but she accepted it. It came to the heroin and she accepted that the four bags there were hers.

I wrapped up the interview and charged her with supply offences telling her that she would appear at court the following day. However, when I was escorting the female to the charge area of the office, she told me that there had been five bags of heroin and not four as I had shown her. I asked her why she had never admitted this, she said that she believed it was better to accept the lesser amount as it would perhaps help her receive a lesser sentence at court.

I was furious by the time I got to the unit room and closed the door so that I could speak to my team. They advised me that none of them was present when the drugs were seized but they all believed that when the target was interviewed within the house about them, she did say something about there being five bags and not four.

I decided that we would say nothing more about it, but we would never assist anyone else to conduct any other searches as this was too much to be involved in. After all, why would I trust a ned who was making these wild accusations. What we all thought about the drugs was that someone had stolen them within the house. We knew who we all suspected but there was no way we were prepared to go to the bosses as that individual could have been investigated if it was in fact true.

They decided that as a team, they would stick together and it would always be the case that they knew nothing of what had taken place within that house. There was a lesson for us all, trust no one as others take advantage and this could have resulted in serious consequences for innocent participants. Later that day, I spoke with the Sergeant of the uniformed team "off the record" and explained what I suspected. I told him that the person should never be allowed to work in plain clothes or be involved in drug searches. He agreed and I never heard anything else about it.

It proves that to help other teams there needs to be trust and this incident had totally ruined ours with anyone else. We didn't want to put ourselves in that position ever again.

The suspect officer approached Caroline a few weeks later and said she wanted to do another search with uniformed colleagues but needed assistance from us. The Sergeant had not been approached yet. Caroline said immediately "fuck off, never ask us again."

The day arrived for my panel interview. I was very nervous but made the conscious decision to go with the flow and wait to see what questions I would be asked. There was no particular question that would be asked so therefore, no one was in a position to assist me.

However, from a personal perspective it was a very emotional time for me as my aunt (mother's side of the family) had been down visiting my mum and other sister and she ended up in hospital with Crohn's disease but took a massive aneurism and died. She lived in the far north of Scotland and was being buried on the very day I was due to have my panel interview.

I had not told anyone in my family about the panel but I had to make a choice about whether I travelled 300 miles to attend the funeral or take care of my future career. I chose the latter as I would not have been considered for another panel for 6 months so for me it was a selfish choice but one I made for the right reason. I felt extremely sad at not being able to go but I concentrated on what was right for me and my own family. There was also the fact to consider that my relationship with my own family wasn't great and I couldn't deal with the possible animosity had I gone. In hindsight I know that I did what was right for me. It's not often I think of myself but this was one occasion I did and I am glad I did it that way.

The panel consisted of two superintendents and a chief superintendent. Luckily for me, as I was a CID officer and would be suited, I wouldn't have to salute them on entering the room, whereas uniformed officers had to salute when they approached senior officers whilst wearing their full uniforms. When I went into the room, I shook hands with the bosses and sat down.

I remained bolt upright in the chair whilst the others sat there half slumped, as though already bored! I answered their questions to the best of my ability and there was no contentious questions asked of me. At the end of the forty-minute interview, I was told to leave and sit outside the room whilst they discussed my progress. After about five minutes, I was allowed back into the room where one of the bosses told me that they had decided that I had done well enough to be given an acting uniformed sergeant rank in the near future.

The reason for this was they felt that the experience in uniform would stand me in good stead for my future career and in fairness, I had very limited actual uniform experience as I had been in CID roles for most of my police service. They thanked me for my contribution and I was free to go.

In all, I wondered what all the fuss had been about as I felt that it had gone very well and at least I had achieved the object of the interview—the possibility of becoming a sergeant. I told the others about my interview and they listened intently to my recounting story question by question. At the end of it, they too conceded that the interview seemed very straightforward; no doubt I would be promoted in due course, leaving them to re-establish themselves with another gaffer.

There were still plenty of searches to be made and yet more information had come to our attention concerning a guy who was selling Cannabis Resin in large amounts from his house in a private estate within the Robroyston area of Glasgow. The problem with this was that no one knew what he looked like and there was no photograph held on record of him.

We knew that we would have to keep watch for his luxury jeep coming in and out of the estate in an attempt to find out where he lived. The reason for this was simple; we would require to know his address prior to obtaining a search warrant. Through conversation with an associate who worked for the housing department, on my inquiring about whether she knew of this guy, she informed me that he stayed across the road from a friend of hers and she would get me the right address.

This again proved the importance of maintaining as many contacts as possible with other people who work in various non-police agencies. Within an hour, she had phoned me and told me his address and who he lived with. All we had to do was try and catch him with some drugs. It was decided that we would spend a couple of days watching for his jeep and try to follow it to see where he went. The three days allocated proved useless and it was decided to leave him for now, as we were getting no place fast.

We still had many other houses to search and we kept the bosses happy by doing as they asked. One morning, three of the team was already in place within a high-rise block in Balornock and they were monitoring the activity of addicts calling to buy drugs. After a while, I was asked to attend with the bag containing the warrant and the other items necessary for the search.

I parked the car and managed to gain entry to the block. As I entered the lift, I became aware of a female standing next to me and she started to talk to me. "So how are you then, Dale, is this your day off?"

"No Lizzie, I'm working, anyhow, surely you don't think I would be coming up here on my day off?"

"Well, I heard that you were supposed to be shagging some burd up this block!" I laughed and told her that this was just idle gossip. It was quite surreal at times and the conversations I had with known criminals in that they were very pleasant to talk to at times and were willing to have random conversations with me.

It suddenly dawned on me that the female I was talking to was the sister of the target whose house I was about to search. I asked her where she was going and she told me that she was off to see her sister who lived in the block. I knew that she would be the ideal person to get us into the flat. Knowing that both she and her sister were drug addicts and they were often wanted on warrant. My recollection was that there was currently a warrant in existence for Lizzie, so I decided to use this to my advantage.

When the lift door opened at her floor, I followed her out and into the landing area. There the other three who seemed very surprised to see me with Lizzie joined me. I told her that the deal was for her to get the door open and after that, she would be allowed to go and I would turn a blind eye to the fact that she had an apprehension warrant for her. This type of bargaining is frequently used but in fairness, Lizzie was a nice girl who happened to take a bad turn in the road and chose drugs.

She was angry, but in true Ned style, she agreed to go along with my request. She knocked on the door, then whistled the whistle that all addicts do when trying to score drugs from dealers. The voice from within asked who it was and on hearing that it was her sister, she opened the door.

In poured the four of us and Lizzie ran off down the back stairs. Once inside, the usual wrestle with the police ensued and the female was placed in handcuffs. The boyfriend, however, was fighting like fuck with the three guys there including me, but we eventually overpowered him and thereafter began the usual ritual of pre-search information.

The female was searched but no drugs were found on her. Ian and I searched him, and when it came to looking up his ass, it was my turn as we would share that aspect of a search among the team of guys so it wasn't the same person having to look up rear orifices all of the time.

I immediately saw something plastic hanging down from his ass. I couldn't risk losing the drugs, as often I would ask the guy to remove them but this time I asked him to squeeze as though he was going to the toilet. At first he said no but when I mentioned about getting a warrant and a doctor to assist, he squeezed. Luckily, I had on plastic gloves but nothing prepares a person for what may be secreted up inside these dark places.

Once it was out, I saw that there was a large amount of heroin inside a shit-covered plastic bag. I almost spewed from the smell and the sight before my eyes, as Ian almost had a heart attack laughing at the look on my face.

This was truly one of the hazards of the job and one that I hated. However, we got the result we were looking for. In all, there were forty bags of heroin secreted there. We knew this, as one of the team had to count them out later at the office, wearing a facemask similar to those worn by doctors.

Whilst I could have asked him to remove them, sometimes the ned would just pop them straight into their mouth, which just makes the whole process rather complex. If I had followed the letter of the law, I should have taken him to a police office and arrange for a police casualty surgeon to attend who would then ask for the bag to be removed by the suspect. If the suspect refused then a Sheriff warrant would need to be obtained to have the casualty surgeon to remove them. So, rather than do all of that, I broke with tradition and try to get him to assist us, which he willingly did. Obviously, the case was reported that the suspect had removed them voluntarily but I suppose we were only bending the facts slightly—well, he assist us.

The female in the house was really pissed off when she found out that we had been allowed into the house through the sheer cunning and treachery adopted by her sister. She swore that she was going to break her legs for double-crossing her in that way. They were both charged with drug offences and remanded in custody as she too had outstanding warrants.

At court, they both pled guilty to supplying heroin and sentenced to three years each for the supply charges. Another easy search although quite potentially one of the most horrid I ever had to deal with! The next morning, having driven up to the private estate where the other guy we were looking for was staying, we drove around on the off chance that we would see him. As luck would have it, he drove right past us and didn't even give us a second glance.

Trying to remain calm but at the same time trying to keep him in our sights, I followed him at a distance. He drove all of five hundred yards and stopped at a fast food outlet to buy a roll and sausage. I stopped alongside him and detained him from that place and took him back to his house so that we could search it for drugs.

Within five minutes of the search, we recovered a large amount of Cannabis Resin as well as about twenty thousand pounds in cash. In all, the search lasted for about an hour and resulted in the arrest of a major drug dealer who was wanted by most of the Force Headquarters squads who didn't even know where he was living prior to his capture by us.

The downside to this was that several bosses were angry at our intervention as they had wanted to monitor his whereabouts for a while to see if he would lead them to bigger targets. However, these other squads never registered him as a target, so therefore, we were quite entitled to target him.

They were too busy trying to be so uptight about the fact that a small unit like ours could get the target they had secretly been after for six months. He later received four years for the supply charges, again confirming that we were a first-class group who were working with virtually no fancy equipment that they had at their disposal.

The only thing we never truly exploited was the use of informants on a regular basis, ours was more sporadic than planned as I was always of the belief that they were fraught with danger. Many good cops had fallen foul of informants and I was determined not to do the same. Having given one particular guy a let off with a warrant as a favour, he promised to return the favour by getting us a handgun.

This was the ultimate 'turn' that a unit such as ours could hope for, as the bosses would be delighted to rid the streets of something such as this. One dark cold evening, the phone rang in the team room and it was Joe. He told us that he had gotten his hands on a handgun and that he was prepared to give it to us, although this meant that it would be 'found' by us at a predetermined spot.

This may sound unorthodox, as there would be no arrest made, but the main concern was that at least the gun would be off the streets. Off we went to the agreed spot and there hidden behind a disused building was a .38 revolver. We immediately called out the armed response team who would have to ensure that the gun was safe, with no bullets inside.

Having done this, we removed the gun to the police office and sent out a telex to all other police offices detailing our 'find'. Within an hour of the telex being sent, it was ascertained that the gun had been stolen several days before from a farmhouse in Ayr. I began to panic, as I knew that the guy who had phoned us was a prolific thief and my mind was racing to the very fact that he had probably broken into that house himself and stolen the gun.

Perhaps he thought that this was a good way to pay us back for our generosity in not jailing him on a warrant. I phoned him and asked him where he had gotten the gun but he assured me that he had paid to get it so that we would leave him well alone. I had no option but to accept what he was telling me and let the bosses wallow in their self-belief that we were a truly outstanding unit who could get every result imaginable! We, however, were happy that the guy who got us the gun had nothing to do with the break in, although I still sometimes wonder about that one.

It really got to the stage whereby we, as a team, had accomplished many varying degrees of house searches and recovered an excessive amount of drugs and cash but there was still lots of other work to be done. I felt that I had achieved so much running the unit and that the more mundane searches annoyed me more than anything did. Perhaps I was becoming quite arrogant to the fact that I needed more stimulation to entice me to stay.

One area left particularly untouched by us was Blackhill. The reason for this was quite simple. The majority of dealers worked in the streets selling anything from heroin to pieces of Cannabis Resin and Valium tablets. One night, one of the team received an anonymous phone call from a man, saying that someone was selling heroin from his house and that he had about five thousand pounds worth.

A warrant was quickly obtained and before long, we were on a side street planning our attack. The only problem with this house was that it was a new local authority house and the door had a five-lever mortice lock securing it. This meant that it would have taken us about ten minutes to force it open, therefore, we decided to enlist the help of the local beat cops.

The plan was for them to knock on his door on the pretext of making an enquiry with them, hoping that he would answer. They stood a better chance of having him open the door than we did!

The two cops did as requested, with another two of the team hiding at the side of the building. On cue, he opened the door and the four of them piled into the house and detained them. This was also a good PR show for the beat cops as it proved that they could manage to keep abreast of who was selling drugs and that it wouldn't be tolerated. The guy was furious and would have tried to fight but my guys already in his house were much bigger than he was and he obviously decided not to fight.

However, he became verbally abusive and no amount of persuasion could stop him. It all centred upon the fact that he didn't want to be strip-searched, which was a clear indication that he had something concealed down his pants. The beat cops carried out the search on him and found four bags of heroin inside his pants.

The street value was about one thousand pounds, so we were all quite chuffed with the outcome, although we still had to search the house. Our unmarked car was left parked outside the house and we were keeping a brief eye on it, as this area was notorious for vandalism so we had to ensure that it didn't happen to our car, as the bosses would be livid. When the kitchen was searched, Caroline found a further four bags of heroin in the freezer, inside a plastic bag containing frozen chips.

The guy was furious and the colour virtually drained from his face. He knew that we had him well and truly done. He seemed such a strange-looking individual, insignificant even, but he was selling the drugs on behalf of a 'big' drug dealer. His only hope was for us to try to do a deal with him, but this would mean that he would have to surrender his supplier to us. I knew that obviously, he would have to consider it, otherwise he would be looking at doing three to five years for the supply charges we would libel against him.

When I presented him with the facts, he initially agreed to assist us as far as he could and he would go along with our request. Back at the office, I spoke with the duty officer responsible for the detention of arrested people. I asked if he would perhaps release our prisoner if he provided sufficient information to lead us to his supplier.

The prisoner played along with the plan, but when he discovered that there were five charges against him, he refused to cooperate with our plan. I didn't think that he would anyhow, as he was a friend of the supplier. This didn't faze me, as it was common for all prisoners to grass on other criminals and he was no exception. He did give us other information but nothing that we didn't already know.

Due to his lack of cooperation, he was detained in custody pending his appearance at Glasgow Sheriff Court the next day. At the trial, he pled guilty and was sentenced to four years. Perhaps if he had assisted us, we could have eased that burden of the sentence by advising the judge that he had helped us; however, his stubbornness cost him dearly!

We were getting to the stage that the novelty of good searches was long gone. I personally needed to get back to the CID to move on with my career as I had taken the unit as far as I could, plus we had little or no equipment with which to help us and this was particularly frustrating. We even had to use our own mobile phones when out on jobs and this was also causing us no end of spiralling phone bills.

With annual leave taking its toll on our personnel, we were left very often with only three people on the team and this was not enough to do any searches. This became our particularly quiet spell, the first of our time together. I was happy with this as it meant that we could just take it easy and perhaps finish a bit earlier, as opposed to working very long hours.

The usual routine at this time was to have two of us in one car and the other out, single-manned. The bosses didn't like us to drive around with too many people as it made us look like Neds. One night, I was within the car myself and kept in touch with the other two by radio, using a channel only used by us and not known to other police officers or civilian staff. This was to prevent us from being listened to by criminals using scanners.

We used the opportunity to carry out surveillance on other potential targets. I was awaiting the return of Ian and Caroline and whilst within the car, I saw a criminal I knew walking towards me. He frequently provided us with information in return for money when the result was confirmed. This was a well-organised arrangement and the bosses knew of it.

He was a registered informant and was known by the pseudonym JJ as we called him. I allowed him to come into the car and so began a brief conversation about local addicts and where they were buying their drugs. Out of the blue, he started to ask me about why I never wore my stab proof vest! I was so taken aback that I felt my stomach churn. I didn't know what to say, all I could think about was what would I do if he stabbed me! I told him that I always wear one anyhow, it's just that it's not on view for everyone to see.

He didn't seem convinced and then proceeded to tell me that he had heard that some of the major criminals in the area wanted to get both Caroline and me. By that, he meant that they wanted to hospitalise both of us because of the damage we were doing to their dealers.

I was shocked and asked him to tell me more. He said that one story doing rounds was that there was a bullet with my name on it. As well as the fact that I was going to be stabbed or have my legs broken. Finally, he admitted that he was asked by a local drug dealer to stab me, enough to get me off their beat, but not to murder me.

I was petrified, alone in the car with a known vicious criminal, and I had no idea how long the other two would take to rendezvous with me, as had been previously arranged. In the apprehension of what he had told me, I had inadvertently switched off the radio linking us all together. Just at that, Ian and Caroline appeared beside the car. I was never as pleased to see known friendly faces in all my life.

JJ opened the car door and as he left, he put his head back into the car and told me to watch my back and not to go out in the area alone for fear of "getting it". I was visibly shaking so much that Ian had to drive me back to the office to have a coffee to settle my nerves.

I recounted the story to them and watched the look of fear etched on their faces. I didn't know what to with the information. My immediate thought was that if I was to tell the bosses, they would probably immediately move me to another area due to the threats made. The same would probably happen to the unit as they wouldn't take that chance, or so I thought.

We decided that we would keep that information to ourselves and not tell the bosses just yet. Within a couple of days, I decided that I would tell the DI. He seemed quite flustered when I spoke to him and I asked him what was wrong. He told me that he was aware of the story as he had already been up to Barlinnie prison to interview two prisoners whose telephone calls had been monitored by staff, during which they had been talking to others saying that I was "going to get it". He said that he knew but it was nothing to worry about. I was flabbergasted. Here I was worrying and the bosses knew all along and they had done nothing to protect me!

When I told him this, he told me that I was overreacting! I told him that I was going to speak to the boss about it and he panicked. His reaction confirmed that he hadn't told the bosses about what he was investigating. I asked him how long he had known and he told me that it had been a month. I had been left in danger, as had Caroline. I stormed out of his office as I was going to punch his face in.

I was in the situation that if I approached the senior bosses of the division and told them what I knew, they would have no hesitation in moving me from the team. I wasn't sure if I really wanted that but I also had to think of my own safety. Having spoken with Caroline, we decided that we would keep it to ourselves in the meantime and we would all ensure that none of us was left on our own when out doing searches.

Another way around that was to ensure that we limited the number of drug searches in our own area and concentrate on the other areas of the division to assist them with searches. This was agreed by the bosses and I never told them the reason why, only that it was agreeable by my team to help the others increase their own detection figures.

We were well ahead of the others in that respect and it would serve the purpose, as I now knew that within the next month, I was going to request a move back to the CID full time. Our first job was in Easterhouse and this was an area known to me but I had only worked there a short time so the criminals in that area wouldn't know me or any of the others in my team, as they had never worked there at all.

We were as pleased to work there due to the situation, as the team based there was to receive our help. I knew the guy in charge of that unit, John as we had both worked together in our time with the CID and he was instrumental in the Janitor murder along with me in solving it. We were very similar in that we both lacked in patience although we more than compensated in our ability to do the job.

When we got to the office that evening, John told us that we had to search a house not far from the police office, looking for a large amount of Cannabis Resin. It was thought that the house we were going to, was supposed to be a safe house and we would have no problems there. As we weren't known in the area, I volunteered for us to get to the house and ensure we gained entry.

Having knocked on the door, I was surprised to find out that the occupier was about seventy. I went through the motions and told him why we were there. He seemed surprised that we would be at his home and I didn't feel particularly confident about the search. John and his team were equally as surprised when they saw him too. It was decided that we wouldn't waste too much time doing the search and we split up to speed up the process.

John and Caroline went into one of the bedrooms and then I was asked to go in. When I saw the wardrobe lying open, I almost laughed my head off when I saw crisp boxes stacked to the top. However, when one of the boxes was removed, my laughter changed to disbelief.

They were completely full of blocks of Cannabis, similar to bars of soap, only brown in colour! There were twelve boxes crammed into the wardrobe and on opening the other wardrobe, we were astonished to find that there were another eight boxes also full to the brim with the 'soap bars'.

I had never seen a haul quite like it before and ate my words about the likelihood of obtaining a result of that magnitude. The old guy initially maintained that he knew nothing about the drugs. However, due to the huge amount seized, it was hardly an excuse as the haul took over most of the bedroom. He eventually said that perhaps the drugs belonged to his son who stayed in another area of Easterhouse and that he used to come in and out of the house as he pleased.

This obviously made more sense as there was no way the old man was directly involved in that type of drug activity due to his age. Having secured the address of his son, we endeavoured to obtain a warrant to see if we could incriminate him in the crime.

Having managed to search the son's house, we found absolutely nothing to link him with the drugs but we decided to detain him for questioning anyhow. Back at the office, we set about interviewing the father and son team to see who we could pin the charges on. The son continued to deny the allegation, which resulted in us having to charge the father with the supply charges.

All that we could do was hope that the drugs would have the fingerprints of the son, otherwise, it would be left to the old guy to take the rap. That was exactly what happened and at court three months later, the father was sentenced to four years in prison for the supply charges libelled against him. The son allowed his father to take the blame and remained unconnected with the haul.

It was quite good to be estranged from the Baird Street Neds although I found that the Easterhouse criminals were more unlikely to approach the police when requested. They were twice as likely to run away than they were to stand and await us.

They seemed so much less respectful towards us and that in itself was very frustrating, as we were all used to the criminals doing as we asked. Nonetheless, we assisted the other team for a week, allowing them to catch up with the backlog of searches they had tried to do. No matter what we did, I couldn't take my mind off the threats made against me.

I was fearful for my safety and no matter where I worked, I now knew that I had to break free from the team. It was the only way that I could perhaps regain some sense of normality as the fact that I was perhaps on the list of criminals who wished me harm.

Enough was enough; I decided that I would remain with the team for another two weeks in order to clear up a few last minute searches so that my replacement would be able to start afresh. I still had to tell the bosses but the next day, I was going to officially request a move back to the CID.

Chapter 12
Case Against Horatio

Throughout my time attached to the proactive unit, there were many times that a particular name cropped up concerning the supply of drugs. The only difference being, the list of drugs became bigger each time this guy's name was mentioned to us. The list included cocaine, amphetamine, heroin, Temazepam and Cannabis Resin. In truth, I was quite astonished that this guy had the contacts to source the drugs, let alone the mental capacity to ensure that he kept on top of whom he thereafter passed the drugs on to.

I suppose in his defence, he didn't dabble himself too heavily in the stronger drugs like heroin or coke, fearing that he would become addicted himself, as is what normally happens with the vast majority of dealers. He was more of a 'Hash Head' or Cannabis man, as well as the fact that he also liked alcohol. Frequently, he would be seen about the streets drunk and shouting abuse at those in the immediate vicinity.

Horatio had quite a record of convictions ranging from Breach of the Peace to having already served eighteen months for supplying Amphetamine Sulphate (Sulph) from his house. This didn't put him off in any way as he saw the drug game as one where he could make plenty of money from those less fortunate than himself. In many respects, this was a good philosophy as it meant that he could save some money for a rainy day.

One night in particular, yet another anonymous telephone call came to our room saying that someone was selling drugs from a house in the Balornock area. The address was confirmed from our own records and it wasn't the first time that we had heard about this particular guy. With basic information, one of the team left to obtain a warrant from a Justice of the Peace.

Having obtained the warrant, we drove to the locus, or as close as we could and decided to just press on the ground-floor flat buzzer and give a false name in order to gain access. This was common and it was decided that Caroline should try to get access for us whilst we hid at the side of the flat. She buzzed and when answered by a male on the intercom, she asked for "Jellies". This is the street name for Temazepam capsules.

The poor unsuspecting guy inside the flat pressed the buzzer, at the same time he also opened the door to the flat. The five of us piled in after Caroline and entered the living room. Three must have been about ten young people all seated in the living room. After their initial surprise, I took charge of the situation and told them all who we were and why we were there. The young guy identified himself as the son of the householder, his mum, who was out of the house.

So began our usual search of the house and its occupants. Shortly after we arrived, the buzzer sounded and Caroline did what she had to do in order to entice the caller into the house. It was Horatio. He tried to run away but was grabbed by two of the team and dragged into the house. No one wanted to acknowledge who he was or why he would be at his house. After all, we let him in, not them.

Horatio was strip-searched as were all of the occupants and he was eventually allowed to go, as everything was fine with him. Some of the other occupants were also allowed to go as they were under sixteen and that left only about four others. The search of the house revealed a large amount of cocaine, heroin, several hundred Temazepam capsules, Valium tablets and a few thousand pounds in cash. All in all, it was quite a good haul for a search, which was a spur of the minute decision.

The brave wee seventeen-year-old admitted that the drugs were all his and had nothing to do with his mother who was still blissfully unaware that her beloved son had been arrested for supplying drugs.

However, the burning question in all of our minds surrounded his supplier. The poor wee guy was terrified but eventually told us, in confidence of course, that it was Horatio and that he had called there to uplift his money from the deal. It was good news as at least it confirmed what we already suspected. Horatio was supplying drugs around the area but it was also good news as it meant we had taken some of Horatio.

The only other thing we could do was try and catch him. The teenager meanwhile was detained in custody to appear at court the following morning. Several weeks later, whilst two of the team were out patrolling the Barmulloch area of Glasgow in an unmarked car, they stopped a fight in the street and one of the males involved was wanted on warrant.

The usual wheeling and dealing ensued by the troops and the male gave them a "turn" (information) in place of being arrested. They decided to let him go, as it was more of a friendly banter fight with one of his mates so no one was injured.

In respect of the outstanding warrant, well, that sort of thing happens every day with criminals and we knew that he would eventually be caught by some other police officers. I later met up with the troops who told me about their meeting and what they had learned in exchange for his freedom.

It appeared that Horatio was storing his drugs in a "safe house" directly beneath his sister's flat. This made sense, as we knew that he was also staying there with his sister as his own house was being decorated. The seed was set and it was decided to do the job properly and obtain a Sheriff's warrant for his house and that of another supplier of his who was back dealing despite having been arrested three times in the previous months by us. So much for the judicial system, allowing a drug dealer back out on the streets despite her having been charged!

Trying not to get too excited, the warrants were applied for and obtained the following day. It was decided that Kelly's house would be searched on the Friday and Horatio's house on the Saturday.

On the Friday morning, it was decided that Kelly's house would definitely be searched, as when I checked out the answer machine within our room, there had been yet another phone call from the local housing office complaining that Kelly was still dealing drugs from her house. We didn't just rush out the door to get to the house, oh no, we sat back and had our routine breakfast as we did every day.

After tea and toast and a chat, we started to prepare the 'kit' bags containing all of the plastic bags and rubber gloves and other paraphernalia required for a drug search. Included in the bag was a couple of bulbs, in case there was a room without one. Various types of screwdrivers as it is quite common for dealers to even stash drugs behind light switches and sockets within a house.

There was only me, Caroline and Ian available as the others in the team were on holiday. I requested the assistance of Chick to come and help. This was the same Chick who was with me during the death of Albie Ferrie. He duly obliged and the four of us set off to search the house. Having parked the car a short distance away from the high-rise flats, we walked in pairs towards the block.

It was planned well and instead of taking the lift to the correct floor, it was decided that we would converge on the rear stairwell to formulate our plan.

Once on the stairwell, we could see the floor above where Kelly lived. Within a couple of minutes, it was clear that she had drugs in the flat as a deal was done on the doorstep, although we couldn't see who did the sordid deed. Chick said that he was up for a laugh and volunteered to see if he could buy drugs at the door using marked notes. This ploy is frowned upon by the PF's department as there is a certain element of 'agent provocateur' involved in it.

Nonetheless, we decided to go for it anyhow. Using two marked ten-pound notes, the correct protocol was used in that the serial numbers of the notes were noted in Chick's police notebook. This is always done to confirm that the notes used correspond with the notes later seized during a search. He wrote his initials on them before going to the door. The main reason for doing this was that the door of the flat was solid and without it being opened for us, we would probably not have been able to get through it!

Off he went closely watched by us as we were going to pile in through the side door whenever the door opened. True to form, the door was answered but the difference being, the man invited him into the house. This is definitely risky and really, Chick took a great chance in going into the house. After all, we didn't know who was inside.

What I should have said was that Chick looks like a smaller version of Fred Elliot from *Coronation Street*, not the stereotype junkie heroin user expected to turn up trying to buy the stuff. Within a couple of minutes, the door reopened at which point, we all piled into the flat detaining the man and woman inside. It was actually executed very well and went without a hitch. Chick even managed to score his two bags of heroin. He was well chuffed. Especially when he was the fattest junkie in Balornock. Just proves that dealers do sell to anyone.

The search was successful and a large amount of heroin was seized as well as money, including Chick's twenty quid of marked notes. Kelly and the man were arrested and taken to the police office to wait being interviewed. All in all, it was a good result as she had three pending cased for supplying drugs so it was going to be a long weekend for her as she was to be detained for court that Monday morning.

Even the interviews went well and she admitted dealing in heroin from the flat. Benjy on the other hand denied being involved and gave a statement to the effect that Kelly was selling the drugs, he was just there to protect her. He wasn't exactly squeaky clean himself. He had previously been convicted of abusing children so he too was in breach of his bail conditions in that he was still involved in crime. He was also detained in custody to allow the PF to make the decision about being released.

However, both parties knew that they were to be kept in custody, as normally happens. They decided that they wanted to talk all about drug dealers and suppliers. They gave vital information regarding our next target, Horatio. They confirmed the previous information about his safe house. All that was left was to do the paperwork for this case prior to going off duty. Yet another long day at the office!

The next morning (Saturday), there was only Ian, Caroline and myself working. Three is never enough to carry out a drug search, as it is never known who might be in the target house. After having the usual breakfast and laugh at everyone else's expense, we arrived at the topic of the house search. It was decided that we would enlist the help of a couple of uniformed officers to carry out the search, as Saturday mornings are usually quite quiet.

As luck would have it, a couple of the old team were on duty in uniform and we asked them to assist with the search. We would call on them once in situ within the house. Again, the kit bag was picked up as we left the office to go to the flat.

Having gained entry to the house without any problem, I radioed the control room asking for them to attend the flat. Within the house were two females, both of them the sisters of the tenant who happened to be in another house with her boyfriend. Caroline explained to the girls exactly why we had called at the flat and that we were going to search the house for drugs.

Neither girl seemed alarmed, and I immediately knew that there were drugs in the house and that they knew where they were hidden. This job was left to Caroline and Pauline to entice the girls to confide in them regarding the drugs. This was done under caution whereby both of them were asked about the drugs and they gave answers that were written down. The drugs were apparently stashed in the toilet behind a bath panel. Sure enough, there in a red metal box was a large amount of Amphetamine Sulphate or Sulph as it is known by drug abusers.

It was clear that the girls knew the drugs were there but immediately, they informed us that the drugs belonged to someone else, but they were terrified of this guy. We continued to search the house. In particular, in one of the bedrooms, there was a wardrobe and bed. Nothing else. Apparently, the tenant hadn't yet managed to buy carpets for the house. Nothing unusual though as this is quite a regular occurrence in this particular area of Glasgow.

In general terms, the house was a mess and it had a really bad smell. Again, this is just a hazard of the job. However, on searching the wardrobe, I found a plastic carrier bag full of clothing. I opened the bag fuller for a closer look. I discovered that the smell was coming from the bag. I looked inside and pulled out about six pairs of ladies knickers with dried in shit caked to them. I almost threw up. It was the most disgusting thing I had ever smelled in my whole life.

They all burst out laughing but as soon as the smell drifted over in their direction, they started to retch from the smell. I asked the younger sister whose they were and she calmly told me that her older sister, who was in the other room, had a toilet problem. The problem being she was too damn lazy to go to the toilet. She just shit in her pants. Of course, I thought she was joking.

She wasn't though, as Caroline later told me about searching the girl. She had dirty pants on and when asked about them, she just said that she does it all the time. I mean, this girl wasn't eighty, she was eighteen, for fuck sake! What kind of person does that?

I was quite amazed at how calm the girl was about the fact that she was walking around with shit caked into her pants. She seemed unfazed at our surprise. Alarm bells were ringing as I thought that perhaps she was not on a normal par with the rest of the world. I asked her if she had any mental problems but she assured me that there was nothing wrong with her. Each to their own, I suppose.

The uniformed officers took the two girls, including shitty pants, back to the office so that full statements could be obtained from them regarding the drugs. Our job wasn't over yet. We still had Horatio to arrest. It was known that he would be at his sister's house. At ten-thirty in the morning, Caroline, Ian and I all went to the flat above the previous flat, which had just been searched. Again, we managed to gain entry to the house as Horatio's sister opened the door. She wasn't too happy but at least we got in.

Once there a search of that house began and in Horatio's bedroom, we found a piece of Cannabis Resin, as well as a set of house keys. On trying these keys, it was found that one key fitted the lock of the sister's house. The other key fitted the house that had the drugs stashed in the bathroom.

Bingo, the link we needed to prove his association with that house. He was arrested and taken to the police office. He was in good spirits and we had the usual laugh that we always have when dealing with him. It was the type of relationship whereby any time we had occasion to meet him, we always had a good laugh with him. He was always respectful, which was surprising as we tended to make his life hell by hounding him, obviously because he was dealing drugs.

Back at the office, I spoke with the uniformed officers who had kindly taken statements from the two girls. They told a story to the effect that their other sister, the tenant of the flat, was being paid twenty pounds a week to keep the drugs for Horatio. She had given him a key to the house so that he could come and go as he pleased. They were adamant that they never knew what drugs were there, as they had never touched the tin.

The reason she allowed him to keep the drugs at her house was because he had threatened her that if she did not do it, he was going to rape her. She was terrified of him. It seemed quite strange that someone would do this but I suppose having never been in that position, I don't know what I would do if I were afraid of someone like him!

He was well known as a bully so I suppose there may have been some substance to that allegation. Only time would tell, as it was important for us to get the tenant so that her version of events could be ascertained. Ian was left to label all of the productions at the office whilst Caroline and I left to go to Maryhill in Glasgow where it was believed that the tenant was staying with her boyfriend.

Having eventually found the house, Caroline and I knocked on the door, expecting to be told to "fuck off " as normally happens. However, on this occasion, a young girl answered the door, but on seeing us, she tried to close it again quickly. I managed to push against the wooden door and invited myself into the house. Once inside, her boyfriend confronted us, who was shouting abuse at us for coming into the house without a warrant.

Although this is normal for occupants of houses to shout at the police that they need a warrant to enter. I suppose in effect, this is right, except where the police are in immediate pursuit of an offender or where they think that a crime has been committed in that place or where they intend to arrest a person within that house.

In actual fact, we were there for none of the above as we merely wanted to detain the tenant of the other house in connection with the drugs found at her house. All that the police normally do in this situation is to allow the householder to ramble on, then try to make them see sense. This was what I did at this time and eventually told him to shut up so that I could explain why we were there.

I detained the tenant, more for effect so that she would realise that we meant business. I suppose though she was really in a deep shit as the drugs were stashed in her house.

I was hoping that she would grass on Horatio, as this was the best way for us to gain evidence. We left the house with the tenant and took her back to our office for questioning. She was terrified. Although Caroline did an excellent job to put her at ease, as well as to tell her that we didn't want any lies from her. When we arrived back at the office, she was processed in the way that all detained persons are, only this time we locked her up in a cell as opposed to a detention room.

This was again to put the fear of God into her. I hoped that it would work and only time would tell. When we saw Ian, he had finished all of the productions with the case and we decided to have lunch prior to interviewing the tenant and Horatio. However, our work wasn't over yet.

Horatio provided another address as his home when he was arrested. This meant that we were duty-bound to search that also to ensure there was no drug paraphernalia, like money or tick lists, lying around. We had to leave the office, or at least Caroline and I did. She had contacted a local JP to see if we could call there to obtain a warrant to search the house. Obviously, we couldn't just go there without one.

Again, we were not following procedure, as we should really have telephoned the duty PF to ask for permission to do this. I decided as normal that we would just cut out the middleman and obtain the warrant from a JP and I would justify it later if need be. Prior to obtaining it, having never been at the flat in question before, police regulations state that a recce must be carried out to ascertain who the householder is and to see what the name on the door is. This is because that name must be written on the warrant.

When we arrived at the concierge building, we spoke with one of the concierge and told him why we were there. He told us that there was a spare key to the flat with them and if we wanted, he would give us it later to use. We then went up in the lift to check the name on the door. True enough, the name "Horatio" was written on a piece of paper attached to the door.

We had a key so therefore we wouldn't need to force entry or call a joiner to open the door for us. We went back downstairs and held on to the key, to ensure that no other persons would get in. The concierge also confirmed that Horatio was the sole tenant of the flat. Armed with all the relevant information, I informed him that we would be back soon to search the flat.

Caroline obtained the warrant from the JP, having sworn on oath that the details were correct as is standard practice when obtaining such a formal document. We met up with Ian and attended the concierge again. This time though, I asked if one of them would be an independent witness to the search as it would have been illegal for us to conduct it without someone else being present. One of them agreed and we all made our way up in the lift to the flat.

The flat itself was in the process of being decorated and didn't contain any furniture, although it was clear that there was plenty of money being spent on it. The search commenced and the concierge was present as we searched each room. It looked as though it was a waste of time until Ian decided to start searching a fruit machine, the kind normally found in pubs and gaming arcades.

Found in the back of it, after having removed a wooden panel, was a plastic bag containing brown powder. Immediately, we all suspected this to be heroin, based on our experiences as police officers. This was shown to the concierge and placed into a plastic bag. He signed a label attached to the drugs confirming that it had been found in his presence.

Nothing else was found in the flat and we left the concierge station with the drugs and the key, deciding that this was also vital evidence. At last, we could sit down for half an hour prior to carrying on with the interviews. We were mentally shattered at this point as we has already searched three houses that day as well as having carried out other investigations regarding Horatio.

It was decided that the first person to be interviewed would be the tenant of the flat where the drugs were previously found.

Armed with a wealth of information, courtesy of her two sisters, Caroline and I started to interview her under taped conditions. Possibly, we could have obtained a statement from the tenant as opposed to interviewing her under caution. However, I thought that it would be better to do it this way and thereafter leave the final decision to the PF to decide whether to use her as a witness or an accused for allowing her to use her house for storing drugs.

When I started the interview, I didn't really know what to expect. I had warned her before the interview that she should really be considering her own position and to ensure that she told the truth to take the blame away from her. When she started talking, she wouldn't shut up. She went on to tell us that she was afraid of Horatio and that to some degree, he had threatened her. This confirmed what the other two sisters had already told us. She told us that he took a spare house key and promised that he would pay her twenty pounds each week to keep the drugs in her house. She reluctantly agreed as he told her that if she didn't do it then he would rape her.

This seemed far-fetched but she had no witnesses to this threat and even if she had, no one would speak up against him for fear of reprisals. She said that he had only paid her on about three occasions but he had kept the drugs there for about six months. She was too afraid to ask him for the money so she left the house to live with her boyfriend and left Horatio to come and go as he pleased.

She knew nothing of the type of drugs kept there and she had never touched the bath panel or the tin box containing the drugs. All that was now left for us to do was to interview Horatio before allowing the tenant to the leave the police office.

Along with Ian, I interviewed Horatio regarding the drugs found at the first house, the safe house. He denied knowing anything about the drugs and of having ever touched the box.

When I asked him about paying the tenant for keeping the drugs at her flat, he also denied this. In fact, he said that he would be making no comment about anything. This made the interview more difficult as no matter what questions were asked of him, he continued to deny any knowledge of anything.

When I asked him about the heroin found in his flat, he turned white. "I'm not putting my hands up to smack, I'll get three years for that."

"Who put it there then, the smack fairy? It was in your house so it must be yours."

"No comment, Mr Dawson."

"Listen Horatio, it's time to put your hands up to what you've been doing."

"I've nothing to say about any of the drugs." The interview terminated with him being charged with various offences against the Misuse of Drugs Act 1971. Again, he made no comment and he was taken to the charge bar where the duty officer was told of his charges. However, whilst at the charge bar, he made come comment about the safety of the witnesses, in particular the tenant. Basically, it involved her and a "bullet". These comments were said in the presence of other police witnesses and knowing Horatio, I was genuinely fearful for their safety.

I wrote the case against him and put in these additional comments in order to inform the PF of what threats he had made. It had been yet another long day. The case against Horatio was complete. Now all that was required was to await the decision on the Monday by the PF.

That Monday afternoon, whilst at work, I received a telephone call from the PF assigned the Horatio case. She had decided that she would oppose bail and ask the sheriff to remand him in custody. This was due to the fact that he had previous convictions for drug supply, but more so due to the alleged threats made against the witnesses. He appeared from custody and was remanded to a prison for seven days.

During this time, I was asked by the PF to submit all of the statements in support of the case. These statements were dictated by me and sent via the typists to the PF's office. I did the statements for my police colleagues, as is the usual way with petition cases. After the seven days, he was committed for trial within 110 days, the normal time given for petition cases to be called back to court. He was sent back to prison to await his trial. He was at last off the streets and more importantly, off our hands for a few months at least.

During the time that Horatio was remanded in prison, the PF has about thirty days in which to compile the full facts and present them to Crown Office in order that the charges libelled against him are confirmed. It is also during this time that the witnesses are precognosed by a civilian within the PF's office. (Precognition is when someone goes over a previously submitted statement and attempts to illicit the facts about the evidence—only done for cases likely to appear at a Sheriff and Jury trial.)

It was Pirrie who was allocated this task. It was, however, her first case. She telephoned me at my office at least three times a week to ask ridiculous questions about the statements and other matters connected with the productions. It was also a priority to speak with the witnesses and it was arranged that we would take them to the PF's office to ensure that they would attend. As organised, the witnesses attended and went over their statements confirming what they had said. This is necessary as it allows the PF to hear what the witness will say at court.

I too was asked to attend for a precognition with Pirrie. When I attended there, I took my police issue notebook as this contained the information required to allow me to re-enact the houses searched. It is the duty of the precognition officer Pirrie to ask me questions based upon the statement already submitted by me. She was incompetent. She did not know what to do and just read over my statement, making about three amendments to it. At no time did she ask any relevant questions concerning how access to the flats was obtained.

This was never put in any of the statements as these are considered irrelevant facts by police officers. The time to address these issues is at court when asked by either the PF or the defence lawyers. I left after having my meeting with Pirrie, feeling a little perturbed by the idea that someone as inexperienced as she was had to arrange all this paperwork to bring a criminal to court.

Two weeks had passed since my own precognition and I had by now left the proactive team to take up duties as acting uniformed sergeant at another police office. This was the first time in about five years I had been in uniform. This was also a tester to ascertain whether I would be suitable for promotion. It was to last six months and I couldn't wait.

I left the team to look after all of my paperwork as my office was now on the other side of the city. They were still being pestered by Pirrie concerning trivial matters about the case against Horatio. No other police witnesses had been precognosed by Pirrie, although she should have interviewed both Ian and Caroline. Perhaps everything was straightforward.

I hadn't been with my new shift long when one night shift someone had left me a note asking me to attend the PF's office the following day for a precognition with Pirrie. I was quite taken aback as I had already provided her with the details required. I went along the following day to be met by Pirrie's boss, Youngston. The same guy who had been in charge of the Albie Ferrie case. He was abrupt and serious-looking. I went with him into a room and he started the conversation off by telling me that I should consider my answers very carefully.

Alarm bells rang but I tried to hide my suspicions. Indeed, it was him who was suspicious of me. I answered his questions yet at the same time questioned him as to why Pirrie hadn't asked me when I saw her previously. I knew exactly what had happened. It involved the key taken by Caroline and I. Youngston tried to insinuate that I was hiding facts about the key.

Suffice to say that I told him that if Pirrie had asked me how I got into the house, I would have told her. I immediately felt threatened by him as at the back of my mind, I thought that perhaps he was trying to get me to incriminate myself by telling him that I had broken the law.

This couldn't have been further from the truth as we had conducted the whole scenario against Horatio correctly. The reason for that was simple, we had taken about a year to reach this position with Horatio, so obviously we were going to ensure that everything was correct. Feeling pissed off towards Youngston, I couldn't contain myself any longer. "If you suspect that I have done something wrong then caution me properly. Furthermore, why is Horatio still in custody if you suspect that there has been improper conduct?"

He was livid with me for questioning him in this way. "I don't suspect that at all, Mr Dawson, I'm merely trying to ascertain the facts!"

"Well, the fact is I did nothing wrong so I have nothing further to add to your questions, Mr Youngston." I got up and left the room, making my way towards the elevator to get the fuck out of there. I was feeling quite anxious due to the insinuations made by him. On reaching the outside of the PF's office, I actually started to laugh to myself. He thought that I was trying to hide facts of the case from them. Nothing could have been further from the truth.

I had gone out of my way to assist with the investigation, as I always did with every case. My own reputation with members of the PF department was outstanding and I knew many of the PFs by first name. On many occasions, I had been commended on my report writing skills, having the ability to decipher the facts and thereafter writing these in a condensed manner. He had really pissed me off with his arrogant attitude. I immediately thought that this was his futile attempt at getting back at me for raising several issues with him during the Albie Ferrie death. *Oh well*, I thought, we will just have to wait and see what happens at the trial.

The first thing I did was to speak with my colleagues concerning the second precognition. They too were quite at odds regarding this, as it was so uncommon for this to have happened. Neither Caroline nor Ian had been contacted with a view to attending for a precognition, so surely this would have been the best thing to do in order to clarify matters? It never did happen and we all went back to our duties pending the trial of Horatio.

Several weeks later, armed with the case papers, we all attended at the Sheriff and Jury court in Glasgow. Whilst there we awaited the call to give evidence. This can be quite a harrowing time for witnesses as waiting to face the unexpected can be quite nerve wracking. Probably the only thing that keeps police officers sane at this time is the banter.

This case was no different. We had all prepared in advance about our evidence and the events of that Saturday were as fresh in our minds that day as they were the day of the house searches. Even the civilian witnesses were there and we anticipated a long few days sitting around waiting to be called.

About eleven o'clock that morning, the court officer appeared telling us that Horatio has pled guilty to supplying the Amphetamine Sulphate (Sulph). His not guilty plea to supplying the heroin had been accepted by the Crown. This is commonplace, however, as it makes matters easier for the court officials. It was all over. We wouldn't be called as witnesses after all.

Ian, Caroline and I all went into court to listen to the verdict. He was sentenced to eighteen months in prison for his crime. This was a good result and it meant that the people from the Balornock area of Glasgow could walk around the streets without fear of being persecuted by Horatio. What was still very much a matter of conversation between us though was the very idea that Youngston had attempted to coerce me into ruining what was a very good case against a drug dealer.

The issue again came to our minds about the fact that Crown Office had left Horatio in jail yet in the background there may have been doubt concerning the authenticity of the evidence. Surely if it had been suspected that there was foul play on our part, the whole case would have been thrown out? Normally, in this type of situation, where there is some dubiety about a case, the accused would have been released on Bail and his case would have been deserted "pro loco".

This means that the case against him would have been put off, pending a thorough investigation to clarify matters. What we all thought was that the case against him was obviously good and Crown Office were happy to accept the guilty plea tendered by him. I wouldn't like to think that in these days of the

Human Rights Act, Crown Office allowed an accused to plead guilty to charges, which might not have been apt.

This guy was sentenced to eighteen months in prison for a crime he maybe didn't commit. Is that not a miscarriage of justice? The answer quite clearly is yes. However, he did commit the crime and the sentence was just and fair, in our opinion. Therefore, Crown must have been totally satisfied that we had carried out the investigation against Horatio properly!

At least it was over and the right result was achieved. Back to working the deprived areas in the hope that Horatio's sentence would have a significant impact on the drugs market, not! This was a small-time dealer in a very small part of what has sadly become a lucrative market for would-be drug barons.

Chapter 13
Finger of Suspicion

6 December 2000 should have been a day that would be considered by cops as an easy day in the job in that I was to attend Baton Training, which as the name suggests refers to the use of the police baton. This was a bi-annual event, which was a necessary evil in the toils of policing, as an officer has to qualify to prove that he/she is capable of using the baton if required. As well as this, an officer would also have to retrain to use their handcuffs.

It was considered by most who attended it to be a mundane task, albeit the police personnel who did the training were excited about the whole process; each to their own, I suppose!

My own qualifying date was well past as was the case with the majority of CID officers who kept putting the task off for as long as was possible. I had been forced into attending but the only glimmer of light that day would be the fact that I may be finished around one o'clock (1300); not bad as we were to start about nine o'clock that morning.

On time, I finished my task for the day and afterwards, I sat in the general CID office having a coffee with the lads and just chilling out. The phone call taken by the clerk told me that I was to remain within the office as a detective inspector (DI) wanted to see me urgently and he was on his way from London Road office. I assumed that it was perhaps something to do with the possibility of a Force panel interview as I was at that time awaiting promotion.

I sat content with the group and had a good laugh at absent colleagues' expense, telling and listening to the gossip of whose marriage was on the rocks due the vast amount of infidelity, just a hazard of the job and thankfully not one I fell into the way of. Eventually, the DI walked into the office. I have decided not to mention him by name, as it seems quite a pointless exercise.

What he did was not in accordance with the 'rules' of the management. However, it is a fair assumption to make that the management make and break these rules to suit them anyhow. He summoned me with his index finger to follow him into an interview room along the corridor from the general office. He looked really pissed off but I never thought much of it as he was like that all of the time anyhow. We both entered the room and he closed the door telling me to sit down, and so began his tale of woe.

It would appear that some jumped up snotty cow at the PF's office with whom I had previously had contact with due to the case against Horatio was not pleased with the information I had provided during the preparation of it prior to the report being sent to Crown Office. The seasoned detective that Miss Marple had become decided that I was lying to her and she went to her boss.

Between them, they added two and two but poor schooling on their part made them add it up to five. The accusation against a female colleague and me was that we had planted drugs in a house prior to a search taking place and we disposed of a videocassette tape that had been seized during the investigation by me. The female at the PF's office, Pirrie, had only recently been seconded to the precognition office and this had been her first case.

Without, I have to add, any proper training in how to take concise statements. To suggest that I was in shock was an understatement. I was livid at the very thought that my reputation was being tarnished by a female civilian clerk at the PF's office was baffling to say the least. I quickly gathered my composure and asked the DI what to do and what advice could he give me.

I should have known his response. He told me to tell the investigating officers everything and cooperate fully with them. He further told me that I should return the videocassette tape as it was lost and if I had it, I should just give it to him. Anger setting in, I had to grit my teeth as I felt like punching his face in there and then. Not only was he telling me to answer all questions put to me but also to hand over a tape, thereby confirming my guilt in the alleged crime. Not likely, matey was my response.

I could hold back no longer and started shouting at him. Not that it was his fault, but he was trying to entice me to provide them with evidence against my colleague and myself. "Fuck you. Do you think I am that stupid, DI? I try that every day with criminals and if they admit to crimes, that is what seals their fate at court! I am not about to do that with myself, anyhow, I did nothing wrong so if you want to ask me questions then get me a lawyer."

He stood up and told me to be keep my voice down, after all he was trying to help me! Confused, yes I was, he was trying to stitch me up but at least the job had taught me to know that when the police ask questions of a suspect, it's because they do not have enough evidence!

He gave the impression that he wanted to help me but really he wanted me to admit my guilt. I took several deep breaths and told him that the tape was returned by a colleague and that we did not plant drugs in the house, they were the drugs of the tenant.

I asked him who was investigating the case and he told me that it was a Detective Superintendent "H" and Detective Inspector "S" and that they would be in touch with me soon to interview me. I was taken aback as the latter officer was a man I knew as we used to work alongside one another several years before this. Probably what annoyed me was the idea that in ten years as a police officer, I had never had a complaint made against me for any reason, until now, that is.

I left the room and walked past a row of familiar faces that must have heard the shouting coming from the room and they were desperate to find out what was wrong. I kept on walking and made my way to my car where I contacted my female colleague and arranged a meeting with her straightaway.

I was angry with the DI for treating me like an idiot, as well as being apprehensive concerning what the future may bring because of the investigation.

As I drove away from the office, I felt like crying, I was furious about the whole situation.

Tucked away in a café in Glasgow city centre, I started telling Caroline about my earlier meeting with the DI. She too was shocked at the suggestion, as we both knew that what was being suggested was totally wrong. Between us, we decided that the only way to see the investigation through was to stick together and tell them nothing. We were both worried and being well aware of what lengths the police will go to in order to gain evidence, the very thought terrified us.

However, if we stick together, we can cope. Or so we both thought. Suspicious of the whole incident, my head was spinning as I thought of who was out to get me. I did feel even at that time that this investigation was personal, I was to be the victim.

The PF had sent a letter to the Chief Constable who thereafter handed it to the Complaints and Discipline who would then allocate it to the two senior officers to carry out the investigation. How do I know this? Shortly after having been told of the investigation, I received a phone call from the City Housing office in Balornock telling me that two officers had been there asking questions about me. I was surprised, as it was my belief that I should have been served with official police forms telling me that I was the subject of an investigation, yet this never happened.

The investigation had commenced and they were already playing dirty; I instinctively knew that it was going to be a long fight. So many emotions went around my head.

Now after the FAI about Albie, here I was being told that I was again under the police microscope as they attempted to gain evidence against me. Was this the reason? Was it police revenge for not toeing the party line at that incident and now this was an ideal opportunity to get me this time? Call me cynical but this was my belief then as it is now!

Not once during the FAI, either after Albie died or before my attendance to give evidence, did the management of the police ask how I was or if they could assist in any way. Yet again, I was faced with this investigation and needed support; none was given. It was becoming clear to me that I was alone, no one wanted to know. It is true that when someone points the finger at you then you are left to deal with it.

This is a regular occurrence with the police. In effect, senior officers wash their hands of people in situations like mine. I just didn't realise it before! They only think of themselves and don't care for their staff. The events that happened changed my life forever. I suddenly came to see that there is more to life than the police.

Without doubt, my family has become the most important thing in my life. Perhaps I had lost sight of that for a time when I worked long hours as I strived for promotion. I was neglectful as far as they were concerned but that was all about to change. I never envisaged changing views on my career; here I was, faced with another investigation looking at me doing my job, no job is worth that amount of scrutiny. I was treated badly by the police with the death of Albie, but things were about to become much worse. I hoped I would be able to remain strong; at least I had the support of my wife.

Although I learned of the enquiry through unofficial channels, the point to be borne in mind is that the police were conducting an investigation into an officer who was awaiting promotion. Would this stop the process? Yes. I estimated that the enquiry should take no more than six weeks to complete, as there would be only about ten statements to be obtained from those involved in the case, including the Justice of the Peace who issued the warrant to search the house in question.

Several times over the next few weeks, I felt that I was going insane and my paranoia had increased to such an extent that I was hardly using my mobile phone, fearing that my calls were being monitored. Not only that, even at work I was looking around to ensure that there was no form of surveillance on me. They were really getting to me.

Even meeting up with those I had worked with in the proactive unit was done under secrecy, as we did not want them thinking that we were sticking together with these accusations. Most people would ask why someone would go to these lengths if that person did no wrong. Quite simply, the police work with the philosophy that a person is guilty before proving otherwise. Why is that? Well, it is probably the belief within the police that if there is a finger of suspicion by someone towards a cop, then they too are more than willing to point the finger, even if that person is a colleague. No smoke without fire!

The enquiry commenced on Monday, 4 December 2000 and I was told of its existence on the 6 December. Not only did I know of it but other officers were also aware of it. Senior officers were asking questions of me and my colleagues, but other senior officers were looking at other drug-related cases that we had been involved in between January and June 2000.

Quite a task as we were previously one of the most successful proactive units in Strathclyde and our detection figures were outstanding. The reason for them doing this was that they were trying to ascertain if the drugs found at Horatio's house were wrapped in a similar type packaging as those found in other searches.

They firmly must have believed that I or we were responsible for planting drugs in other houses. The reason I know all of this is that I was kept well informed by friends who were also assisting with the investigation as well as from what they heard on the grapevine about the case.

I heard nothing else of the enquiry and thanks to Strathclyde Police, I had the worst Christmas that I have ever had. Likewise, the New Year was not something I was looking forward to and I found it difficult to cope. Attending at relatives' homes for Christmas celebrations whilst trying to put on a brave face as though I didn't have a care in the world was traumatic. I felt that my world was crashing down around me.

By the turn of January, I was finding it extremely difficult going to work, pretending that nothing was wrong. The only person who kept me sane at this time was big Mike, without his help, I do not think that I would have managed to keep up my appearance at work for so long.

At home, my long-suffering wife was well aware of how I felt and she could see that I was having great difficulty sleeping and concentrating on things. She couldn't understand why I could not just walk away, although if I had done that, the enquiry would still have been there, as well as the fact that I saw that way out as being defeatist.

I tried to remain strong and weather the storm, patiently waiting to see what was going to happen. On 17 January 2001, I was night shift with Mike when the same DI who had told me of the investigation came to see me about half past eleven (2330) to go over my appraisal with him.

This was the first time I had seen him since he had told me about the investigation as he never returned my calls. My annual appraisal was two months overdue and now he felt it necessary to complete it! I wondered why they were trying to push to have it done now.

He told me that the reason for its delay was that he had been too busy to do it. Truth be told, I did not want an appraisal to be completed and sent to Pitt Street, the force headquarters, whilst the enquiry was going on. As well as the fact that I would have to complete a form saying how much support I was receiving from my supervisors when in actual fact, their support was non-existent.

I found it very difficult being pleasant to him and after about five minutes, I told him that the appraisal was shit and that I would not be signing it. I went on to explain to him that I was not coping coming to work each day and didn't know how much longer I could do it. I said that it was affecting my ability to work and it was causing me problems at home.

He told me not to worry and that the investigation was rubbish and would go away soon. This was not enough for me; I was aware that he had been assisting in collecting other cases for the investigation team and I knew that he was still working behind the scenes on it. He assured me this was not the case, although quite clearly he was telling me blatant lies. I had enough.

I told him that he had better find out what was happening with the investigation and inform Mr "H" to contact me. When he left the office, he again assured me he would do his utmost to find out what was happening. I knew I would never hear from him, and I was right. He never even asked if he could assist me in any way or how my family was coping either. This just confirmed to me how the police treat its staff. How could I trust someone like him? This was the same guy who tried to coerce me into telling all to the bosses when asked at the time of the Albie death! He was telling lies and couldn't wait to leave the office that night.

I had been very patient with the investigation and my detective abilities were severely disrupted and I could not cope with day-to-day life in the job. I had been allocated an attempted murder that resulted in seven people being arrested. I had to organise the houses to be searched, and the interviews were to be conducted by other colleagues.

Again, I relied wholly on Mike, as I could not deal with the case. Normally, I would have loved an investigation such as this and I would have been pivotal to its conclusion. I realised that I couldn't go on much more at work. As I had heard no more from the elusive DI, I decided to take matters into my own hands. I thought that if I approached a senior officer then perhaps this would allay my fears. Wrong!

On Monday, 29 January 2001, I called at London Road to speak with the Deputy Divisional Commander. As the title infers, this person was second in charge of the division and in this case, she was responsible for the day-to-day running of police matters as well as all personnel issues. A person of the rank of Superintendent holds this job.

Maggie was sitting in her office dealing with paperwork. Police etiquette stipulates that anyone wishing to speak with Maggie and others in that position must make an appointment, albeit they do say that there is an open door policy but it is still expected that officers make suitable arrangements prior to attending.

It has always been my viewpoint that in order to get answers, the only way is to go straight to the person dealing with the problem. I couldn't wait any longer as I had been patient, this was about to change. I decided to meet the problem head on, rather than delay it unnecessarily. I spoke with the personnel assistant who, after much sounds of sighing coming from Maggie's room, showed me into her office. On hindsight, I didn't really know what to expect, however, I did not expect to be rushed or feel intimidated.

"What is it, Dale, I'm busy, you know!"

Quite taken aback by her abruptness, I immediately spurted out, "I'm here to speak to you about some welfare problems I have and to see what you can do to help me!" She sat back in her chair and at last, I had her attention. I then continued with my fears concerning the allegations and asked her what she knew about them.

She tried her best to lie, sorry should I say, to convince me that she knew nothing of the investigation and this was the first time that anyone had mentioned my name concerning it to her. I was immediately incensed at her as having already read the Police Procedures Manual prior to my visit to her, I knew that she was lying.

According to Procedures, when the police receive a letter of complaint, it is sent to the Deputy Divisional Commander, i.e., her, who would thereafter submit a preliminary report to Complaints and Discipline with seven days of the letter being received. Therefore, I knew that she was lying to me, as this report would have had to be completed by her.

I told Maggie of these facts and she brushed it aside by saying in a very indignant way, "I know nothing of this investigation; however, I will try to find out some information for you!"

I could tell that she was bluffing her way out of it with her attempt at denying the accusation. I then told her that other senior management in the division were aware of the investigation and that I found it strange that this type of personnel issue was never divulged to the person allegedly in charge of personnel issues.

She was furious with me for having the audacity to speak out of place to her. The really strange thing about this is that I knew that she was in charge of about six hundred officers in her division and she expected me to believe that she did not know anything about the fact that one of her officers was the subject of an internal investigation. It did not make sense. Therefore, she was lying!

As I had hinted that others were aware of the investigation, she demanded to know who they were, but I refused to tell her. I only confirmed that some were of the same rank (Superintendent) and others below that rank. She again said that she would contact Mr H to ascertain the extent and nature of the investigation and she would telephone me at my office later that day.

This was obviously a clear indication of her own guilt that she knew of the investigation and as I had challenged her, she was about to look stupid. True to her word she did, several hours later, she telephoned me.

All that she did confirm was that I was being investigated and that Mr H would be in touch soon with a view to conducting an interview with me, but as he was busy, it could not be ascertained when this would be. She also told me that Mr H was going to speak with the PF later that day concerning the report to be submitted. How spooky was that? The very day I ask about the investigation, Mr H was to attend for further instruction?

Alarm bells were sounding. However, I thanked her for finding out the information and ended my conversation with her. It was only after the phone call that I began to wonder about Welfare issues. Here I was struggling to come to work and she made no attempt to pacify me, nor did she ask me if there was anything that she could do to assist me. What a job!

Time and time again, I heard stories of how the police turn their back on officers who ask for help, yet I never believed it, until now, that is! How did I feel? Absolutely gutted, bewildered. I had asked for help and none was given, I didn't know how I would manage to continue with day to day work as well as having to go home trying to make out that everything was fine when quite clearly, it was far from fine.

The police quite clearly were not interested in how I felt. This was only a couple of months after the findings of the FAI were made public, albeit no blame was left upon the police but it again confirmed my belief that the police management did not wish to know what was going on. How many times does a person have to cry out for help?

I did discuss things with my wife and I decided that if I heard nothing in the forthcoming couple of weeks, I was going to go off work with stress as I genuinely could not take any more of work. On hindsight, I should have gone to see my own doctor but I kept putting it off as I thought that this would be admitting defeat. I'm no quitter, or so I thought.

The crime in January was particularly violent, which made matters worse. I was shying away from enquiries although one on particular could not be ignored.

The particularly vicious attack in the Wellhouse area of Glasgow was my real breaking point. It required my full attention and I could not give it.

As I mentioned earlier, Mike helped me deal with this case but I knew that I was no longer coping. It was then I realised that I had come to the end of the line. I was not coping at all and it would get worse if I was to continue at work. Each day was worse than the previous, my wife noticed this and told me to make the decision, either stay at work or escape whilst I still had part of my sanity intact.

I sat down with Carmen one night in early February and told her that I had had enough and that I was going to report sick. I'm not sure whether she could believe her ears, at long last after about eight weeks, I was beginning to see sense.

On 9 February 2001, there was a lunch for a trusted colleague who was due to retire. All of the CID would be there, about sixty would attend for a final lunch to say farewell to Laidlaw, a great detective and friend to all. I told Carmen that it was to be my last day at work. I was going to report sick during the lunch then have a few beers with trusted colleagues, perhaps to help relieve the stress as it has helped others to cope so why not me?

Carmen was pleased that I could see it was the right thing to do, but displeased that I was going on a drink binge. I suppose she was worried but I couldn't see that then. Mike was the only other person I told of my plan. I suppose it could be said that I planned to go sick. Yes, I did, but only from the point of view that I did try to weather the storm but as I had been given no form of support, I could take no more. I did this for no one else but me.

I went to work as normal that day and told Mike for certain that it was to be my last day. It felt quite strange being at work knowing that by two o'clock that afternoon, I would be 'on the sick'. It was the right thing to do in the circumstances and I had convinced myself of this, I still stick by that decision to this day. Why should I remain at work when I was being given no support from my employers?

Prior to leaving the office with Mike to attend Laidlaw's lunch, I spoke with the duty officer. A sergeant with whom I had never had a crossed word and therefore, I trusted him to assist me. I told him my tale of woe and whilst sympathetic, he was also annoyed at the lack of support given to me by the police but then he laughed as he questioned his own sanity regarding the very idea that they would have been sympathetic.

I asked him to write me through the sick book as being ill with 'work-related stress'. I also asked that he mark clearly on the form that under no circumstances were senior management to contact me during my absence, as this would make matters worse. All contact was to be carried out through the Occupational Health and Welfare department.

He assured me that he would await my telephone call later that day. I arrived at the lunch and saw the DI who had ignored my request for help. I felt like going over and punching him but Mike kept me on a tight leash. I sat beside a couple of the guys I was friendly with, although they were still unaware what was going on. I kept looking at my watch so that I could make that all-important phone call.

Two o'clock and I left the table to make that call. As agreed, the sergeant marked me off sick. I felt relieved, as I no longer had to worry about work. Whatever else came along I could handle. At least I did not have to worry about going to work each day.

The only reason I stipulated that time was because the sergeant was about to go off duty and the next duty sergeant probably would not even look at the sick book. Therefore, no one at the lunch would know I was off sick. Wrong, the over-efficient late shift sergeant saw the sick book and went running to Maggie, telling her that I had reported sick with 'work-related stress'. Was she annoyed? Yes; what an understatement.

She contacted the DCI on his mobile during the lunch, telling him to come back to the office straightaway. The shit was about to hit the fan, the management panicked. As the DCI left the pub, he glanced at me with a look of disgust. I immediately knew that before long, questions would be asked regarding my situation.

I felt a great sense of glee, almost as though I was relishing the prospect that at last, I had made them sit up and take notice of my situation. To hell with the police! I never genuinely believed that so much hassle would engulf me. I suppose I just thought that I would be left well alone now that I had reported sick and that the investigation would come to a conclusion soon.

However, I never for one minute went sick due to the fact that I was being investigated, it was solely due to the lack of support and if the truth is told, I was genuinely suffering from stress. I left the lunch along with a few others as we decided to go to another pub and drink for the rest of the day. They were still blissfully unaware of what was boiling in the background. I walked with Laidlaw, who was one of the all-day drinkers, and talked to him openly about the events of the previous couple of months.

He was shocked, even further gobsmacked when I told him that I had now reported sick. Although in fairness, he did sympathise with my situation and said that if I thought it was the right decision to make then he would help me in any way he could.

This was the right thing as far as I believed, hearing an older wiser monkey tell me that gave me a little more confidence. We all entered the pub and joined together in drinking a few beers talking the usual police drivel that takes place at these social occasions. The general conversation is generally about either whom is shagging whom both in the job and out, as well as whom the management is shagging, or who made most overtime last month!

I suppose I did come into the latter two categories here as I was well known for working long hours and obtaining good results with enquiries and I can safely say that I thought that the management was trying to shag me! My work friends were still unaware of my own problems and this was going to remain the way, for as long as I could manage.

Standing huddled together about twenty feet away from my group, were four gaffers who, it appeared, were whispering about things that only gaffers whisper about. Suddenly, one of them, the infamous DI, left the table and made his way to a phone situated at the end of the bar, glancing over at my crowd as he walked past us.

Call me paranoid but I got the distinct impression that I was the subject of the look of disdain from him. He made his call and then again looked at me as he walked back towards his own drink buddies. A brief conversation took place between his own crowd and he made his way from them towards the door, looking at me and shaking his head as he left. Mike said to me, "I think they know you're off sick, wee man!"

One of my colleagues noticed what had taken place and asked me if everything was all right. Before I had a chance to say anything, my mobile phone rang. It was Caroline. She sounded agitated. She asked me what was going on as she had been summoned to see Maggie concerning the investigation. I briefly told her what I had done that day and she said that perhaps that was the explanation why she has been contacted to attend there immediately.

Obviously, Caroline was wary of what would happen when she went to see Maggie but I tried to allay her fears by telling her not to worry and that she would be at least told what was going to happen to her concerning the investigation. She said that she would contact me whenever she was clear from her meeting.

On returning to my friends in the pub, I instinctively knew that Mike had told them all what was going on. The only thing is that they were all supportive and agreed with my decision reporting sick whilst the investigation was being carried out. Little did they know that I reported sick because I couldn't take any more of the pathetic behaviour shown to me by the police.

A few more beers were the order of the day and nothing specific was mentioned about the allegations against me. This suited me fine, as I didn't really want a post mortem about it all. What I wanted was just to shut it all out and get drunk. My only concern was for Carmen, stuck at home, no doubt worrying about her soon to be drunken husband.

I had called her earlier and tried to reassure her, but I'm not entirely convinced she believed I was fine. Although at least she was not concerned about me being drunk, but I decided not to tell her that the management were aware of my position.

A short time later, Caroline phoned me again telling me that she had been to see Maggie. Apparently, she told Caroline that I had reported sick and that she had nothing to worry about, the investigation was only concerning me and that she was a witness against me. She also told Caroline that if she needed any support, she would help her in any way she could. What a difference from the way in which she had dealt with me!

Perhaps if I had been spoken to and told what was going on behind my back, I would never have reported sick in the first place? Suddenly, Caroline's tone changed. She seemed to be quite strange towards me.

"Is there someone else there, Caroline?"

"Yes, the DI wants to speak to you."

This was the same DI who had previously been in the pub. He was now back at the office. I was livid, as I had specifically asked that senior management did not contact me. I suppose I could have hung up but I did not want to make matters worse for Caroline so I decided to listen to what the DI had to say.

The DI started by telling me that I was being stupid and that I should just come back up to the office straightaway and the whole situation could be sorted out. I told him no, as he had had plenty of opportunity previously to reassure me and he had done nothing to allay my fears.

Maggie was also as bad as the DI. She too was previously in a position to assist me yet she did nothing to help me either. The DI further told me that the investigation was rubbish and was going nowhere and that they (the management) were prepared to forget the fact that I had reported sick. I asked how they could do this when an official police document had been completed on my behalf.

He said that Maggie was prepared to destroy the sick form if I went back to the office right away. If I refused then there would be no way back for me as she would 'go public'; i.e., she would inform personnel department of my sickness on Monday. I was really pissed off as it was becoming clear that they could manipulate the situation to suit themselves yet they were not prepared to help me when I requested it previously.

I told him to fuck off and leave me alone as requested, I was sick and that was it. I also said to pass on the 'fuck off' statement to Maggie. He didn't know what to say. I hadn't finished with him though. I also told him that he was out of order making Caroline contact me on the premise of him having no bottle to contact me directly himself.

He tried to calm me down saying that he would arrange for me to be picked up and taken home if I wished, but before he could continue, I hung up. I had nothing more to say to him about the situation.

I re-joined my friends in the pub and continued as though nothing was going on. The drink must have been taking effect, as I didn't appear to be bothered about the whole sorry situation. No wonder people become alcoholics, as it sure does help ease problems!

"Kiss my arse" was my genuine thought after the phone call with the DI; after all, I had asked him for help prior to all of this and again, none had been forthcoming. Here they were wondering what my next move would be, yet at the same time they were trying to gain lost confidence in me, and to take control of my current situation.

I think deep down I was trying to blank out what was going on; I just wanted to try to forget what was going on around me. Caroline phoned me to say that she was going to come to the pub to meet up with me in an effort to confide in me regarding what she had been told by Maggie. I remained in the pub but at Mike's suggestion, it was decided that perhaps we should move on so that if the management did attempt to trace me then we would be elsewhere.

Glasgow being such a vibrant city has many bars and hostelries along its many streets and alleyways. A real bevy merchant would be spoiled for choice in this particular locale, as it is quite simply awash with decent pubs with good promotions to entice revellers. The eight of us left and walked all of fifty yards to another trendy pub to continue with our bevy session. It was decided that this would be the last place as it was quiet and friendly, we settled in for a long night ahead.

Just after seven o'clock, Caroline and another couple of the guys joined me in the pub. By this time I was well on the way to being drunk, although I was well aware of what was going on around me. I had again phoned Carmen and told her everything was fine and that I would be home soon. Caroline looked grey when she came in, and those of us who know women would find this strange as invariably they cover up well with vast amounts of make-up when going out on the town.

It would seem that despite her best efforts, make-up could not disguise the effect the situation was having on her. Apparently, Maggie had told her that she had nothing to fear as she was a witness and that the investigation did not focus on her. She was offered welfare support and counselling if necessary. Obviously, this rattled me even more, not only was I now the prime suspect, but why was I not offered any support? I was mad, not at Caroline, but at the system. I felt betrayed as I was a hero one minute and now master villain. The police had already found me guilty!

In their eyes, I had done something ethically or morally wrong, quite what I'm not sure. Caroline did her best to attempt to entice me back to work, saying all I had to do was phone the DI and they would destroy the already completed sick form. She also said that both the DI and Maggie told her that the enquiry was nonsense and would go away, I was ruining a good career for nothing.

All of this went over my head; as far as I was concerned, I had made the right decision and I would stick by my decision until the end. It has been said that I am quite a stubborn person and would stick to my principles rather than swallow my pride and admit that I was wrong. However, even if that is true, I am glad for the decision I made that day. The most important thing of all was that I knew even then that I would have the full support of Carmen, this meant more than anything did to me, as I knew she would stand by me no matter what.

It seemed that the subject was closed as I decided that I was going to get drunk and I really felt no need to speak about it all night. There was a large crowd of us all standing around chatting and laughing although on hindsight I can't really remember much of what the conversation was about. Not through the drink, but probably with the fact that my mind was racing despite my protestations that it wasn't.

The bar was very busy and I noticed quite a lot of other police officers that were known to me. In truth, this pub was a bit of a police haunt due to the fact that there was never any trouble in it, and the beer was cheap by Glasgow standards. I was told by Mike that there was a night out for someone who had been transferred from London Road office (my own headquarters) and that there would no doubt be a lot of other police personnel coming in also.

I never gave it a thought as friends surrounded me and we were all having a good time. Until however, in walked the DI, apparently he was there to see the person who had been transferred. Suddenly, anger overtook me and I felt like exploding.

Again, Mike kept me on the straight and narrow telling me to leave well alone and not to even get into a conversation with him. Obviously, he was right as I probably would have been jailed myself for the harm I wished on this DI. What was I saying about the fact that the pub had a good reputation for no trouble within?

A call of nature was necessary and I left to go to the toilets, which were downstairs in the pub. No sign of the DI so I thought he must have been away chatting to some other people. Wrong, standing at the top of the stairs was this vision, the DI.

Immediately, I thought to myself, *Did he fall or was he pushed*? I laughed as I approached him wishing that I could push him downstairs and make it look like an accident. He looked at me as though I was mad, quite possibly I was but I managed to remain composed.

"Look Dale, get back to work, this investigation is a lot of shite and is going nowhere. You have a career to salvage."

I looked at him and felt sick, I almost hooked him there and then, I was so pissed off at him. I brushed past him and headed to the toilets, turning around on my way down to say, "You follow me down here and I'll break your scrawny neck, ya wee prick."

I went into the toilet and no one followed me in. As I walked back upstairs, I could see him skulking at the side of the passageway, like a robber waiting on his next victim. "Persistent fucker you are, eh," I said as I was about to walk past him.

He grabbed my arm. "Look, we need to talk." I told him to let go of my arm. Mike appeared, he had obviously been watching from the side lines.

"Dale, come on, let's go, he's not worth it."

However, the diplomat inside me told me to stay and listen to what he had to say to me; after all, I had nothing to lose.

I did listen for all of about thirty seconds when my own zero tolerance kicked in. All I could think of was how he had made me feel when I asked, rather, begged him to help me yet he still did nothing. I told him that what he did was a disgrace, both him and Maggie. However, he didn't disagree with me and listened as I ranted and raved at him. Not that it was going to make any difference to my situation, as I was not about to give in to mindless drivel.

Perhaps I needed to hear myself relay my own thoughts and fears on the subject and how badly I was being treated, yet he never once attempted to apologise for how he had dealt with the situation. This confirmed my suspicions, he had been sent down to the pub to look for me and attempt to bring me back to work.

They would then be able to offer me support and thus tick a box of an official form to say that they did what was expected of them! I took great delight in telling him to stick his sympathy up his ass and that hopefully at a later date, he would have to account for his actions.

Again, he attempted to tell me that the investigation was crap and would go away, quite simply I did not believe a word he had to say. I walked away with my head held high, thinking that I had won. Of course, how stupid is that! No one ever wins in any conflict against a major organisation, particularly one such as Strathclyde Police.

They have all lied to cover up their mistakes as well as to cover their own backs and each other's! I remained in the pub for about half an hour after that, I could no longer force myself to remain in the same room as him. I left and made my way home to Carmen, at least I knew she would be waiting with words of wisdom, my God but I needed words of wisdom that night to keep me sane.

Having managed to return home safely I told Carmen of the day's events in great detail. I'm not sure whether she did actually listen to me or whether she was just glad to see me back home in one piece! Sometimes going over and over events such as these may be seen as being beneficial, not in this case. On hindsight, I truly believe that the more I discussed the events, the longer lasting the potential was to go completely off the rails due to an out of control situation. I went to sleep that night with too much on my mind, as no doubt did Carmen.

Probably the worse situation for me was that I knew the way that the police operate, they would stop at nothing in order to gain the necessary evidence. On the other hand, I also had first-class knowledge of the way in which the PF's office dealt with reports.

One of the reasons for that quite simply is that they both have personnel dealing with reports when in actual fact they do not have the mental capacity to reach a logical decision. There always appears to be flaws in the whole legal system and every department will pass off the blame to another party. One would expect learned people to be just that. Wrong, they are too afraid to make decisions fearing that "their careers" will suffer as a direct consequence.

Accurate but wholly unrealistic when another person's livelihood and reputation is at stake, no-one cares. Saturday morning and the mother of all hangovers, especially with a two-year-old daughter who just wanted to make a noise and play. Up and about the house attempting to take stock of the earlier events of Friday, but I was still content with the decision to sign off sick. Mike phoned me to ensure that I was still alive and well.

But this was a double-edged phone conversation. He had been contacted that morning by the DCI asking him to contact me to convince me that it was still not too late to change my mind. Again, Mike had been told that the investigation was rubbish and would go away, I still had my career to salvage. My position remained the same.

I would not be bullied into making any rash changes to an otherwise volatile situation. However, the most frightening angle attempted by the DCI via Mike was that if I resumed from the sick, they would destroy all record of it, I would not be disciplined for drinking whilst on duty on the Friday afternoon. I was shocked at this as after all, about fifty other colleagues had also been out drinking that day whilst technically still on duty and I can only assume that they would be fine and nothing would be mentioned to them about it.

Mike did take my side and told me that he had informed the DCI that we both had signed off work that day to say that our tour of duty had ended and if need be time off could be deducted from us for that. What was forgotten though was the fact that the DCI as well as other high-ranking officers had also been drinking that day so therefore, how could they justify attempting to discipline me?

I told Mike to inform him that I was sticking to my decision. He did agree that it was outrageous to even suggest doing that to me, but this is the organisation's way of attempting to strike a balance between their fuck up and failure to assist a colleague when asked.

I bid Mike farewell and attempted to enjoy my newfound free time, whilst still on full pay. In the coming few days, I began to realise that there was more to life than having to work twelve to fourteen hours a day. The havoc it plays on a person both personally and psychically now makes me wonder how I managed to sustain that kind of life for so long.

My family became more important and I was determined that if I at least learned that from this situation then it would all be worth it! I made a conscious decision that no one would know I was off, and so began over two years of lying and deceitful behaviour towards my family.

I didn't particularly like the idea of doing it but the reason behind it was quite clear to me. I did not want anyone knowing that I was off sick as I felt a failure and perhaps also felt that to some extent I was letting everyone down. I know that really all I wanted to do was to protect them from having to endure the torment felt by Carmen and I at this time.

I did not want family members asking every time I met them to explain what stage I was at with the police investigation, thereby at least this way, I was perhaps making life a little easier for us. Over the coming weeks, I received lots of phone calls from concerned colleagues asking after me as well as providing me with information concerning the on-going investigation. I tried to treat the information as being of assistance to me but what it was doing was eating away at me inside.

I became full of hatred towards the police due to the way they had dealt with things and I blamed my wife when things went wrong. I know that it was not her fault but whom else could I blame? She was there for me; the police wasn't. I decided to start keeping a diary of events in order to formulate a case against the police for the way I was being treated.

At times this helped, other times it almost drove me insane and I tried very hard to focus on the facts as I heard of them and then once committed to my PC, tried to distance myself from the events documented by me.

This was Carmen's idea as she said that it would perhaps make an otherwise stressful situation seem like fiction. Many times having documented my feelings I re-read the events and I can honestly say that it made me feel better. Well, for at least half an hour, then the anger would again take over and I would be on the lookout for a target to ridicule.

I genuinely believed that if I vented my anger on another person then perhaps it would make me feel better about myself. I lost all confidence in myself. Prior to this happening I was easy going and happy, content with life. After the events I totally changed, and not for the better.

Caroline and her now husband Alan are both friends so I also knew that it would be a difficult situation for them to deal with. Albeit she had been told that she would be used as a witness against me, neither of us knew what to expect when it actually came to the crunch. Knowing both Mr S and Mr H, I often commented that whilst they were senior to me, they would never be as good a detective as I was.

Having worked with S several years before, I knew how devious and underhand he could be. Yet strange as it may seem, I half hoped for some backhand information from him, as he has been known to do that type of thing with previous enquiries. But I never did realise why he never spoke of my investigation to anyone, this was something that I was quite astonished at as he is quite loose with his tongue when discussing things like this with his own cronies. I began to think that perhaps there was some major conspiracy against me by other high-ranking officers in the job. This was at that time paranoia on my part, or so I thought.

For the duration of the investigation, with Carmen's help, I managed to keep on top of what was going on. The idea to keep a diary and a close record of every phone call would no doubt assist me later, that was what I kept telling myself at that time. Phone calls from friends helped, as at least I felt that they believed in me. It was always my belief that this type of investigation was supposed to be discreet and confidential.

However, this emphasises my point when I say that the police cannot keep secret when dealing with cases such as mine. It always comes back to the poor unsuspecting victim, in this case me. Again the frustrating thing for me was that these officers involved were not half the detective I was and I suppose it is partly due to their own shortfalls that I managed to learn of the information as they gathered it.

Some of the phone calls I received were from witnesses involved in the case. They were horrified at the accusations against me and they were non-police personnel. This was reassuring as at least they did not believe the lies that the police were attempting to pin on me. What I found quite annoying was the fact that some of these witnesses were visited about five times by the police, each time they went over the story time and time again in the hope that the witness would slip up and perhaps say something derogatory against me.

I have been involved in many high-profile murder investigations and the most I ever had to clarify points with a witness would be twice. The reason for this quite simply is that I do the job properly and can gain the information quickly and concisely. It was an indication to me that the police, or should I say in particular Mr S, was out to get me.

Meanwhile, Caroline was on annual leave with Alan, at this time, they were supposed to be planning their wedding. This should have been a happy time for them both and the reason for the annual leave was also to enable them to recharge their batteries prior to going back to work. Not on this occasion for Caroline.

Mr S continually harassed her via the telephone. Even her mobile was being tried as he attempted to make arrangements to interview her. She reluctantly answered and he told her in no uncertain terms that she was to make herself available for interview, despite the fact that she was on holiday.

Furious, she said that she had other plans and if it was that urgent, he could have contacted her at any point prior to her taking annual leave. Through his manipulation, he expected Caroline to conform, but she is also a strong-willed character and told Mr S that she would be contacting the Police Federation for advice prior to agreeing to any interview.

He was furious. Her refusal to bow down to his bully boy tactics would no doubt have made her an enemy for life as Swindle is the type of person who does not agree with junior staff answering him back. But as Caroline was quick to point out, she too had rights and he would not bully her into a position that she did not feel ready to undertake. An agreement was made for her to attend at Govan police office on 22 February for her interview as a witness at 11 o'clock. Why Govan?

This was a worrying piece of information to me as I was aware that a major incident room had been set up there and that the incident was being recorded on the HOLMES computer system. This is a system that is only used in extreme cases. Normally, this is used for protracted murder investigations whereby it is thought that it may take a long time to solve and would involve a lot of work. The system makes it easier to retrieve information, the name meaning Home Office Led Major Enquiry System.

I was shocked to learn she would be interviewed there, as prior to going off sick, I knew that there was an ongoing incident being carried out at Govan. I contacted a friend who told me that he had heard of this investigation and that it was on the HOLMES system—this confidential investigation was called "Operation Window".

This goes to prove how incapable of keeping a secret operation those involved in the police are! I was also told that the police were trying to attain itemised billing for my landline and mobile phones. I was furious as it would need a warrant from the Secretary of State for Scotland to have this done. This made me wonder just how far the police were prepared to lie against me in order to obtain information, as they would have to swear an oath that the information given by them was correct.

This proves how corrupt some people become in an attempt to gain promotion. This was one of my near breaking points as I was paranoid about using these phones and became so paranoid that I would barely leave the house. Again, Carmen calmed me down by saying that this would prove nothing. She could be phoning my friends to find out for me and even if they did show any association chart, then it would not prove who made the call.

I saw sense, but I was still wary when using any phone, as I am aware that the police can in fact listen to phone calls as they are being made. Prisons also monitor calls of criminals for information purposes within the prisons. I resorted to radical measures. When I wanted to speak to Caroline or close friends about the investigation, I would either meet them or alternatively phone them from a phone box.

I was forced into buying another mobile phone in order that I could maintain some form of contact with my colleagues in emergencies. I can safely say that the police never went to these lengths to investigate murder suspects during my time working there, even during high-profile investigations such as the murder of a McGovern family member in Springburn—he had been an alleged gangster and drug dealer.

My world was falling apart as I felt as though I had no rights at all. My Human Rights were never once taken into account and they were violated throughout the whole investigation. I did not know how much more I could take! At times like that, one's mind can race ahead and get to a point where you feel that it could explode; I felt like that 24/7 and often thought about running away.

At this point, I feel that I should clarify something; these investigating officers obviously forgot that despite the fact that they had been promoted during their own police service, they did bend the rules and indeed the laws of Scotland during their careers. They were of an era where the police were well known for adopting evidence and confessions by illegal means, hence the large number of people claiming that the police 'fitted' them up.

What they clearly did not realise was that in my working career over ten years or so, the police were clever, well-educated professionals who did not have to resort to the measures once frequently used by those in the bygone era like Mr S and H. I was most certainly not of that ilk and I had done a very good job for the police as had my colleagues. My philosophy was always that if evidence was there then I would seize it, if there was none then so be it.

I most certainly was not going to put my reputation and livelihood in jeopardy for some jumped up Ned who would make accusations at the drop of a hat. It would appear from gossip in the criminal world that on occasions, the police carrying out drug searches would miss some vital evidence. Whether that was bravado on the part of the Ned involved or perhaps the police did miss drugs during the search.

Although I must confess that after searching the same house for the second time, we recovered about twenty thousand pounds worth of drugs; we never found drugs the first time because we failed to look under the floorboards the first time. This surely proves the point that even the police make mistakes!

I am firmly of the belief that Strathclyde Police does not know how to treat its staff. Those who form part of the senior management team do not possess the skills necessary to identify when issues pose a potential threat to a person. When an officer like me approach them and ask for help, then this should be provided and the problems should be addressed, not left to fester and work itself out because that will never help any situation.

The people put in charge of personnel do not have any personnel qualifications. They are police officers who have been promoted, they are not personnel managers. In the police organisation, they automatically assume that their rank gives them imaginary powers and they expect others around them to adhere to their every whim.

Well, sorry to disappoint you all, there are those of us who do not agree with your moralistic high ground and we do have principles and find it difficult to tolerate irate tantrums from ranking officers, every individual has the right to express their opinions.

The sad reality is that the management is so caught up in their own careers, they tend to lose sight of the magnitude of the effects that their decisions may have upon a person. A word of advice to those rankers, who believe that they know it all—you don't.

When I signed off sick, I specifically asked that no senior officer should contact me at home. I felt that they had failed in their duties previously and I did not wish to be bombarded with unnecessary telephone calls full of pity, yet also asking when I would be returning to work. You see, that is what happens, they are not in the least concerned for a person's health, they only want to find out how long that person will be ill for.

I was well aware that the management was desperate to speak with me. The reason quite simply was that they had fucked with the way they had dealt with my situation. A simple message also to Maggie and others—no, I did not make a statement by going off sick, as you all put it.

It is not a feeble attempt at speeding up the investigation, although they did make headway with it after I went off sick. What I did was merely prove that they do not know how to treat staff, the only thing that they can do is lie and deceive.

Any trust and respect I had for my occupation is lost. In fairness, the only thing they did right with me was not contacting me as requested. Although it did leave me in the dark; if I needed any answers, I contacted the Health and Welfare department who asked relevant questions on my behalf.

Frustrating is too mild-mannered an expression for my feelings during that bleak time. Here I was being investigated yet word from Maggie and others was that the investigation was rubbish and would go away. Would it not have made more sense to tell me that when I asked for help in the first place?

Apparently, the investigation was of a confidential nature. Bullshit; everyone in my division was aware of it thanks to the loose tongues of those involved in it. The rumour going around the office was that I had planted about five thousand pounds worth of drugs in a house, bought no doubt with money stolen from previous searches.

But then the police are well known for embellishing a story so that the poor sod on the receiving end, i.e., me, was already guilty before even interviewed. I was mad at the way my reputation was in tatters because the police could not keep the matter confidential. Loose tongues make light work!

Again, I was faced with the prospect of not knowing what was going to happen with the enquiry. I had decided to leave things well alone, albeit it was very difficult coming to terms with the fact that I was still as much in the dark about the matter. Until Caroline contacted me to say that she had to attend Govan on Thursday, 22 February 2001 for interview.

Mr S had told her to attend on her own, as she was a witness. She contacted the Federation and a representative agreed to accompany her that day to ensure that she was treated fairly. When they attended at Govan that day, S basically attempted to coerce Caroline into speaking to him without the Federation rep being present.

His reason was that it was in case she wished to tell him anything of a confidential nature during the interview. I will translate that; he meant that he wanted her to tell him what he wanted to hear so that they would have a good case against me for wrongdoing. However, Caroline told him that the rep would remain with her and if he did not like it then she would leave the office.

To suggest he was a little bit annoyed is an understatement. He started shouting at her and tried to intimidate her again. So much for fairness! Caroline said to me that she thought S would have a heart attack, he was ranting and raving so much. A sight I wish I could have seen, the very idea that he was being told that he couldn't manipulate her was obviously making him angry.

The interview went ahead whereby she provided a statement to him and another female detective. The Federation rep was also present. After four and half hours, Caroline was told that she could leave. She was a witness and S told her that the complaint was against the police and not against any particular person. He was looking into the workings of the proactive unit and she was to assist with the enquiry as a witness. We were all witnesses in a happy big witness world! This was interesting, I assumed that the complaint was against Caroline and myself. Oh well, I must be wrong then!

Caroline emerged from the interview physically and mentally drained. As Caroline told me, "I felt as though you had committed a murder and I saw it, they wanted me to tell them about events that never occurred." Despite the fact that she had taken along with her a federation rep, she had quite clearly received a hard time from S and the female.

It would appear that issues which required clarification were continually put to her in an attempt to see if she would tell them that I did something wrong and she couldn't wait to bare her soul about it all. Caroline told me that it felt as though the police were clutching at straws, they had no evidence and only with her telling them what they wanted to hear would there be any form of case against me.

This was despite the fact that she had been told that we were all witnesses but at the same time, S was attempting to gain evidence against me, a so-called witness. It made no sense and at last, Caroline could see that. We were both of the opinion that the police were on a mission to get me, no one else, just me. But at what cost? Any cost at all, obviously they banked on the weak link being Caroline, a wee lassie with little service and through their intimidation, she would no doubt tell all, as she was afraid of the police hierarchy.

Wrong; Caroline was strong enough to withstand any accusations against us, although it would be tough. Never once did the police consider for one moment that perhaps they were barking up the wrong tree. This was beginning to seem more of a conspiracy to get me, why I still do not know, I can only form my own opinion on that one!

Basically, S asked Caroline to recount the events of 3 June 2000 and how we came to conduct various searches. However, as Caroline pointed out, an operational statement had already been submitted in relation to these events and she apparently told them that she would only answer questions in order to clarify matters, which she did.

This was not good enough and would account for the long interview she had to endure and from what I have been told, S wrote down what he wanted, not what was directly being said by Caroline as should happen when a statement is noted from a witness. In particular, Caroline was asked about returning a videocassette tape sometime in June 2000. She clearly stated that she had returned the tape to the concierge station, but she did not know to whom it had been returned.

This doesn't mean that she never returned it, she did. I should know. I was in the car and asked her to drop it off for me. Quite clearly, the reason for this was the tape contained nothing of any evidential value, for both the PF's benefit or for our own intelligence purposes.

The fact that she failed to get a receipt for its return would prove to be my downfall; why was I accountable for that action? Suffice to say that Caroline was left as much in the dark as she had previously been, as nothing was really explained to her about the investigation. Swindle told her that he would be in touch if he needed more information.

The other poor unfortunate person involved in this 'ménage à trois' was Ian. Yet another totally trustworthy good cop who had worked with me for about six months. He, like the rest, could be left to his own devices as he was very shrewd when it came to dealing with Neds, a particular asset that is a must in the line of proactive policing. Ian knew what was going on with the investigation as we all kept each other informed.

There is nothing wrong in this as, after all, we were all witnesses and the police discuss matters before any form of interview takes place. He was to attend Govan on 26 Feb 2001 for interview and he arranged to take the same Federation rep along with him for moral support. S was not available for this interview and it fell to two other detective sergeants who had been transferred from another department to work on this investigation.

From what Ian told of his interview, it would appear that he escaped relatively unscathed as he had a lesser part to play in the recce carried out prior to the warrant being obtained by Caroline for the final search. Quite relieved as he was, he still felt that there was a hidden agenda with the police. He too was told that the investigation was not against any particular person and that it centred upon the workings of the proactive unit. Good, perhaps I will be a witness too?

As all of my contact with the police was through the Welfare Department, at my request they arranged for me to attend for an interview at Govan police office on Friday, 2 March 2001. The only difference was that I had to attend on a voluntary basis, meaning that I had to attend of my own free will. I immediately knew that I was a suspect.

You see, when a person falls into this category then the suspect can attend at a police office and sign a form to say that they have attended there for interview voluntarily. Failure to do this may result in the suspect being detained under the terms of section 14 of the Criminal Procedure Scotland Act 1998 and that person may be detained for a period of up to six hours. The last thing I wanted was to be detained, so I agreed to attend at ten o'clock that Friday.

The arrangement seemed quite strange to me, as this was all organised on Thursday, 1 March 2001, the day before my interview. All I knew was that I was to attend an interview. What the interview was all about was still as much of a mystery to me then. What should have happened was that I should have been served with an official police document detailing that I was the subject of an investigation and what the nature of the allegation was against me.

The police never did carry out this procedure. The reason I knew of the existence of this particular process was that I had managed to access the Police Procedures Manual detailing what the police do in certain circumstances. Quite clearly, again the police were neglecting the correct way I should have been dealt with.

It really did not surprise me in the slightest and even the Federation were surprised but I felt that I was having to be held accountable for my actions, so surely whoever was failing to adhere to the correct practices should also be held responsible. This was not to be the case and I was left very much in the dark about the whole sordid process.

Mike spoke with me that afternoon and told me that he had spoken with the DCI earlier in the day. It seemed that there had been significant news regarding the investigation that would help my case, although what the precise nature of this information was Mike was unsure.

Between us, we ranted and raved with each other trying to assume what the good news would be that would affect me. No reasonable explanation was forthcoming so I knew I would just have to wait until the interview to find out. After all, I didn't know what my interview would be about!

I contacted Caroline telling her of my impending interview with S. I wasn't alone. She too had been summoned to speak with her Divisional Superintendent who told her that she had to attend at Pitt Street that afternoon to meet with S again. When asked why she was to attend, she was informed that she had to clear up other matters that had been omitted during her last interview. More worrying for her was that she was told that it was an official order. This means that her failure to attend would have resulted in her being disciplined for 'failing to obey a lawful order'.

This would have meant that she could face a fine or even lose her job if she did not attend this interview. Naturally, she was concerned but agreed that she would attend as requested. But a moot point was that she had under no circumstances to bring along with her, any member of the Federation, as they would not be allowed into the interview. Caroline was incensed. Again, she was being bullied into a situation that was beyond her control and one that she could do nothing to prevent.

Having spoken with me about this, Caroline and I both worked out that this was a final chance to see if S could get her to tell him that I had committed a crime whilst doing my job. Although in fairness, neither of us could see how it was possible to carry out this process when she was being treated as a witness in an investigation yet she was being ordered to attend during her tour of duty. From a fairness perspective, Caroline should have been treated the same as me as we were both at that house doing the recce. Again, the fact she wasn't confirmed that this was a conspiracy against me!

Basically, what S was doing was trying to prove that he was calling the shots and that Caroline was defenceless to do anything about it. She was to be at Pitt Street at two o'clock and along with her boyfriend Alan, we would meet afterwards to find out what was going to happen next.

Awaiting her return from the interview was a painful experience. Alan and I both drank about a gallon of coffee going over various scenarios about what they would be asking Caroline. After almost two hours, she emerged and joined us in the café. It would appear that the reason for this final interview with her was merely to bully her into selling me down the river. The feeble attempts by S and the same female detective sergeant who had previously interviewed Caroline, both took it in turns to tell her that anything she said could be in confidence and that they would protect her from being prosecuted.

Worst of all was the very notion that these people wanted desperately to have me arrested for planting drugs. Caroline stuck to her story, the truth as it happened, but still they refused to believe her. Caroline was still of the opinion that they too wanted to get her but they really had nothing to go on with either of us.

Again, a statement was noted from Caroline but she refused to read it over and most importantly, she refused to sign it. They asked her many of the same questions previously asked the week before. I think that this was more of the police trying to assert their authority by proving that they can deal with officers in any way they see fit.

Nothing was said to Caroline about this new information obtained, so this made me think that it really had little or no bearing on my investigation at all. I left Caroline and Allan to return home, many bad thoughts swimming around inside my head about my impending interview. I knew that I would have to prepare mentally for the next day's meeting.

I would have to suggest that S probably expected me to attend there alone for interview but if a Ned is in trouble with the police for any reason then they instruct the services of a lawyer to attend to be present during that interview.

Police officers are no exception to that rule, so with the help of my solicitor from Levy & McRae, I arranged to be interviewed. I knew the lawyer as I had used her previously at the FAI regarding Albie Ferrie. I knew that I could rely on her. I patiently waited in the foyer for S to attend. When he did meet me, he attempted to shake my hand, as though he was pleased to see me. This was no pleasure meeting here. I was meeting the man who was attempting to frame me for acting out with my police powers. My lawyer, sensing the agitated manner I was adopting, urged me to remain calm and dignified throughout and not to get into any precarious situation with S.

I tried so hard not to just kick his head in, perhaps it would have given me a great sense of achievement but I maintained my composure.

The other officer present was a detective sergeant whom I did not know. This fact I was quite relieved at. The only thing I knew for sure about that interview was that I would be making no comment in answer to the questions asked. The reason for that is as I have already stated, the police only ask questions when they have insufficient evidence to charge a person. I was no different and I was going to maintain my silence throughout.

The interview started and my lawyer sat beside me. The questions were already prepared by S and he read them from documents he had before him. Each time my answers remained the same, "On the advice of my lawyer, I do not wish to answer the question."

This may seem easy to do but having been in the situation whereby I have conducted hundreds of taped interviews, I knew that this reply would annoy the hell out of those asking the questions. The easiest thing to do is answer, but I was not going to allow them to gain the slightest shred of evidence against me. The questions asked of me were quite mundane and I had easily anticipated what they might have been, mainly about my movements on the day of the search, i.e., 3 June 2000.

However, the second-last question threw me. I suppose it was more of a statement from S rather than a question having reflected on the events. He stated to me that in fairness, he had to tell me that there was no direct evidence to link me with the drugs found during the last search. Relief is too short a word to describe how I felt. Yet at the same time, I was boiling with rage as the realisation of what he said sank in.

Basically, this meant that there was no DNA evidence to suggest that I had planted the drugs. I was devastated, although I'm not sure why, as I knew that the police had suspected that I had planted those drugs. But to be actually told that they now could disprove the allegation was supposed to make me feel better. It made me angrier as it confirmed to me that the police basically had found me guilty before the investigation commenced.

I felt really angry and had to be told to sit down as I found myself rising to my feet as though about to do something stupid. To this day, I still don't know what I would have done to S had my lawyer not grabbed hold of me, ushering me to sit down. I again made no comment regarding this but it did throw me right off the way I had been coping mentally with the interview. I started to shake and I felt sick. One last question was asked of me:

Q. Did you attend that flat prior to obtaining a warrant, enter, find the drugs then put them back and leave to obtain the warrant?

At last, the idea of what I was suspected of hit home. This was the good news on Thursday that the DCI had mentioned—the fact that the evidence linked the drugs to Horatio. I was quite relieved, the police had nothing to pin on me at all and they were clutching at straws and trying to formulate a jumped-up charge to justify the lengths that they had gone to with the investigation.

I smirked, but S repeated the question to me thinking that I hadn't heard it. I replied that again on the advice of my solicitor, I do not wish to answer the question. However, at the end of the interview, I was advised that a report would be submitted to the PF for consideration and they proceeded to charge with the offence of Attempting to Pervert the Course of Justice.

The interview was over. Forty minutes of rubbish, but I was glad it was over. All of the allegations against me surrounded the fact that I had attempted to pervert the course of justice by interfering with a set of house keys, disposing of a videocassette tape (the same one Caroline had returned) and withholding information from the PF. I felt so stupid. I was being persecuted by the police for doing my job. I had done nothing wrong other than not answering questions *not* asked by the PF.

I mean, that the incompetent civilian who had conducted the first precognition never asked me relevant questions concerning the search of the house. Yet I was being held responsible for her inability to do her job properly. Only it is so true or I would find it totally laughable.

This investigation cost thousands of pounds in money, not taking into account the wasted police man-hours and paper to look into the actions of someone who did nothing wrong. It was a complete farce, and not one I will ever forget.

Again, I had to leave the diary well alone. I refused to update it as it was way too much for me to comprehend just how bad it made me feel towards the police, as well as the mental issues going on with me surrounding the whole hypocrisy of the organisation of which I was part of. Part of the reason why I failed to keep the diary entries at that particular time was the way the status of both Caroline and I had been dealt with. In particular, when I thought of her status, it was clear from the outset from what we had both been told, she was a witness and I was the suspect.

However, what was unclear was the way the police had dealt with her. At all times the police maintained that Caroline was only a witness, yet she was treated differently from me, in the respect that having had a statement noted from her, she was again taken to be interviewed, only this time without an independent witness being present.

This sort of thing happens with major investigations as the police attempt to exert their authority by bullying witnesses into confessing to a sequence of events. Caroline was no different, so the second statement submitted contained exactly what S wanted it to contain, regardless of whether it was fact or fiction, as far as we were concerned. Caroline did not sign this statement but its content was unknown to either of us as my own lawyer could not access a copy of it.

Another major issue for me concerned this alleged letter of complaint by the PF to the Chief Constable. I approached my lawyer several times in order to obtain a copy of it so that it could clarify the status of Caroline and I, as I firmly believed that the complaint was against us both, as opposed to the inference from the police that I was the only suspect.

Although, when Caroline and Ian were originally interviewed, S told them that the complaint was not against any particular person. Therefore, S was lying to Caroline and Ian so that he could gain evidence. This reaffirmed my belief that he had not changed, even after all these years. He was still trying to bend the rules to suit himself!

What I was told by my lawyer was that the letter was a Crown Production and I would only gain sight of it if I was to be arrested and the matter was to be brought to court. With this in mind, I resigned myself to believe that it was possibly best that I did not receive a copy of it as it would mean that I would have to go to court. A prospect that I did not particularly want, as that would infer some element of guilt as the Crown obviously must think that there was sufficient grounds to bring me to justice.

I decided not to press for a copy of the letter and as my lawyer also stated that there did not appear to be any evidence against me so therefore the likelihood of ever being arrested was negligible. After being informed that the matter had been reported to the PF for consideration, I awaited the result of their findings into the investigation.

Meanwhile, I was left to just get on with things and had to try to forget what had previously happened. Quite how I was supposed to do this I'm not sure but I intended to try. The only positive thing was that I remained off sick from work and I intended to spend time with my family to make up for the years of having never being at home.

I was so totally disgusted with the way the police had dealt with me that I decided to err on the side of caution, not attempting to think of possible outcomes for fear of going insane. Probably one of the worst things to do in a situation such as mine is to listen to the police tittle-tattle that ran amok after I was interviewed.

Again, rumours were abound that I was going to go to jail for planting drugs and that the police had loads of evidence against me and that I could expect three years at least. This, as one could imagine, did nothing for my already failing self-confidence.

I now know that the reporters of the information felt that they were assisting but really it was like pouring petrol on an already blazing inferno. Having been informed that the police were trying to gain itemized billing for my home and mobile annoyed me greatly. So much so that I contacted BT and Orange, who were the providers of my phones and I asked whether the police had requested this information; both denied that it had happened so I should have felt easier, but I didn't. I used my other new mobile more often as again my paranoia was getting the better of me.

The fact that my investigation was on the main HOLMES computer irritated me and I knew that it was correct as during my interview, S asked me about certain events and he read from statements that were on paper only associated with that particular computer system. Obviously, I knew this due to my experience of major investigations in the past.

That did not bother me now as I was beginning to believe my lawyer that the police would be hard pushed to present evidence as they couldn't see it going any further. This waiting game was one of the most arduous experiences I have ever had to endure. I became irritable, or should I say even more than previously, and everything annoyed me whilst being at home. It is only on reflection that I see just how bad I had become.

I don't mean that I was abusive in any way, just that I was not the same easy going person as before and I flew into mad rages for no apparent reason. Life was hard, surely it must get better, I kept telling myself, By the end of March 2001, I was feeling lower than I had previously. Again, stories were circulating concerning the investigation and at least about ten other senior officers were well aware of the ins and outs of the investigation; so much for confidentiality!

One DCI who worked at Govan police office even had the audacity to comment to a friend of mine that the case was nonsense and there was no evidence against me. He had read the report that had been sent to the PF and it was, in his opinion, a lot of rubbish. Where is the fairness in that; after all, he did not work on the investigation against me.

What kind of organisation allows its matters to be conducted in this way? I'll tell you—Strathclyde Police. An organisation famed for its Investors in People accreditation. One that is fair, and treats staff worse than any other major organisation I have ever known. The sad thing is that the police carry out their own investigations into the police so where does a fair process come into the equation? It clearly doesn't and the sooner independent investigators take over this draconian way of investigation, the better.

Previously, there have been cries for others to investigate the police but the organisation does not wish it to happen. Probably the reason is that they would have to be more accountable for allowing cronyism to take over during this type of farce. I fully believe that it is high time an outside team of investigators took over this role in order to provide a fair system for decent cops in the job. Not only that, but the general public deserve to know how the police treat its staff.

I attended the Federation offices so that I could receive some advice from them regarding the way the police was treating me.

The rep I saw was a constable whose sole purpose is to advise officers of all ranks regarding police procedures. Having gone there, I left with the impression that I knew far more than he did concerning procedures and he was as helpful as a chocolate teapot. He is in effect the same as most high-ranking police officers, only out to help provide an easy life for himself and has no loyalty to me, only the organisation. It was quite pathetic to say the least.

I needed help and was referred to the Welfare Department. This would be the same Welfare who had not returned any of my calls for about four weeks. What a system! I was off with stress and no one wanted to know. So much for the caring side of the police! Except for a first-class GP, I received no noteworthy help or advice at all from the others.

I wanted advice from the Federation regarding the possibility of suing the Chief Constable over the way I was being unfairly treated and all that I received from him was, "It's probably best not to rock the boat, they won't be pleased."

At this point in my life, I decided that I could take no more and I decided to resign. Having voiced this idea to Carmen, she laughed and quickly pointed out that even if I did resign, I would still face the prospect of criminal proceedings, so the problem would not go away by resigning. Again, I saw sense and decided yet again that I was in this for the long haul, regardless of the outcome. As if things weren't bad enough, Mike contacted me to say that I was to be served with papers regarding the allegations. This meant that the police were at long last going to inform me exactly what I had done wrong.

I believed that this should have taken place prior to my interview but alas, perhaps the police had made a mistake? I agreed to meet Mike along with a detective sergeant who had to officially 'serve' this document to me.

I met up with them in Glasgow and saw that the document only informed me that I was the subject of a report to the PF, no other details were listed. I remained as much in the dark as before. This meant that it was official, I was an accused person, awaiting the outcome of the findings by the PF's department.

That same night, Caroline contacted me at home to tell me that she too had been served with the same document I had received. This also meant that she was reported for alleged criminal conduct to the PF despite the fact that she had never been interviewed as a suspect in the same way I had. She was a witness throughout yet now she was an accused like me.

This made no sense, as my own policing experience taught me that if a person is to be a suspect then they should be treated as such and not as a witness. Therefore, the complaint by the PF was obviously against us both and the police were trying to use Caroline as a witness against me but they had no evidence against me so they just decided to report us both for the crime. (Attempting to Pervert the Course of Justice).

This emphasises my belief that the police reported what they wanted to report, hoping to get me, and if they failed then they may perhaps get both of us. If it was suspected that Caroline was responsible for some form of criminal conduct then why did the police treat her as a witness? This was definitely a case of double jeopardy.

The police were covering all bases in that they had treated Caroline as a witness expecting her to conform to their way of thinking. The very fact that she refused to fully cooperate with them thereafter made them put whatever facts they had to the PF but stipulating that she refused to comply with their requests and therefore should be treated as a suspect along with me. The very idea that they would even consider using her as a witness against me made me chuckle! The reason for that is quite clearly, they had no evidence against either of us but perhaps using Caroline against me, they may have had a very flimsy case. This placed me in a false sense of security regarding the case as at that particular time, I began to feel that I would be fine and the whole sorry mess would disappear.

It was by no means over as the long wait on a decision being made by the PF to prepare the case and then send it to Crown Office for final consideration was far from over. What never really occurred to me at the time was that the PF now had another opportunity to examine the facts at hand prior to the case being submitted to the Crown Office in Edinburgh. I genuinely believed that someone there would uncover the truth, this being that there was no case to answer.

During the Horatio case, Caroline should have been precognosed, as well as Ian. This would have set the record straight regarding what had actually happened. As this had never taken place, I felt that at least this time the PF would speak with them both. Again, how foolish I was, never was it even a consideration that they should be spoken to.

It would appear from sources who worked at the PF's office in Glasgow informed me that what would happen would be that the case would be read over and then sent to Crown Office as soon as possible in order that a decision be reached. This again reiterates my idea that the so-called experienced Fiscal's department made a huge mess of this case by failing to carry out the proper procedure in relation to their preparation of the case.

It may be due to any number of explanations from the staff being too inexperienced in dealing with cases, or indeed down to good old incompetence. I would have to suggest that it is a case of the latter as opposed to the former!

There was a whole catalogue of catastrophes with my investigation and the blame cannot lie solely at one door. Of course, the police are very much to blame for their clear and direct victimisation of Caroline in an attempt to get at me as well as their blatant discrimination against me. Also, there was the ineptitude of the personnel at the PF's office who quite clearly acted above and beyond their remit. This all points to the idea that there are so many mistakes being made by these people in authority against ordinary members of the public who are treated worse than common criminals, and may have their reputations totally ruined by these power-mad freaks.

This makes a mockery of our criminal justice system, as quite frankly, these decisions can be wrong. What is more astonishing is that the employees of the Crown cannot be held responsible for their actions, yet a public servant such as I has been made to be more than accountable for my actions. Both the police and the PF's office must address a review of these laws to prevent other innocent victims becoming scapegoats for bungled investigations.

Again, I have to highlight the fact that one of the major problems with "Policing the Police" is that at present, this responsibility rests with each force concerned. There are still occasions that another force will investigate another force area, but this is only when those under the spotlight are in fact senior officers.

In my particular case, the investigation was left with two senior officers from Strathclyde, one of those being a person who had previously worked alongside me and did not particularly like me. Is it the case then that this was quite clearly a conceited effort on his behalf to get at me due to his dislike for me? Or alternatively, is it the case that other senior officers, being friendly with Mr H, asked him to dig that wee bit deeper in an attempt to get at me due to my behaviour against them?

In particular, I would point to the death in custody of Albie Ferrie and my lack of agreement to conform to every whim of the newly promoted Detective Superintendent H. I have to suggest in very strong terms that either of these remain firm possibilities as to why I was victimised by the police.

It is a clear indication that those non-conformists such as me are more likely to fall foul of an organisation such as Strathclyde Police. Another bizarre fact was that the PF who complained regarding my actions when dealing with the case against Horatio was Y. The same man I had a fallout with over the FAI concerning Albie Ferrie as I refused to be bullied by him at that time.

It was becoming clear to me that this was a major conspiracy by the police and the PF's office! This reaffirms the point at hand that it is about time an independent commission was brought into play so that all complaints against the police be handled in a fair and true way, as quite clearly that does not happen at present with this force, I am testament to that.

Having been told that I am now the subject of a report to the PF, I started to try to work out how long I would have to wait until I learned of my fate. A friend spoke with a PF who said that they (the PF) had about six weeks to prepare my case prior to it being sent to Crown Office in Edinburgh for a decision. This meant that it would be ages before I would find out what would happen, if anything.

That said, I thought that surely Caroline and Alan would be spoken to by the PF and that would clear up all ambiguities on my behalf. This again never did happen, although it should have. Yet again, this system in place to protect the innocent until proven guilty fell apart. Perhaps that was because Caroline was also down on that report as an accused person and this would therefore prevent them from speaking to her until a decision was reached.

I felt for sure that they would speak with them to prevent any further undue stress on my family and me. Meanwhile, I was secretly going mad with worry as at any time, I could have been arrested. I was afraid and it was beginning to show. I became a virtual recluse. The only time I ventured out of the house was to take my daughter to and from nursery.

I needed some form of escape so I decided that I would continue with my studies. I spoke about it with my GP, who suggested that this would perhaps be advantageous in the circumstances and would provide me with something else to do in case I ended up out of a job. I had already passed the first two credits of my degree course and this was a welcome boost, as it proved to me that I was capable of undertaking study despite enormous pressure.

Carmen, as always, was very supportive and encouraged me to try to lead as normal a life as possible whilst all of the upheaval through my work continued to play havoc on our personal lives. This was a good decision and helped me enormously, as I was required to submit four thousand word essays and this ensured that I maintained some form of normality. It was also a difficult time as

I found it very difficult concentrating on my studies although Carmen assisted me with the typing required for the submission of the essays.

As though trying to keep up appearances with other family members and neighbours wasn't bad enough, I had the added pressure of having problems with my own family. This was due to a family rift with two of my. It was as though they felt threatened by us and possibly of the material possessions as we stayed in a nicer house—at least, that was how I viewed it. It had reached such a state that they now no longer had any contact with us both. This I could really accept but what made matters worse was the very fact that for almost five years, they also ignored my own daughter by walking past her in shops or the street.

This infuriated me and added to my already surmounting problems. It was eating away at me like unwanted fungi. I did attempt on several occasions to reach the bottom of the problem but to no avail. It would appear that I was just destined to be left alone to get on with my own life. I could really have done with my family around me at that time and if they had been supportive I would have told them. But that wasn't the way it was. It was a dark, bleak time for me and Carmen, she was the one who helped me through it.

The very fact that Carmen and I lived in a nice house in a decent area was obviously an excuse to mask the real reason they were all too busy forming opinions of us that they never once stopped to ask if things were alright.

They remained blissfully unaware that I had major work-related problems and I decided that I would keep up the pretence of it all. After all, I could hardly tell family members of my predicament when they refused to speak to me. This was partly from a pride point of view, as well as anger at the way in which they were treating me.

I knew that I would never tell them the heartache that Carmen and I had to endure for that period of our lives. Even after many years, the situation is as bad as ever, but they are still none the wiser as far as my situation is concerned, even my own mother had no idea and thought that I was still working.

Right or wrong, I decided that it was my tale to tell and thought that maybe one day I would tell her about that chapter of my life. I was not ready for that to happen. All I can say is that without Carmen to keep me on the straight and narrow, I don't know where I would have been; to her, I am eternally grateful.

As far as my employers are concerned, I fully believe that I am fighting against a culture, which is incestuous, arrogant and more concerned with covering their own backs than admitting mistakes. There is a great big club of which I am not a part, the rules for them are conspiracy, collusion and face-saving. How can I compete against that? The institution that is Strathclyde Police is much too big to take on and win!

Chapter 14
The Result

I knew that the coming months waiting to find out what was going to happen to me would be full of roller-coaster emotions. I could not prepare for the final result, as I was too busy running over and over in my mind what was possibly going to happen. I knew that the report had been completed by the PF and was already at Crown Office in Edinburgh, thanks to a friend who made discreet enquiries for me.

Meanwhile, I had to pretend that I was working and continued with my web of lies and deceit to members of my family and Carmen's family. My mother believed that I was still working shifts and I told her that I was back working in plainclothes, in case anyone saw me at a time I was supposed to be working.

It was difficult at home also, as I had to ensure that my car was not there so as not to arouse suspicions with my neighbours. One ironic thing there was the fact that my lawyer lived in the same street. She obviously knew that I was not working but I trusted her not to tell anyone, and she didn't. I made a conscious effort to ensure that my car was away for long periods of time from my home and even left it at close friends' homes in order to make it look as though I was still working.

The strain was enormous and I even stopped going to my local supermarket, fearing that I would meet colleagues who would only keep asking about the investigation and I just wanted to block it out. However, I very quickly realised that not all of my colleagues would be that interested and not all of them continued with their phone calls to me. I knew before I went off that only a small number of them would remain in touch with me, and I was right.

This did not bother me as for the first time in years, I started to unwind, despite what was happening. This may seem quite bizarre but I was actually managing to enjoy my home life without having to cram everything into two days off as I had done for the previous ten years.

I soon formed the opinion that there is a life outside the police, but I had been just too wrapped up in the job to see that. That is without doubt a problem with the job. Whilst still attached to it, there is no way of seeing beyond that which is in front of you. I was like that, but not anymore.

I could do things with my wife and family that I never managed to do before. Even to get up and go away for the day before this was a military operation, ensuring that I had no court or had to work due to a murder investigation. I became a father at last; my daughter was three years old but I had virtually missed most of the memorable experiences due to working for an organisation that bullies and ill-treats its staff.

I missed the chat with the guys at work but not the actual job. This itself was a difficult thing for me to grasp, as I had been so focussed before, but now I was being paid not to go to work. I decided that I would make the most of it whilst I could.

It wasn't all about day trips and fun time; quite the opposite. I still had the veiled threat of the outcome of the investigation to attempt to deal with. By now, I was hovering on the brink of despair. What was quite strange was the fact that my mind kept coming up with negative outcomes of the report yet I did not believe what was happening.

A great reality check for me was my daughter. It really is amazing how children can help in a situation like this. I was heading for a nervous breakdown but in reality I knew that she would help me cope. Between Carmen and my daughter, I had to hold on as it would be a long drawn out process but they made it all seem worthwhile. I still kept in touch with some of the guys from work but the contact was beginning to reduce.

I now saw a different way of life. There was more in the world than the Police after all, and I could now see that? The lies and deceit to my mum and my own family meant nothing to me, as I wanted to protect myself from the barrage of questions. The last thing I wanted was to have to explain what happened. It is only when a person becomes embroiled in something of this magnitude that you can really identify with the thoughts going around in my head.

I often commented to friends that I felt like a fraud, living the alleged life of a police officer without actually having to do the job. An old cop who used to work in the intelligence section at Baird Street had previously been a sergeant but the toils of alcohol led to him being demoted. This was obviously in the days that those convicted of drunk driving faced much stiffer punishment from the police organisation.

However, Stuart had never told his mother of his demotion and the poor old soul went to her grave thinking that her son had done well in the job earning promotion. This made me think that perhaps he had the right idea, deciding to spare his family the indignity of his erroneous ways. I decided that I would also stick with that plan. After all, it didn't do Stuart any harm.

The toughest thing of all was the way the police had treated me. I must have thought that I meant something to the force. Quite clearly I did not, as I was being treated disgracefully by the management. All I had to hope for was the result from Crown Office, surely that would vindicate me.

Before long, it was June 2001 and I had not received any form of contact from the Welfare department, or even the police. I should not have been surprised as I was now finding out that the departments within the force are really lackadaisical when It comes to dealing with members of staff who are off sick.

I got fed up phoning the different departments to find out information. They never returned any of my calls and I was basically left to my own devices. I decided to take matters into my own hands and started to go to a library in order to research various elements of law as I was convinced that the report was flawed.

When I asked the Federation for advice, it seemed that they were thinking more of the police than my situation. Very often, I was given wrong advice as I had previously researched the Police Procedures Manual to ascertain where the investigation had been conducted wrongly. As I have mentioned earlier, there was no formal contact made to me regarding the allegations against me. This should have been intimated to me long before my interview but as the police seem to be a law unto themselves, this procedure was never carried out.

My visits to the library occupied my time and ensured that my car was away from home thereby fooling my neighbours that I was still working. The only people who knew what was going on were close friends not associated with the police. This was comforting as at least I could hear unbiased views from them. They were horrified to find out the way I was being treated by my employers.

In particular, one female friend works with a law firm in Edinburgh and she looked into various employment issues on my behalf. It would appear that I was being victimised and harassed. I decided to investigate this further. I discovered that I wasn't the subject of a normal employment contract, as other employed people are. I was governed by "Conditions of Service", which meant that the police could really do as they wish.

The reason for this is that my employment is similar to that of the Armed Forces. They too are answerable to their employers by way of a disciplined service, which means that normal employment issues do not come into play. I was being treated badly and I could not do anything about it.

On Monday, 19 June 2001, my lawyer contacted me to say that she had been in touch with the PF's office and the report had been returned from Crown Office. However, the PF refused to tell my lawyer of the outcome until they had informed the police. Alarm bells were ringing.

I was petrified, but my lawyer tried to pacify me by telling me that this was normal procedure and I would probably find out later that day, or even the following day. I suppose at least the end was in sight, so I had to be thankful for that!

On the Tuesday, I received a call from one of my friends at work telling me that the DCI was looking for my mobile phone number and he was going to ring me. I seized the opportunity and tried to contact him but he was unavailable. I left a message asking that he ring me as soon as possible.

By early evening, I was panicking, as I had not heard from him. Carmen reassured me that I was being paranoid and that he perhaps was too busy. No news is good news? Yet another sleepless night lay in store for me as I worried about what the next day would bring, hopefully an end to this torment.

Wednesday, 21 June 2001, my father-in-law's birthday. My daughter was excited about this and couldn't wait to see him to sing "happy birthday". I awoke just after eight, although I never slept much having seen every hour of the clock that night. As all parents know, when a three-year-old awakens then that's it, no going back—"Get up, Daddy, it's Granada's birthday."

I got up and tried to be pleasant, a difficult task, as I am not a morning person. Straight downstairs to begin another day. God but kids are so funny, she was singing and dancing already despite the fact she had only been out of bed about ten minutes. How I wish I could be like that!

About a quarter to nine (0845), I heard a knock at the door. Thinking that it was the postman with the mail, I opened the door and saw two familiar faces, H and S. My heart sank. I felt nauseated. I could feel the blood draining from my face.

"Can we come in and speak to you, Dale?" DS H sounded very formal as he uttered these words.

I was taken by surprise and stuttered something, I can't to this day recollect what it was. I showed them into the living room and grabbed hold of my daughter, taking her upstairs to Carmen who was about to come down to see who the early guests were.

I returned to the two men awaiting me. This was the moment I was dreading; had they come to my house to tell me that it was over?

DS H stood up. "I'm afraid I have bad news for you. I have a petition warrant for your arrest on the grounds of attempting to pervert the course of justice."

I reeled back onto a chair in disbelief. "And you bastards came to my house to arrest me in front of my wife and daughter? Why did you not arrange for me to hand myself into a police office, that's what normally happens."

Carmen came bounding downstairs. She had heard what he said, albeit she stood there staring in disbelief at them. I turned to see her and our daughter attached to her. I was livid. Bad enough being arrested, but to be arrested from home was beyond contempt. Not that I had expected different treatment as a police officer but I am aware of other officers who have been in this situation and arrangements were made through their lawyers to attend at a police office at an agreed time.

I tied to remain calm but I was not succeeding. H handed me a copy of the charge, which ran to about half a page of nonsense. It contained the details of the one charge alleging that I had stolen a videocassette tape, interfered with a set of house keys and withheld information from the PF, all in an attempt to pervert the course of justice.

I suppose what this amounted to was the culmination of the hard effort made by S and Co as they strived to get a result. The only difference being the charge, it made no sense and was pretty ambiguous. I had been charged with stealing a videocassette yet these officers who had attended my home in order to arrest me made no effort to search my house for this item.

As an experienced detective, I would have thought that this should have been given priority, as this was a petition warrant. (This type of warrant should result in an accused person being tried at either a Sheriff and Jury trial or at the High Court. The sentences at these courts are greater than those at the Sheriff court.)

They made no attempt to carry out this procedure. I was really angry but sensing that Carmen was afraid, I did my best to remain calm. I asked if I could shower and change prior to leaving the house and was told that it would be best if I wore a suit for my appearance at court later that day. I was to be taken to East Kilbride police office to await transportation to Glasgow Sheriff Court.

I went upstairs to shower and Carmen came to ask if I needed anything. I asked her to bring my mobile phone so that I could phone my lawyer as well as a few of my colleagues to let them know. I contacted my lawyer but she was in a meeting. When I told the receptionist what had happened, she told me that my lawyer had already been informed by the police shortly before; she was going to meet me at the police office later that morning.

After showering and changing, I went back downstairs and asked H about Caroline, I was trying to ascertain whether she had been arrested. He told me that it was only me who was to be charged over the allegations. I suppose at least she won't have to endure this degrading treatment by colleagues.

It was time to leave Carmen and my daughter behind. I told Carmen to meet me at the court later that day and I had already contacted one of my friends from work to meet her, to ensure that she would not be alone at the court. The friend I had contacted was Caroline's partner. I knew that if he was going to be at court, Carmen would be all right. He would take care of her!

The Sheriff court is not an ideal place for anyone, especially someone who does not work for the police, nor has any clue as to the type of person who would be there. The waiting area would be full of drug addicts and criminals all waiting on their families emerging from the cell area within the basement of the court.

I was glad that at least Ian would look after Carmen, awaiting my return. I kissed my family goodbye and made my way to the unmarked police car parked outside. I turned to see my daughter waving furiously at me, obviously thinking that Daddy was away to work with his friends.

How wrong she was; I was heading for a cell like a common criminal! On reaching the police office in East Kilbride, I felt sick. I hadn't spoken to them en route there. After being processed at the charge bar, I was shown into a waiting room within the CID corridor to await my lawyer.

At least I wasn't locked up in a cell, things weren't as bad as I had thought. Two officers from the Serious Crime Squad were left to babysit. The female officer I had met before as she is friendly with Shona—Aileen—was trying her best to break the monotony of the wait with idle chitchat.

I was given coffee and allowed to use the phone. What I should say is that this is not standard practice for arrested people but at least I was being fairly treated under the circumstances. I phoned Carmen to ensure she was okay.

She told me that my lawyer had contacted her to say that she would be at the police office to see me shortly. Ian had also been in touch with her to say that he would be at the court to provide her with support, of this I was quite relieved. Only one other problem, our daughter.

Carmen had arranged to take her to her mum's house, but her biggest test would be whether she could pretend that all was well without having to worry her mum. She decided to come clean with her and tell her the truth. Probably, a wise move on her part.

All arrested people must be fingerprinted, and I was no exception. This was carried out by Aileen; I did not have a problem with her but I did have a major issue to deal with—my arrest from home in the presence of my family. This was a matter that would not simply go away, I needed to ask H or S.

My lawyer arrived and I was allowed a meeting with her prior to having the charge formally read over to me under taped conditions. Anne was aghast, she did not understand the charge, nor could she believe the very idea that I had been arrested. As far as she could see there was no case to answer, yet I was arrested. It made no sense to either her or her legal colleagues. I was formally cautioned and charged on tape but I made no reply to it.

After this, I was informed by H that I was to be suspended from duty pending trial over the charge libelled. I handed over my warrant card to him and he walked out of the room, grinning. I sat and said nothing, but inside, I felt like slitting his throat! My lawyer told me to ignore him, as quite clearly he wanted to aggravate me, and it worked.

After my lawyer left, I met Aileen again. She told me that she wanted to take a DNA sample from me. I refused and then H appeared. He told me that it was in my best interest to comply as if need be, he could ask the court to have me remanded in custody to allow them to appeal to the court to have it taken from me, with or without my consent.

I asked him why this was so as the crime did not fit the criteria, he told me that it was just in my interest to agree to it. I was mad and began venting my anger at him telling him that I knew about the DNA evidence linking the drugs to Horatio. He was livid with me. I'm not sure whether it was because I shouted at him or due to the fact that I had mentioned the DNA as this was supposed to be confidential.

He stuttered and tried to regain his composure and told me that if I had already been told that information then I should comply with the request. I told him that no one told me, "I just worked it out by myself, as I am a good detective." Although I had been told this, he had now confirmed the information. He reacted again by saying that he would make sure I was detained at court if I failed to comply. Yet again, I was being bullied into a corner, not one I wanted to go into so I had to comply. After all, I had a wife and daughter to think of.

I was taken to Glasgow Sheriff Court, my appearance was to be at two o'clock (1400). We arrived about five minutes early and I was taken right through for my appearance before the Sheriff. Inside the court were my lawyer, the PF and the clerk of the court who is responsible for the paperwork side of things, such as bail papers, etc. This is also called the custody court, as those who have been kept in custody at police offices appear in the afternoon in front of a sheriff. It is decided in this court whether a person is released on bail or kept in custody. I hoped that I would be the former as opposed to the latter.

Had H done the dirty on me and requested that I be kept in custody? The PF read over my charge to the Sheriff, then my lawyer asked that I should be released on bail, and it was agreed. That was it, all of a minute or so and I was to be freed on bail pending trial.

Well, not quite, I was taken back to the cell area where I knew some of those criminals in the holding cells. I was terrified that I might be placed in a cell beside them. I was put in a cell on my own and the door was closed over and locked. I felt humiliated. I asked the police officer to leave me in a room, and told him that I too was a police officer and that I was not going to run away!

He told me that he was only following orders. I never asked him anything else as I felt at my lowest ebb yet. I tried to contain my feelings but it was very difficult. I could have cried, but I didn't. I just sat in silence going over the events of earlier that day. H had done his best to get to me. This was obviously his way of proving that he had clout in the police. I was the fall guy, probably due to my lack of respect for the wanker, but fuck him and the job!

After about twenty minutes, I was released on bail and walked along the basement corridor towards the lift. I reached the ground floor and approached the main doors of the court when I heard a familiar voice—"Dale." I turned to see Carmen, Ian and Caroline walking towards me. I turned away and walked in the opposite direction, too afraid to look back. Carmen ran and caught up with me, she knew I was relieved to see her, despite my tears.

I couldn't put into words how I felt. The sheer relief of being released on bail was overwhelming. The whole day had passed by quickly although I can account for every second of it. Before, I would have been laughing and joking with colleagues about things in general, yet there I was being watched over by detectives from the Serious Crime Squad before appearing at court as a common criminal. I was at my lowest peak yet and my self-esteem was at rock bottom.

I wanted to sit down and cry but again, my pride took over and I tried to be calm, for Carmen's sake. I jumped into Ian's car and the four of us headed to Merchant Square in Glasgow, famed for its art deco cafés and bars. I didn't feel like alcohol, I made do with a coffee and recounted the sordid details to three ghoul-like faces before me. It's harder for a police officer to comprehend the very notion of being locked up in police cells, as we are the people responsible for locking others up!

Yet when it happens, it seems much worse as I was the unfortunate soul who was left awaiting my release. Although Ian and Caroline were sympathetic, it meant nothing to me, as deep down I was quite angry at Caroline for not sticking up for me fully. Had she told the full story about the tape being returned and that we did nothing wrong then perhaps I wouldn't have been in this horrid situation.

I knew that I was being harsh in blaming her but had she not danced around the issue concerning these matters and answered the questions then maybe I would not have been arrested. I will never know, but there is still the anger at why I was the only person being held responsible for the actions of two police officers.

In real terms, the reason for this was that there was insufficient evidence to substantiate the charge against us both and perhaps there was a petite amount against me, hence the reason that I was arrested as opposed to us both! After about an hour, we left and Carmen and I made our way home to collect our daughter. The journey was short but took forever as we kept talking about the events of that day not knowing what would happen in the future.

I was also suspended, which meant that I would not be allowed to enter a police office without being escorted around it. This was also quite a feeling; I felt as though I had been sacked, although I knew that this wasn't the case. The police had been a huge part of my life for ten years yet now I was being cast aside with all and sundry already saying behind my back that I was guilty.

A question that Carmen had not asked was about the outcome of the arrest. What would happen if I went to court and was found guilty of this charge? Quite clearly, I would have been sent to prison. I dreaded the question being asked of me, as I knew that Carmen would freak if she found out that I might be taken away from her and our daughter!

We collected our daughter and went home; I wasn't up for visitors and just wanted to be left alone. However, my phone was in meltdown with friends leaving messages of support, which on hindsight was a comfort to know that some people believed in me. After having arrived home, one of my non-police friends turned up at the door swearing at me for having let him down. I completely forgot that I had agreed to assist him with his moving house that very same afternoon.

I laughed, obviously I had forgotten about that as I had other trivial matters to attend to! I explained my predicament to him and his face was a picture. He couldn't believe that he had been ranting and raving at me like a lunatic and I had just been arrested. At least I could laugh, which was good, I suppose under the circumstances. I knew from that point on that I would get through it with the help and support of Carmen and my friends.

He left the house and agreed that we would delay the house move until the following day when I could concentrate more on helping him.

Life had to go on, as those who have small children will know! My daughter would never know that I had work problems, as I wanted her life to be as normal as it could be for a three-year-old. I was determined to try to enjoy life and appreciate my family a bit more now that I had time to do it. Perhaps not the ideal way in which to do it with the veiled threat of jail hanging around my neck, but I would at least try.

My own family would not know of my dilemma as I made a conscious effort to avoid telling others of what was going on. The only other thing was the prospect of them finding out through other police officers with loose tongues and perhaps that would be the only way they would find out about me.

This was a chance I was prepared to take. Even Carmen's family was to remain in the dark, apart from her mum and dad who now knew, albeit they were very supportive of us. Breaking the news to other non-police friends was difficult and they were all amazed at just how badly I was being treated, this was like a bad nightmare and not one many people would like to have!

The first thing to do was to sit down with my legal team to discuss the way forward. What made matters difficult for me was the fact that I was frustrated because I was on one side of the legal fence and knew how the police operate.

Suffice to say, I also knew how defence lawyers acted as well as the PF's office so my mind was in overdrive as I tried to direct my defence team.

The precognition agent attached to the law team assisting me was an ex-detective inspector who had retired from the force and was now taking statements for a living. He was a great help and proved to be excellent at his job. Wullie is forever in my debt for his attention to detail, which assisted me greatly.

I met with the senior partner of the law firm who was also aghast as to why I had even been arrested, as there appeared to be no reason for my arrest, as the jumped-up charge made no sense. He tried to assure me that they would uncover the real truth that had been "overlooked" by S and H when they did their report to the PF concerning me, thereby leading to my arrest. I felt quite relieved that even my legal team believed that there must have been a hidden agenda to get at me for some reason, only time would tell.

Over the coming weeks, the phone calls from police friends stopped and the realisation that I would have to get on with my life without them was slowly dawning on me. Only a select few still keep in touch and they are my friends, not those who meet me and try to 'fish' for information about my predicament. I was slowly going mad with worry as I was concerned about my future and I noticed that I was trying to cope alone, shutting out Carmen in the process, but this did not deter her in the slightest, she put up with my mood swings and tearful bouts without complaining, the good-hearted saint that she is.

After a couple of months, that dreaded question came from Carmen about the likely outcome. I had always decided that I would keep as much from her as possible but somehow I could no longer keep up the pretence.

I told her that if it went to court and I was found guilty then I could expect about eighteen months to three years in jail. She was horrified at the prospect of me having to endure that, even though we both knew that I had done nothing wrong. What she never gave a second thought to, was her own wellbeing and to what she would do should that happen! This was typical of her, never thinking of herself, always thinking about others, in this case—me.

I did try to tell her that this eventuality may never happen but the look on her face told a completely different story. I knew that she would be worried but I felt that it was important to tell her the truth rather than lie and be shocked should that prospect of jail arise.

At this time, I also had an insurance policy that had just matured. Under normal circumstances, this would have ensured a great summer holiday for us all with enough left over to stick away for a rainy day. Carmen is terrific in every way. In particular, she is great with money. She ensured that we had sufficient savings to help us if we ever needed money for a rainy day.

However, on this occasion, I knew that we would have to forfeit a holiday as we would have to hang on to the money just in case we needed it. Carmen suggested that we go on holiday but I had an alternative use for the money. I never told her the use that the money would go to but eventually, after having stalled her several times over the issue of a holiday, I told her why I felt we shouldn't touch the money.

You see, should the really bad situation happen whereby I was imprisoned, then there would be enough to pay our mortgage and council tax for at least two years. When I told her this, she burst into tears. I think it dawned on her that I thought there might even be a chance this might happen.

Really, what I was doing was erring on the side of caution. I only wanted to ensure that my family would be able to cope financially should the worst-case scenario happen.

Time would tell whether this would be the case or not but the waiting game was pushing me further and further into the depths of despair?

My defence team started working on my case and set about interviewing the same witnesses already interviewed by the police. When a person is accused of a crime and engages the services of a lawyer, the company then presents their own case to the crown.

In order to do this, precognitions have to be carried out. This is the interview of all witnesses although it is always the situation that people will speak to the police but not to defence agents. They become somewhat wary of lawyers who represent criminals. I knew that I now fell into that category and perhaps some of the witnesses would speak out against me.

This was at a time when my paranoia was in overdrive and I felt as though everyone was against me and no one was for me. With the exception of Wullie, who was responsible for carrying out the precognitions on my behalf. From the outset, he believed my story and he set about tearing away at the lies reported against me by S.

I was asked to call at the lawyer's offices in order to speak to Wullie about the case. When I arrived there, he seemed quite agitated and I found out very quickly why he was that way. Wullie started ranting and raving about how I had been set up by the police and the PF's office and how they had all conveniently forgotten to reveal the truth during their reports to Crown Office.

It would appear that Pirrie, who was responsible for my own precognition, had omitted to do a concise statement. Not only that, she had failed to report the truth from one of the main witnesses in the case. She had actually put words into his statement, which suggested that I had been up at the house of Horatio for about twenty minutes. She misread the fact that this was the time taken to actually search the house with the warrant.

But you see, incompetence was her middle name and what she reported was taken to be fact, when it actually was fiction! Wullie has spoken to witnesses who clearly made the allegation against me weak and full of faults. For the first time in a long while, I was beginning to regain my own self-belief again. I had started to doubt what had in fact happened that day of the house search and had my mind set for a long trial awaiting a verdict by the jury. Wullie had single-handedly proved my innocence.

He had spoken to the lawyer in charge of my case and he too now started to believe my story, although it would have been nicer had Peter believed me when I had told him the facts myself. This confirmed what I always suspected. Lawyers only listen when they have to! Wullie had one problem though.

Pirrie was stalling having a statement taken from her. She obviously realised that she was about to be found out. Not only her though, but her boss at the PF's office was also stalling. As I had mentioned earlier, he was the same guy who had been in charge of the Albie Ferrie case and I had previously had a bust up with Y over that case several years before. This confirmed my conspiracy theory, although Carmen believed that I was losing my mind due to the pressure of it all. I was still adamant that I was right though.

Eventually, Wullie managed to obtain statements from Pirrie and Y but they refused to fully cooperate by providing as full and detailed a statement as had been given to the police. Peter, my lawyer, had to write to the PF stating that they were refusing to cooperate in order for them to provide a statement. Quite clearly, they were still not telling the full fable previously reported against me to the police.

However, four months after my arrest, I felt that the case was looking stronger in my favour and Peter tried to tell me that I would walk a free man from court. But he seemed to be missing a vital point. I didn't want to have to go to court fearing that my name would be circulated in the press, as I would have been unable to conceal my identity. If my identity came out then my wife and daughter would also suffer. Not only that, my family would also learn of my predicament but I did not want that to happen.

Towards the end of October 2001, I received a letter from Peter. It said that they had received notification from the PF's office that my trial would be the 21 January 2002 at Glasgow Sheriff and Jury Court and I should make an appointment to come and see him. I was gutted; it was getting closer to the deadline of a court appearance and I knew that if found guilty in this court, I could be sentenced to up to three years in prison.

I was frantic! Tears flowed like they never had. Carmen found me heaped in a corner of the kitchen, sobbing uncontrollably. She read the letter and tried to console me before walking away, leaving me to ponder my future in jail!

It seemed that I would have to go down the path of appearing at court and set about trying to cope with my feelings about that. I often joked that I would be "passed about like a scud book" amongst the other prisoners. I had to explain to Carmen what I meant by that. I suggested that all the rough sex-starved cons would probably have their way with a good-looking cop who was jailed for allegedly planting drugs in order to get a result.

This joke didn't go down too well with her although I was only trying to make light of a very stressful situation. I met with Peter and he discussed how he was going to conduct my defence. I quickly interrupted him by saying that I wanted a QC (Queens Council) to represent me as I felt that it needed a person who would make the jury perhaps take notice to the idea that this was a serious allegation against a police officer and was a situation not to be taken lightly.

He was not too pleased with my request and told me that I may not be granted that under the terms of the insurance policy. You see, I did not have to pay my legal expenses as I contributed to a fund, which covers instances such as these. I reminded him that I was allowed to have the services of a QC as it was going to a trial by jury. The QC is trained to defend in cases presented at this type of trial and also the High Court. I suggested the services of someone who had been recommended to me and Peter was reluctantly agreeable to attempt to secure Paul's services for me. What Peter didn't realise was that whilst I was suspended from duty, I had carried out my own enquires into the legal system and I knew what I could do and what I could expect from my law team. I was, after all, fighting for my freedom.

Despite all of these things happening to Carmen and me, life must go on as normal as possible for our daughter. It was horrendous as at times I felt like running away but I knew that it was not her fault that her dad was under great pressure so therefore I had to try even harder to cope for her sake.

I had no contact from the senior management of the police. Welfare never once phoned to ask how I was and the Police Federation. Well, least said about them, the better!

They are all only concerned with themselves, officers who come under scrutiny are a burden and they wash their hands of people like me. As I had been lying to my own family that I was still working, I had to ensure that I kept a low profile fearing that my big secret would come out as I still did not want anyone to know. Carmen and I had to plan Christmas for the wee one as well as having to put on a brave face for everyone else. The last thing we wanted was false sympathy.

We were both living on our nerves and I wondered how long both of us could keep up the pretence as it was really wearing me down. I was determined though not to discuss the situation with any of my family due to the way they already were towards me. The last thing I needed right now was for them to either gloat over my misfortune or offer false sympathy to me. We tried to carry on our Christmas preparations for the sake of our precious daughter.

Again, Peter wrote to me telling me that I was required to attend for an interview at his office. This time though, it was to be with Paul the QC. His services had been secured and he wanted to speak to me. The week before Christmas (2001), I went to speak with Paul and I have to say that he came with a great reputation but I was still wary of meeting with him. The reason quite simply was that I dreaded what he would have to say about my chances concerning the trial that was now only about four weeks away.

I arrived at the office and was summoned to speak to Peter. He told me that he was appalled at my case and as to why I was even arrested he could find no logical explanation. "Have you actually read my case papers then, Peter?"

"Oh yes, I read them last night. I—"

I interrupted him, "Why has it taken you so long to do that when I have already had six months of worry over this, could you not have told me this sooner?"

He didn't know what to say. "I don't read the case papers until it's drawing close to a trial." I was fuming, I had worried all this time when in actual fact, I had needed him to reassure me long before this time yet he was just probably too busy to be bothered to read my file.

I should have been relieved that he was on my side but I was so angry with him. He tried to explain that this was standard practice but I was too incensed at him and I left his room to await the arrival of Paul. I tried to regain my thoughts but I was having great difficulty in doing this.

Wullie appeared and spoke with me but I think that Peter probably sent him to speak to me to ensure that I had calmed down before my next meeting. It worked. Wullie made me see that Peter and his other aides were busy and they had many more clients other than me! I think though that I was really about to have a breakdown; I couldn't take any more and was trying to blame someone for my problems.

Out of the blue, Paul appeared and whisked me off to a side room where I began recounting the whole sordid story to him. My autopilot mode took over as I had recounted the story so often I could do it almost without taking a breath. Paul sat intently listening and taking brief notes. After I finished my story, he started to hit me with questions and I replied as well as I could under the circumstances. What he couldn't believe was the fact that I had never been the subject of complaint in my whole service and that I was awaiting a promotion. The summing up he made was very accurate.

He believed as I did that this was some sort of vendetta by either the police or the PFs office and that there would be no case to answer as they had no evidence, that is if what I had told him was accurate, which it was.

I felt actually good again, my QC believed me so I knew that this was good. Yet at the same time, I felt sad. Sad because the police must have desperately wanted to get me so bad that they would "sex up" a report to make me out to be a bad guy, which I wasn't.

Paul was also convinced of my innocence as he said that it was strange why I was being dealt with in this manner and my colleague Caroline, who had been with me throughout, was being let off without anything happening to her. It made no sense to him and I was told to go home and forget about it as he hoped that we wouldn't have to even bother with a trial!

I left the office with many thoughts that day. More or less the same as I had experienced for almost a year but fresh ones raged in my mind about this conspiracy against me. When I got home, I told a very relieved Carmen the diagnosis from Paul and she too seemed quite upbeat about the case for the first time. There was one snag, however; I was due to be served with my indictment.

This is the formal paper served on an accused approximately 28 days before a trail. It outlines the charge and the likely penalties should a guilty verdict be reached. This was approaching the 28-day period though and still there was no sign of it being served on me. Then came the phone call from Caroline that was about to alter the path of events.

Caroline had been summoned at long last to provide a PF's precognition. The same one that she should have had before the trial of Horatio, although that had never happened. She should even have been precognosed before I was arrested. She told me that she spoke with the senior PF dealing with my case and she recounted her version of events but he was unaware as the full contents had not been put in her original statement taken by S in March.

Perhaps she was liberal with the truth at that time due to S being so devious towards her. She told Jack everything, but I don't think he wanted to hear the truth as it changed his case against me. From what Caroline told me about that interview, he was trying to frighten her into telling him what he wanted to hear as opposed to what she had to say.

However, she again reminded him that his bully tactics would not work and if he had a particular course of action he wished to take, then feel free and do it, otherwise write down what she had to say. He reminded her that it was his job to reach the truth and if need be she could be precognosed on oath in front of a Sheriff. He must have believed that this would scare her in some way.

In actual fact, this made her more determined so she agreed to his threat. But he backed down and listened to what she had to say. The very fact that when S noted a statement from Caroline, there was a Federation Rep present yet this was omitted from his report to Crown Office should clarify that he had his own mission to accomplish. The reason for the Rep being present with Caroline then was to ensure that she would not be bullied, yet she was, and now she had told Jack about this, he too was in a panic.

You see, Caroline told him that she would give evidence to the effect that she was bullied by both the police and now him. He refuted that allegation and again reminded her that he was trying to learn the truth. After about an hour, she left the interview and she believed that Jack now knew that the report S had submitted was falling to pieces.

I listened intently to Caroline and she seemed more positive about the situation than she had previously. This again was reassuring to me but I still had to wait to see whether I would be served with the indictment or not. I told Caroline of my earlier meetings and she too tried to settle my mind concerning the likelihood of a trial.

When I came off the phone, I told Carmen of the events as recounted by Caroline, but she tried to ensure that I wasn't building up my hopes too much that the case would be dropped against me. Sometimes clinging on to a brief glimmer of hope is all that a person has of remaining calm; I was no exception.

I waited with baited breath every day for the knock on the door awaiting the indictment. Right up to Christmas Eve, yet it never arrived. I did try to enjoy Christmas but it was impossible. Not only did I have to put on a brave face but I was also thinking about the prospect that perhaps next Christmas may be spent in prison away from my wife and daughter.

As if that wasn't bad enough, the fact that my own family had stopped speaking to me also made matters worse as I kept thinking about why they were doing this to me and my own family. Although my own mother knew of the rift that had developed, she made no effort to change the situation and this too was deeply upsetting. Carmen knew that I was trying to be brave but my mother-in-law also knew that deep down, I wasn't coping with the strain of everything.

She did try to reassure me but I was deeply depressed by the whole situation and as far as I was concerned the whole Christmas period could not come to an end quick enough!

I found myself putting on a brave face at Christmas for the sake of my daughter but deep down, I was aching as I found the 'season's greetings' were a great bind to me. I did make the effort but I truly believe that I was on automatic pilot and I was just going along with the festivities whilst at the same time distancing myself from my family.

At times, I imagined that I was watching all of the actions of others like watching a rerun of an old epic film. I think I just floated around in a trance eagerly awaiting its end. Although Carmen told me that our daughter thoroughly enjoyed herself so I suppose it was bliss knowing that she was unaware of the torment being experienced by her parents. Even after New Year, I still had not been served with the indictment.

My emotions were at boiling point and when one of my friends Drew phoned me, I convinced even him that I would not have to go to court. His attempts at telling me to be careful not to believe that this would happen fell on deaf ears as I thought that I was right and no one could tell me differently.

However, it started to affect me, as it was all I could really talk about to Carmen. I was insistent that it was all about to come to an end. "What a disappointment it will be if you're not right?" Again, Carmen was trying to tell me not to be too sure of what might or might not happen, after all, nothing else had ever gone in my favour before!

Due to the extended holidays enjoyed by members of the PF's department and all other office staff, including my own solicitors, it couldn't come quick enough for them to get back to normal business. I contacted Peter, my lawyer, on 8 January 2002 and advised him that I had still received no indictment and asked that he contact the PF to ascertain what was happening.

I dreaded the return phone call, especially if it meant that my trial date was now off until later, as is normally the case with most criminal trials. Invariably, they are postponed at the last minute for even minor reasons. Alas, 1145 that morning, the phone rang. Anxiously, I answered; it was Peter.

My heart was racing like a train and I felt physically sick and had to sit down on the bed awaiting his retort to my question. "Are you ready for this, Dale?"

"Go for it, what did they say?"

There was a brief pause. "Crown office have decided that there will be no proceedings against you due to a lack of evidence."

I suppose it was a blessing that I was sitting on the bed! I couldn't speak to him, as I was dumbstruck. "What does that mean?"

"It means that it is all over, you will not be served with an indictment after all and obviously, you will not have to go to trial as they have dropped the case against you!"

It took a few minutes for it to sink in. I was free at last! I quickly pulled myself together and asked Peter why they had decided to drop the case against me. He explained that the PF he spoke to told him that apparently Pirrie and Y had added two and two together and assumed that it made five.

He went on by saying that I should never have been arrested in the first place. If the police had carried out their investigations properly, then I would never had been in the position that I was forced into. I asked Peter if I could sue the PF for making the mistake, but he told me that Crown Agents cannot be sued, so I would just have to accept what happened and get on with my life. I thanked him for telling me so quickly and put down the phone.

Obviously, I was angry yet relieved at what Peter had told me but there were so many emotions running around in my head and I felt numb. No time to dwell on my own thoughts straightaway, as I had to break the news to Carmen.

I ran downstairs and saw Carmen preparing our daughter for nursery. I couldn't hide my excitement. Carmen took one look at me and burst into tears, without me even uttering a single word to her. She instinctively knew that it was over. And it was!

Chapter 15
Second Bite of the Cherry

At last, after the torment of the previous year, I could perhaps attempt to regain my self-esteem and confidence. I was still reeling from the fact that all of this could have been avoided if only the bosses had done their job. I had an appointment with my lawyer to discuss what had happened and also to talk about the possibility of suing them.

When I went to see Peter, he had already made brief enquiries with the PF regarding the investigation. He confirmed that an error had been made at their end and I should never have been arrested in the first place. This was the most harrowing thing to accept as what he was in fact telling me was that all of this could have been avoided. When I raised the prospect of suing them, Peter told me that I couldn't sue the PF's office, as they can't be held to be accountable for their actions, unlike me!

I was annoyed at that but had to accept it. I also raised the prospect of suing the police for their treatment of me but Peter told me that I should leave well alone and just accept what has happened and put it down to a bad experience and move on with my life.

I left his office, feeling annoyed and angry. I could do absolutely nothing about what had happened and I couldn't accept this. It was eating away at me like most other things had in the past but I just couldn't shake it off. There was still the minor problem of the suspension. I was technically not allowed to go near a police office and I still had no warrant card or police notebook and the stigma of being suspended was all too much to bear.

I left his office feeling low and again felt like resigning from the job. I tried to busy myself with other non-police things and I still had my studies to keep me going. My degree was the only thing that seemed to keep my mind off what was happening. Carmen was, by this point, heavily pregnant and ached for me to become normal again. The truth of that being, I never envisaged ever being normal again.

I knew that I had to get out of the job and prayed that I could manage to keep myself going and pass my exams so that I would have at least something to show for time off. I was finding it difficult to concentrate and relied on Carmen to help me with my studies and she typed most of the essays, which were required to be submitted. I suppose the only real reason to carry on was our daughter.

After the initial period of realisation dawned on me that I would no longer have to worry about court, I started to relax and the calls from some of my work colleagues still kept me going. One Thursday morning, the post brought more good news. At last I could begin to move on, as I was no longer suspended. The Deputy Chief Constable had rescinded it, after Peter had contacted him ordering it to be done. It was now more than two weeks after the notification of my innocence. Included in the letter from the police was a letter telling me that I had to telephone my police division with a view to having a return-to-work interview.

My stomach heaved at this prospect, as it seemed that I had no option but to return to work. The following day, I drove to the office to have the meeting with the new Deputy Divisional Commander. He had replaced Maggie who was now in a promoted position elsewhere. Strange how the police manage to reward those who don't do their jobs properly, Maggie, H and S had all been promoted within a short timescale of each other—perhaps for a job well done in trying to ruin a good guy's life!

When I entered the building, I felt sick and awkward, not knowing what to say to people. I walked up to his room and never saw anyone, of this I was quite happy. The new guy was actually very nice and tried to make me feel at ease and even sympathised with me. It didn't work though.

I was angry and vented this anger at him; at least he listened to me. He agreed with many aspects of what I had claimed was wrong and he even provided me with other pieces of information, confirming several aspects of the investigation. I left his office feeling slightly better that at least he had listened and didn't belittle me in any way.

After I had left there, I made my way to the CID office to speak with the DI. I met with a couple of the guys who were delighted to see me and I had my first cup of coffee back there. After a few minutes of idle chitchat, I went to speak to the DI who told me that he was glad to see me and that he expected me back at work a few days later. I was shocked, as I had no intention of going back right away.

After all, I was still entitled to annual leave covering the period of my suspension. I was entitled to about six weeks' worth of holidays and I was going to make sure I got them. Reluctantly, he agreed and so I left the office knowing that I had plenty of holidays and didn't need to go back to work for almost two months. I still felt uncomfortable knowing that I would have to eventually go back to work, back to an organisation I didn't trust.

We were both determined that we would enjoy my time off, but Carmen gave birth to our son during my annual leave, so I knew that I would be spending time at home. Just after the birth and we were settling into our home routine, another bombshell arrived through the letterbox in the form of intimation of another investigation. This time, it was a discipline investigation into allegations that I had not carried out the correct procedures.

This meant that I was open to more scrutiny from the hierarchy. My pleasure at becoming a father again was short-lived. When I inquired as to how long it would take to complete the investigation, I was told that it would only be a couple of months at most. I knew that the worst-case scenario would be sacking, the best being I would be given a warning. What surprised me most of all was that I didn't even know what I was supposed to have done wrong. Indeed, I had been accompanied by other colleagues, and I assumed that they too would be investigated. All I could do now was wait and see what occurred.

I contacted Caroline to see if she too was the subject of the discipline investigation. She knew nothing about it and confirmed what I thought, I was the only person who was being investigated and it was clear in my mind that someone somewhere was definitely out to get me! Having contacted the Police Federation to find out what was happening. I knew nothing of the context of the investigation and requested that they find out on my behalf.

Within a couple of days, I was notified that the investigation would centre around the search at Horatio's house and the fact that I allegedly failed to inform the PF of certain things during the investigation. I was back to square one, I felt as though I would never get away from the fact that I was being persecuted by my employers when, as I have maintained, I did absolutely nothing wrong.

They were quite clearly determined to make my life a misery and attempt to push me over the edge. Carmen tried her utmost to keep me upbeat but the Federation dropped another bombshell. It would seem that it had been decided at the Discipline Branch situated at Pitt Street that at the conclusion of their investigation, they may enforce a statutory condition upon me that I would be required to resign if found guilty.

Again, it seemed as though they were determined to rid the force of one of its finest detectives. I was devastated that I was potentially looking at being forced into resigning and if I refused, they would quite simply just sack me, leaving me with no income and more importantly, no job.

Although some of the guys were still in regular contact, this too was beginning to change. Some of the guys had stopped their contact and I was slowly losing my mind with worry again. I thought that all of my worry was behind me and now I was again looking at potentially being sacked. I had to fight back but in truth, I was worn down.

God knows how poor Carmen felt as I tried to hide my feelings but it was becoming too difficult. After about two weeks of wallowing in more self-pity, I made an appointment to speak with someone from the Federation offices and decided that I would fight them all the way. On speaking with the Federation, it was ascertained that it would all rest on whether they would be able to prove anything against me. He told me that the investigation should only take a couple of months so at least by about June, I would know my fate.

They couldn't really do much to assist, as they would have to await the outcome like me. I also paid a visit to my lawyer who was also of no assistance, he too told me to just sit back and await the conclusion of the investigation. I struggled to live from day to day as the whole sordid events were still praying on my mind and trying to work at the same time was almost impossible to do.

My family was still unaware of the pressure we were under and I was glad about that as I couldn't have coped with their constant questions about what was going on in my life. My only release was the fact that I had my studies to contend with. This was actually a welcome release as I could channel all my energy into completing them to the best of my ability.

Carmen assisted me with the typing required although our own house was so busy with the children that the weeks just seemed to disappear. Again as with the other investigation, I received little snippets of information from friends and non-police colleagues about what was being asked of them. It seemed that this investigation, like the criminal one before was attempting to uncover some form of wrong procedures on my part.

The Chief Inspector dealing with the enquiry was going over old ground by visiting those already visited by S and Co in the previous one. Although the Federation assured me that this was standard practice and was 'in fairness to me'.

This expression always made me laugh, as there had never been any fairness as far as I was concerned and this enquiry was no different. Caroline was still not in the frame anywhere and quite clearly, it was definitely me they were trying to get!

The only difference this time was that she couldn't really be used as a witness against me as she was implicated every bit as much as I was. Not that I particularly wanted her to face the same scrutiny but why was I being made to be accountable for the actions of others when they could quite easily be to blame for this as I was.

I decided that I also wanted to raise a formal complaint against the police, in particular against H and S for the way they had dealt with my criminal investigation. Senior bosses tried to sweep it under the marble flooring lining the corridors of power at Pitt Street!

I refused to be fobbed off and requested that it be dealt with in a proper manner and warned that failure to do so would result in me seeking legal action prior to going to the press with my allegations. Eventually, I received a letter from a Chief Superintendent (CS) who told me that he would be investigating my complaint and that he wished to meet with me 'on neutral ground'.

I agreed to this but requested that a representative accompanies me from the Federation and so the meeting was set to take place within a hotel on the outskirts of Glasgow. Once there, I managed to tell the CS what my actual fears and complaints were against those involved. He listened intently and took brief notes and seemed interested.

I, for once, felt that at long last someone was prepared to listen to my side of the story. In particular, I told him that I wanted to see the actual letter of complaint to see if it did in fact name me specifically or whether, as was intimated by S, the complaint was against the Proactive. I had my doubts as to whether he would be upfront with this information or whether he would hide the truth.

I left the meeting feeling quite satisfied that at least he would try to answer my questions. Meanwhile, the other investigation had come to a complete standstill and despite me asking the Federation to chase up the officer in charge, they too seemed to be hitting a brick wall.

When I kept moaning at them to find out for me, I was shocked to find out that the reason for the delay was due to a 'complaint'.

Again, I was furious and knew that perhaps I had made matters worse for me but I still needed answers. When I asked who was holding up the investigation, I was shocked to learn that it was a female Superintendent who had been my DS prior to her undertaking her current position. We had worked together on the "Janitor" murder as she was the senior officer who had led on that failed murder investigation, despite the fact that I had actually helped solve the whole thing. How strange it was to be investigated by the same female who had assaulted someone during the janitor murder. If that is not double standards I don't know what is?

I was shocked that 'JJ' was allegedly behind the delay as I got on very well with her, or so I thought. I thought that perhaps she would be on my side, but then again, I couldn't trust anyone and as I was about to find out, she wasn't on my side.

Again, being impulsive, I decided to try and find out myself what was happening and telephoned her boss, to find out why my investigation had come to a halt. He was most helpful and assured me that the investigation was still proceeding and wasn't at a standstill. I told him that the female Superintendent had informed the Federation that it wasn't going to go any further until my complaint against the police had been dealt with.

He seemed angry, both at what she had said and that I had found out about it! By the time I had put the phone down and spoke with Carmen about the conversation, my mobile started to ring. When I answered it, I knew who it was, the Federation rep.

He was ranting and raving and telling me how I was out of order making that phone call to the boss in charge of the Discipline Branch. I calmly told him that if he had assisted me in the way he is supposed to, I wouldn't have to go behind his back and get answers myself.

Again, I had managed to fall out with someone else. Why? Well, I believe it was because I was doing my own work and not relying on them to do it for me. I was actually feeling quite happy for the first time in a long while. I felt that I was perhaps taking charge of my own destiny and knew that it would probably go horribly wrong, but I was prepared for that happening.

Having heard nothing from the Federation for over two weeks, I was concerned about what was happening but then I received a letter from the CS who was dealing with my complaint. He answered my questions, albeit briefly, and confirmed that I was in fact named in the letter of complaint as was Caroline. However, their get out was that the whole criminal investigation was led and directed by the PF. Therefore, they couldn't be held to be accountable if they were directed by Crown Office.

He failed to answer as to why I was the only person investigated other than to say that it was decided that it would serve the investigation better if Caroline was used as a witness against me. He went on to further say that at no time did the officers involved, i.e., S & H, make any concerted effort to put any blame directly on me.

Only that they had conducted the investigation in a professional and appropriate manner. This was supposed to answer my questions but it was probably the best I would get under the circumstances. At least I knew that I was right all along when I assumed that the complaint did mention us both, (Caroline and I) and that the police had singled me out as the main instigator of the alleged misconduct. It made me so angry to think that I was the scapegoat and held to be accountable.

I reluctantly phoned the Federation and updated them of the outcome of my complaint and asked if they could find out for me what was going to happen with the other enquiry, now that the complaint was dealt with. Within a couple of days, I received a call telling me that a result would be known by the June at the latest. I was ecstatic, as this was now four months after the start of it. I geared myself up for the result and after consulting with friends regarding potential outcomes I patiently waited on the letter arriving through the letterbox.

June came and went and by mid-July, I again contacted the Federation to find out what was happening. This time I was told that the female Superintendent had told them that no decision had been reached and that it may take longer, perhaps by September.

I was furious. She again appeared to be trying to delay my agony and preventing me from moving on with my life. The ironic thing was that she was now dealing with other people's livelihood and pontificating against others. The reality being, she was not without blame herself for breaking the law and I knew this to be the case. My anger returned, fiercer than ever and I wanted everyone to know that the person who was delaying this investigation was actually more guilty at breaking the law than I was!

Carmen had to listen to me moaning and she knew just how frustrated I was becoming and I knew that I had no control over the delay. Trying to work and pretend that life was normal to those on the outside was becoming more and more difficult. I was on the verge of losing my mind and nothing could make it any easier to cope with.

Even work itself was frantically busy and I had no interest in the job or the bosses around me. I knew that I needed a change and I craved the chance to do something other than the job as a police officer. I knew that the only way of escape for me was to complete my studies and perhaps look to alternative employment.

However, before that would ever happen, I would have to ensure that I remained in situ pending this enquiry reaching a conclusion.

At long last, I received a call from Ian telling me that he was to be interviewed by Discipline regarding the enquiry and almost directly after he had called, I was informed by Caroline that she too was to be interviewed. They both told me that they would tell the Chief Inspector the events and that I was in no way to blame for any of the allegations.

It was now October, eight months after the enquiry began and no other enquiry to my knowledge had lasted that length of time. Even those who probably should be investigated as a result of a conviction at court, or even of committing other offences against the Discipline Regulations!

It took until the end of November to contact my lawyer to have him write to Pitt Street asking what the delay was and why the enquiry was taking so long. I received a phone call from the Federation telling me that the end was in sight. All that remained now was for the formal document telling me what the offences against the Discipline Code was, and what options would be open to me.

I knew that at all costs I didn't want to have the option on for the 'requirement to resign'. I had no idea what the charges against me would be. The only thing I knew was that Caroline was not included.

I made an appointment to speak with my rep from the Federation to discuss the options open to me as well as the discussion regarding the offences against me. He seemed quite upbeat and this to me was a good sign that perhaps it wasn't going to be that bad. I read over the first page of the paper detailing my own personal details.

The second page was more of a shock. It contained seven offences against me. I was livid and could hardly read the allegations against me. They varied from theft or alternatively losing a police production (video tape) to failing to disclose information pertinent to a case. In a word, it was the biggest lot of crap I had ever read.

I remained calm and asked the representative for my advice. However, unbeknown to him, I was actually taping the conversation, as I required a safety net in case I was going to be forced into a corner. Obviously, this is not common practice and I don't know what the outcome of that would have been if I had been caught!

He started to explain to me that the Supt at Discipline (JJ) had decided to split up the allegations to allow her to present more charges against me. He explained that if I accepted it this way, the Supt would keep out the requirement to resign from the conduct form. In other words, if I accepted the allegations against me, I would be able to keep my job. If I disagreed, I would be forced to resign, or even sacked.

Here it was, I was being blackmailed. I asked him to explain it to me again and he duly did. He explained in depth the charges and also named the Supt who was making the decisions. I told him that I felt as though I was being forced into admitting charges I didn't commit. I also said that I got the impression that a gun was being held at his head to force me to make this decision.

He agreed and thereby confirmed the fact that I was being set up. I told him that I would accept three charges and no more. If she wanted to leave in the requirement to resign in the conduct form, I would ask for a full hearing of evidence. In essence, I was in no position to haggle, but I was fighting for my reputation and most importantly, for my job.

I left the office furious at what had taken place, yet strangely enough I was also chuffed as I had taped the conversation and therefore, I had a bargaining tool if required. I drove away from the office and couldn't wait to stop and listen to it. When I was about five miles away from the office, I stopped in a lay-by and listened with anticipation to the tape recording.

It was clear and concise and depicted the verbal events within that office. The tape even ended with the rep providing his name as the phone had rang during my visit and he had identified himself when answering. I was quite relieved as I had managed to get away with my deceit and it was good to know that it would perhaps help me if required.

A short time later, I was contacted by the rep and advised that reluctantly the Supt had accepted my offer and there was to be no requirement to resign. I was delighted and at least I wouldn't be forced to leave my job. I arranged to sign the revised conduct form the following day and all that remained now was the actual Discipline Hearing. I was given a provisional date for mid-December and I couldn't wait to get it over with.

Eventually, after a couple of weeks, the day arrived for the hearing, which was taking place at the Force's HQ in Pitt Street, Glasgow. Carmen came with me as usual for moral support and as she was not allowed near the hearing, decided to wander around the shops.

As previously arranged, I met with my Federation Rep Joe at a hotel near the HQ and we thrashed out the way ahead and how I was to conduct myself during the hearing. I was advised that the Chair of the meeting was a Chief Superintendent whom I used to work with during my time at Easterhouse. Kenny was a real nice guy and I hoped that this would perhaps go in my favour as I had had a great working relationship with him during my time there.

At the last meeting with Joe, I had signed the conduct forms that confirmed that I was admitting 3 disciplinary offences and this hearing was a formality in that it was meant to actually impose some form of punishment. This ranged from verbal, written, final written warning or even a pay reduction of one grade if deemed appropriate. I was advised that it would likely be a written warning.

Joe would speak on my behalf and I was merely to be present as the female superintendent 'JJ' was presenting the case against me to summarise the allegations within the disciplinary papers. Joe did say that I would be asked if I wished to comment but as he was speaking for me, I should just say no.

Once the facts and defence had been presented, I was to await a final decision by Kenny. So the scene was set for my hearing. I walked into Pitt Street agitated and I felt physically sick at the prospect of having to endure this. Having never even had a complaint against me during my career other than this, I didn't know how I was going to get through the hearing.

I was left outside the hearing room pending the arrival of the others and when they did arrive, Kenny nodded to me as he passed and I was again left outside the room whilst the scene was set for the hearing by JJ. Eventually, I was marched into the room and I was taken aback by the magnitude of the size of the place.

It was a huge mahogany collection of tables joined in an oval manner. The Chair was at one end, I was shown to the opposite end and someplace in between on either side sat JJ and Joe. In front of me was a desk with a microphone and I was aware of a set of recording equipment behind JJ—which was later to be used to record the whole process. It was one of the most intimidating rooms I have been in, up there with a cell although the size was at the opposite end of the spectrum. I was embarrassed and anxious at the same time and wanted it to be over.

It began with introductions, which were all formal with name, rank, number and place of work being relayed by all attendees for the benefit of the tape and I was advised to speak loudly and clearly if asked to clarify anything so that it could be caught on tape.

In fairness, I was well aware of how to speak during taped recorded conditions as I had conducted hundreds of interviews like that during my career. JJ began with the scene setting of the events of that day some 2 years before when I was supposed to have been searching a house and all that I was alleged to have done.

It was a surreal experience listening to someone speak about my actions and I was unable to interrupt. JJ's version was certainly different from my recollection, but after all, I was there at the incident, she wasn't. She was basing this story upon her own version and it did not mirror the actual events as far as I was concerned.

After this, Joe was allowed to present my case although he had a watered down version of what we had discussed and I was angry that he had not followed my instructions about what to say on my behalf. After all, this was my chance to present my version. This infuriated me and when I looked over at JJ, she appeared to be smirking at what Joe was saying.

I thought about how smug she was and yet she was not within sin herself with her behaviour during her career of alleged assaults and bullying behaviour. Joe finished in no time and asked that my unblemished service and reports of commendation be taken into account and that was it. Over in about 15 minutes in total, or was it over?

Kenny thanked them both and following the protocol, asked me if I wanted to say anything. Having listened intently to the 3 allegations made against me for neglect of duty regarding not following correct warrant protocols and only obtaining a Justice of the Peace warrant as opposed to a Sheriffs warrant, not recording a police production correctly (cassette tape) and not returning said tape, I wasn't happy. Joe had done a good job of putting up a defence for me but not to my high standard and so I said "yes" to the question posed by Kenny.

JJ immediately responded that Joe had spoken for me and I should not need to say anything. However, I responded saying that I had waited 2 years to defend myself and felt that this was an appropriate time to do so. Kenny said that he understood my frustrations and normally, no one does respond but if I felt that it would assist in the decision making process, he would allow it. My heart was pounding and underneath, I was sweating like hell. JJ threw her pen down in disgust as I put my hand into my pocket and removed my prepared speech.

You see, I was prepared for it, I just didn't know whether or not I would follow it through but having listened to the other two, I felt that I had nothing to lose. I started to speak slowly and concisely, taking each allegation in turn and gave my version of facts and attempted to overturn any attempt made by JJ to insinuate that I had in fact done something wrong.

I don't know where I got the strength from but I did it. I read all four and a half typed pages as though defending a murderer at the high court. At the end, I thanked Joe for his continued support and also thanked the Chair (Kenny) for affording me the courtesy of the right to reply.

So it was done, the hearing evidence stage in support or otherwise of the allegations was over and we were adjourned pending Kenny reaching a decision. Kenny left the room and JJ looked at me in disgust and barked at Joe that she wanted to speak to him in another room.

This other room was about 3 doors away and I was in the main hearing room looking out over the towering blocks of Glasgow's office district and pubs—God, how I wished I was in a pub and not in there! I could hear JJ shouting and ranting like a lunatic at Joe for allowing me to prepare a speech.

Joe tried to explain that he knew nothing about it but she wouldn't even let him speak. She shouted over him, swearing like a trooper and telling him that she would never do a deal with him again at a disciplinary hearing and "that wee prick" (must have been me she was referring to) had wasted it for others who were due to have hearings. Joe took the verbal assault on the chin and eventually, he was thrown out of the room, out of her sight.

When Joe came into the hearing room to get me, he suggested that we go to the side door so he could have a fag; obviously, he too was feeling the pressure. I apologised for doing what I did but when I explained why I did it, he fully understood but wished I hadn't. In truth, I couldn't give a shit if I had ruined it for someone else, I was only fighting my own corner at this stage and was only looking out for myself.

I waited for over 2 hours on Kenny making a decision, again Joe was sure that it would be a written warning but warned me that I could also be reduced in salary by one pay grade. Either way, at this stage, I couldn't have cared less, I wanted it to be over. Eventually, JJ appeared at the door and advised that the Chair was on his way and he had reached a decision—the wait was over.

Kenny arrived and we resumed the format of the hearing and the tape recorded conditions were started again following the break and a description of the reason for the delay in the decision making process. It seemed that Kenny found it difficult to reach a satisfactory conclusion as he had listened to the sequence of events as presented by JJ and Joe but was mindful of also wishing to take into account my own version of events.

He did however say that the reason for the delay was due to my version of events and how unprecedented it was to allow this information as I had chosen to have Joe speak on my behalf. He did state though that he had decided to also take my views into account.

He read the decision formally and I was advised that I would receive a copy of the outcome in writing at a later date. In summary, he expressed his concerns and disappointment in me appearing before a hearing and had also taken into account my unblemished career and how well respected I was. He felt that I had been through enough anguish and anxiety and did not want to exacerbate this further and with that in mind, he decided that I should be administered with a verbal warning.

JJ exhaled her disapproval and her body language was clear for all to see that she was fuming at the outcome. The least punishment available was given. A verbal warning—in real terms, not even a slap on the wrist. To me, it proved how he too must have believed my version of events and that all of this was a complete waste of time.

Obviously, I could not believe the outcome as I was expecting more of a punishment; albeit I still to this day refute any suggestion of the allegations made that I did anything wrong, but at least it was minimal. My feeling of dread was more of elation now but I had to contain this and ensure that I was respectful to the process I was involved in.

The look on Joe's face too showed how surprised he was at the outcome but nonetheless, it was a major victory for me. The process was brought to a close and I was free to go. I thanked Kenny for his time and assured him that I would not be back before a hearing again.

I walked out of the room, back along the narrow corridors and made my way to the back stairs. I leapt down two stairs at a time to get to the outside of the building. I needed fresh air, my heart felt like it was going to burst in my chest. I pushed open the door and walked into a bright bustling Pitt Street and slumped into a corner of another building and cried uncontrollably. At last, the events of the previous 3 years had concluded, my life and job still intact. It was over.

Chapter 16
Life After the Trouble

Although the hearing was now over, I still had major problems within myself as my thoughts and feelings were eating me up inside. Whilst there was initial elation at the outcome of the hearing, I struggled to deal with day-to-day life because of the past events. Trying to move on from one major event in your life is difficult but when it comes to dealing with a succession of events within a close period of time, it is enough to test anyone.

at me like a parasite. No amount of comforting words or deeds by Carmen or my children could console me. I needed to get a grip and quickly.

I still needed answers about why I was the victim and scapegoat in all of this. Why was Caroline not treated the way I was although she was in fairness not dealt with appropriately by H and S during the investigation. I still needed to know why I was picked upon when clearly the complaint was against two of us.

Caroline was forced into giving statement after statement in an attempt at getting her to admit my guilt, when we both knew that there was no guilt. S did his best to try to frame me for something I didn't do as he had to obtain multiple statements from witnesses, perhaps due to incompetency because after all, surely a good detective manages to illicit the full facts on the first occasion? At least, I did when I was doing my job.

My excessive drinking was becoming a worrying habit as I sought solace. I knew that I needed to look at options for my future career and decide what I wanted to do. Having managed to pass my degree I knew that now there were options open to me and at times in the depths of despair I lost sight of the fact that I had a wonderful wife and children who wanted me there.

At times, whilst I lost that reality check, I often wonder how I could have stopped thinking about them especially when they were and remain now as the pivotal source of my being. I think on reflection that I had complete apathy with myself and that was all I wanted; I needed to wallow in self-pity, self-doubt and fear for the future.

Focus was the only think that Carmen kept saying to me, I kept looking for excuses and threw things at her about how it was a conspiracy and everyone was conspiring against me which was obviously how I saw it but in actual fact it was hatred that was making me feel that way.

I was now on annual leave yet again. You may find it strange to think that after almost 3 years off work, I would welcome annual leave. I needed time to sort myself out and try to concentrate on what to do next. I needed the space without distractions but my head was full of the events and I could not erase them.

I caved in and the time came for me to return to work. Carmen had supported me through all of this but the actual walking through the door of the police office I had to do myself. I returned to Easterhouse to work and the team had totally changed there, as had the DI. Yet another new face but the new guy was decent and sympathised with me greatly.

Mike was still there so at least I had an ally and I was to work alongside him, which was of great benefit. The initial few days were a haze to me and in fairness, those around me were more concerned with my story and wanted to know the ins and outs of what had taken place but I would not speak about it.

As far as they were concerned, the matter was over and I wanted to get my head down and get on with the job. The only difference for me was the fact that this was a struggle for obvious reasons. Working with Mike, we went from one investigation to the next but in truth, I was heartbroken and knew that I could no longer do the job I loved.

You see, I was dedicated and enthusiastic before all of this but now I was spent. I had no will or desire to do the job anymore and at the back of mind, I was afraid that JJ or H or S would try some other means of getting at me and who knows, they had gone to great lengths before, perhaps they would do it again!

One night whilst sitting at home, Carmen tried to get me to open up and yet again, this fell on deaf ears. I had become so withdrawn and empty, despite the fact that she was the one keeping me functioning. I also knew that she too would only be able to take so much shit from me. She snapped at me to pull myself together.

In fairness, throughout the whole time that the events were going on, she never once lost sight of an end goal of getting through each stage. But even now, she was at a point where it seemed pointless trying to get me to move on. So came the suggestion about a move down to England to be closer to her family. After all, I had no real support mechanism in my own family to speak of so we were at the stage that there was nothing to keep us there any longer.

In fairness, I had never given that thought as a possible option for me. In that instant, I actually felt an awakening within. She was as usual, right again. I needed to focus on something positive and to plan for moving on, whether another job or indeed, another area to live.

The children were of an age where a move would be of no real consequence and they would be closer to family members who actually wanted to see them. It made sense and so for the first time in a long time, I tried to focus on us and our future.

The weeks passed and I discussed the possibility of a move with Mike and he said that he agreed, especially under the circumstances. I needed to draw that line and get on with my life. I didn't discuss it in any great detail with him. Despite the fact I liked Mike and liked working with him, I had lost all trust in everyone in police circles. Once that trust is gone, there is no way back.

One night, we cemented the deal and I took annual leave and went to visit my in-laws and we started to look around the area for schools and properties. As Carmen knew the area, I knew that she would choose one that suited our needs and those of the kids. The area was known to me from all of my previous visits and whilst I had never quite thought about a move there it was actually very appealing. It was a completely different way of life and my only concern was that I would struggle to slow down.

I was probably caught up in the excitement of a possible move, our house was up for sale with several interested parties we were within sight of a move. I went on a night out with some colleagues and there was other cops there too. Several of them being nosey bastards were raking up the past and wanted to know about the events but I kept trying to say that the matter was finished so I am not talking about it.

The comments came thick and fast about "getting away with it" but more importantly, several kept saying about how I should still be trying to get answers from management about "why me"? This had an adverse effect on me and I again wanted and needed answers. Having been advised that I couldn't do anything against PF because of the fact that they, as Crown Agents, couldn't be sued.

The police complaint I raised concluded that the whole investigation was at the insistence of the PF and therefore this was an easy get out as the police could blame them for the course of action adopted. I had already sought advice from a lawyer and he too advised that I would get nowhere with any claim. Faced with the prospect of having to accept what happened, I had to do something about it— but to do what I didn't know. The only solution I could see was to pack up and move away from my current life.

I obviously was not over what had happened to me and all of my emotions came flooding back. But this time, I felt completely overwhelmed by it all and I think I now started to grieve over the previous 3 years events.

Carmen was also struggling to deal with me and I can now appreciate that it must have been an overwhelming position for her to be in, trying to deal with me, the children and holding it all together for us both. I took another couple of weeks off. I think on reflection, it was during that period I finally realised just how much it had all affected me.

I quite frankly couldn't forgive, forget and move on. I needed to have closure and actually draw that definitive line in the sand. We had received an offer on our house and so the decision was made, I was going to resign.

Again, being secretive, I chose not to mention this to anyone and we both planned the move with military precision. Well, at least, Carmen did as she was the organiser, the project manager to beat all project managers. We had discussed my resignation and I had a prepared letter with me as I really wasn't sure when I was going to do it. I suppose I was putting it off and knew that it would happen when the time was right.

During an early shift one morning, Mike and I were working on a robbery enquiry and it involved an 85-year-old female who had answered her front door only to be bundled inside. Then she was bound and gagged while the male intruder ransacked her home and made off with her life savings of £2500—her funeral money, enough to ensure that her family were not out of pocket.

It was a truly despicable crime against an innocent and vulnerable lady. This was someone's mum, gran, aunt, etc. and here in the end stages of her life, she was treated like that in her home. In fairness, I had no contact with the lady as someone else had taken her statement. Through good detective work, we actually managed to secure an arrest and we were due to interview him. I declined the prospect of the interview as I felt utterly disgusted in what had happened. I suddenly realised that my heart and soul had been ripped out of me and I could no longer do the job.

I left work that afternoon and called in at my local shop and there, walking towards me was Bob, a guy I knew from one of the uniformed shifts when I had been in the CID at Baird Street. I hadn't seen him in all the time my own issues had been going on.

I stopped to speak to him with the usual how are you greeting and he just looked at me. He started to breathe really strangely and he was trying to speak to me. He was unable to however, he attempted to ask me how I was but he stammered his way around a garble of mixed up words.

I started to laugh at him and thought he was at it. Tears welled up in his eyes and I immediately knew that something was wrong. Realising I had made fun of him by laughing at him, I ushered him towards the coffee shop instructing him to sit down and I would get him a drink.

On returning to speak to him, I handed him the coffee and before I got a chance to do anything else, he handed me a piece of paper. I opened it and read the contents. It said that because of stress at work (police-related) he had developed a severe stammer that made it virtually impossible for him to effectively communicate. I didn't know what to say to him.

For the first time in a long while, I knew that there was someone worse off than me. I was totally shocked and despite his current predicament, he managed to say, "How you?"

I felt humbled and sad so I went into ramble mode and spoke about what had happened to me over that time. He nodded and periodically said the odd few words like "I've heard" or "I know". As we finished our coffee and walked towards the car, he shook my hand and said thanks.

I was again totally thrown at his selfless approach to me and I turned to him saying that we should go for a beer the next night. He agreed and so we arranged to meet up as he lived only a couple of streets away from me. The next day at work, I decided whilst writing off a report that now was the time. I had decided that I was going to resign.

I calmly walked into the DI's office telling him I needed to speak to him. He looked up at me and told me to sit down and close the door but I didn't want to. In fairness, he was okay with me and had never done me any harm but I didn't want to have a long drawn out conversation with him. I was blunt and to the point.

"Here's my resignation letter, it's not up for discussion." I handed him the envelope with the letter and turned and walked away. Naturally, he followed me out to the main office but there were other detectives around and he obviously didn't want to say anything in front of them. He asked me to come back into his office but I said I would speak to him later. He left me and I returned to my desk to start finalising all of my outstanding work and reports.

Although I had been back at work, my actual workload was quite light and I had been working with others so I knew that it would be easy for me to do. At that moment, Mike walked into the office; before I got the chance to do anything, the DI grabbed him and took him into the office.

I jumped up and went into his office and told the DI it was my news to deliver, not his. So it was, the discussion I didn't want to have I had to do. Mike was gobsmacked and they both tried to persuade me to think about it but as I stressed to them, I had my mind made up and I intended to finish at the end of the week. Obviously, the DI said that I must serve 4 weeks' notice but I said that I wouldn't be doing that, I was leaving in 2 days' time.

Obviously, it was hectic as the DI left the office to run down to Baird Street to tell the bosses about what I had now done. Within an hour, the DS and DCI walked into the office. Mike was still the only other person who knew what I had done. I was summoned into the office to speak to the DS, DCI and DI but I didn't want to discuss it and it was my choice to make.

Before they got the chance to say anything, I told them that I had no intention of entering into a conversation with them, I was leaving because of the way the police had treated me and I had lost faith in the career I had planned with them.

I continued, "I am emotionally drained by the whole experience and I deserve the right to move on if I choose. Whilst you may believe that I am doing this because it is still raw but it is still raw and will remain a major part of my life and I am ready to move on. Let me be clear, leave me alone to finish my paperwork and I will be leaving—end of conversation, gentlemen."

I didn't give them a chance to say anything, walked over to my desk, grabbed my car keys and left the office. The DS shouted after me but I kept walking and made my way out of the office. I went home and told Carmen that I had resigned; she was surprised, relieved, amazed and delighted. It was always to be my decision and Carmen had said that if I left, it would be my decision as it would be unfair if I was to blame anyone and the tough decision was to be made by me.

However, I did it for me and I also did it for us. That night, I went for a beer with Bob and although it was tough as he struggled to speak, it didn't stop me from speaking and I told him of my plans; obviously, I knew he wouldn't be able to tell anyone!

He actually brought me more paperwork, it detailed his story of how he was being bullied within the police by his superiors and the stress resulted in him developing the severe and almost life-changing condition. We had a good night and he listened and spoke periodically and very briefly.

This was part of my final decision making process as I realised that others were also going through a hard time within the force and it confirmed my thoughts about leaving as there was no guarantee that something like that would not happen to me in the future. I instinctively knew that I was not prepared to find out.

Perhaps it was fate that led me to that decision; if I had not met Bob, I am not sure I would have made the decision at that time but I believe that fate deals the cards and my hand was played now—time to leave.

I returned to work the following day and again, the DI tried to get me to change my mind but I stuck to my decision. He said that I had until the end of the day to decide or else it would be passed to Pitt Street. I told him if he didn't fax it immediately, I would use my copy and do it. He was angry at me but followed my wishes and sent the letter.

I was asked at the end of the day to attend Pitt Street on what was to be my final day for an exit interview. I declined and said that I wouldn't be attending the exit interview. There was no requirement for me to do it and I was not going; they were, of course, trying to make me work my notice but after my continued pleas to leave immediately, they succumbed and I was able to finish. I don't know how I felt as I left as I had my mind focussed on escaping.

Ultimately, it took me a few days to realise that I had actually left but I had no time to dwell on it as I had way too much to do with the impending move. The day arrived, the van appeared and we loaded up all of our belongings. We had only told a few people of our move as I intended to move with as little fuss as possible. I never told my own family that I was going as I needed to get away; I would worry about that after the event.

I still had not told my own mum of the previous 3 years and so many emotions were going around my head that I knew I never would. I did however visit her and told her that we had sold up and were moving to start a new life in England.

Obviously, she was stunned and annoyed that I had never told her but I said I had my reasons and so as not to worry her, I decided not to tell her. An emotional farewell ensued and I left her with more unanswered questions than answered. But it was what it was; I had to think of myself and my family.

Friends are regular attendees at ours now that we are settled. I am truly thankful to the friends who were aware of the sequence of events and who helped me immensely; words cannot express my gratitude to them for their support. To my colleagues involved along the way and were subjected to horrendous treatment, I salute you but in some respect, I am glad that it was me and not you.

Having moved away to begin my new life, I was afraid of how I would be in trying to move on. It has taken me several years to settle and I still carry many scars of the events I was subjected to but it is what it is.

I am happier, more settled than I have ever been and would not have gotten through it without my beloved devoted wife—Carmen, this is for you; a final chapter has drawn to a close and now, we will be able to move on.